signal to noise

Also by Carla Sinclair

Net Chick
The Happy Mutant Handbook (co-author)

signal to noise

carla sinclair

Harper*Edge*
An Imprint of HarperSanFrancisco

HarperCollins Website: http://www.harpercollins.com/harperedge

HarperCollins®, 📖 ®, HarperSanFrancisco™, and HarperEdge™ are trademarks of HarperCollins Publishers Inc.

FIRST EDITION

Library of Congress Cataloging-in-Publication Data
Sinclair, Carla.
    Signal to noise / Carla Sinclair.
    1st ed.
    San Francisco : HarperEdge, 1997.
        p.   cm
  PS3569.I51985 S54 1997
  813/.54 21
  ISBN 0–06–251533–0 (cloth)
  ISBN 0–06–251534–9 (pbk.)

97 98 99 00 01 ❖/RRD 10 9 8 7 6 5 4 3 2 1

To Mark

My deepest thanks to my husband, Mark Frauenfelder, and my mom, Jackie Bly—Mark for his inexhaustible enthusiasm and willingness to read every version of the book, always offering insightful remarks; and Jackie for the many wonderfully bizarre and humorous story suggestions.

I'd also like to thank my editor, Eamon Dolan, and agent, Karen Nazor, for all their work in making this book happen.

Other thanks go to:

Joe Bardi, Colin Berry, Mel Bly, Gareth Branwyn, Melissa and Tim Connelly, Laura Curtis, Nicole Goguen, Sally Kim, Terri Leonard, Tasha McVeigh, David Pescovitz, Sarah Polen, Kathy Reigstad, Kelly Sparks, Kristin Spence, and Nina, Lew, Wendy, Calvin & Daria; and Shalini, Marny, the Daves—and everyone else in South Park.

Also, thank you Malcolm McLaren for the lyrics in chapter 9, which come from the songs "Mon Dié Sénié," "Walking with Satie," and "Driving into Delirium" (all published by Chrysalis Music/L. Gorman) from the album *Paris* (Gee Street Records Ltd./Island Records).

1

Jim Knight lights another cigarette and looks at his watch. Noon on the dot. If Rhiannon isn't here in five minutes he'll split. Jim skims the table of contents of *New York* magazine, oblivious to the tree-branch-filtered sun overhead. No article about him and his recent promotion at *Signal* magazine. Damn—they interviewed him over two months ago. Maybe next issue.

A weathered bicyclist wearing tight Lycra shorts and a yellow bandanna around his head rolls by with a shaggy sheepdog. He scowls at Jim's cigarette. Jim scowls back. The rider secures his bike and dog to a nearby bench and saunters into Caffe Centro. Jim reskims *New York*'s contents.

"Hey Jim," says a breathless voice.

"Hi Rhiannon." Jim sneaks another glimpse at his watch. 12:04.

Rhiannon places her cappuccino on the small green metal table before she takes a seat.

"I would've gotten here earlier, but I got stuck talking to Raymond. Guess who's going over to watch *Project Bluebook* at his house tonight?"

"Who?"

"Darren!" she says.

"Darren who?"

"Guess!" Rhiannon urges.

Jim doesn't want to play this guessing game with Rhiannon. He doesn't care who's going to be at Raymond's weekly *Project Bluebook* party tonight. He just wants to hurry and discuss the DNA-computing article she's proposed so he can get back to the office.

Jim flicks the ashes off his cigarette and pretends to concentrate.

Rhiannon's bangs are extra-short today, cut above her eyebrows, and in the noon sun her face is Morticia Addams pale. She's wearing a long black lace dress, tall skinny granny boots, and strange spiky earrings, which she says represent the pagan calendar. When the *Washington Post* wrote an article about *Signal* magazine, they went on and on about Rhiannon, referring to *Signal's* section editor as an "Edwardian beauty." They didn't even mention Jim, though as features editor he's got a much higher position.

She takes a sip of her cappuccino, still eager for Jim's guess, but he's already forgotten the question. His colon twists sharply as a dozen thoughts bounce off his mental to-do list. He's got a 12:45 meeting with some PR people who claim to have software that allows users to exchange video-email messages over 14.4 modems. At 2:00 he's got an editorial meeting and at 3:00 he's being interviewed by CNN. He also has to fire the receptionist, Mara Brown, who insists on leaving every day at 6 PM sharp, always screws up phone messages, and has been caught a few times taking Odwalla out of the refrigerator without sticking two bucks into the tin box. She's not a team player.

Jim also has to drive his fiancée, Mandy LeMattre, to the airport at 4:45. Mandy works at *Signal* too, as senior account manager in the advertising department. She's flying to New York tonight to help set up their new East Coast office. And then there's the email. Jim's got over 100 messages to answer and he's expecting a Bill Gates article from a new writer—a lengthy piece that he'll need to edit. The list goes on.

"We don't have all day," Rhiannon says, "so I'll just tell you: *Darren Cooper* is going to be at Raymond's tonight!"

Jim perks up. Shit, this is great. Jim's been trying to get together with Cooper ever since the Canadian author got into town last week.

"What do you mean, Cooper is going to be at Raymond's?" He likes Raymond, but Raymond and Jim are worlds apart. At *Signal* there are two echelons, and as Jim sees it, the two don't mix very well. Those in his own echelon, which include the publishers and top editors, have cocktail parties and go to private business retreats and meet the digital world's movers and shakers, while the rest of *Signal*'s crew, which include Raymond, go to raves and smoke a lot of dope and read zines. Jim doesn't understand Raymond's connection with Cooper.

"He wants to watch *Project Bluebook* with us and take notes for his next book," Rhiannon says.

Jim's head is spinning. When he and Mandy were drunk one night they came up with the idea of writing a book, using photographs and interviews, that would depict the life and culture of Silicon Valley. They would interview engineers, venture capitalists, and entrepreneurs, and Darren Cooper would write the book's foreword. It would be like a real-life version of Cooper's novel, *Cube Farm*. Mandy would take the photographs that would run throughout the book. Tonight would be the perfect time to pitch Cooper about the project.

Rhiannon waves at a *Signal* intern passing by. Jim doesn't remember his name, but he doesn't like the greasy strands of red hair hanging over the eyes of this acne-scarred student. Or the dusty maroon sweater that reeks of sweat and pot. Or the caveman-style Birkenstocks that half-cover his and too many other feet in San Francisco.

A girl comes out of Caffe Centro with a plate in her hand. "Tuna sandwich?"

"Yeah, that's me," Rhiannon says, taking the plate from the girl. "Didn't you order anything?"

"No, just my cappuccino," Jim says.

Rhiannon is now explaining her DNA-computing article to

Jim. He peeks at his watch, wonders what time *Project Bluebook* starts. Whether it's at 8 PM or 9 PM, he'll probably have enough time beforehand to edit the Bill Gates article—assuming he gets it this afternoon as promised—*and* tackle his email. And if the TV show starts at nine, he may even have time to research next month's cable-modem piece. But he'll never get his work done sitting here at the cafe. It's 12:32.

"So what do you think of my DNA idea?" Rhiannon asks, taking a bite of her sandwich.

"Uh, it's fine. Go with it, Rhiannon. It'll be great."

"Are you sure? Don't you have any suggestions? I don't want to write the whole thing and then have you rip it to shreds, like you did with my artificial-life piece."

"I don't know, Rhiannon. I'll need to see the article before I can make suggestions. Hey, do you know what time *Project Bluebook* comes on?"

"Jim, I thought we were meeting today so you could help me with my piece."

A group of twenty-somethings approach Jim and Rhiannon. They're all fresh and good-looking, like MTV people. One of the girls, her hair dyed red, smiles at them.

"Hey you two!"

"Hi Clare!" Rhiannon says.

Jim forces a smile. "Hi!" He's glad these slackers, who work in the same building as *Signal,* pass him and enter Centro before he has to add anything to the conversation.

"They're so cute," Rhiannon says, looking at them through the cafe's window.

"I guess—for a bunch of trustafarians living off Daddy's money, wasting time on their useless zines." Jim rolls his eyes. "Their office is such a goddamn mess that it's embarrassing for *us.* I mean, with all those windows on the ground floor everyone can see their pigsty, and it's the first impression people get when they enter our building. They're overgrown teenagers who haven't entered the real world yet."

Rhiannon's eyes widen. "God, Jim, I thought you liked their zines. Especially *Going Gaga.*"

4

Jim hates *all* zines. Sometimes *Going Gaga* has a good article or two, but who has time to rummage through a bunch of quirky crap just in hopes of finding one interesting piece? If these zines are truly great works of journalism, why doesn't a large publishing house like Condé Nast invest in them? Like they did with *Signal*.

Signal is the shit. It's the only magazine covering the *culture*—the people, business, ideas, and art—of technology, and the digital scene is where it's at.

12:37.

"Rhiannon, I'd better run. Your piece will be fine." Jim drops his cigarette and steps on it.

"Whatever," Rhiannon says. "Oh, *Project* starts at 9:00."

Jim grabs his jacket, slips *New York* under his arm, leaves Rhiannon sitting at the small metal table.

Jim walks along South Park, south of Market Street, the hub of San Francisco's "Multimedia Gulch." South Park and its surrounding neighborhood are the Hollywood of the digital world. The area is infested with magazine, Web and CD-ROM companies. *Signal* and Caffe Centro are within two blocks of each other, both situated alongside the park.

As Jim walks back to his office, he ignores an old man walking on his hands near a picnic table, a short-legged mutt barking for his owner to throw a ball, the lunch crowd sitting on the grass eating sandwiches and sipping lattes in to-go cups, and a couple of five-year-olds screaming around a swing set. A gentle breeze caresses the treetops surrounding the park.

Spasms wring Jim's colon and he picks up his pace.

2

"Darren Cooper is going to be at *Raymond's* tonight?" Kat almost squeals. She can't fathom why the world-famous author whose books have inspired her to try to become a serious writer herself would be at Raymond's. Raymond is just a hippie kid who works on *Signal*'s Website.

The Caffe Centro waitress brings two turkey sandwiches to the table.

"Yeah," says Clare, "and it's totally cool with Raymond if you come."

Clare is the editor of her own zine, *Going Gaga,* which she promotes as "high weirdness for the techno-savvy." She ran it with her husband, Gerald, for five years out of a small bungalow in North Hollywood. Every year it doubled in circulation. Then 10 months ago *Signal* sprouted from nowhere and offered Gerald a job as associate editor. So they moved to San Francisco and Clare continued *Going Gaga* in the same building as *Signal,* two floors below.

6

"I'll definitely be there," Kat says, peeling the cheese slices out of her sandwich and tossing them aside. She wouldn't miss Cooper for anything.

Kat, who bartends at night, started interning for Clare three months ago. She didn't want the job at first, since *Going Gaga* doesn't make enough money to pay anybody. But Clare promised Kat free lunches and Kat figures it's a place to get her feet wet in the publishing world.

Kat glances over at the friends she and Clare walked into the cafe with—Mike, Mike, and Mary. They run *Force,* which they insist is a *maga*zine, and share their workspace with Clare. They're sitting two tables away with their literary agent, talking about their book proposal.

Kat looks around at all the Lisa Loeb and Clark Kent types sitting around her, tapping on their laptops to the beat of hip-hop jazz. Everyone in this cafe has a goddamn book deal except her.

Rhiannon enters the cafe and tosses her empty plate and cappuccino mug into a plastic busing tub. She sees Clare.

"Hey girlie, what's up?"

"Hi Rhiannon." Clare stands up and hugs her friend. "Do you know Kat? She's my intern."

Kat hates the word *intern.* People automatically label you as a desperate inexperienced dork.

Rhiannon smiles politely at Kat, then starts talking to Clare about her new boyfriend. Of course he works at *Signal* too, as their music editor. South Park is so incestuous.

Kat feels like a nobody in front of most *Signal* employees. If only she could get something published. Everyone in South Park acts like it's so easy.

"Oh shit," Rhiannon says, "I'm running late. Nice meeting you," she says to Kat. *Right.*

The Mikes and Mary are laughing with their agent, who also represents Clare. The meeting looks as if it's going well. Kat hears the agent, Carrie Rozan, tell the trio she should have good news for them in the next day or two.

Both Mikes are cute. Mike Moony is tall and dark and rides a motorcycle, but Kat never goes for his type. Too much of a boy, who likes to go camping with the guys, who stands up girls. But she did kiss him at a party once. They were both

7

drunk and flirting with each other, as usual. Moony was sprawled over a large blue swivel chair, teasing Kat that he'd never seen her with anyone and that she must be asexual. Without thinking, she bent down and stuck her tongue in his mouth. He grabbed her and pulled her onto his lap, and although he smelled a little sweaty, she continued to kiss his mouth, and then his neck. After a few minutes she got bored and jumped to her feet, hoping someone else was around for her to talk to. No one else was in the room, but she saw Mike Yoke standing outside, staring at them through the window.

Mike Yoke is the shyer of the two. He has curly brown hair, a high forehead and artistic hands. He seems to harbor lots of secrets, whispers when he talks. Kat would fuck him in a minute if she had the chance. But he never goes out with girls who look like her—birdlike but curvy, with Asian features and chopped black hair.

"I'll be right back," Clare says. She heads for the bathroom. Kat feels a little funny sitting alone. She eats her sandwich and looks around the crowded cafe.

Now the meeting with Carrie Rozan is breaking up. The agent gathers her notes and shakes hands with Mary and the Mikes. Mike Yoke stands up with her, and as she turns to leave Yoke locks eyes with Kat. He winks at her.

She forces herself to swallow her food, and by the time she smiles back Yoke is already bending over his table, whispering something to his friends. Kat nervously stirs her coffee, hopes Clare returns soon.

"Hey," Yoke says, catching Kat off-guard. Instead of sitting in Clare's empty seat he squats next to Kat.

"Hi." Kat hates herself for being so nervous. She's never at a loss for words when she's talking to Clare.

"We just had our meeting with Carrie," he says.

"Yeah, I noticed." *Say something clever.* Kat takes a sip of her coffee.

"Where's Clare? I wanted to thank her for hooking us up with her agent."

8

"She'll be right back." Kat looks at her cup. *Say something!* "Hey, do you know who Darren Cooper is?"

"Of course. I just reread *Taquitz Canyon*," Yoke says. Kat has his attention.

"Well, he's in town and he's going to watch *Project Bluebook* with a bunch of us tonight at Raymond's house. Raymond works at *Signal*. Anyway, if you're interested I'm sure you could come."

"Really?" Yoke's eyes are shimmering, and Kat hopes it's really okay if he comes.

"Yeah. I'm probably going to get there around 8:45." Kat wants to ask him if they should ride together, but that would seem so datelike.

"Wow, this is great. Where does Raymond live?"

"Somewhere in the Mission. Clare knows his address."

Yoke stares at her like he wants to hear more, and just for a moment Kat feels connected, in-the-know. She relaxes a bit as she takes another sip of her coffee.

3

"This is so typical," Rhiannon says, slamming her notebook down on the table.

"Maybe he forgot," another editor says.

Jim ignores them. He brought his laptop to the editorial meeting and does his email offline while they wait for Jerry, the editor-in-chief, to show up. He can't understand why the other 12 editors and writers get so upset every time Jerry is late or forgets about their weekly meeting. Why don't they use this time to edit an article or make some calls?

Jerry finally breezes into the conference room and takes a seat in a corner. His hands are empty—no notes, no pen, no pad of paper. No one would ever guess he was the founder of *Signal*. He looks like an eccentric '70s-vintage rock musician, with long gray wavy hair, a handsome beaklike nose, and casual drapey cotton clothes. He's wearing Tevas today.

Jim quickly shuts down his email program and opens a new document in Microsoft Word to take notes.

Everyone quiets down, waiting for Jerry to start the meeting, but he only cocks his head and flashes his trademark "mysterious smile." Jim is about to mention Rhiannon's DNA article, just to get the ball rolling, when she speaks up.

"I came up with a few good titles for my junk-email piece.

Should I read them out loud?" Rhiannon wrote a feature about spammers and junk email for the issue that's being Fed-Exed to the printers tomorrow night.

She turns to a page in her notebook tagged with a Post-it note. "Well, I thought—"

Jerry gets up, in typical drooping-shoulder stance. "Kill that piece," he says.

Silence. Rhiannon's eyes are wide, protruding like cones.

"What!?" she finally shouts.

"That topic sucks," Jerry says. "It's already been done."

Papers are rustling, someone's keyboard is tapping notes. Jim sits still. He's learned that Jerry's decisions, no matter how erratic, stick like cement.

"What the hell are you talking about?" Rhiannon argues. She's been at *Signal* even longer than Jim and should know better. Her feature is history.

Jerry looks at his watch and takes a step toward the door.

"But you saw my story last week and *okayed* it!"

"What do you want us to replace it with?" another editor quickly asks. Editorial meetings are slated for an hour but sometimes last only five minutes, depending on Jerry's day.

Jerry looks quizzically at each editor, skipping Rhiannon. When his eyes lock with Jim's they intensify, expecting support from the editor's pet. Tensing, Jim babbles, "Too bad I haven't received the Gates article yet." It's scheduled for next month's deadline.

"That's what we'll replace Rhiannon's piece with," Jerry says, waving a satisfied index finger at nothing in particular. He massages his chin.

"Jim, turn in the Gates feature tomorrow by noon. In fact, I want another editorial meeting tomorrow morning—let's say 10:30." Jerry strides out of the room, quietly shutting the door behind him.

11

"Goddamn it!" Rhiannon says, pounding her fists on the table. "This is so fucked! I worked my ass off for that piece." Her voice cracks and a red-rash necklace blisters across her collarbone.

Rhiannon was *Signal's* first employee, working for free when Jerry and his partner Chelsea Simmons started out. She and Jerry butt heads all the time, especially over feminist issues, but Jerry looks to her for advice on what he calls "*Signal's* internal culture." When it comes to infrastructure issues and office politics he'll listen to her, but only *he* makes decisions on the magazine's content.

Now the group is bashing *Signal's* editorial system. It's irrational. It's tyrannical. It's unprofessional. It's a farce. The editors and writers are almost chanting, like an angry coven conjuring up a hex.

A sharp pain shoots across Jim's gut and he folds up his laptop. He feels bad for Rhiannon, but he's coming out of this meeting in worse shape than she is. He's got to edit and deliver a piece he doesn't yet have by tomorrow morning. He'd ask someone to back him up with an alternative piece but knows no one would willingly help him out. They all think he's an asshole, just because he plays the game.

Jim runs to his desk and pops a Rolaid. Then another. He checks his email, praying for the article. Thirteen new messages since he last checked, but nothing about Gates. *Damn it!* Jim reminds himself that the article wasn't due until this afternoon, tries to focus on something else.

He opens up a message from the production manager. It's a spam to everyone who works at *Signal:*

To the selfish slobs who need to learn the meaning of "community kitchen" (and you know who you are): How long does it take to fill the Brita water pitcher? Two, three seconds? Maybe Mommy cleaned up after you at home, but she's not refilling the Brita container for us here. There's no use having a Brita if it's not refilled. Once the filter dries up, it's destroyed and we have to buy a new one. At this point we're all drinking lead and chlorine, thanks to you. The solution? It's *reeeal* simple, kiddies. After you pour the water into your glass, REFILL THE PITCHER. Hope that's not too difficult.

Delete. He brings his own bottled water and doesn't have time for kitchen politics.

A message from Chelsea catches Jim's eye. She represents the other half of *Signal*—the business half. While Jerry oversees all creative content, Chelsea keeps the machine running.

Jim, can you stop by my office? I have something to ask you.

Jim immediately gets up. He doesn't usually talk to Chelsea, usually has no reason to. What could she want? His stomach flutters, not in its usual stabbing way but in adolescent puppy-crush style. Chelsea is a lot like his fiancée, Mandy, with a shiny dark bob, fast speech, and perky business suits. If they were four-legged animals, Chelsea would be a gazelle and Mandy a show horse.

One night Jim and Mandy went through the list of *Signal* employees, asking each other whom they would make out with if they didn't know each other, and Chelsea was at the top of Jim's list. It's not just her looks. She's got a quality that Mandy doesn't have. Something dark, demented, out of control. None of the dupes at *Signal* see this. How could they? At work she's the sharpest, most composed, self-possessed person on staff. She knows how to play people. But there have been a few overnight business retreats and after-hours parties where Jim's seen her other side. Times when she's stripped down to her bra and undies, danced wildly around a campfire or coffee table, sat in Jim's lap and asked him to feed her.

A breathless intern approaches Jim. "A CNN crew is here to interview you."

Jim tells the intern to have them wait.

"The reporter seems like he's in a hurry," the intern says.

"He'll wait." Jim walks away, heading toward Chelsea's office.

A couple of pens lie on the floor next to someone's desk and Jim grabs them, stashing them in his shirt pocket. A rare commodity at *Signal*. Jerry has made it clear that the company will not supply pens to its employees. Jim keeps his pens locked in his desk drawer.

13

Anyone who steps into *Signal*'s workspace is bewitched. A loft with high lumber ceilings, brick walls, and oversized windows looking out at the bay. A constant beat of lounge or world music reverberates from small speakers placed throughout the office. Everybody works in the same large room at long rows of tables set up as they'd be in a high-school cafeteria. Only Jerry and Chelsea have their own private offices in a corner of the loft. The energy at *Signal* is seductive, passionate, giving the illusion of an artist's studio, a place of clay and oils, sculptors and painters, not Internet geeks. Once people stop by they never want to leave. The whole world wants to work at *Signal*. No one sees its dysfunctions until the intoxication of landing a job there has worn off.

Chelsea's door is cracked open so Jim pokes his head inside. She's signing checks.

"Chelsea?"

Chelsea starts, her head snapping in his direction.

"Oh hi. What's up, Jim?" She gets out of her chair and perches on the edge of her desk.

Jim wonders if she remembers inviting him to her office. He grabs a chair and sits in front of her.

"Well, uh, I got your email."

"Nice shirt." Chelsea runs her angular hand down his rayon sleeve.

"Thanks. Heh."

"I wanted to talk about your gig tomorrow night. Are you still playing?"

Jim blushes. How does Chelsea know?

He plays clarinet with a jazz group once in a while. He used to play every week but Mandy hates it. Takes too much of his time, she says, and she doesn't like the trendy lounge crowd. They're drugged-up losers. But when the group doesn't have a clarinet, he fills in. Tomorrow will be nice since Mandy's going out of town.

"Yeah, 8:00. At the Slow Club." Jim wonders if Chelsea's had a boob job.

"Good. Jerry and I are taking a few people out tomorrow night. You've met Dusty Lawson and Andrew Garrett. We thought we'd hear you play, and then you can join us for drinks. We'd like you and Dusty to form a strong working relationship." Chelsea cocks her head while she talks.

Jim gets a little nervous around her digerati chums, who always run over his sentences with illuminating facts of their own. Andrew Garrett is a futurist business consultant, a renowned author, and the man who invented The EGG (Electronic Global Gathering), which is hands-down the most respected online service in existence.

Dusty Lawson is a stylishly outlandish character who fights for cyber-rights, jets around to fulfill prestigious high-tech speaking engagements, writes trippy sci-fi screenplays for Hollywood, and owns thousands of acres of oil land in Texas. Jim's glad he'll be on stage most of the evening.

"Thanks Chelsea. It'll be great to see you there. How did you know I was—?"

Chelsea looks over Jim's head, toward the door.

"Chelsea? Can I talk to you for a minute?"

Jim turns around and sees the production manager—the same guy who wrote the Brita spam.

"Hi Euclid. What's going on?" Chelsea waves him in. He leans against the desk next to her. With a quick tilt of her head she swings her hair to one side and looks at him. Jim shifts in his chair, wishing the mumbling weirdo with the pierced eyebrow and long fingernails would get the hell out.

Euclid asks Chelsea if she remembers the generous software company that gave *Signal*'s art department an expensive computer program for free.

"Yeesss?" Chelsea asks, waiting for the punch line.

"Well, I thought it would be nice to give them some *Signal* tote bags and sweatshirts to show our appreciation."

Chelsea sits back down at her computer. She opens up a folder. The list of *Signal* merchandise. She lays a long index finger on her pursed lips as she thinks.

15

"They can each have a cap," she finally says.

"A cap?" Euclid unconsciously rotates his eyebrow ring.

"Yes. They can each have a cap." Chelsea perches herself back on the desk and looks at Jim. Euclid pivots so that he's facing her.

"But Chelsea, these people just gave us a 10,000-dollar gift. A cap would be *insulting*. How about just the sweatshirts?"

"I only want them to have the caps."

"But *why?*"

"Just a capricious decision."

Euclid moans. She ignores him and he stomps out of the office. The door shuts loudly behind him.

"I've got a lot of work to do," Chelsea says. Her attitude has changed. She's standing erect and waits for Jim to leave.

"I guess I'll see you tomorrow night," he says.

"Yes, at the Slow Club. Thanks for stopping by."

4

Kat catches another typo and marks it with a red pen. The sun beats her back like a shiatsu massage. Working in the park makes it hard to concentrate. Clare also lies on her stomach, next to Kat. They're each proofing half of the next *Going Gaga*. Once they finish their stacks they'll swap, see if they can find mistakes the other missed.

The words are beginning to blur. Kat needs a rest. She sits up and crosses her legs.

"What are you doing?" Clare asks.

"Just taking a breather."

Clare sits up too. She stretches her neck. "We should really try to finish this by tomorrow. I want to get this printed in time for ZineFest." Clare notices an error on the front page of her stack and quickly circles it a bunch of times.

"Relax. We have plenty of time," Kat says.

Clare is too high-strung, too caffeinated. She's got eight whole weeks before the big night.

ZineFest is an annual zine convention that takes place at Club DNA. It's a good place for zinesters to publicize their zines, sell crap like T-shirts and subscriptions, network with other writers and small-press publishers. *Going Gaga* and *Force* will share a table.

"We don't have *that* much time, Kat."

Whatever. Kat watches an old lady lug some bags of groceries into a peppermint pink Victorian house. She's probably lived across the park forever. Kat wonders what the biddy thinks about her neighborhood's recent metamorphosis. A few years ago South Park was a skeleton of its current gentrified self. Most of the Victorians had slumped around the park like propped up corpses, office buildings had been beaten to boards and broken glass, even criminals stayed clear of the area. Yet there was a small core of locals—artists, old-timers, low-income families—who took pride in their quiet community. They liked things the way they were. And they hated the onslaught of entrepreneurial digeratis-to-be who enthusiastically found they could rent lots of space for next to nothing.

The tension between the locals and the flocking multimedia youth is subtle. More obvious is the disparate picture seen from the center of the park. Historic houses shuffled between freshly stuccoed Euro-cafes and Gehry-esque condos. Roadsters parked behind blanket-filled grocery carts. An old kook junk collector's open garage confusing patrons on their way to the chichi gift shop next door. Cappuccino aficionados slurping foam, backs turned to the halfway house next door.

South Park's transformation is still in progress. Empty lofts are snatched daily, construction is rampant, twenty-somethings are becoming rich—and famous. Kat feels the pulse, wants to be in the center of it. But for now she fidgets in the periphery.

"Do you want to be famous?" Kat asks Clare.

"Of course. Doesn't everyone?"

Clare is pretty, says her background is half Egyptian, half English. But she's too fragile, with paper-dry skin and purple crescents always hanging below her eyes—eyes that are bloodshot today. She works seven days a week, like most people around here. It can get depressing, the way Clare and her husband devote every waking hour to computers and work. But it's part of the culture. *Going Gaga* doesn't make a profit, barely keeps itself afloat. Clare expects it to bust into the mainstream soon. She's *sure* it will.

Kat wants recognition as much as anyone, wants to be the people around her. If only she could find a groove.

"Oh!" Clare exclaims, waving her hand.

Kat sees Yoke and Mary on the sidewalk in front of a designer boutique, waving back. Mary says something to Yoke and they start walking toward the park.

"We can't talk long," Clare whispers. "We have to finish these articles."

Kat remembers tonight, Darren Cooper *and* Yoke, and feels like it's Christmas Eve. She pictures herself on top of Yoke, his hands under her shirt. Mary and Yoke are in the park now. *Act normal.* Kat looks only at Mary.

"Working hard?" Mary asks sarcastically.

"We are," Clare says.

It took over a month before Kat and Mary exchanged more than two words. Kat thought she was an arrogant bitch, but it turns out she's just really quiet. Like Yoke and Moony. Must be a Chicago thing, where they all grew up. Mary's actually down-to-earth and really smart. Besides her eggplant-dyed hair she looks granola, with hairy legs, no makeup, poncho-type clothing.

"Where are you guys going?" Clare asks.

"My friend at the *SF Daily* is subletting his furnished apartment, right over there." Yoke points across the street. "The red door." The apartment is between the designer boutique and Pepito's, a burrito joint.

"You want to live around here?" Clare asks.

Yoke shrugs his shoulders. "Maybe. Mary's thinking about it too. The place is 3,000 bucks a month, so a bunch of us would have to rent it together."

"We just want to check it out," Mary says. "Want to come with us?"

Kat nods her head. She likes living by herself but wants to

19

see what these fixed-up lofts look like. Anyway, she's sick of sitting in the park.

"Sorry, we can't. We have so much work to do," Clare says.

"I want to go, Clare. I'll be right back," Kat says.

Clare snaps a sigh and widens her eyes, something she does when she's stressed. Kat pretends not to notice.

It feels good to stand up. She follows her friends toward the shiny red door. They cross the street and pass the door, continue walking toward the end of the block.

"Hey, what are we doing?"

"We have to get in through the back," Yoke says.

They turn right, then another right down an alley.

Kat gags at the ripe stench of dumpsters lining the back of a building.

They get to a black gate secured with a massive padlock. "I think this is it," Yoke says loudly, competing with a chorus of screaming saws, falling pipes and pounding hammers. Kat feels her bones jump with each clank of a hammer. Men in yellow plastic helmets cling to all sides of the building next door.

Yoke slowly tries the combination. "21-00-13," he says to himself. He yanks on the lock but it doesn't open.

"Huh?" Yokes tries it again. "Damn!"

"Are you sure you have the right combo?" Mary asks.

"Let me try," Kat says. "21-00-13?"

"Yeah," Yoke says.

Kat spins the dial and the lock pops open.

"Cool!" Mary says.

They enter a small cement patio that looks like a zoo cage. Mary walks to a nondescript door.

"That should be unlocked," Yoke says.

Mary jiggles the handle and it turns. They climb a flight of steps and enter a huge sunny loft.

"Shit! Careful you guys," Yoke says, pointing to wet mud tracks they've all stamped on the gray Berber carpet. Kat wipes her feet on the corner of a step.

"Wow, this place is huge." Kat figures it's at least three

20

times as large as her one-bedroom apartment, with just a few wood-and-metal vertical beams that hint at where one "room" starts and the other ends. A couple of Japanese paper partitions are propped up to make space more private. The kitchen and bathrooms are made of red-and-black granite. The front room has bay windows overlooking the park. Kat looks out and sees Clare scribbling away. She laughs and points her out to Mary and Yoke.

The furniture is modern and sparse, sleek and cold. A tall cubicle hutch is attached to a wall with a wide-screen TV and a stacked stereo. Yoke turns on the radio.

"Sounds pretty good," Kat says.

"Mmmm. I smell chicken," Mary says. She looks in the oven. It's empty.

"I smell it too. Probably the burrito place downstairs," Yoke says.

Kat's hungry again. Centro lunches never fill her.

Mary opens the refrigerator. "Hey, there's a six-pack of Coke in here." She takes a can.

"We shouldn't take those," Yoke says.

"Why not? No one lives here." Mary offers one to Yoke and he accepts. She takes two more and tosses one to Kat. A couple of low black cotton couches that look like they open into futon beds sit across from each other in the middle of the room, with a lacquered wood table in between. Kat settles down on one, Mary and Yoke on the other.

Kat props her heavy boots on the table. Her skirt is short so she crosses her legs. Parched from her hour in the sun, she guzzles the Coke.

"This place is so Ikea," Mary says.

"I hate it," Yoke says, playing with a remote control. "It's too high-tech, too '80s."

He accidentally turns on the TV set. *Rosie* is on. Yoke flips through the channels and stops at E! Something about fashion models. He hits the mute button so they can still hear the radio.

21

"This place would make a better office," Kat says.

"Yeah, but I'd hate to hear that obnoxious jackhammer every day. It's so annoying," Mary says.

Kat finishes her drink, crunches the can and tosses it into the kitchen's wastebasket.

Yoke and Mary are slouched forward, staring at the muted telly. Kat wonders if they ever get excited about stuff. She rests her head back on the couch.

"What happened at your meeting today with the book agent?" Kat asks.

Neither Mary nor Yoke answers right away.

Finally Mary says, "A couple of people are interested in our proposal. We might get an offer in the next day or so."

"That's great!" Kat says. "Which publishers?" It's a challenge now, to see how much information she can get these two to divulge.

Yoke looks at Mary before speaking. "I don't know. A couple of editors are still thinking about it."

"Like who?"

"We really won't know anything for the next few days." Mary crosses her arms. End of conversation.

What's the big fuckin' deal? Are they afraid she'll jinx it for them? Kat wants to ask what kind of advance they're hoping to get, but skips it. She'd love to make Yoke come, jungle-fuck style, make him shake, scream, contort his face, lose his mind.

"How long does your cousin want to sublet this place?" Kat asks.

"You mean my *friend*. For a year, I think," Yoke says, sitting back. He puts his feet up on the table, bumping his Coke can.

"Shit!" he says. There's Coke all over the carpet.

Mary and Yoke jump up and look for paper towels but can't find any. Kat runs to the bathroom for toilet paper and sees a black towel. Perfect.

22

"Here, use this."

Yoke mops up the puddle as best he can. The huge stain looks like a table shadow.

"Oh great. I'm dead," Yoke says, standing over it.

"Just cover it with a couch," Kat says. She moves her couch closer to the window and slides the table over. Mary shoves the other couch over the spot.

Kat likes the new arrangement. Not so symmetrical.

"Let's go," Yoke says, turning off the TV.

Kat hangs the towel back up, folding it so the spongy side is hidden.

Outside the temperature has already dropped. They walk back toward the park.

"Did anyone turn off the radio?" Mary asks.

No one answers.

5

"It's clearly evident that we've moved from a second-wave agrarian society to a Tofflerian third-wave information society. Fewer and fewer people are pushing around atoms, and more and more people are pushing around electrons."

"Great! That should do it," says the fat uptight CNN reporter.

Jim shakes hands with the CNN crew and rushes to his desk. 4:30. The interview lasted a lot longer than expected and he still hasn't fired Mara.

He runs to his computer to check on the Bill Gates article.

"Are you coming to Raymond's tonight?"

Jim's heart does a flip. Mara is standing by his side, intruding in his personal space. She's chirpier than he's ever seen her. *Fire her now.*

"It'll be a big group tonight since Darren Cooper's going to be there." Mara's cheeks are red and her nostrils flare.

Before Jim can respond Mandy taps him on the shoulder. He hasn't seen her all day. She's holding a large suitcase with wheels, ready to be taken to the airport.

"Hey babe, time to go," she says. "Ready?"

"Hold on!" Jim wishes Mara and Mandy would back off. He scrolls through his email. Still no Gates piece. The goddamn writer *promised* it would be in today. Sweat beads sprout on Jim's upper lip.

"Did you know Cooper's going to be at Raymond's tonight?" Mara asks Mandy, her words shooting out like machine-gun bullets.

Mandy glances at Mara as if she were a peasant, then at Jim with a you-haven't-fired-her-*yet?* look.

Might as well get it over with. He takes a breath, forming the best firing phrase in his head, but as soon as his mouth opens the girl runs off.

"Hey Anny, did you hear Darren Cooper's going to be at Raymond's tonight?" Jim hears her say.

Mandy lifts the handle of her suitcase. "We have to go."

The airport. The Gates article. Darren Cooper. He'll fire Mara tomorrow.

Mandy raises the window of the BMW. It was warm this morning but cold fog is starting to roll in.

"Why on earth haven't you gotten rid of Mara? The new girl starts next week." Mandy adjusts her shoulder pads.

"I barely had time to eat lunch today, let alone fire anyone. I'll definitely do it tomorrow." Jim wonders if he can shape up a poorly written piece someone submitted last week about Marimba's Kim Polese, in case the other doesn't come in tonight.

Mandy lights up two cigarettes and offers one to Jim. "Going to Raymond's tonight would be a great way for you to hook up with Cooper. You could take him out for a drink after they watch their TV show and tell him our idea."

"Yeah, I know. That's what I'm planning to do." Of all nights. That fucking Gates article. Jim tries to clear his mind. He tells himself that even if he doesn't receive the piece until tomorrow morning he'll be able to edit it in time.

"Good!" Mandy says. "I wish I could be there tonight. If you can get Cooper alone it'll be great."

Whenever Darren Cooper walks into *Signal*'s offices, the

editors dote on him like he's the next Tom Wolfe. Jim's tried to explain his idea to Cooper a few times but can't ever get a word in without some jackass hovering around. Jim likes the author's writing well enough but likes his status even better. It's Cooper's name that'll help sell their book.

"Get off the freeway!" Mandy yells.

Jim almost misses the off-ramp and cuts off a bearded man in a truck. The man nearly falls out his window giving Jim the finger.

"Damn, I've got a run in my nylons," Mandy says.

Everyone on the sales staff at *Signal* wears designer clothes, and the women in advertising are all "hose and heel gals." Mandy wears more makeup than any of the others. As senior account manager she says she has to look professional. She comes from a wealthy blue-blood family from Boston and looks the part. Jim met her in the Harvard business library two years ago when he was doing research for the *Boston Herald* and she was finishing up her MBA. Then they both moved to San Francisco to work for *Signal*. She doesn't care that he comes from a working-class family. She admires his sophisticated taste, GQ-WASPy looks, and unabashed drive to succeed. He's attracted to her pin-up body, take-charge personality, and pre-occupation with her career. Given his demanding schedule, Jim feels lucky he met Mandy before he got the job with *Signal* and that she's as busy as he is. He just proposed to her and they set the date to coincide with their second anniversary of dating— August 15, two months away, and one month before his 30th birthday.

Jim has to brake at a green light to avoid running down a drunk pedestrian who's taken over the intersection. The inebriated fellow is pretending to be a traffic controller. With exaggerated hand movements, he's directing cars from all directions to either stop or proceed. Jim goes heavy on the horn.

26

"Move, pissant!" he belts out his window.

Mandy chuckles, then says, "Aw, Jim, the poor guy looks homeless."

"Asshole!" Jim hollers at the man.

The drunk is oblivious to Jim's and others' noise, but a police officer on a motorcycle finally intervenes and talks the man into stepping up onto the sidewalk.

When they get to the Oakland airport Jim pulls up to the unloading zone.

"Hope you don't mind that I'm not going in with you," he says. "I need to rush back to the office and call a goddamn writer before I meet up with Cooper." Jim will get that Gates article if he has to bang down the writer's front door.

"No problem. I'm going to miss you."

"Me too."

Jim takes Mandy's heavy suitcase out of the trunk and she pulls a new pair of panty hose out of its side pocket before he gives the case to a Skycap. He tells her to call when she gets to New York, though it'll be after 2 AM by the time she gets to the hotel.

"Now you be a good boy," she says in a baby voice.

He smiles and kisses her goodbye. She abruptly breaks away and straightens her blouse, saying she'd better hurry so she can change her nylons.

Jim pulls out of the unloading zone and merges with the flow of airport traffic. As he tries to shift into third gear a ferocious metallic scream emanates from his engine. He tries it again and the gearshift vibrates frenetically before another scream erupts. He tries second gear, and then first. Same result. *Shit.* He hits his steering wheel with a closed fist. Tries again. More metallic screams. *Shit!* His first reaction is to find Mandy, but on second thought he decides to find a pay phone. Triple-A will be more helpful.

Jim flicks on his hazard lights, locks the doors, looks for a telephone. He sees a line of four phones, all taken. He lights a cigarette and waits.

6:00. That drunk really put him behind schedule. A large red-headed woman slams the receiver down and huffs away. Jim throws his half-smoked cigarette on the ground and grabs the phone. He pulls out his Triple-A card and dials the 800 number. Busy. He dials again. Still busy. Jim's colon somersaults and he fishes out another cigarette. On the third try he gets through, only to get a recording telling him to hold the line. *Fuck.* He takes a long drag and waits.

6

The phone rings and Kat slowly picks it up, careful not to smudge her wet nails. It's Mike Yoke. He's about to catch a bus and wants to make sure she's going to be at Raymond's by 8:45. Says he doesn't really know the people who work for *Signal*, feels a little awkward going over to Raymond's, and doesn't want to get there before Kat and Clare show up. She tells him to stop worrying, she'll be there in 20 minutes, and hangs up.

She takes a deep breath, feeling like an idiot for being so nervous. She checks herself out in the mirror and hopes her butt doesn't look too big in her blue velvet stretch pants.

A gust of wind shoots through an open window. Kat notices fat raindrops slowly amassing on the glass, threatening to fuck up her transportation. She refuses to drive her scooter in the rain—last time she skidded on an oily puddle and ripped up her knee. Kat grabs the portable phone and drops onto her couch, tossing her legs over the armrest. She calls some friends who live three buildings down from her. Danny writes a column for *Signal*—a job he does from home—and his girlfriend, Kimmy, works as an assistant designer at Esprit. The girl answers.

"Hello?"

"Hi Kimmy, it's Kat."

"Hi."

"What are you guys doing tonight?"

"Not much, just eating dinner." Kimmy sounds lazy and Kat apprehensively tells her about Cooper, how she can't get to Raymond's on her scooter, and asks if they want to come. Clare didn't seem to care that Kat had invited Yoke. Two more people shouldn't make a difference.

Kimmy muffles the phone, then drops it. "Whoops!" Kat hears her say. "Sorry about that. Sure, we'll go. Danny's all excited. When do we have to leave?"

"Now."

Kat throws on a black leather jacket, steps into her motorcycle boots and locks the door. Without an umbrella she runs through the rain to Kimmy and Danny's apartment. It's an old Victorian in the Lower Haight, a neighborhood filled with hole-in-the-wall bars, coffee shops, tattoo and piercing joints, cheap food, and vintage clothing stores.

"Boy, don't *you* look spiffy," Kimmy says when she sees Kat in her blue velvet pants. Kat's wearing more eyeliner than usual and has exaggerated her lips with a brownish-blackish-red lip-liner. Her short wet hair is slicked to one side. She compliments Kimmy's new knee-high boots.

They pile into Danny's decaled vw van, an odd choice for a guy who sports a crew cut, black horn-rimmed glasses and green polyester pants. He seems more like the Nash Metropolitan type. Danny found the van at a garage sale in Berkeley for 500 bucks. He hasn't had any problems with it, says the man who sold it to him was desperate for cash. The van's skinny wipers are moving at full speed.

"Oh, can we stop for beer? It's on me, to pay for the ride," Kat says.

"Think we can stop for beer and still get there by 9:00?" Danny asks.

They have only half an hour before *Project* starts. "I don't

30

know. Maybe we can get it afterwards and hang out at your house for a while, if you want."

"Yeah!" Kimmy says.

"What about work tomorrow?" Danny asks.

"Who cares? I can get by on a few hours of sleep," Kimmy says.

Kat snickers. Kimmy always wants to go out and party with friends and Danny always balks, complaining about work the next day. They get to Raymond's street and circle the block a couple of times, then the next few blocks before they find a parking spot. All three crowd under Kimmy's umbrella while they run to Raymond's.

Danny rings the doorbell and puts his arm around his mod girlfriend. Kat looks into the front door's little square window and sees Raymond loping down a flight of steps.

"Hi," Raymond says in a mellow stoned voice. He has long dark curly hair pulled back into a ponytail, with loose strands flying all over the place. He's wearing lots of purple. "Come on up."

Kat's head is filled with cotton, as if she's semiconscious and hyperaware at the same time. *Should I let my arms hang down by my sides or should I cross them?* They get to the living room, which isn't nearly as crowded as Kat had expected, and she sees Him sitting on a couch, talking to some chick that Kat doesn't recognize. There's an empty space on His left side, and before Kat knows what's going on, she's sitting in it.

Cooper glances at Kat, starts to turn back to the chick, then looks at Kat again and smiles. "Hi."

"Hi!" *Shit.* She sounds too enthusiastic, like a goo-goo-eyed fan.

Now he's back with the chick. Kat sits there looking for something to do. Kimmy and Danny sit on some pillows across the room. Danny casually talks to Kimmy but glances at Cooper every three seconds or so. Kat notices for the first time that Mike Yoke is in the room. About 10 people are scattered around, talking, drinking beer, eating pizza.

Raymond catches Kat's eye. "Want something to eat or drink?"

"Yeah, do you have some beer?"

"Sure do." Raymond hands her a bottle of Heineken. "Have you met everybody?"

"No, I don't think so," Kat says as calmly as possible.

Raymond makes introductions to everyone. The chick Cooper is talking to lives upstairs from Raymond and goes by the obnoxious name of Boom. She has a short brown shag and laughs very loudly. Cooper laughs too. Kat hates her.

Raymond says to Cooper, "Kat works with Clare on *Going Gaga*. You know Clare's husband, Gerald, who edited your story for *Signal*."

Cooper turns his back on Boom. He smiles again at Kat. "Really? I love *Going Gaga*. Is Clare coming tonight?" Kat adores his Canadian accent.

"Yes, she's supposed to be here." Kat feels good about the way she said that. Then her mind draws a blank.

Yoke has inched his way over, and Kat introduces Yoke to Cooper as the editor of *Force*. Then another blank. *Got to keep the conversation going.*

Cooper seems excited to be talking to them. Kat figures he wants to learn more about the San Francisco zine scene as well as *Project Bluebook* for his next novel.

"I'd like to talk with you guys about what you're doing. Think we could get together sometime, maybe for lunch?"

Kat wants to pinch herself. *This isn't happening!*

"Well," she nearly stammers, "we're meeting at my friends' place, Kimmy and Danny's, after *Project*." She points to the couple. "They live pretty close. We're just going to have some beers, and you can join us if you want."

Kat and Yoke look at Cooper as if he's about to call out lottery numbers. He shrugs his shoulders. "Yeah, all right."

Adrenaline shoots through Kat's body, the cotton in her head gets thicker. "Okay, wonderful!" she hears herself saying. She never uses the word *wonderful*.

Clare and Gerald arrive just as *Project Bluebook* starts. Clare smiles at Kat and Gerald waves to Cooper. Boom grabs Cooper's arm and starts explaining the show's basic premise.

Kat can't concentrate on *Project*. First of all, everyone's shouting at the TV screen, which ruins the creepy alien ambience the series usually creates. The escape from reality works only when there's no extraneous noise. Of course Cooper is the bigger distraction, though Kat's a little calmer now that she's been sitting next to him for a while. He's looking away from her to watch the program, and to hear Boom's *Cliffs Notes* of past episodes. Kat looks at the left-rear corner of his head, which, like Yoke's, is covered with molasses curls. She can't believe she's only inches from the head that defined a generation. His thin physique shifts as the chick babbles on about *Project*'s parasite grays and HAARP scientists, and Kat wonders if the TV program is at all interesting to Cooper. She wants to do him right here on the couch.

A phone rings by Kat's foot and she jumps. Raymond dives for it.

"It's for you," he says to Cooper.

Everyone continues to look at the television set but attention is locked on Cooper, who talks in a hushed voice.

After a minute he hangs up and apologizes, says he has to go and pick up some publicity photos.

"At *this* hour?" Raymond asks.

"Yeah, the photographer is leaving for Connecticut tomorrow morning, so I have to get them tonight."

Before he gets up Kat asks him about their after-*Project* get-together. He says he'll try to make it after he picks up the photos, but if he's not there by 11:00, they'll have to do it another time. She writes Danny and Kimmy's address and phone number on a napkin he's been holding.

"Thanks." He squeezes her arm and leaves.

Kat forces her next few breaths.

Mike Yoke leaps into Cooper's empty seat.

33

7

It's 9:48 by the time Jim hails a taxi from San Francisco's Embarcadero Center. He jumps in the cab and gives the driver Raymond's address.

"Is it okay if I smoke?" he asks the driver.

"Okay by me. Just crack the window."

Jim hasn't had a cigarette for three hellish hours. After finally getting through to a human at Triple-A, it took someone almost an hour to show up. The guy towed Jim's car to a shop in Oakland. Then, finding the airport's cash machine out of order, Jim was forced to take public transportation into the city.

The next two hours were a total waste: waiting in the rain for the AirBART bus to take him to the BART station; getting on a BART train only to have it break down; shuffling to another train that was headed in the wrong direction but would take him to a station where he could transfer to a train heading in the right direction; then waiting 20 more minutes for the tracks to clear so the proper train could take him into San Francisco.

Jim exhales a lungful of smoke and slowly rotates his neck three times in each direction. He won't be editing any articles tonight, but at least he'll still be able to talk to Cooper. Later tonight he'll check his email for the Gates article, which *must* be in by now, and then he can get up early tomorrow and tackle it when he's fresh.

The taxi pulls up at Raymond's apartment in the Mission District. Jim looks into the cab's rearview mirror to comb his hair before he pays and gets out.

He's a little hesitant to knock on Raymond's door. Although only a few years older than Raymond's crowd, Jim feels a generation away. But Darren Cooper will be there, and *Project Bluebook* must just be ending. Maybe he can whisk Cooper away to a nearby tapas bar.

He knocks on the door, looks into its little square window and sees Raymond coming down the stairs. Raymond looks at Jim through the window and cocks his head, obviously perplexed. He opens the door.

"Hi Jim. Uh, what are you doing here?" He smiles crookedly.

Jim smiles back, acts like there's nothing odd about this visit. "Hi Raymond! How's it going? Guess I missed *Project Bluebook.*"

"Uh, yeah, you did. Want to come up?" Raymond motions for Jim to enter.

Jim saunters in, leaving wet tracks on the wooden steps. He makes his way to the living room, eyes darting around for Cooper. The room quiets down as heads turn toward him. Jim recognizes Danny as one of *Signal*'s freelance writers and nods, forgetting his name.

Danny says hi, introduces Jim to the group. Jim doesn't see Cooper.

"Want a beer?" Raymond asks.

"Okay. Yes, thank you." Jim takes the bottle and chugs several gulps.

"So what brings you here?" Raymond asks.

Everybody in the room is staring at Jim. He's the only one wearing gabardine pants and penny loafers. He doesn't want to take off his jacket, wonders where the hell Cooper is. He finds himself standing right in the center of this slacker crowd and sidesteps to a less conspicuous spot near the wall. He can see the kitchen and notices Mara, the receptionist he was supposed to fire. She's leaning against the table, making out with one of *Signal*'s shabby interns. He wonders what she'd do if he fired her right now.

"Well, I uh, I need to talk to Darren Cooper, and I heard he was here. I hope you don't mind my barging in like this."

"Hey, no problem," Raymond says as he lights up a joint. "Want a hit?"

Jim stares at the joint. He's smoked pot before, but it's been a few years. He used to get high sometimes with an old girl-friend of his but never liked doing it in public. Made him para-noid.

But he knows everyone here already thinks of him as an arrogant geek, and before he can think of a way to *just say no*, he says, "Sure." He wonders if Cooper is high.

Jim takes a hit off the joint and hopes he doesn't cough it up. The marijuana crackles as it burns. Jim holds in the smoke for a few seconds, then exhales. He pulls it off. Everything is cool. He gives the joint back to Raymond.

"You just missed Gerald and Clare," Danny says.

It would have been nice to have seen Gerald, who's got one foot in each social group. He hangs out with Clare's zine friends and *Signal*'s "lower echelon" all the time, but since Gerald is an associate editor at *Signal,* he and Clare also enjoy occasional parties and fancy dinners with the *Signal* elite.

"Oh. What about Cooper? Did they leave with him? Where is he?" Jim hopes he doesn't sound desperate.

Raymond has sucked in a lungful of marijuana smoke and can't answer.

36

Danny fills in. "Cooper left a little while ago to pick up some photos." He looks at Kimmy and Kat. "In fact, we better go back to the apartment before he gets there."

He doesn't know if it's the pot, but Jim's suddenly frantic.

He doesn't have a car. He hasn't eaten. He's wet and he doesn't know these people. He feels alone. And he's just *got* to see Cooper tonight.

"Want to come with us?" Kat says to Yoke and Raymond. Yoke grabs his jacket, says he'd love to join them. Raymond decides to hang out at home for the rest of the evening. Boom, who isn't invited, tries to lock eyes with Kat, then with Danny, but no one pays attention to her.

Danny, Kimmy, Kat and Yoke all get up and thank Raymond. They walk by Jim and he knows it's now or possibly never.

Jim lunges toward Danny. "Hey, do you think it would be okay if I came along?" he asks in a lowered voice, hoping no one else can hear him.

"Well, I guess so," Danny says without enthusiasm. "Do you know where I live?"

"Actually, I was hoping I could get a lift. My car's in the shop."

"Oh." Danny stares at Jim.

Kimmy comes to the rescue. "Sure, you can come along with us!"

8

"Don't forget to stop for beer," Kat says to Danny. "It's on me."

The van has two benchlike seats in the back. Kat is sitting next to Yoke in the first one, Jim sits by himself in the rear.

Kimmy, riding shotgun, turns around and tells Kat and Yoke about a new line of T-shirts she's designing. She's calling it "Nrrrds" and she'll start off with eight different nerdlike characters, each enclosed in a rectangle with a name, abbreviation, and number, as if they're part of the Periodic Table of the Elements.

"That's a great idea!" Kat says. "And you should put them on really thin Ts, and use ugly pastel colors—peach and powder blue and Easter-egg green."

"Is this something you're doing for Esprit?" Yoke asks.

"No, it's my own thing."

How do people ignite their ambitions? Kat wishes she had some great project in the works, but even creating something as low-key as a zine seems like such a complex undertaking. Kat wouldn't know where to start.

Yoke says he has a cousin who prints shirts and could probably give Kimmy a discount.

"Thanks, that would be great. I'll make sure to get his number from you."

As Danny makes a sharp turn, Kat leans into Yoke. She feels his warm breath on her cheek and fantasizes that he grasps her, flips her around, smothers her with his flesh. The van straightens out and she slowly separates herself from him. She's surprised Yoke turns her on as much as Cooper did.

The van arrives at Danny and Kimmy and Kat's street.

"Are we walking to the liquor store?" Kat asks, wishing she'd worn a sweater under her jacket.

"Yeah, hope you don't mind," Danny says. "That way I only have to park once."

Kat looks out the window and notices the rain has stopped. She hears someone cough behind her and turns around to see Jim. She'd forgotten about him.

"What are you so anxious to see Cooper about?" she asks.

Jim is hunched forward with his arms crossed. His shoulders are nearly touching his ears.

Yoke turns around to hear his response.

"Just business."

"What kind of business?"

Jim pauses, looking out the window. "Uh, he wrote a short story for *Signal*. We just have some things to discuss."

Kat wonders why this guy is so stiff and vague. So self-important. She's bored with him and turns back around. Yoke follows suit.

After searching for seven minutes Danny finds a parking spot. The van's butt sticks into the red but in San Francisco you take what you can get. As long as you're not blocking someone's driveway, parked under a "No Parking" sign, or negligent with your parking meter, you're usually okay.

The group climbs out of the van and heads toward Haight Street. Kat shivers, hating San Francisco's incessant chill. Even when it's a sunny day you can always bet on a frigid evening. This never seems to bother anyone else.

The *Signal* editor quietly offers Kat his jacket. She thanks him, surprised at his thoughtfulness.

They enter a liquor store on Lower Haight and Kat grabs two six-packs. "Is this enough?"

39

"Uh-huh," Danny says. He picks up a bottle of Absolut.

"Here, I'll pay for that," Kat says. "You drove."

"No, that's okay. I'll get the vodka," Danny says.

Jim walks out of the liquor store before the others and lights up a cigarette. Danny grabs the two bags of liquor and hands one to Yoke.

Kat pulls the jacket around her when they step back into the cold. A faint spicy fragrance lines the collar and she automatically categorizes Jim as a *man* rather than a *guy*. He'd have more fun hanging out with her dad than the gang he's with tonight. Yoke waves his hand across his face to shoo away Jim's smoke. Jim doesn't notice.

They pass a store called Body Manipulations.

"That's where my friend got branded," Danny says.

"Branded?" Jim asks.

"You know, like when a cow gets branded," Kat explains.

"Yeah, I know," Jim says.

"I'm thinking of getting it done," she lies, to shock Jim.

"Why?" He looks angry.

"Because it's cool."

"Oh God," Jim moans.

Kimmy nudges Kat. "Ooh! What kind of design are you going to get?"

"I'm still deciding." Kat wants to change the subject.

She notices Jim's large Rolex watch and wonders if it's one of those imitations you can pick up in Singapore for 10 bucks. Her uncle gave her one when she was 14, a decade ago. She wore it for a week then gave it to a friend at school.

"What time is it?" she asks.

Jim looks at his watch. "10:45."

"We've got to hurry," Kat says.

9

"Welcome to our humble abode," Danny says to his three guests.

They enter the Victorian flat and follow Danny to the living room. Jim immediately sinks into a red vinyl armchair, the cleanest looking seat in the room. Danny sits in a wooden rocking chair, and Yoke and Kat make themselves cozy on a worn fuzzy couch. Kimmy asks everybody what they want to drink. Beers all around except for Danny, who has a screwdriver.

Jim thanks Kimmy for the beer and drinks it slowly. Doesn't want to be too smashed when he talks to Cooper. The beer melts his muscles.

Danny unscrews the lid of a white hair-gel container that's sitting on the coffee table and pulls out a bag of joints.

Jim doesn't want to do this anymore and looks at the front door, wondering when Cooper will rescue him. *Please knock on the door.* He doesn't want to smoke any more marijuana, but doesn't want to be the only one who refuses. *Hurry up Cooper!*

Danny lights up, makes a weird snorting sound as he holds in the smoke. It bothers Jim. This isn't his scene.

Now Kimmy has the joint.

Kat is telling Yoke about a ham-radio club she used to belong to whose members met virtually by sending Morse code messages to each other.

"Now I have this habit of tapping out words with my fingers while I talk on the phone," she says.

Jim looks at Kat and can't believe that this cute chick, who laughs like a girl and whose eyes are lined like Cleopatra's, is interested in such a prehistoric geek hobby.

"Here Jim," Kimmy says as she passes the joint.

Shit! "Thanks," he says as he takes a quick toke—just enough to please the gang. He passes the joint to Yoke, who passes it to Kat without taking a hit. No one says anything to Yoke.

Jim chugs down the rest of his beer and it hits him hard. He sinks into the red vinyl.

Kimmy walks over to a tall CD rack, plucks out a disc and pops it into a boombox. A sultry British male voice purrs over sensual drums and a Middle Eastern–style synthesizer. Sounds like jazzy spy poetry, something they'd play in a James Bond movie. *"I grabbed her cute arse so close and sank my desperate mouth at the heavy oily sex."* Jim's never heard music quite like this before. It takes him away, to a sweaty place without screeching modems and 404 errors. *"I pass old hotels with sexy curtains. Life and love and death. . . . I always get a kick out of Paris."* French voices whisper in the background.

Everyone is talking and laughing but no one sees Jim. He's invisible to the four people in front of him. He's watching a play, a farce about twenty-something culture. The girl with the short black hair who calls herself Kat is the star. Her lilting voice and animated features have everyone mesmerized. Her blue velvet pants are now the topic of conversation. Her side-kick, a fellow who goes by Yoke, pets the velvet pants, and they all fall into hysterics. The hosts of the show, Danny and Kimmy, keep the drinks a-pourin' and the joints a-burnin'.

42

Another bottle of beer appears in Jim's hand. He swallows its cold contents.

Jim looks around the room and sees tall stacks of books and magazines. A thick bouncy wave passes through his body. Sounds and colors are turned up a notch. *"I first saw Paris in Soho when I was 13, sitting on a coffin drinking coffee. I wore black on black."* An old framed movie poster of Tarzan hangs on the wall, and Jim is transfixed by the deep red bustier of its featured actress, Monique Van Vooren, whose pointy breasts look as dangerous as the whip in her hand. Another swell of bouncy air cuts through Jim's body. He then sees a mannequin propped below the poster. It's wearing a clear plastic shirt with a bull's-eye in the middle.

"Like her shirt?" asks Kimmy, who's suddenly standing over Jim.

"It's so weird," he blurts.

"I made it," Kimmy says.

Jim looks at Kimmy and notices her features for the first time—a large oval face, high cheekbones, small pouty lips, hazel feline eyes, all framed with short blond hair. She's wearing a blue synthetic-fur jacket that's cut off at her waist. He's amazed at how beautiful she is.

He wants to respond but forgets what they were talking about. He looks at her, waiting to see what she'll say next. She laughs, then slinks over to Danny and sits on his lap. They rock back and forth in the wooden chair. Another joint is passed around, but this time Jim doesn't resist. When Kimmy hands it to him he puts it to his lips and slowly fills his lungs with resinous smoke.

Kat is now telling the group about the day Clare and Yoke were taped on MTV's *faux cinema verité* series, *The Real World.* Judd, the cartoonist on *The Real World,* had called Yoke, hoping *Force* would run some of his cartoons. Yoke had been nonchalant with the cartoonist until Judd told him he was part of *The Real World*'s San Francisco cast. Judd said he hoped Yoke wouldn't mind the camera crew coming along if he came in with his portfolio. Yoke immediately perked up, told Judd to come over.

43

Clare, sharing an office with the *Force* guys, desperately wanted to be on MTV and asked Judd if she could look at his portfolio as well, but Judd ignored her. So right when the cameras were rolling, Clare butted into Judd's interview with Yoke, told Judd that *Going Gaga* was looking for artists like him. She held her zine up to the camera while she talked to him, not realizing it was upside down.

"The funniest part is that she'd just gotten out of tooth surgery," Kat explains, "and her lips were still all fucked up and numb, so she looked pretty scary. But she was determined to get on that show."

Everyone breaks into laughter, including Jim, who's never seen *The Real World*. Once he starts laughing he can't stop. His insides are convulsing. The conversation moves on to Mike Moony's date with a girl who works at Caffe Centro. Jim looks at the mannequin with the bull's-eye and bursts into more convulsions. He sees an orange Bakelite kitchen clock on the wall—one just like his grandmother used to have over the stove—and it makes Jim happy. He smiles at it, half-expecting it to smile back. He notices that it's 11:05 and he's not sure if he's surprised because time's gone by quickly or slowly.

A phone rings and Danny picks it up. "Hey, how's it going?" he says.

Kat's laughing at something Yoke told her. She's adorable when she laughs. Her wrinkled-up nose reminds Jim of a girl he had a crush on in the seventh grade who'd always crinkle her nose when she was confused about something. Kat's nose is still wrinkled and tears stream down her face as her body shakes from the chortles.

"Don't you live in Pacific Heights?" Danny shouts to Jim. Danny has a hand over the telephone's mouthpiece.

"Yeah. Who's that?"

44

"Cooper. He's in Pacific Heights. We thought maybe we could party at your house."

Cooper. Jim had almost forgotten. He doesn't know what he wants to do. He can't talk to Cooper about his book idea with all these people around. But he doesn't know how to separate himself from them. He needs a cigarette.

"Well?" Danny asks, looking at Jim.

"Does he know where I live?"

"Not until you tell me," Danny says impatiently.

Jim gives Danny his address, not really sure what the plan is. He feels the old panic missile ramming against his colon but doesn't let it through. He watches Kat and falls into another fit of hysterics.

The panting British voice continues to throb over the stereo: *"We walked those streets until we were too drunk to know which corner to turn, driving ourselves into delirium."*

10

Kat is riding shotgun in the van this time and Yoke is driving. Danny and Kimmy are making out on the first bench and Jim quietly sits alone in the back.

"You okay to drive?" Kat knows they're all more loaded than Yoke is and doesn't know why she asked that.

"I'm fine, just had a couple of beers."

"You don't smoke pot, do you?" She hasn't seen him take a hit all night.

"No. I had a bad experience once. Went to a brunch about a year ago and there was tons of food. But you know me, not much into variety when it comes to food, so I just had a bunch of brownies. No one told me they were hash-flavored."

"Wow, you must've really tripped," Kat says, giggling.

"It wasn't funny," Yoke says. "I'd never been high before and it really freaked me out. I was stoned for days. I've never gotten high since."

They ride in silence for a while. Kat's a little embarrassed, feels like she's put a negative spin on her rapport with Yoke. She should listen to what people are telling her, not try to be so cute all the time.

The houses are now gigantic as they cruise up Divisadero, through lower Pacific Heights, then into Pacific Heights proper.

"Where am I going?" Yoke calls back to Jim.

Jim tells him to make a left on Jackson.

"Wow, where are we?" Kimmy asks, as if she's just woken up from a deep sleep. Danny is still kissing her neck.

"Stop!" Jim says, forcing Yoke to brake hard. "This is it. Just pull in the driveway, all the way to the back."

Kat can't believe how large and manicured the yellow Edwardian house is. "How the hell can he afford this?" she says under her breath.

"I don't know. These houses cost millions," Yoke whispers as he parks the van in the two-lane driveway.

They get out of the van and Jim escorts everyone to a guest cottage in back of the main house. It's also yellow and Edwardian in style, but much smaller, with two bedrooms, a den, a living room and a small dining area. It has a huge deck overlooking the bay and the Golden Gate Bridge. The place reeks of spice potpourri.

Kat and Yoke smirk at each other. Of *course* he doesn't own the big mansion in front.

"This place is great!" Kimmy says as she and her friends give themselves a tour, Jim tagging behind. "How much do you pay for this?"

"2,095 a month," Jim says. "That includes a parking space." Usually renters pay an extra hundred bucks or more per month for a parking spot in the city.

Jim turns to Danny with unfocused eyes. "When's Cooper coming?"

"I already told you in the van, around 11:45 or so."

Kat wishes Jim weren't here. He's so out of place.

"Have anything to drink?" Kimmy asks.

Jim shows off his fancy wet bar in the dining area, which is stocked with expensive wines, brandies, aperitifs, beers, and dry mixes. Thin glass shelves above the bar's sink are stacked with hand-blown goblets, martini and shot glasses and a bowl filled with plastic swizzle sticks. He pulls out a beer.

"Help yourselves," he says, disappearing into the living room.

47

"A wet bar. Can you believe this?" Kat whispers. "He never left the '70s!" She imitates his stiff peacock walk.

Kimmy screams a laugh. "Oh, but he's being nice, letting us raid his stash."

"You have to admit," Danny says, "the guy's a definite dork."

Now Kimmy starts imitating the peacock walk, and Kat doubles over with laughter. The pot from Danny's place picks up a second wind. Tears roll down her cheeks as Kimmy struts toward her. Kat sees Yoke chuckling to himself and she hears herself roar. Her stomach's starting to cramp.

Kimmy opens the mini-fridge and rummages through the wide assortment of bottles. "So what'll it be?"

"I'll take a beer," Yoke says.

"Why don't we make some mixed drinks?" Kat suggests, drying her eyes with a cocktail napkin. She checks her eyeliner in the bar's mirror, then looks at the liqueur selection.

"Look, he's got curaçao. We could make something exotic, like blue Hawaiians," she says.

"Yeah!" Kimmy exclaims. "You guys sit down and Kat and I will surprise you with tonight's Pacific Heights special."

Danny and Yoke straddle bamboo chairs near a round glass dining table.

"How do you make blue Hawaiians?" Kimmy asks.

"Easy. It's just curaçao, pineapple juice, ice, and rum." Kat looks in the mini-fridge but doesn't find any pineapple juice. She uses orange juice instead. After she pours the ingredients into the blender Kimmy pushes "blend" and the machine jumps and whirls and shrieks until the ice is as fine as sand.

The girls pour the blue liquid into large martini glasses and top them with paper umbrellas and swizzle sticks that they've speared into lemon and lime wedges. Since there's a lot left over Kimmy makes an extra one for Jim.

"Might as well bring one in for him," she says.

"Maybe it'll loosen him up," Kat says.

They each grab a glass, Kimmy holding two, and make their way into the living room. Jim is on the phone.

48

"You said this afternoon. . . . Yeah, I know, but now it's due tomorrow. . . . Okay, one hour. I'll be waiting for it." Jim hangs up. He squeezes his eyes really tight, exposing his gums while he does it, and Kat uses every ounce of willpower not to burst into another round of hysterics.

"Don't you ever break from work?" Kimmy asks, handing Jim the blue drink.

"Where are the tunes?" Danny asks in a booming voice as he wanders over from the dining area. Before Jim computes the question Danny's already flipping through a stack of CDs.

Kat looks over his shoulder. Benny Goodman, Glenn Miller, Duke Ellington, Xavier Cugat.

Danny finds an old cassette of Herb Alpert and the Tijuana Brass Band.

"Cool," he says, popping it in and pulling a joint out of his pocket.

The doorbell rings and Jim practically leaps over the coffee table to get it.

"He's here," Danny says, lighting up the joint.

Kat feels the cotton again. They all follow Jim. Kat takes a sip of her drink, trying to look casual.

Jim opens the door and Kat gasps. Jim jerks his head in, creating a double chin.

A grinning, gnomelike man in a black cape stares at Jim. The fellow's eyes are glazed behind wire-rimmed glasses, his teeth large and gapped, all the way to his molars. His hair is shiny, straggly and long.

"Heh," the man snorts.

"Sir Kengo!" Danny says, running over to the new guest. "What the hell are *you* doing here?"

Kat *knew* he looked familiar. Sir Kengo is a legend in the Bay Area, a brilliant, eccentric psychedelia-doused writer who started a trippy tech-culture magazine called *Zenith*. This was way before *Signal* was conceived. Kengo's been on all the talk shows, has posed for *Newsweek* and other mass-press publications, and has written several books of cultural criticism. *Zenith* and *Signal* act like each other doesn't exist.

Jim finally moves out of the way, letting in the new arrival.

"I was with Cooper—" Kengo says in a nasal voice, smiling broadly when he sees Kimmy and Kat. "Hi there," he says to the girls, interrupting himself.

"So where *is* Cooper?" Jim says, looking at the front door.

Kengo helps himself to someone's blue cocktail on the coffee table. He falls into a green recliner. "He told me you guys were having a party. Said he's sorry he couldn't make it."

"Couldn't *make* it!" Jim exclaims. He leans on the armrest of a couch.

Kat waits for her heart to sink but it's relieved. She's actually excited. Yoke is practically her date for the night, and now she's partying with the one and only Sir Kengo.

11

If Cooper's not coming, what the hell are all these people hanging around for? Jim sits uncomfortably on the armrest of a couch while his guests rearrange the cushions and Kat stretches her legs over his coffee table.

Why can't he feel like he did at Danny's? Mellow, happy, outside himself, the way he used to feel as a kid. Everything was magical at Danny's place, but as soon as the van pulled up to his own house his spellbound mood flipped 180 degrees. Now everything is dismal, heavy, his thoughts jumbled and murky.

Danny relights his joint. *Not this again. Kick them out.* Jim looks at his watch. 11:45. He'll let them stay for 15 minutes, then tell them he has to work. Yoke passes the joint to Jim. He doesn't know why he feels pressured to smoke when Yoke doesn't have to. But maybe it'll lift his spirits again. He wants the furniture to smile at him. He takes a hit and hands it to Kengo, who sucks the joint hard.

"Guess what I brought?" Kengo says while exhaling. Danny flashes a knowing Cheshire smile.

"What?" Kimmy asks, taking the joint.

Kengo pulls out a syringe and a sealed ampoule full of clear liquid.

Heroin! Jim's chest pounds. *Get out!* Jim violently shakes his finger at Kengo. "You guys can't do that here," he says.

"What is it?" Kat asks.

Kimmy exhales a cloud of smoke and giggles.

"We need a plate," Danny says, looking around the room.

Didn't they hear him? No one even looks at Jim. He can barely breathe. He watches Kengo gleamingly eye the stuff like a mad scientist, feels like part of a grotesque cartoon show. He stands up. "YOU'RE NOT DOING HEROIN IN MY HOUSE!" he shouts.

Everyone freezes. Jim wonders how loud his voice sounded. *The Dating Game* theme echoes in the background.

Kengo pushes his loose granny glasses in place with his pinkie. "Heh-heh." The recliner chair looks like a throne.

Suddenly Danny snorts with laughter. "It's not heroin, you geek, it's ketamine."

Everyone chuckles. Jim feels his cheeks throb. He hasn't felt so out of touch since high school. He's happy to see Yoke fidgeting nervously with his empty cocktail glass.

"What's it like?" Kat says, getting off the couch to get a better look at the bottle.

"It's mild, but so fuckin' rad," Danny says. "It's just a monkey tranquilizer. Makes you feel like you're floating."

"It only lasts 45 minutes," Kengo says.

Oh great. Another 45 minutes. Jim can't kick them out after his uncouth outburst. Thank God Mandy isn't around. Jim is surprised at all the drugs these people do.

"Don't let the needle scare you," Danny says to the group. "That's just to extract the stuff. We'll snort it."

"Oh!" Kat says, sounding relieved.

Jim opens a bottle of beer and puts it to his lips. He can taste each ingredient separately—the malt, barley, hops. The cold bubbles wrap around his tongue and slide down his throat with a tickle. His body warms up, reminding him of the joint he just smoked.

52

"Okay guys," Jim says calmly, trying to sound like this is all normal to him. "Do the ketamine, but then we'll have to break up the party. I still have work to do."

"Aren't you going to try it?" Kat asks, squinting though the lights are dim. Her eyelids are thick and flappy.

"I don't think so," Jim says. *No fucking way.*

Danny gets up and walks to a wood cabinet near the stereo. It's filled with antique dishes and Fiestaware. He grabs a blue-and-white English saucer that Mandy inherited from her great-aunt.

Suppressing a gasp, Jim asks Danny to use the Fiestaware instead.

"Oh, sorry," Danny says, putting the saucer back. He takes a yellow salad dish.

Kengo spears the syringe through the rubber seal of the bottle, filling it with the transparent fluid. He flicks it a couple of times with his middle finger as a doctor would to pop the air bubbles, an unnecessary act since they won't be shooting the stuff. Then he squirts the ketamine onto the plate. Kengo repeats this process several times until the plate is brimming with the watery substance. Everyone watches intently like astute pupils in a chemistry lab. Even Jim is curious.

Kengo then hands the plate to Danny.

"I've got to microwave this now," Danny says, excusing himself from the living room.

Jim peeks at his watch. 11:55. He should receive the Gates piece in 30 minutes, assuming the writer keeps his promise. While they fry their brains with monkey downers he'll work on the piece. He'll pull an all-nighter if he has to. A couple of waves bounce through him. His joints become elastic.

Kat walks over to Jim, places a hand on his shoulder. Electricity shoots up his spine. "Jim, would it be okay if I brought in a six-pack from your mini-bar?"

"Yeah, sure," he stammers. He remembers her cute crinkled nose and hopes she'll laugh again. A bonfire ignites in his gut.

Jim looks at Sir Kengo, who's asking Kimmy about some costumes she designed for avatars that modeled in a virtual fashion show. Kimmy says it went really well, her two-dimensional clothes made the front page of the business section in the *LA Times,* and companies are calling her to design more virtual garments. Jim makes a mental note to bring this up at tomorrow's editorial meeting.

"Sir Kengo, what have you been working on lately?" Jim asks.

Kengo twirls a strand of hair with his fingers. "Well, I just starred in an art film. In fact, I have the video with me, just picked it up when I saw Cooper." He reaches inside his cape and pulls it out, sets it on the coffee table.

"Really?" Kat says, bringing in the beer. "Can we watch it?"

Danny's behind her with a plateful of white crystalline powder. "Ketamine time."

Jim tenses. Yoke grabs a beer and stares at the desiccated drug.

Kengo opens his video case and pulls out a stubby straw. It's instantly poised between his thumb and index finger.

"I can't believe I'm finally going to try this," Kimmy says, taking off her blue fur jacket, revealing a shiny blouse covered with sparkly stars.

Danny asks Kengo if he brought a razor.

"Oh yeah," he says, opening the video case again. He plucks the razor from under the tape and gives it to Danny.

Danny takes a few moments to scrape up the dry crystals that have stuck to the plate, then chops the stuff. Scrape, chop. Scrape, chop. The white grainy pile reminds Jim of cocaine, which he snorted once at his frat house but never felt the effects of. He's mesmerized by the ritual.

"Done," Danny says, as if he's just performed surgery. He hands the plate to Kengo, who christens it with his straw. His eyes stare vacantly at Jim as he inhales the drug. Jim looks away. While Kengo's still holding the plate, about to take another sniff, Danny reaches over and shovels up a small mound of powder with the tip of his car key. It's immediately up his nose.

54

Jim glances at his wrist. 12:15. He wants to check for the article before the plate reaches him. He stands up.

"I've got to see if some important email came in. Just make yourselves at home."

"Aren't you going to try any?" Kat asks again. It's her turn with the plate.

"No, I'll just take a beer," he says, reaching for another bottle. He wishes he could carry her away from this decadent crowd. Someone sticks a joint in his face and he takes it. Just one more hit.

"See ya," Kat says as Jim walks toward his den.

12

Kat leans against the headboard of Jim's king-size bed, listening to Kengo. He's telling her and Kimmy—and Yoke, who's sitting on the edge of the bed as if he's about to bolt, fucking up Kat's ketamine experience—about the young woman who produced his film. Her husband is a billionaire who owns major companies all over the world; he's around 70 years old—twice his wife's age. Kengo says he wants to marry a rich porn star who would fund his films and buy him drugs.

Danny's trying to work the VCR so they can watch Kengo's tape.

"Damn it." He gets behind the TV set and fiddles with some wires.

"It shouldn't be *that* complicated," Kimmy says, interrupting Kengo. Danny ignores her.

Kat's body is already coming down. In the living room she'd thought she was going to faint, or lose control, not in a mushroom mind-trip way but physically, sensorially. She'd floated for a while, felt like she could almost touch the ceiling, but it wasn't a blissful drift. More like she was being sucked into a vortex, a weird pressurized zoom. She wanted to scream off the intensity, hold on to her limbs, which threatened to painlessly dislodge themselves and spin away. She couldn't even look at Yoke, couldn't let extra stimuli distract her from taming the trip.

Now that she's calmed down, her bones feeling rubbery and relaxed, Yoke is weighing on her. He hasn't said more than two words since Kengo got here. Hasn't smiled, hasn't looked at her. It's like he thinks they're all degenerates for doing drugs. Like alcohol isn't a drug. Like get off your high horse.

Kengo is describing an exotic dancer he knows, Trixie, who pulls a prank in every city she works. One time she was staying in a hotel room next to a bickering couple, the woman scream-ing that her man didn't pay enough attention to her, that he was flirting too much with some bimbo in the lobby. So when they left their room, Trixie pulled out some random chick's X-rated eight-by-ten—Trixie always packs a stash of other peo-ple's publicity shots, which are handy prank props—and with a red felt pen wrote . . .

Kat tries to keep an ear on Kengo but notices out of the cor-ner of her eye that Yoke has the phone on his lap. He's calling someone.

Kimmy and Danny laugh. Kat forces a chuckle, oblivious now to the punch line. Her ears are cocked, one on Kengo and one on Yoke, like the independent eyes of a chameleon. She hears a few words of each conversation but misses the messages of both. She does manage to respond with the proper smiles and surprised eyes to Kengo's story, and she gathers from Yoke's blasé tone that he's bored.

"Hit the VCR button," Danny says to Kimmy, who's holding the remote. She hits it and the TV turns to complete static. Danny takes the remote from Kimmy and punches all sorts of button combinations.

Yoke gets up and walks to a stack of neon-orange paper on the dresser. He takes a sheet off the top and reads it to himself. Kat joins him.

"What are those?" she asks.

"Flyers. Wow, Jim plays in a band."

57

Kat reads a flyer from the stack.

Mel Green and the Hot Band
Special appearance on clarinet by Jim Knight
Slow Club . . .

"Look," Kat says, showing her friends the flyer. "Can you imagine Jim on the clarinet?" She puffs her cheeks and bulges her eyes to look like a fat horn player. Danny roars, and as soon as Kimmy grabs the flyer Kat feels *faux pas* written all over her face. Yoke must think she's such a big-mouth bitch. He folds up the flyer and sticks it in his pocket.

"I'm going to take off," he announces.

Kat's heart drops. She blew it. The floaty ketamine high is squashed to a mere rocking in her skull. Her head's bobbing without actual movement. She tries to smooth over her last catty remark. "Jim is really surprising. A *Signal* editor *and* a musician. Pretty cool."

She's not sure if she made any sense, but Yoke smiles.

"Are you sure you want to leave?" Danny asks. "I think I've almost got this thing working." He's checking to see if the remote has batteries.

"Yeah, I'm going to crash at a friend's house. He lives close to here." Yoke zips up his windbreaker. "Thanks guys. It was fun. Hope you get the VCR to work."

Kat offers to walk him to the door.

"Hey," Danny says to Kat. "While you're out there, ask Jim how to get this fuckin' machine to work."

Kat and Yoke walk silently toward the front door.

"Well, I hope you had fun," she finally says.

"Yeah, I did." Not much enthusiasm coming through.

"Sorry if you were bored when we did the ketamine."

"No, I wasn't bored. I'm just not into that kind of thing, you know?" Yoke gets to the front door and stands there with his hands in his pockets. Kat hates the awkwardness, that should-we-kiss-or-shake-hands? moment when a date gone awry comes to an end.

"Guess I'll see you tomorrow," Kat says, backing up, letting him off easy.

"Hey," Yoke says, looking at the ground. "If you're not doing anything tomorrow, want to see Jim play? I like the Slow Club."

The ketamine kicks in again. *This isn't happening.* She's living a movie with a twist ending. Kat concentrates on keeping her facial muscles slack, trying to contain her giddiness. Her body keeps stretching like taffy.

"Sure. I've never been to the Slow Club. Sounds like fun."

Now she wants him to leave before she does something stupid.

But he just stands there, gazing at her. His cheekbones are sharp, accentuating the hollowness in his cheeks. His mouth is slightly open, lipstick-red. Does he expect her to kiss him? She takes a step toward him. *Fuck me.* He reaches for the door.

"Okay Kat. See you tomorrow." Yoke slips out without even a handshake. Cold air whips in and slaps Kat on the face.

She stands alone near the mini-bar. She doesn't get the game. He broods all night and treats her like a stranger, decides to leave before the party's over, then asks her on a date but splits without touching her. His strategy is twisted, too amateur. She's used to holding the cards, playing dealer. Her brain is numb.

She doesn't feel like facing the bedroom gang just yet, then remembers the VCR. They want her to ask Jim about it. Kat bets the *Signal* dork-editor has never fudged with the gaming rules, doesn't even know they exist. She's never dated a straight player before, doesn't think she would. Yoke's tactics are incredibly annoying but at least they stir her, challenge her. A date with Jim would be like a round of Mother May I?

"Jim?" Kat says, knocking on the den door. No response. Kat slowly turns the knob and pokes her head in.

Jim swivels his chair to face her and she involuntarily

59

gasps. His face is misshapen, distorted. His head seems to have shrunk, accentuating his glazed, small frantic eyes. On his computer screen glares the *Wall Street Journal* home page.

"You okay?" Kat asks.

"No. I don't know." Jim looks at a wall as he talks. "Everyone expects so goddamn much out of me."

Kat's caught him at a rare moment. This workaholic pressure-cooker has finally sprung one of his valves. With all of her stimulated senses on edge she waits for him to continue.

"It's just, I've got this stupid article that finally came in and it doesn't work. It's *shit,* and I'm supposed to make it good by tomorrow morning." He stands up, bashes himself into a wall, then sinks to the ground. Kat can't help her morbid fascination, wondering how far this will go.

"I'm being pulled in a thousand directions at once," he sputters, "and I've been sitting here, listening to you guys party in the other room, asking myself, 'Why am I doing this? What the hell is it all for?' I mean really, what *is* it all for?"

Oh boy, now it's getting too philosophical. Kat tries to lighten the mood.

"God Jim, *look* at you. You've got a fancy house, a job that anyone would envy, you're young, you're good-looking." Well, he *would* be good-looking if it weren't for his pale rashy skin, uppity expression and Army-boy haircut. She does like his strong nose, crooked David Bowie teeth, and pillowy lips when they're not screwed up with stress.

"Here," she says, grabbing an unopened bottle of beer by his computer. She doesn't know what else to do.

"But you don't understand," he says, getting up, oblivious to the new drink in his hand. "I never have any *fun,* can never just hang out like you're all doing. I can't even remember the last time Mandy and I went on a real date. Everything is always business, and not even *my* business. It's all so someone else can become a millionaire. How goddamn bizarre. I'm just a cog, part of a machine that doesn't even know I exist. I feel so fucking smothered."

"Hey, stop it," Kat says, wishing she hadn't come into his den. "We're all just cogs, even the millionaires. It sucks that you never have fun. *That*'s got to change. But your work—well, you work for a great magazine, you should be happy." Kat can't believe this Pacific Heights professional who doesn't even know her is spilling his guts like this. She wants him to feel better so she can get back to the gang.

"Everyone I know works as much as I do. That's the scary part," he continues, gesturing dramatically now. "It's not like I can look at someone else as a role model. *Every*one is working seven days a week, *every*one is stressed. Email is supposed to make things easier, relieve me from bullshit phone calls, give me more time, but in reality it's just sucked away any free time I might have had left. It's insane."

Kat thinks about the people she knows. Some of them work as hard as Jim and are as stressed as he is about it, while her other friends aren't working enough and feel like desperate losers because of it. She fits into the latter category.

Jim suddenly notices the drink in his hand and knocks half of it back with a few swigs. He absentmindedly sets the beer on an ashtray that's sitting on a tall stand. The bottle isn't stable and tips over, breaking into large wet pieces on the hardwood floor. Jim scrunches his face, looks like a decaying jack-o'-lantern.

"Relax, I'll get it," Kat says as softly as she can, hoping to calm him down. "I'll be right back."

She runs toward the kitchen, wondering how weird this would be if she weren't high.

13

Jim stares at the *Wall Street Journal* Website, the page his browser defaults to when he first starts Netscape. He doesn't know how many times he's seen this site—maybe 600.

Jim stands up, then sits back down, rolling his chair away from the mess on the floor. Is Kat coming back? *Kat.*

He wonders if he scared her off with all that talk about email and the pressures of life. He wishes his mind would sober up because it's been playing too many games with itself, and every time it loses his soul becomes heavier. One of the games his mind is playing right now is that he's infatuated with Kat. She would have seemed so insignificant to him yesterday, but now he pulsates for her—her soothing voice, her fresh energy, her seductive tomboy clothes, her wrinkled nose when she laughs. Her effervescence brings him back to treehouses and lemons and the plastic wading pool that used to refresh him and his friends on blistering Orange County summer days.

He picks up a framed desk photo of himself and Mandy. It was taken at his cousin's wedding. She's wearing a pastel-pink silk dress with pearls around her neck and she's smiling at Jim in the picture. He remembers deciding that day that he would marry her. He's very much in love with Mandy, he reassures himself. She keeps both of them moving forward with their careers and their future. He knows this is a good thing.

But he wonders where Kat is, needs to be with her, just till his mind clears up. Did she forget about his mishap? What's she doing? He must find her. He pulls a fresh pack of cigarettes out of his desk. It would be nice to have a smoke on the deck, with her, in the cool damp air.

As Jim staggers toward the door, a wave of nausea rushes up to his tonsils. He takes a deep breath, sits down on the floor. The wall across from him is undulating; the ground is rocking.

Kat enters with a roll of paper towels.

"You're back!" Jim says, meaning to leap up but falling back to the floor. "I didn't think you were coming back."

"Yep." Kat rushes past him, squats over the wet floor. "You know, you're just paranoid tonight. It happens sometimes when you party too much. You'll be much better tomorrow." She hasn't looked at him since she entered the room. Jim watches her long fingers carefully pick up the pieces of glass and throw them into a nearby wastebasket. "Be careful," she warns him, "there might be some slivers left on the floor."

Jim gets up with her. "You're so nice," he says, almost in a whisper. He wants her to look him in the eye.

Kat gives him half a smile, staring at his chest. "Well, so are you." She runs her fingers through her hair, side-glancing at the open door. "I better get back to the others."

"Wait!" Jim lunges between Kat and the open door. "Want to see *Signal*'s new Web page?" Jim is desperate to keep her near him. When he's with Kat his pot paranoia is replaced by a carefree isolated presence where nothing but the two of them and goodness exists. He can't let her slip away.

"Actually, we're trying to watch a video. How do you switch your TV to the VCR?" Kat looks beyond him.

"The VCR?" Jim doesn't know what she means. Another lump bulges in his throat and he inhales as deeply as he can. The beer is fighting him. *Keep it down.* She says something else to him. Gibberish. He hears himself laugh, has no idea what's so funny, wonders if he's sitting or standing. Her face is narrowing, serious-like. He laughs again. Her mouth shrinks. Shocked, Jim realizes she's getting upset.

"Don't be upset with me, Kat."

"What's your problem?" Her hands are on her hips.

"I'm sorry, I . . ." What are they talking about?

Now she's wiping his face with the corner of a paper towel. What's wrong with it? Tears? *Shit, what's going on?*

"You feeling better?" she asks.

He's missed something big. How long has she been here?

"Much better now that I'm alone with you." He could kick himself for allowing those words to slide out. He tries to save the moment.

"I mean, you're just so nice, and—God, I don't know what I'm trying to say."

Kat looks at the door. "Then don't say anything. Maybe I should—"

Before she can finish her sentence Jim grabs her and holds her tightly to his chest. She smells like a pineapple boat, feels like an electric blanket for a short moment, all warm and soft. Then she bristles and wrestles away. He hears a thud and realizes it came from the area on his chest where Kat shoved him.

"What are you *doing?*" Her eyebrows form a sharp V over her delicate oval face.

She's beautiful even when she's upset. Jim's stomach rumbles, some glands around his throat tingle and throb. The nausea has come back in the form of a tidal wave. Before he has a chance to apologize he bolts for the bathroom, makes it to the toilet just in time. He can't remember when he last ate, is surprised that his stomach has so much to offer. Tears blur the room and he wipes them away with the back of his hand. Once his insides are purged, he unsteadily gets to his feet and reaches for the sink, but can't find it. His brain starts to spin, the room becomes small, and then it's dark.

14

"Hey, what's going on?" Kimmy asks, bursting into the den. Danny follows her in.

"I don't know," Kat says. She stares at her friends for a minute, walks past them toward the bar, contemplates a beer, decides against it.

"We came to see what was taking you so long. We saw you guys hugging, then the next thing we knew he was flying across the room. What *happened?*" Kimmy asks.

"We weren't 'hugging.' The fuckin' jerk grabbed me and pressed me up against his chest, and his breath got all hot and thick. I didn't know what he was doing but it freaked me out, so I pushed him away. He's totally fucked up right now, wasn't making sense."

"Where'd the fucker go?" Danny asks, looking around the room, bouncing slightly the way a boxer does during a fight.

"I think he went to the bathroom. Let's get out of here," Kat says, feeling flat. "It's getting late."

"We just have to wait for Kengo. He's on the phone," Danny says, still pumped up. "I want to talk to Jim, see what his fuckin' problem is."

Kat whispers to her friends how Jim nearly cried on her

shoulder about his whole life, how he knocked over his drink and freaked like a baby over it, how he tried to trap her there by showing her his stupid Website, then how he laughed and sobbed simultaneously, spewing a huge mess of tears and saliva on his face.

"It was gross," Kat says.

Danny leaves the den, ready to start something with their host.

"Oh brother, the *Wall Street Journal*," Kimmy says as she points to his computer screen.

Kat sits in front of the Macintosh. "Let's see what he's got bookmarked."

Kat scrolls through Jim's online dog-ears while Kimmy peers over her shoulder: Yahoo, Altavista, Cool Sites, The Palace, *Playboy, Business Week, New York Times, Signal,* Personal Stuff . . .

"Figures, he's got *Playboy* on here," Kat snorts.

"Oh, I'm sure Danny's got *Playboy* bookmarked too," Kimmy says. "Want to take a look at it?"

"Not really. I wonder what he's got in here," Kat says, scrolling past *Signal* and opening up the folder headed "Personal Stuff." She turns to Kimmy and whispers, "I hope he's still in the bathroom."

Kimmy drags a chair from across the room and sits beside Kat.

The only site listed in Jim's personal file is one called El Tropical, and Kat feels slightly disappointed. She had hoped she'd catch him with a bunch of slimy-sounding URLs.

She accidentally lifts her finger off the mouse with the cursor on El Tropical, calling it up. Judging by the short time it takes for the page to download Kat figures Jim must have an ISDN line.

66

WELCOME TO EL TROPICAL!! BET SMALL, LOSE SMALL, BET BIG, **WIN** BIG!!!

Below El Tropical's blinking slogan is a roulette wheel that turns, a dollar slot machine with enticing icons of fruit that keep spinning, a craps table with jumping dice, and a card table with flashing signs that alternate from *21* to *Baccarat*. Kat clicks on the spinning fruit and a new page appears—one that contains an enlarged version of the slot machine, with the numerals 1 through 5 written below. *Return to Casino* is also offered.

Kat clicks on *5,* and five "dollars" are entered into the slot. The fruits wildly spin, then a peach, watermelon and banana line up.

–5. Would you like to spin again?

Kat hits *Return to Casino* and goes back to El Tropical's home page. She then chooses *21.*

Minimum Bet: $10. Maximum Bet: $20,000.

Danny walks into the room. "Looks like Jim is still in the bathroom, and Kengo just needs to make one more quick call. I think he's taking care of his long-distance business here."

The girls ignore him, engrossed in their virtual piece of Vegas.

Kat yawns. "So how much should I bet?"

"Hmmm. I wonder how much we have?" Kimmy says. "It's no fun if you don't have a kitty to start off with, you know, like in Monopoly. No fun if you have nothing to lose."

"It doesn't look like it matters," Danny says. "This game looks pretty cheap to me."

Kat doesn't see any rules or a personal-assets folder. "Oh well, let's see what happens." She bets 50 dollars, and gets a 10 and a nine. "19!"

The virtual dealer gets two nines.

+45. Would you like to bet again?

"Might as well bet 20,000 dollars," Kimmy says.

Kat places the bet and receives an ace and a nine. "20!"

"Or a 10," Kimmy says. "You could double down and hope for another 10."

Kat ignores Kimmy, and the dealer gets a jack and a seven. "I won again!"

"Well you would have *doubled* your chips if you'd drawn

67

another card. You would have gotten the dealer's jack." Kimmy sounds a little irritated.

+20,045. Would you like to bet again?

Kat bets another 20,000 but this time gets two sixes. She takes a hit and busts with 22.

Kimmy gets up. "Let's get Kengo. I'm bored." Kat hears her kiss Danny.

+45. Would you like to bet again?

Kat bets another 20,000 and gets an eight and a six. She takes a hit and gets a two. She stands on 16. The dealer shows 21.

-$19,955. Would you like to bet again?

Kimmy and Danny leave the room.

Kat plays another 11 rounds of maximum bets, winning only one of them. "This stupid piece of shit," she says, thumping the desk with her fist.

NOTICE: You are approaching your financial limit with El Tropical. Your next bet may not exceed $885. Would you like to bet again?

"Fuck you," Kat says to the computer as she clicks on "file/quit."

Kat stands up and looks at the computer's clock. 1:05. Kimmy runs back into the room. "Jim's not answering the bathroom door, and it's locked!"

Kat runs after her friend to the bathroom door. Kengo and Danny are trying to unlock it with a bobby pin.

"Oh my God, what did I do? I wonder if I pushed him too hard. Maybe he had a heart attack or something!" Kat wails.

"Are you getting it?" Kimmy asks Danny.

"Yeah, I think so."

"Oh my God. Oh shit," Kat says. "What did I do?"

Kat tries to push Kengo out of the way. "I can unlock it," she says.

68

Click. "I got it!" Danny says, pulling the bobby pin out of the lock-release hole in the doorknob. Danny tries to open the door but Jim's body blocks it.

"Oh my God, he's on the floor!" Kat shrieks. No one pays attention to her. "What if he's dead?"

"Honey, can you slide his legs toward the sink?" Kimmy says to Danny.

Danny slips his leg into the door's slight opening and gently tries to push Jim's body out of the way, but the small bathroom doesn't offer any extra floor space.

"Somebody call 9-1-1!" Danny cries. Kengo and Kat both move for the phone, but before they pick it up it rings.

Kengo stares at Kat. "I wonder if that's one of my girlfriends calling me back."

"Well don't just *stand* there!" Kat screams, grabbing the phone.

She takes a deep breath, and in a shaky voice says, "Hello?"

After a pause, a woman says, "Is Jim there?" Each syllable is icily enunciated.

"Uh," Kat's voice wavers, "he's not available right now."

"What do you mean? Who is this? I want to speak to my fiancé." The barbed voice sets Kat into a frenzy.

"I uh, I can't talk right now. Jim's uh, not available. Call back tomorrow!"

Kat slams the phone down before the woman can say another word.

"Who was that?" Kengo asks.

"Oh God, that was his girlfriend—Meg, or whatever her name is."

"Yeah?" Kengo's eyes light up with the drama.

"Well, I just blew it with her. I didn't know what to say."

"I think he's okay!" Kimmy screams from the other room.

The phone rings again.

"Oh no, that's probably her. Don't pick it up," Kat says to Kengo. They watch the phone as if it were a time bomb.

"You guys," Kimmy says, coming into the room, "he's snoring in there. Looks like he just passed out. Aren't you going to get the phone?" She reaches for it on the fourth ring but Kat juts her arm out, signaling Kimmy not to pick it up.

69

"Just let the machine get it," Kat says. "It's probably his girlfriend again."

After the machine noisily clacks, Kat's assumption is confirmed. "Hello? Jim? What the hell is going on? *Hello?* Who just answered the phone?" Mandy's voice is an octave higher than before. She pauses for a full five seconds, enough time to compose herself.

"Jim, I'd appreciate a call ASAP. You know where I am." *Beep.*

15

"Hello, Jim, are you there? It's 11:00 in the morning your time. I just called you at work and they said you hadn't shown up yet. I'm starting to worry. Listen, whatever happened last night, we can talk about it. I'm sending you email now. Please get back to me soon. Love and kisses." *Beep.*

The left side of Jim's face is cold, and as thoughts begin to formulate he realizes he's on the floor. He rolls onto his back and whacks his hand against the sink's cabinet. "Ouch!"

He tries to sit up but the weight of his palpitating head forces him to remain on his back. He looks at the yellow cracked bathroom ceiling and wonders how he got here. He hears his watch clink against the tiled floor and lifts his wrist up to eye level.

11:03, Tuesday.

Tuesday?

As if his heart had been suddenly connected to jumper cables, Jim leaps to his feet, tears off his stale clothes and jumps into the shower, lathering up before the water has a chance to become warm. The icy stream is just what he needs. Pieces of last night start parading before his eyes. *Rain, Raymond, never-ending rounds of joints and beer, a headless man-*

nequin wearing a clear shirt. Everything is jumbled. He tries to make sense out of the events. *Darren Cooper.* The thought of Cooper unlocks a new thread of events. *Mission: Darren Cooper, waiting for a tow truck in the rain, melting in a comfortable red chair at someone's apartment, blue velvet pants. . . .* When Kat comes to mind something in his chest flutters and he wants to jump to a new thought. He has an uneasy feeling about her. He reluctantly digs deeper, and more murky details materialize. *Kat's wrinkled nose, sitting in the back seat of a van, feeling like an idiot, giving Kat and her friends a tour of his house.* Jim turns off the shower and stares at the wet wall. *His house.* How could he have invited them over? What happened here? When did they leave? But the rest of the night disappears into darkness. He can revive more of the earlier night's particulars—*walking with strangers to a liquor store, looking up at a blond angelic face*—but the tour of his house is where the tape runs out. He doesn't even know if Cooper ever showed up.

Jim quickly shaves, throws on a robe and grabs a dried-up croissant from the fridge. He then slides a filter full of Starbucks coffee into the Krups machine. While the brew is dripping he lights a cigarette. A red blinking light catches Jim's eye and he sees that four people have called him. He hits "play."

"Hello? Jim? What the hell is going on? *Hello?* Who just answered the phone? [Pause.] Jim, I'd appreciate a call ASAP. You know where I am." *Beep.*

Jim's colon feels like it's just shot up his spine. He stops the tape and rewinds it. But before replaying Mandy's shrill message he concentrates until his brain hurts. A blue cocktail races through his mind but he can't remember anything else. He hits "play" again.

"Hello? Jim? What the hell is going on? . . . " Jim decides 72 he's heard enough of message one and with a shaky finger pushes "forward." The tape stops at message two.

"Hello, Mr. Knight, this is Keith at Otto Mobility. Your car won't be ready till tomorrow. Your whole transmission is being replaced. Give us a call if you have any questions." *Beep*. Keith doesn't leave a number.

Message three. "Jim? Are you there? You'd better be on your way in. We *need* to drop that Bill Gates article into copy-edit today. We have our editorial meeting at 10:30, and then I want to meet privately with you and Kenneth at noon. Where are you?" *Beep*. Jim sucks hard on his cigarette. His watch says 11:20. Missed the first meeting.

Four. "Hello, Jim, are you there? It's 11:00 in the morning your time. I just called you at work and they said you hadn't shown up yet. I'm starting to worry. Listen, whatever happened last night, we can talk about it. I'm sending you email now. Please get back to me soon. Love and kisses." *Beep*.

Jim pours himself a cup of black Starbucks before it's finished dripping. After he guzzles a cup he rushes around the house, looking for Mandy's phone number. He remembers jotting it down on his computer and races to the den.

Kat, broken glass, pineapple boats. Jim stops in his tracks, looks around the den for signs of last night. Everything seems to be in order except for a couple of empty beer bottles, a leaking straw wastebasket, and a chair that's been moved across the room. He puts the chair back, then lifts the basket filled with drenched paper towels and races to the kitchen, leaving a trail of beer drops behind him. He throws the reeking mess, including the basket, into the sink.

Jim rushes back to the den. He looks on his computer's desktop and opens up a "memo window." But he can't find Mandy's number. He decides to email her. She'll probably log on before she checks for phone messages anyway.

He puts out his cigarette and remembers a bottle falling from the ashtray last night. He remembers crying but can't remember why. He shifts uneasily in his chair. His modem sounds its usual ditty and a heap of email messages appears on his screen. He quickly scrolls down to the bottom, sees "Billing info/accounts@tropical.com." Above that last message he sees "No subject/Mandy@signal.com." He double-clicks and reads,

73

In case you forget, I'm at the Parker Meridian. But I won't be back at the hotel until tonight. Email me and let me know what happened last night. I *need* to talk to you ASAP. Last night was very strange. I'm feeling strange. Bye.

Jim hits "respond" and writes,

Baby, *don't worry* about a thing. Last night was strange for me too, and I'll tell you all about it when we talk. I'll call you tonight. I miss you. Love, Jim.

Jim hopes he can get his story straight before he talks to Mandy. He types "I love you" in the subject line and hits "send."

11:30. A private meeting with Jerry in half an hour. Jim rips off his robe as he runs to the bedroom. He opens his closet door and then slams it shut, horrified by what he's seen in its inside mirror. Jim slowly turns around, sees crumpled bedsheets, scattered pillows on the rug, empty glasses and bottles everywhere. His armpits drip like leaky pipes. What *happened* here last night? He tries to push Kat's delicate Asian features and velvet-covered butt from his mind. His bowels on the verge of explosion, he runs to the bathroom.

16

Cold fog seeps into Kat's skin, through her muscles and joints, into her blood. She hugs her body and steps quickly to the *Signal* building. Her head feels fuzzy from last night, and as she glances through the windows that look into the offices of *Going Gaga* and *Force,* she's astonished to see Yoke opening up a bottle of champagne. With a wild-eyed smile Clare notices Kat and runs to the intercom to buzz her in.

Kat slowly passes through the cement-and-wood lobby and into the workspace. She wishes she'd bought a cup of coffee before entering the building.

"Kat!" Clare shouts. "You're just in time to celebrate! They sold their book! They're getting a 50,000-dollar advance!"

"Well, we'll have to use *some* of that money to pay our artists," Yoke says, grinning.

Tacky is the name of their proposed book, which will take a look at American culture in the '90s. With their dry-wit sensibilities it could be pretty hilarious. Mike, Mike and Mary will do the writing, and they'll hire outside artists to help illustrate it.

"Congratulations, you guys. That's really great," Kat says. A small lump knocks around in her throat and she tries to swallow it. She's happy for them, but their success is yet another reminder of how stagnant her own life is. She's the only one in the room who's never had a book contract.

"Here, have some champagne," Mike Moony says to Kat as he hands her a plastic cup full of bubbles.

"Thanks," Kat says. She touches her lips to the drink, then puts the cup down on Clare's desk. She looks at Yoke, who's slugging back his share of champagne.

"How can you drink so much?" she says to him.

"What? It's only half a cup," he says.

"But I mean after last night."

Yoke grabs the champagne bottle and slowly pours himself another full cup, grinning at Kat the whole time.

"Want to come out and celebrate with us tonight?" Moony asks her. "We're going to the Slow Club."

Kat looks at Yoke. He shrugs his shoulders and says, "Yeah, Kat's coming. I already asked her last night."

Back out! Going tonight is a wrong move. It's *so* Yoke to invite his friends on their date. He obviously doesn't cream for her, won't give up anything for her. But then Kat rationalizes that tonight he *should* celebrate with his friends, this is a huge deal for them, she shouldn't be so selfish. And he wants her to be a part of their revelry. Damn it, she'll go.

Clare's phone rings and she goes to her desk to answer it.

"Well," Mary says to Kat and Yoke, pulling her long hair into a ponytail, "how was it last night?"

"Yeah, what was Cooper like?" Moony asks.

"'What a night' is all I can say." Kat takes off her coat and tosses it on the floor.

She and Yoke begin to relay last night's events, starting from the beginning when Kat boldly sat right next to Cooper on the couch. Yoke explains how genuinely nice Cooper was, how he wanted to meet them at Jim's but got tied up.

"Oh, but *you* missed the high drama," Kat says, interrupting Yoke. "After you left, I went to ask Jim about the VCR and he totally freaked." With intoxicated giddiness the trio waits

76

for her to continue. They're like kids around a campfire listening to an urban legend. "At one point he started *crying . . .* "

"No way," Mary says.

"Oh my God." Kat notices Jim through the windowed wall. He's having trouble fitting his key into the front door of the building.

"Speak of the devil," Kat says.

The Mikes and Mary turn around and laugh. Kat wishes Clare would get off the phone. She'd enjoy this.

Jim finally unlocks the heavy door and walks past the first-floor office. He glances over at everyone through the glass that separates the lobby from the workspace, sees Kat and visibly tenses up. She waves at him and he motions for her to come over.

"What's going on?" Mary asks, emphasizing each word.

Kat leaves her friends to see what Jim wants. His eyes are milky and swollen.

"Hi Jim. How are you feeling today?"

He steps away from her.

"Shitty. I've taken three aspirin this morning and my head is still pounding."

"Well, you were pretty loaded last night."

Jim shifts around on his feet, has one hand fumbling in his coat pocket. "Uh, well, that's what I wanted to talk to you about. I can't remember much of anything about last night, and I, I wanted to know what happened."

Kat sees her friends sneaking looks in her direction. She laughs, both at her friends and at Jim's anxiety.

"What's so funny?" Jim asks, horror-stricken.

"Nothing. Thanks for the party last night. It was fun."

"*What* was fun?" His upper lip twitches. "Kat, tell me what happened."

"Well, we partied at your house, you got carried away, then you passed out. I never would've tagged you as such a lightweight. You should probably take another aspirin. You don't look so good."

Kat turns around, leaves Jim standing alone in the lobby. She hears him call her back, asking what she meant by "carried away," but she doesn't respond.

"What did he want?" Yoke asks.

"Who knows? He's all paranoid about last night. He doesn't remember anything."

A new intern for *Force* buzzes the intercom and Mary lets him in. Yoke, Moony, Mary and the new guy all gather into their own circle.

Kat stands alone and watches Yoke while he explains to the intern how the magazine is put together. His voice is soft and Kat can't really hear what he's saying. He looks over at her and she quickly makes herself busy. She sits at a computer across from Clare, who's still chatting away on the phone. Sounds like she's talking to a *Going Gaga* editor who lives in Virginia. They usually meet on the Internet at their "virtual office," as Clare likes to say.

Kat notices a stack of envelopes waiting to be stuffed with zines. Busywork is just what she needs.

17

"Saw you at the party last night," Mara says to Jim as he enters *Signal*. Mara is sitting at the reception desk, putting copies of her headshots and acting resumes into envelopes pilfered from *Signal*'s supply room.

Jim remembers her at Raymond's, making out with a *Signal* intern. He also remembers he has to fire her and decides to do it now. What better time than when he's feeling his worst?

"Mara, I need to talk to you," he says.

"Hey, don't worry, I won't tell anyone about your delinquent behavior last night." She winks at Jim.

Jim feels like a train that's jumped its track. "What do you mean?" He barely keeps from stammering. He thought he'd remembered everything that happened at Raymond's house—nothing more delinquent than a quick toke.

Jerry comes running over to Jim. "Where the hell have you been? Why'd you miss the morning meeting? And damn it Jim, copyedit needs the Gates article. *Now*."

"Yeah, I was just going to—"

Jerry plows through his words: "Kenneth and I are going over the masthead in a few minutes. I could really use your help with that. Or did you forget about that too?"

Every ligament in Jim's body feels like a violin's tightened E-string. He fantasizes ripping off his clothes and running across the desks like a madman, screaming nonsense at the top of his lungs. Would Jerry still whine for the goddamn Gates article *then?*

"Let's meet at your desk," Jerry says dryly, sweeping long gray waves out of his eyes. Jim usually relishes sitting at the top of Jerry's star-player totem pole, but when his boss is pissed he has the farthest to fall.

Jim is swept away from Mara before he finds out what her wink meant. Was it something he did? Maybe he said something outrageous. Or maybe she's just teasing him about the pot. His skin turns to ice as he considers the possibility that Mara may have been at his house. Goddamn her. He can't do any firing until he pieces together last night.

As if Jim can't find his own way, Jerry leads him down a row of desks, each sporting a computer and a nerve-racked human, until they get to Jim's spot. "I'll find Kenneth. You wait here," Jerry says.

Jim is glad to be alone. He immediately opens up his email and finds the Gates article, realizes he already opened it sometime last night. Did he work on it? By the looks of the first sentence, obviously not. He scans it, cutting and pasting sentences where needed. The piece is weak. Cut, paste, cut, cut, create a sentence, cut, paste, delete a paragraph, add a few more sentences, create a title, spellcheck. His work is embarrassingly sloppy but he doesn't have the luxury of time. Within seven minutes he has a three-page, barely usable article. If only he had a couple of hours, he could really make it sing. He's a damn fine editor, and that's the reason Jerry depends on him so.

Jim looks around the room but doesn't see either Jerry or Kenneth. He logs into his email and sends the article over to the copyeditor. Done.

80

Jim leans back in his chair and wipes the back of his sopping neck.

An even longer stack of messages than this morning's

appears on his computer screen. Jim scrolls to the bottom to see if Mandy has responded to his earlier e-note. Nothing. He sees the message "Billing info/accounts@tropical.com" again and looks over his shoulder. No one is in eyeshot, so he opens it up.

Ten months ago Jim was climbing fast at *Signal*, excited about his relationship with Mandy and unerring in his touch with financial investments. He was in sync with the cadence of life. And then he tripped.

Betting on sports had always been his Achilles' heel. He rarely missed a game, was going on his third year with a bookie, and logged his winnings and losings in a digital notebook that opened with a password. Though he sometimes bet over a thousand dollars on a game, he always broke even by the end of each year, give or take a couple hundred bucks. Mandy knew he was a sports fanatic, figured he had a few dollars riding on the games with his buddies, but she had no idea how seduced he really was.

Last year had started off with an explosion. He'd happened to win 3,000 dollars in the first two weeks of January. At the same time, he'd just landed his first freelance article for *The New Yorker* and had had his picture taken for a Gap ad. For the next five months he barked orders at his bookie. He was puffed up, riding high, spending lots of money.

But in July everything crashed. After months of trying to catch up to his January success, Jim found himself $17,600 in the hole. He'd never owed so much to his bookie, who was anxious for the loot. Jim was desperate.

During the second week in July the San Jose Sharks, their record sour for the season, were scheduled to play. Jim thought betting against them would be a sure thing, and in his desperate attempt to wash his slate clean he bet $17,600 against them. The Sharks won! The bookie, using language Jim had never heard him use before, demanded cash immediately. Jim had some money tied up in stock, but not $35,200. Mandy could have bailed him out, but he didn't dare introduce her to Jim the Loser.

The only out he saw was Jerry. With his head hanging down to his knees he told Jerry about his predicament. Within 24 hours his boss reluctantly slipped Jim the cash but warned him to never, *ever* let this happen again.

Jim remembers his boss saying, "I really don't know why I'm doing this. You've let me down, Jim. Don't *ever* put me in this position again." A memory Jim wishes he could drag into the trash file.

Jim still owes Jerry $29,100 and intends to pay it all back. No one else knows what transpired between the two men. Like a recovering alcoholic, Jim now steers clear of sports pages and broadcasts. Preoccupied with her own affairs, Mandy doesn't seem to notice her fiancé's sudden disinterest in the games.

But saying goodbye to his bookie left Jim feeling empty. He was afflicted with a craving parallel to a hunger for sex or a deep pang for nicotine. Right after his financial disaster *Signal* had run a feature about an online gambling service called El Tropical. Based somewhere in the Caribbean, this online casino set up a membership with its global players with an internal "bank account." Jim was seduced.

The rules were made clear to Jim before he signed up:

1. Members are strongly urged to wire El Tropical money *before* they play.
2. If members lose more than they have in their casino-held account, they must wire the debt immediately.
3. If members don't have sufficient funds, they may make twelve monthly payments at an interest rate of 19 percent.
4. The first payment must be wired to the casino within 24 hours after playing.
5. El Tropical puts a stop to a player's gambling rights at the discretion of the casino manager.

Although El Tropical had given Jim the okay to bet up to 200,000 dollars, he's made sure to stay within his personal limit of a hundred bucks per week. Lately he hasn't even had time to play, but it satisfies him to know that the tables are at his fingertips.

The last time Jim played with El Tropical was around eight nights ago, and he won 35 dollars. He opens El Tropical's email expecting some sort of form letter explaining what to do in case a member goes overboard with bets. Instead he reads:

> Mr. James J. Knight:
>
> Our records indicate that you have $840 in your El Tropical account. After deducting this amount from last night's gaming activities, the moneys still owed to us total $199,115.
>
> Here is a breakdown of last night's transactions:
>
> 11:46 PM

SLOTS:
>   Spin 1: –$5

TWENTY-ONE:

Hand 1: +50	Hand 9: –20,000
Hand 2: +20,000	Hand 10: –20,000
Hand 3: –20,000	Hand 11: –20,000
Hand 4: –20,000	Hand 12: –20,000
Hand 5: –20,000	Hand 13: –20,000
Hand 6: –20,000	Hand 14: –20,000
Hand 7: +20,000	Hand 15: –20,000
Hand 8: –20,000	

> TOTAL: $–199,955
> ACCOUNT CREDIT: $+840
> _____
> TOTAL DUE: $199,115

> We expect payment in full, or the first of twelve monthly payments of $18,349.76—which already includes the 19 percent interest rate—by

midnight tonight. You may email a Digicash payment to accounts@tropi-cal.com.

Thank you for playing with El Tropical!

Sincerely,

Larry Goines
Casino Manager

Caustic words race to Jim's fingertips as he replies to Mr. Goines, informing him that "if you wish to compete with pro-fessional casinos *and* to keep my business, it would behoove you to replace your current chimp with an actual human who can at least count to three and recite the days of the week." Jim ends his e-letter by demanding an apology and some casino credit or he'll take his digital dollars elsewhere. He then hits "send," chuckling at the most clever thing he's written all week.

A shadow glides across his keyboard. Jim turns around to see Jerry standing behind his chair. He feels his cheeks flush as he ponders his letter to El Tropical, wondering how much Jerry could decipher from it.

"We're meeting in the conference room," Jerry says. "Kenneth is waiting for us there." Jerry's eyes are flat and Jim realizes his boss didn't read a word of his message to Larry Goines.

"I sent the Gates article off to the copy desk," Jim says as he follows Jerry down a row of desks, past the communal kitchen, into a spacious conference room with tall white walls and an industrial-gray carpet.

Jerry doesn't respond. They see Kenneth seated at a large round table. He's the oldest employee at the magazine, in his late 40s, with thinning hair and a pink inquisitive face. Kenneth is up there with Umberto Eco and Marshall McLuhan when it comes to concepts and ideas, and he's considered a kind of Socratic guru at *Signal*. Employees from all positions

84

come to Kenneth when they need advice, which he doles out in the form of "out-of-the-box" questions that lead to deep revelations.

Jerry takes a seat across from him. Jim sits between the men, a few seats away from each. Gerald enters the room, wiping his glasses on his shirt. "I'm sorry, was I supposed to be here?"

"Actually, no," Jerry says, "but we could use your input. Why don't you stay?"

"Oh, okay." Jim has noticed Gerald trying to horn in on his level of responsibilities lately. Nice tactic, pretending he didn't know what was going on. Gerald takes a seat across from Jim.

"As Jim and Kenneth already know," Jerry says, "I need help in cutting the contributing writers list in the masthead. It's too long, and I don't like giving credit to people who say shit about *Signal* to the press. Those people can go to hell. Take Bronson Meads, for example. That asshole was all over the Net, especially The EGG, cutting down our business plan as if we wouldn't find out! People aren't going to trash us in public and get away with it."

Wham! Jim tenses. *Email, the Bill Gates article, Netscape.* As if he'd just been injected with a heavy dose of amphetamines, a suspicion that he *did* gamble his life savings away last night jolts his nervous system. *Netscape.* He now remembers opening up the Web last night but doesn't remember why. He can't *remember* any gambling. Was he showing off in front of the others? Why wouldn't they have stopped him? He imagines Kat and her friends egging him on to bet the maximum, and then again, and again, enjoying a perverse pleasure every time he dropped another twenty grand. *No!* He refuses to believe Kat would do that to him.

"I agree, she should be cut too," Gerald says, moving down the masthead with his index finger.

Jim tries to figure out who they're talking about. "Why should *she* be cut?" he asks, hoping to get a clue.

"Are you a masochist?" Kenneth asks. Gerald snorts. Jim

realizes they mean Sarah, a writer who's poked fun at Jim all over the Net, calling him cheap, bow-legged—which isn't true—and likening him to yes-man Larry Tate, the nerdy ad exec on *Bewitched* who would've wholeheartedly agreed with Lucifer to make a deal.

"I'm glad we're cutting her," Jim says.

Stay focused. When Jerry asks if "the other one" should be cut as well, Jim looks to see how Gerald responds, then nods his agreement, hoping his expression looks sincere. He sees Kenneth taking notes. Jim grabs a pen and writes "masthead" on a blank pad of paper sitting in front of him.

His snide message to Larry Goines. Jim clenches his pen, squeezing perspiration out of his hand. The walls of the conference room narrow in on him. He's *got* to talk to Kat, and once he learns of last night's events he can straighten this thing out with Goines, apologize, explain to him that it was a stupid mistake, say he wasn't lucid last night, he won't let it happen again, he hopes he can be forgiven. He'll tell Goines that he has the utmost respect for him and El Tropical, that he'll be happy to send him a free subscription to *Signal* and any of the magazine's merchandise he wants. With enough groveling Goines might cut him some slack. Jim doesn't allow himself to think of the alternative.

"Jim, are you okay?" Jerry asks, his tone both concerned and irritated.

"I'm sorry. Yeah, I'm okay. Actually, I've got a migraine, but I'll be fine." He sits up straight and concentrates with all of his might. If he can just get through this meeting . . .

18

Almost 5:30. Another batch of twenty-five envelopes to stuff, stamp, label, and seal, then Kat's out of here. All day long she's been listening to Mary and the Mikes revel in the glory of their new book deal. They're suddenly acting all professional-like, conducting *Force* as if it were a real magazine. Mary's been coaching their new intern on what to say to potential advertisers. Yoke is actually cleaning up the piles of clutter that cover the floor.

Clare's been working on a freelance piece for *Signal* and is on the phone with her husband right now.

"Oh my God, you're kidding. . . . I see it! It's parked right outside," Clare says into the phone. "I will. I'll call you back. Bye."

"You guys!" Clare yips with a whispered undertone, signifying that she's got either a secret or some important gossip. Everyone looks at her. "Jann Wenner just walked into *Signal!* Look"—Clare points to the window—"there's his limo across the street."

Kat had seen a cherubic boy-man step out of the limo but hadn't realized it was Jann Wenner, founder of *Rolling Stone*.

"I've got to get some copies of *Going Gaga* to him," Clare says, collecting two current and four back issues.

"What are you going to do?" Mary asks.

"I'll give these to the limo driver, tell him to pass them

along to Wenner. You never know. *San Francisco Daily* once called *Going Gaga* the *Rolling Stone* of pop culture. Once Wenner reads these, how can he resist?"

Clare takes her zines and runs outside. Kat watches her scamper across the street like a crazed squirrel. A car slows down for Clare and she freezes in the middle of the road, not sure if she should keep going or turn back. The car honks and she finally moves forward. The Mikes try to read her lips as she talks to the chauffeur.

Kat sighs and goes back to stuffing her envelopes. Stuff, stamp, stick, seal. Stuff, stamp, stick, seal. Kat hears Moony, Yoke and Mary laughing at Clare's every move, but Kat doesn't look up. After 16 finished envelopes and what seems to have been a long time, Clare saunters into the office, her face as bright as her artificially red hair.

Clare talks in a fast, clipped voice. She says the driver was really nice and flipped through *Going Gaga,* asking her all sorts of questions: How long has she been working on it? What's it about? Where'd she go to school? She felt like he was conducting a preliminary interview.

When her friends go back to work Clare scowls at Kat. "What's *your* problem today?" she asks in a low tone.

"Nothing."

"Bull. What's wrong with you? You've been a downer all day." Clare spits her words like venom. This stuns Kat. Clare is usually so chipper. She must really be annoyed that Kat didn't lap up the Wenner story like everyone else did.

Kat doesn't want to get deep right now. "Back off, Clare. I'm just tired, and I'm trying to figure out what to do with my life." She shouldn't have said that last part, doesn't have the energy for this.

"What do you mean? You're doing *great* here. I thought you wanted to get into journalism." Her voice is getting louder and Kat's sure the others are listening in.

"I do, but it doesn't look like I'm getting anywhere." Kat wishes she could shrink to nothing. How *dare* Clare force her to admit these things out loud.

"Wait a minute," Clare says. "Gerald's given you a lot of chances to write reviews for *Signal*. Reviewing would be great for your resume and you'd get paid, but you're always turning it down. I don't know why you're feeling sorry for yourself."

Kat's PMS-bitch attitude flatlines. She's right. It's not *them*, it's *her*. Clare gives her opportunities, but Kat always has some lame-ass reason why she can't go through with them. She never would've run out to Wenner's limo with her work the way Clare did today.

Kat's face tingles and she tilts her head back, staring at the water-stained ceiling, forbidding herself to cry. She's never seen this stern side of Clare before but it's actually more attractive than her usual Los Angeles happy-shiny personality.

"Yeah, you're right, Clare. I don't know why I can't get motivated to really *do* something." A tear zigs down her cheek and she quickly wipes it with her hand.

"Oh Kat," Clare says. The tear propels her back to her old self. "You're so smart and talented. I know you'll be really rich and successful, and I'll still be chasing after moguls like a crazy woman with a black-and-white zine in my hand."

Kat laughs, attributes most of her moodiness to a post-ketamine crash.

Moony comes over and puts his hands on Kat's shoulders, starts massaging them. His hands are strong, activating dormant endorphins.

"Want to grab a bite with us before the show? We're leaving in a couple of minutes." He works his fingers down her spine.

Maybe she pegged these guys wrong. Moony is the passionate one, Yoke is the one who stands girls up. Her shoulders drop and as Moony climbs back up to her neck, goosebumps flood her back. It doesn't matter anymore. Yoke is cute but nothing to get worked up about. So she loses a game. He doesn't play fair anyway. No biggie.

"Yeah, I'd love to get something to eat," she says, excited now for the Slow Club.

19

Jim's ears are ringing. He doesn't know how much aspirin he's taken but figures it was more than the American Medical Association recommends. Jerry's been ignoring him since the masthead meeting and now he's joking about something with Gerald. They're bantering like old cronies.

Forty-five minutes till he's on at the Slow Club. How the hell can he play the clarinet tonight? He needs to find Kat, see if she witnessed his losing streak. El Tropical hasn't given him much time, his first ludicrous payment of over 18 grand is due tonight. Jim wrings his clammy hands together. He doesn't know what the casino will do if he doesn't pay, doesn't want to find out. Even worse, he has no way of knowing if they're being straight with him. Wouldn't he have some recollection of gambling like a maniac? Screw the Slow Club—he's got to get to the bottom of what happened last night. He needs to find Kat.

He calls Mel, the band leader. After four rings a machine picks up with a sax riff in the background. Mel's smooth voice tells Jim to leave a message. Jim hangs up before the beep. He frantically checks his computer for numbers of the other band members but doesn't have any. Why the bad luck lately?

The Slow Club is in walking distance. He'll run over there and tell them he won't be able to stay due to a personal emergency. He won't even be lying. He puts his computer to sleep, slips on his jacket and grabs the clarinet case tucked under his desk.

He peers in the window of the first-floor office in case Kat or her friend Yoke is around. Of course they're not. The place is quiet, with only Clare at her desk, writing something by hand. Jim is about to sneak by, not wanting to chitchat with Gerald's wife, then realizes he doesn't have Kat's phone number or address—not even her last name. What the hell was he thinking? Thank God Clare is still here.

The first floor is cold. None of the windows are properly sealed and the heater obviously doesn't work. Clare sees him come in and straightens her posture. "Hi Jim!"

"Hi."

She puts down her pen. "Are you okay?"

Jim hasn't caught his reflection recently. But he feels like shit, must look that way too.

"I think I'm coming down with something." He sticks his free hand in a pocket, trying to appear nonchalant. "Hey, do you know how I can get ahold of Kat? I just need to ask her something."

Clare smirks with a raised eyebrow. He prays she doesn't ask him what this is about—he's too beat to be clever.

"Aren't you supposed to be at the Slow Club?" she asks.

"Yeah," he says, not about to tell her he's going to cancel. "I'm on my way."

"Well Kat and Mary and the Mikes are all going there to watch you. You should be able to find her there."

"Oh really?" A surge of energy clears Jim's head. This is too easy. He'd better get down there before they change their minds and go somewhere else. "Thanks Clare. I better run or I'll be late."

"Sure. Have fun."

If he can just pull Kat aside and get her to talk straight with him he'll be able to move forward with whatever problems he may've created. If, in the worst-case scenario, he did fuck up and drop a couple hundred thousand, he'll need to get an attorney. Aren't there laws against operating casinos across international borders? He wonders if he can keep this whole disaster from Mandy.

He remembers an article someone wrote for *Signal* over a year ago about an organization that opposed online gambling and helped people in his position fight preposterous or bogus debts. He'll have to look into that.

The Slow Club is just a block away now. Jim gasps at the possible scenario that he seduced Kat last night. Or vice versa. *Someone* was in his bed last night. How will he react if she tells him they made love? His stomach turns like it did back in his dating days when some knockout babe would lock eyes with him. But then it could've been *anyone* in the bedroom last night. He doesn't even know how many people came to his house. Maybe it was just Mara and some greasy loser under those sheets. Jim charges into the club.

The muggy air inside is webbed with smoke. It's a thrill to be in a public place that welcomes cigarettes. Jim pulls one out, inspecting the crowd for familiar faces. Shit, he doesn't see her. Does he cancel and run back to Clare for Kat's coordinates, or does he take the chance that she'll be here? He lights up and takes a deep draw. Chelsea is sitting at the bar chatting with an older woman. No sign of Jerry or their other cyber-elite colleagues. Jim turns his back on Chelsea and sees Mel Green sprinting over.

"Hey man, we were getting worried about you. Come on, we're all backstage."

"Backstage" consists of a walk-in closet–sized room with one faded director's chair, wall-to-wall torn posters of blues and jazz musicians, and an old stained-glass light fixture sporting a red Coca-Cola logo. The band is clustered in these claustrophobic quarters, tuning up, going over the rundown, talking about adding a new number to the repertoire. Jim steps out, peeks at the audience. He can't go through with this. With El Tropical on his trail he needs to find Kat. *Walk out. Blame it on food poisoning.*

Jim spots Jerry entering the club with his two digi-heroes: the lanky owl-faced futurist and EGG-man, Andrew Garrett; and Dusty Lawson, the eccentric cyber-libertarian oilman. Dusty looks around the club with his perpetual smirk and immediately recognizes a statuesque redhead with a square Germanic face. She screams "Dusty!" and he lumbers over to her, embracing her with his bearlike arms.

Andrew and Jerry see Chelsea at the bar and she points to a table that's reserved for them.

"We're on in five minutes. You've got to get moving," Mel says, tugging on Jim's sleeve.

"Um, I don't know if I—" Suddenly Jim sees her. She's eating a candy bar, pushing her way through the crowd, wearing the same yellow-plaid skirt she wore this morning. She's with the ragged bunch who work with her. "I'll be right back!" he says to Mel, running across the stage to the crowd.

Kat sees him right away. She elbows the girl she's with. Their friends find a table and Kat quickly takes a seat instead of allowing Jim to talk to her alone.

"Hi Jim," she says as he approaches their table.

"Can I talk to you for a minute?" Jim doesn't look at anyone but her. "In private," he adds.

"This is Mary," Kat says, pointing to her friend, "and this is Mike Moony. You already know Yoke."

"Hi," Jim says reluctantly. "Kat, I really need to ask—"

Kat points to the stage. "Is that your band?"

Shit, they're already setting up on stage. Mel notices Jim and runs toward him.

"What the fuck are you doing? We're starting in a couple of minutes. Don't hang us up like this." Mel's ice-blue eyes are unblinking and hard, like marbles.

Kat is tucked into the table, not about to jump to Jim's rescue.

"I've got to go," he says to Kat, "but can we talk after the first set? It's extremely urgent."

"I'll be here," she says coolly. Jim hesitates, then turns from the table and hears Kat say, "Good luck!"

"Yeah, good luck," one of her friends adds. The same person asks his tablemates what they want to drink. Their voices blur as he walks toward the stage.

Jim only has time to put his clarinet together and run through a scale before he's facing the crowd. Chelsea, Jerry and their hotshot guests are sitting only two tables away from Kat's group. Suddenly Jim's nervous. He hasn't felt this way on stage for years, but usually he prepares himself mentally before a gig. Tonight he's thrown himself in front of an audience without even a thought about the music.

The drumsticks tap each other four times and the band begins to play. It's an improvisational tune they've performed a million times before, making it easy for Jim to mechanically jam while mulling over his next step.

After this set they'll get a half-hour break. He'll take Kat aside, making sure they're far enough away from her friends and Chelsea's troupe. He'll ask her if she saw him gambling last night. If . . .

Jim's lost track of his key. Shit, what's the music doing? He stops playing for a moment. Luckily with this kind of jazz a lull from an instrument is acceptable. *Focus.* Jim closes his eyes and listens to the drums, the sax, the other horns. He joins back in, this time keeping his mind on the musical thread. His clarinet sings to him, unchains him, carries him away like a sex-scented temptress. She takes him on a spontaneous ride of rhythmic motion, moody turns, and sudden stops that only accentuate the next burst of movement. His instrument screams, cries, laughs madly, dances with its surrounding sounds, dances with Jim, who at the moment isn't aware of his own existence.

94

20

Kat can't concentrate on anything Mary is telling her. Something about a documentary on midwives. Kat nods, feigning interest. She didn't think Yoke mattered anymore, but it's hard not to seethe at his rude table manners. His back's been turned toward her ever since the music started so he could better talk to some bimbo ex-girlfriend who shrieked with rapture when she saw him. She's got long blond-streaked hair, all one length, tight jeans with a beaded belt, and a tiny red fuzzy cardigan. Moony's flirting with her too.

"Excuse me," Kat says, interrupting Mary. "I'll be right back."

Kat has to get away before she explodes. She dares herself to elbow the bimbo in the ribs as she walks by but chickens out. The women's room is on the other side of the lounge area and it seems like forever before she reaches it. The club is too muggy and as soon as Kat steps into the bathroom she heads for the sink.

The cold water feels good on Kat's wrists. She splashes it on her face, wondering how much cash she has, wondering how much a cab would cost to take her home.

"Do you have a lighter?" a woman says, stepping out of a stall.

Kat looks in the mirror and sees the co-owner of *Signal* behind her. Chelsea Simmons. Kat tries to stand straight and gracefully, like someone with confidence.

"I have some matches," Kat says, pulling out a matchbook she just took from the ashtray at her table.

"Thanks!" Chelsea says. She cocks her head. "I've seen you somewhere. Do you work in South Park?"

"Yeah. I work in your building, on the first floor."

"Oh!" Chelsea pulls out a joint. She lowers her voice—as if anyone in the noisy club would hear her. "Want some pot?"

"Maybe just a hit. Thanks."

Chelsea is petite like Kat, but more polished, more angular, like a slick manga character. Her clothes are rich, cut perfectly to her figure but hanging a bit loose at the same time.

Kat can't believe she's smoking a joint with Chelsea Simmons. And that Chelsea is so nice, so normal. The woman is in her 30s, worth millions by now, and rumored to be quite shrewd. Kat doesn't know what to say but it doesn't matter. Chelsea keeps the conversation going.

"Are you one of the owners of *Force?*"

"No, I work with *Going Gaga.*" Kat's sentence sounds more like a question. "But I'm here with the guys who do *Force.*"

"Oh! I'd like to meet them." Chelsea looks in the mirror, touches her hair. "How do you like the music?"

"It's great," Kat lies. She hasn't paid attention to the band since their first few notes. She remembers laughing hysterically with Mary at Jim's stiffness, but since then she's almost forgotten he's up on stage.

"Jim is fabulous on the clarinet," Chelsea says. "He's one of our editors at *Signal.*" She extinguishes the joint and Kat doesn't let on that she already knows her editor.

Chelsea puts an arm around Kat as if they're old buddies. "Why don't you come to our table? I'll introduce you to everyone."

Kat doesn't understand the special treatment. She hasn't said anything clever enough to warrant this. Maybe she reminds Chelsea of a long-lost best friend. Whatever it is, it beats going back to her own table.

Chelsea is with three guys and another woman at a table filled with Perrier bottles and a couple of wine glasses. These folks are all 20 or 30 years older than Kat. Kat recognizes one of the men, Chelsea's business partner Jerry. Chelsea asks Kat for her name, then introduces everyone to her.

"Hi. Nice to meet you," Kat stammers. *Lawson, Garrett, Fuller.* Like an idiot she just smiles, offers no morsels of higher intelligence.

"She's with the *Force* publishers tonight," Chelsea says, widening her eyes at Jerry when she says the word *Force*. She explains to her friends that *Force* is a start-up magazine on the first floor of her building, that it's really going somewhere. Kat wonders when *Force* graduated from being a mere zine.

Suddenly everyone at the table is facing the band, no one says a word. Jerry's head rocks to the music as if he's shaking his head *no*. Kat looks around the room and notices lots of heads moving like that, instead of the jerkier *yes* motion you usually see at rock shows. Yoke is still talking to the bimbo, who's taken Kat's chair, and Moony is trying to wrestle something out of Mary's hand. They seem young and rowdy compared to the sophisticates she's with now. The blond runs her hand across Yoke's head, messing up his curls. Kat feels the volcanic steam rising again and tries to divert her attention to the stage. She lets the mellowness of the pot take over.

At first the music makes no sense. Kat's never understood jazz. You can't dance to it, there's no center, no obvious structure. She doesn't notice Jim at first, but can't take her eyes off him when she does. He's transformed himself into the music itself, his body pliant and expressive, his face lost in the beat, on the verge of some explosive emotion. Kat listens to his instrument, blocking out the others. At first his deep billowing tones are sad, each note slow and mournful, reminding Kat of a broken man hopelessly in search of something unknown to him. Or maybe it's *her* the music describes. Kat chokes up, hop-

97

ing no one notices how affected she is. She sneaks a peek at her table partners. They seem moved as well.

Suddenly the attitude changes, the clarinet picks up, starts tittering like someone with a mischievous secret. Kat's spirits lift as the music jumps an octave to prance a new riff, which hops and hides and runs circles around the room—perhaps the broken man's breakthrough, his celebration of a life he hadn't noticed before. Kat feels alive, her emotions juiced, and she wants to know more about the clarinet player on stage, so different from the repressed *Signal* editor of last night.

When the band breaks, Mary and the Mikes charge over to her. From their devilish grins—a look Kat's seen before when some exciting business scheme is in motion—she has a hunch they know who she's with. The schmoozers probably know more than Kat what Chelsea's friends do. Kat seethes. Yoke ignores her for a blond slut, then tries to suck up to her when she has something he can use.

"We were wondering where you went," Mary says.

Yoke smiles at Chelsea and company.

Reluctantly Kat introduces everyone, and Chelsea and Jerry are perkier than Kat had expected. It's as if they're all in on something covert. Another trip to the bathroom is in order. Kat excuses herself and notices Moony taking her chair as soon as she leaves. She pulls out her wallet before she gets to the restroom. Sixteen bucks. Definitely enough for cab fare.

She approaches the back wall, hoping to find a pay phone, and walks right into Jim. The emotional fire she felt just minutes before flares up again. She doesn't remember this relaxed man as the constipated stiff she had to put up with last night. He's not the same person—his energy deeper now, more sensual.

"Kat," he says. He looks like he's just been fucked.

Kat wants to experience what he's feeling, wants to be the clarinet. She lets go of the heaviness that's weighed on her since the bimbo showed up and takes his hand, pulls him around a corner, down a narrow hall, near a row of phones and an emergency exit. They can see a portion of the bar from here, but the rest of the club is obscured from view. Jim leans against the wall as Kat closes her eyes and presses against him, finding his mouth with hers. His lips are soft and have a faint woody taste. He wraps his arms around her and holds her tightly. His body is hard and magnetic, vibrating with hers as they kiss. Kat wedges her hands between his back and the wall to get as close to him as possible. She hears Mary nearby and wonders who she's talking to, wonders if anyone can see them. But it doesn't matter. Jim's mouth deepens and Kat gets inside it, he inside hers. The voices in the club fade away.

21

"Hey Jimbo, we're up in fifteen minutes," the drummer says, slapping Jim on the arm. He joins the line at one of the phones.

The spell is broken. Kat's body loosens and she turns her face away. Jim kisses her cheek, catching a familiar citrus aroma. He can't get enough of Kat, doesn't want her to leave. He has fifteen more minutes and wants to spend each one with her. But she pulls away.

A hideous anxiety gnaws at the back of his brain, but he can't deal with it right now.

"Stay with me," he says, meaning now and after the show.

She plunges into him again, her electric tongue charging his nervous system, one hip digging between his legs until he's about to erupt. But this time it's short-lived, she abruptly steps back.

"I have to make a phone call," she says, her voice almost too soft to hear. She walks toward the phones. He follows but then realizes the call might be personal. He backs up, leans against the wall and watches her.

"Are you ready to sit down with us?" Chelsea asks. Jim jumps. He'd completely forgotten about the *Signal* entourage. *Fuck, did Chelsea see him kissing Kat?* If she did, she doesn't say anything about it. But that half-smirk on her face frightens him.

"Come on." Chelsea takes his hand, a subtle flirtatious move that would usually turn him on but at the moment feels like nothing more than a fistful of fish bones.

The small table is overcrowded with chairs and people.

"Hi," Jim says to Andrew and Dusty, who are so engaged in conversation they don't even notice his presence.

Jim guesses by photos he's seen in *Signal* that Chelsea's aging friend—a rendition of Peter Pan if he *had* grown up—is Ethel Fuller. She's three inches from Jerry, firing a sober monologue that doesn't pause for newcomers.

Jim does a double-take when he recognizes the other three people at the table—Kat's friends, sipping Perrier as if they belonged. He shakes his head, wonders if all the aspirin he took is having some kind of surreal effect on him.

Without warning Jerry backs away from the rambling Ethel, makes sure Jim knows everyone. Ethel holds out a limp hand, then launches into a story about a trip to Russia she took last month to lead a panel at an international telecommunications summit. Recognizing her from a photo that had appeared in *USA Today,* she explains, a couple of KGB agents took her to lunch. During a delicious plate of chicken Kiev they asked her if she knew anyone in the US government they could sell some hot state secrets to.

Jim cranes his neck and spots the hall that leads to the pay phones. He doesn't see Kat. Her friends are here, so she'll definitely be joining them at the table. His heart feels like it's going to jiggle free from its arteries.

As Ethel tells her story Jim notices strange looks shooting in his direction, especially from Jerry, who's combining his mysterious smile with a scornful glare. Little man Yoke waits until Jim catches his eye, then shakes his head with disdain while turning back to Ethel. If they saw him making out with Kat he doesn't think Jerry would find it amusing. Mandy is a good friend of his—Chelsea's too. But Jim is sure it won't get

101

back to Mandy. It would bring the morale down at *Signal* if his boss were to get between him and his fiancée. It would be too ugly. Normally he would panic severely over this—he's never cheated on a girlfriend before—but he's too high on Kat to care.

Where is she?

Jim scans the bar but doesn't see her. He flashes on El Tropical and knows he should have asked her about last night but pushes that offensive thought away. He wants her body between his legs again.

Then it hits him. Of *course* they slept together last night. That's why she's so into him tonight. He tries with all his power to remember something about his tryst with her but can't.

"Are you okay?" Chelsea asks Jim.

He wonders what kind of face he was making. "Yeah, I'm fine," he says.

Dusty loosens his ascot and cuts off Ethel's spy story to narrate his own encounter with some CIA spies when he was at an electronic commerce convention in Amsterdam. "They wanted to set up a money-laundering operation for an arms dealer—"

"Oh, this is a good one," Chelsea says, leaning into the table. Kat's friends stare raptly at the adults. Only eight minutes left. Jim looks at the back wall, where two guys are making out.

"Excuse me, I just need to get some fresh air." Jim leaves the table without more than a nod from Chelsea. He hears Dusty boom with laughter at his own story. Jim circles the club like a hawk. His body is out of kilter, won't feel right till he's with her again. He lights a cigarette and steps outside.

What's he doing? He's going to ruin what he's got with Mandy, which is the best thing he's ever had. He needs to calm down, clear his head. Kat is just a wild girl who's wasting her youth, a typical punk who thinks something will fall into her lap. She's got nothing, would just bring him down. With Mandy he's someone on the rise. He's got to get control of himself, stop this fantasy before it's too late.

Jim spots Kat getting into a cab across the street. He drops his cigarette. Adrenaline shoots through his veins.

Jim runs to the edge of the sidewalk and flaps his arms. "Kat! *Kat!*" She shuts her door. "Wait!" Jim tries to run across the street to dive in the back seat with her, but the whizzing stream of cars won't let him. Oblivious to the frantic man on the curb, the cab pulls away.

Jim leans against the side wall of the Slow Club, its cold bricks numbing his cheek. He's only got a couple of minutes now before he's due back on stage. It's time to push Kat out of his mind for good. He'll just take her aside tomorrow to ask about El Tropical. That will be it. It's over.

He stops by the table one last time before getting on stage and can't believe his ears.

"*Force* is just what we're looking for to penetrate the youth market," Chelsea is saying. "Its target audience is younger than *Signal*'s, which opens up a whole new demo to us."

"I've got to see a copy of this magazine," Dusty says.

"Oh, you'll love it. It tackles serious issues geared toward twenty-somethings, issues that aren't usually addressed in the media, yet it's not dry at all. Their sensibility is very smart and critical. The magazine is very well put together," Chelsea says, briefly glancing at each person around the table.

"You want to buy *Force?*" Jim asks. He's astounded at the news. He's never heard mention of this before, and now Chelsea and Jerry are talking openly about buying a zine with their friends. Since when is he out of the loop?

"Chelsea and I have been talking about it," Jerry says to Jim. He looks at Yoke. "We'll need to see a business proposal and conduct due diligence, of course."

"Of course," Yoke says, nodding enthusiastically. Jim can tell the kid doesn't even know what "due diligence" means.

The band members start taking their spots on stage and Jim excuses himself. He rushes to the VIP closet and grabs his clarinet, relieved at the chance to lose himself again.

22

Kat deletes her first paragraph. She's been trying to start a novel, a story she's been thinking about for a long time—a fictionalized account of four real-life suffragettes who fought for their right to vote. It would focus on their personal lives and what it was like to be a feminist at the turn of the century.

It isn't a good day to start such a venture. Every time her fingers hit the keyboard she cringes about last night. Did she really make out with frat-boy Jim? The fact that she was so into it, that it felt so right, makes her sick. Even worse, after she called her cab she saw the Mikes and Mary all smirking at her like they saw the whole thing. They must've thought she was the biggest creep ever. She ran out of the club, never even said goodbye to them.

Then Kat closes her eyes and her chest swells. She remembers the musician on stage and how he moved her, how voluptuous his lips were against hers, how she felt their energies join. *It's just an illusion.* She can't write.

She told Clare she'd be coming in late today, but it's already 3:20—a little ridiculous to head over there now. Besides, she can't face the three Ms, who've probably already told Clare about her vulgar behavior. They must think she's desperate.

She'll cancel with Clare, rent a video and have some Thai food delivered.

Clare picks up on half a ring. *"Going Gaga."*

Kat always thinks Clare's phone greeting sounds silly.

"Hi Clare. It's Kat. Is it okay if I don't come in today?" Might as well not beat around the bush.

"Sure, that's okay." Her words are sharp.

"Clare, it's just that it's gotten so late, and—"

"It's *okay.*" Clare's voice drops to a whisper. "I just over-heard the Mikes on the phone. I think *Signal* wants to buy them."

"What?" No wonder Chelsea was so nice to her last night.

"Can you believe it?" Clare sounds bitter, which surprises Kat. Just yesterday Clare was so ecstatic about their book deal—but then Clare's written a book herself. This is different, now it's competition. Now her peppy friend knows how it feels to be on the other side.

"Going Gaga would be a much better companion to *Signal* than their stupid social-activist zine," Clare hisses. So the truth comes out.

"Did they tell you how they partied with Jerry and Chelsea at the Slow Club last night?" Kat can't help but turn the screw a little tighter.

"They mentioned it in passing," Clare says, then adds, "Did you really suck face with Jim Knight? Mary said she and Chelsea saw you two going at it when they went to the bar."

Kat's not ready for this twist. Her face burns. How can she explain last night to Clare, or to anyone? It's like trying to describe violet to someone who sees only black and white.

"God!" Kat's ambiguous answer gives her a second to catch her breath. What assholes they are, gossiping about her and merging with *Signal* at the same time.

"Kat, are you still there?"

"Yeah, I just can't believe they told you that." Still ambig-uous.

Their conversation is interrupted by call-waiting on Clare's side.

"Hold on." Clare clicks off for a moment, returning right away. "Kat, it's Gary. He wants to know if you can fill in for one of the bartenders this afternoon at 4:00, just for an hour."

Kat usually works only three nights a week and could use the extra money, even if it's just for an hour. She'll still have time for a much-needed reclusive evening.

"Yeah, sure. Tell him I'll be there. See you tomorrow."

"Okay."

Kat hangs up before her friend can ask anything more about last night. Poor Clare. She's been slaving on her zine for years while *Force* just launched nine months ago, and already they're waltzing with the bigwigs.

Chelsea and Jerry must've wooed the *Force* crew after she left. And Yoke probably got all chummy with their high-falutin' cyber-pals too. Shit. Kat is 24 and feels like time is running out. If she doesn't devise a plan to start a future she'll end up an old unaccomplished nobody.

Time to split if she's going to make it to the bar on time. Kat grabs her backpack, keys and helmet. As she reaches the door the phone rings. It's Clare again.

"Hi Clare, what's up? I'm in a hurry."

"Listen, I didn't have a chance to tell you before, but *Zenith* is having a party tonight, and they're looking for a copyeditor. Gerald and I were going to go, but Gerald has to stay late since the adulterous Mr. Knight is feeling sick and has to go home." Kat winces. Clare is already teasing her about Jim. "You should really go to the party. Just drop by after work and then leave if you want. I *know* they'd hire you. They love *Going Gaga*."

It's nice that Clare's trying to help her out. Probably feels sorry for her after yesterday's emotional scene. The last thing Kat wants to do is go to another party, but it *does* seem promising. Like *Going Gaga* and *Signal*, Sir Kengo's *Zenith* covers the culture of technology. But it takes more chances than *Signal*, is aesthetically much more sumptuous than its competitors, and has a passion for neuro-hacking. They've written about topics no one else will touch, like getting high on frog venom, and

106

wire-heading—a way to alter consciousness by pumping electricity through wires attached to one's head. Zenith's publisher,
who calls herself the Empress, is a mysterious sexy woman in
her late 40s who runs the magazine out of her home—an old
Berkeley Hills mansion. This is where the party will take place.

"I don't know," Kat says, fantasizing about eating a yum-yai
salad in bed with an old movie popped in the VCR. "I mean, I'd
love to work for them, but don't you think I should talk to the
Empress at another time? It doesn't seem like they're going to
be in the hiring mood at a party."

"You'll get there early, before they're in full party mode.
The Empress may be hard to talk to, but you already know Sir
Kengo. If you don't go tonight someone else will probably get
the job."

She's right. Kat says she'll probably go and gets the address
from Clare. She can loaf tomorrow night.

The bar is in the financial district and it gets busy around 4:30,
when the business crowd begins clocking out for the day. Most
of the faces are familiar, and Kat feels at ease behind the shel-
lacked oak counter, blending, shaking, and pouring drinks.

"Vodka or gin?" she asks a small man who's just ordered a
martini.

"Gin, straight up. With an olive."

When Kat begins to shake the drink the fellow becomes
frantic, flapping his arms and almost vaulting over to her side
of the bar. "Hold it! You're bruising the gin. My God, please,
just stir it."

Another man, a regular, says, "I'll take it if he doesn't want
it. I've taken a few bruises in my life." He winks at Kat.

Kat slides the bruised martini over to the regular and stirs
another one for the slimsy fellow. The regular asks how she's
doing and before she responds tells her that he and his wife are
pregnant. She congratulates him. The TV is on and Kat hears a
teaser for the five o'clock news. Almost time to clock out. She

107

feels a little funny attending the *Zenith* party alone. It'll be an older, more esoteric group than she's used to and she probably won't know anyone except Sir Kengo. She'll just have to breeze in, introduce herself, stay for 20 minutes or so, then sneak out. She better not be the first one there.

"Are you betting on the game?" the regular asks. Kat doesn't know which game he's talking about.

"No. Are you?"

"Uh huh. I've got a couple of bucks riding on it. I have some of my buddies coming over this Sunday—"

"Excuse me, may I have a cranberry juice?" someone says from the other side of the bar.

Kat turns around and sees Jim leaning over an empty bar stool. She freezes.

"What are you doing here?" she finally says.

"I need to talk to you."

Kat's dying to know what he wants but needs to stay on track for once. "I don't know, Jim. I'm working, and in a few minutes I'm leaving to go to an important party. Can we talk tomorrow?"

"No. Please Kat, I won't take a lot of your time, but I really need to talk to you tonight. It's urgent."

Kat's intrigued. Jim's face is gaunt and desperate, his hands are fidgety, even his clothes look tattered. Is this about last night?

"Okay. But just a few minutes." She hands him a cranberry juice.

Moments later her replacement steps behind the bar and Kat shoves her timecard in the punch clock. Since she was the only one working she gets to keep all of the tips, which amount to 15 dollars and change. She stuffs the money into a side pocket of her backpack and slings the bag over her shoulder.

108

Kat walks over to Jim, who's still standing at the bar, and tells him to have a seat. She sits only inches from him. He moves his head toward hers, comes dangerously near, then brusquely backs up. His new ragged look is much sexier than his former conservative dork-boy attire—kissable, but not quite the same person she kissed last night. His uptight expression gets in the way.

"Actually"—he clears his throat and looks down at the floor—"I was wondering if you have a car. I'd love to get a ride home and we could talk on the way. See, mine's in the shop till tomorrow. I'll pay for your gas."

"You're unbelievable! I only have a scooter and I don't have an extra helmet." Why doesn't this bigshot have a rental car?

"I'm sorry. I guess I can take a cab. I just need to find an ATM first. I only wanted a ride so we could talk privately."

Jim's desperation fascinates Kat. "What about?"

"It's about the other night. I may be in a little trouble." Jim's upper lip is beaded with sweat.

Kat has an idea. She tells Jim she'll take him home if he gives her roundtrip cab fare so that she can go to Berkeley without having to park her scooter downtown and ride BART. She tells him they can talk at his house for a few minutes while she waits for the taxi. But if a cop pulls them over because Jim's not wearing a helmet, *he'll* pay for the ticket. He agrees. They walk in silence for two blocks to an ATM, he takes out $160, then they walk to her scooter. She pulls a small, barely legal, bowl-shaped helmet out of her backpack and hops on the bike. Jim tells her it may be easier if he drives.

"No, I don't let anyone drive my scooter. No offense. I've had bigger passengers than you before. Just get on."

Jim wraps his arms around her waist, his chest leaning into her backpack, and Kat pulls out into the busy street. She thinks about the hard-on he had at the club, and the frosty phone message his girlfriend left the other night, and assumes it's all tangled into whatever Jim is so worked up about.

23

The scooter drones its way up Divisadero at 20 miles an hour. A car blares its horn behind them and Jim tightens his grip around Kat's waist. He was in meetings all day, snubbed by Chelsea, and never got back to Mandy's email and phone messages. His last communication to her was yesterday morning's e-note. He's also ignored three new messages from Larry Goines, the casino manager. Never even opened them up. After his talk with Kat he'll decide which direction to take the situation.

Since he woke up this morning he's been fixated on his memory of Kat's high-voltage mouth. A rerun of last night's scenario starts up again and he tries to stop the film—a difficult task when her body is in his arms.

The houses finally turn to mansions and the scooter loses speed as they chug toward Divisadero's peak.

"Is it Jackson?" Kat shouts through the wind.

"Yes," Jim says into her ear.

Kat swerves onto Jackson, Jim leaning into the turn. As they approach his address Jim notices a Mustang, slathered with primer, parked across the street from his house. It's out of place in this neighborhood. A man slouches behind the Mustang's steering wheel, fingering his small patch of beard.

Another person—perhaps a woman—with dark sunglasses and a baseball cap sits in the back seat. The man in front stops plucking his chin fur and straightens up when he sees Jim. Kat pulls up to the curb.

"Here we are."

The driver of the Mustang says something to his partner and then picks up a cell phone. The partner in the back frowns at Jim, then interrupts the driver's phone call to tell him something. They look like they're arguing. They both take another look at Jim, then converse with each other again.

"You can get off now," Kat says, waiting for him to get off the bike before she does.

Jim looks at his driveway and sees an ashen-complected older-looking man wearing black velvet slacks and a matching tight blazer appear from behind the guest house. His thinning gray hair flies in all directions. He stops in his tracks when he notices Jim. He then shoots a look at the Mustang.

"Go!" Jim says to Kat. "We've got to get out of here!"

"Why? What do you mean?"

"Kat, start the goddamn bike." He clenches her waist with his hands and squeezes her. "We have to get out of here!"

The man slinks down the driveway, then takes a cue from his partners and starts running at an angle toward the scooter. His light-blue eyes burn into Jim's.

"What's your problem?" Kat says as she spins around to face her passenger. Then she sees the anemic man charging across the lawn.

The Mustang door opens from the inside.

Jim leans over Kat, turns the key and revs up her bike.

"Move it!" he cries.

The man in black bounds forward just as Kat pulls out into the street. Jim hears him yell something but the scooter's engine drowns out his voice. He turns around and sees the guy jump awkwardly into the primered vehicle as it struggles to make a U-turn.

"Kat, just do as I say. You've got to . . . fucking shit!" As if

111

he's seeing double, another dumpy car with a man hiding behind the steering wheel is parked a block down from his house. It looks like a tan Mercury, and the driver has a small, triangular head, like a cat's. He's staring right at Jim. As they pass the car he hears its engine start.

"My God! They're *everywhere!* Step on it!" he shouts to Kat.

Kat accelerates without saying a word and turns right, which allows her to speed downhill. At the third block she turns to the left, onto another residential street. Every parked car now scares Jim. He expects each one to rev up its engine and come after him, like a zombie from *Night of the Living Dead.* He's not sure how many of Goines's thugs are planted in the city.

Jim turns his head and sees the Mustang just two blocks behind. The nose of the tan Mercury is peeking at them from the prior street but seems to have stalled.

"Turn another corner."

Kat turns.

Jim peers over his shoulder, sees the Mustang race down the street from which the scooter just turned off. It then screeches to a halt and backs up.

"Turn to your left!"

Kat veers to the right instead, turning into a narrow alley cluttered with trashcans. She passes a few old buildings, then abruptly steers the bike into an open garage. The scooter's foot-peg scrapes along the entire length of the car parked inside. Jim jumps off the bike and pulls the garage door down. Seconds later he hears a car barrel by.

Kat and Jim nervously stare at each other for a moment and then Kat says, "What the hell just happened?"

Jim knows it's not safe to stay in the garage. Its owner must be nearby or the door wouldn't have been open.

112   "Shhh," he hisses at Kat. He puts his ear up to the garage door but doesn't hear anything.

"Kat, we need to go somewhere safe where we can talk. Where do you live?"

"No way. We're not going to my place. This is insane. Who *are* those people?"

"I think they may be with some sort of Mafia. Shit, I've got to go someplace where I can think." Jim traces the car's damage with his finger.

"I can't believe you've dragged me into this. This is so unreal. Why would the Mafia be after you?"

Suddenly the garage door shoots up. Jim dives behind the car and crouches as low as he can, but Kat sits motionless on her scooter. Jim hears a woman's voice say, "Just what in the world do you think you're doing?"

"I, I'm sorry, I, uh, we were being chased," Kat says.

"Who are you?" the woman asks sharply.

Jim hears the sound of heels tapping around the car.

"My name is Kat Astura."

As the tapping heels get closer, Jim inches his way further around the car.

An animalistic wail bursts from the woman. "My *car!* Look what you've done to my car! You low-class scumbag! You'll have to pay for this!"

Jim carefully peeks around the car and is horrified at what he sees. The tall freckled woman with broad shoulders and cropped platinum hair is CeCe James, one of Mandy's advertising peers and racquetball partners from the gym.

The scooter belches and kicks up fumes as Kat screams, "Come on, let's split!"

Jim doesn't budge. He closes his eyes, wishing he could disappear. He wonders if he could slide under the car to the front of the garage and slip out unnoticed.

"Come on!" Kat screams again.

Jim opens his eyes in time to see a pair of black suede pumps step in front of him. He keeps his gaze to the cement floor.

"Oh my Lord. Jim? Jim!" The woman looms over him.

Jim springs to his feet like a jack-in-the-box and jumps on the back of the scooter.

113

"I'm so sorry," he mumbles to CeCe. "I'll pay for the damages." His voice is barely audible over the bike's engine and he doesn't make eye contact with her. He wraps his arms around Kat as she rips out of the garage and heads down the alley.

Jim gasps for air. After they turn onto a main street he tells her to stop.

"We *can't* stop!" Kat blares over the traffic noise.

"Please. I'm going to faint."

24

Traffic is thick and Kat imagines every car that passes by to be the Mustang.

"How are you doing?" she asks. Jim is sitting on the curb in front of a flower shop on Union Street. He's cradling his head in his hands. He doesn't respond.

"We really shouldn't be sitting here like this. Are you okay now?"

"No, I'm not okay. But you're right, we should leave. Only problem is, there's nowhere to go."

"Yes there is." Kat gets on her bike and motions for him to climb on.

She feels his breath on her neck and tells him to hang on. The cold sea air activates every cell in her body as she cruises down Bay Street, and the smell of seaweed and salt water invigorates her mind. Adrenaline floods her body, she feels alive. She's involved in a real-life adventure but feels like a character in a movie, like Thelma or Tank Girl. She knows she can jump out at any time. These men don't know who she is—and besides, they're after Jim, not her. Even the lady whose car she trashed will ultimately be Jim's responsibility.

Kat tries to imagine what Jim could have done to provoke

these mobsters and draws a blank. Must be some kind of bor-ing white-collar crime, the kind of intangible business fraud that Kat never really understands. She marvels that this editor geek, who exhibits such a conservative and rigid exterior, is actually a soulful jazzman leading an audacious double life. She finds this sexy, wonders if his girlfriend knows this side of him.

Turning right on Columbus, they leave the waterside and head toward North Beach, the city's Italian section. They pass Washington Square, where groups of frat-boys, old Italians, Asians, lustful dates, and faded pigeons meet. Kat smells garlic and tomato sauce and roasted coffee beans and dim sum—Chinatown is only two blocks to her right—as they make their way up the crowded street. She sees a pit bull hanging out a window of the car ahead of her and thinks of her own dog, Roscoe, who lives at her parents' house. She wants to wrestle with him.

"Aargh!" Jim squawks as if someone's punched him. Kat slams on the brakes. The truck behind her nearly runs into the scooter as both vehicles screech and skid, filling the air with the aroma of burning rubber. The driver gives Kat the finger as he weaves around them.

"What?" she bellows, her heart pounding as she resumes normal speed so as not to be hit.

"They're behind us!" Jim cries.

She turns her head and sees the Mustang a couple cars back. She accelerates and passes the truck again, not sure if the mobsters spotted her and Jim. But it seems likely—especially given the commotion the near-collision caused. She quickly hangs a left.

"Are you okay?" she shouts to Jim.

"Uh-huh," he says unconvincingly.

116 Kat winds through the city's narrow streets, passes Union Square, crosses Market Street. She pulls over to where the bi-cycle lane would be if there were one, slowing the scooter almost to a halt. Both she and Jim look around but see neither the gray nor the tan vehicle.

"Where are we going?" Jim asks.

Kat pulls into a parking lot and an older woman wearing an orange plastic vest approaches them. Her white badge says "Eileen" on it.

"How long are you staying?" she asks in a raspy voice.

"Probably three or four hours," Kat says.

"I'll need six bucks up front."

Kat turns to look at Jim. He snaps to attention, pulls a twenty-dollar bill out of his pocket, hands it to Eileen.

A stray cat meows at Eileen's feet. "Hold on, Happy," she says to the animal. She gives Jim his change and points to a narrow spot already occupied by two motorcycles. "You can pull her in there."

"Where are we going?" Jim repeats as he and Kat walk back up toward Market Street. Kat unstraps her helmet and stuffs it into her backpack. She lifts her hair with her fingers.

"I thought we'd go to the *Zenith* party. It'll be safe there, and you can tell me what the hell's going on while we ride BART."

Jim stops walking. "Kat, I'm not going to any party. I'm sorry, but that's not something I can do right now."

"Great. Then tell me what you had in mind."

"Why can't we go to your place? I just want to be alone with you. They don't know where you live."

"Yeah, and I'd like to keep it that way. I think this is the best idea. Those guys will never find us if we're on BART. Besides, I need to talk to the editors over at *Zenith,* and I feel like I'm 'on' right now. I'm really pumped up, you know?" Kat rubs her hand down Jim's back. "Don't worry, it'll be fine."

Kat starts walking again and Jim reluctantly follows. She doesn't know what she'll do once they leave the party. If she's smart she'll ditch him, let him fend for himself. He must have a friend who can put him up for the night.

They ride the escalator down to the station, buy tickets from a machine, wait for 10 minutes, then board a train headed for Berkeley. Rush hour has ended and they find an empty seat for two. Kat lets Jim slide in by the window—she's

117

claustrophobic unless she has an aisle seat. After a few moments getting adjusted and gathering her thoughts Kat faces Jim, who's already looking at her. She has the urge to kiss him again but restrains herself. She does put her hand on his leg.

"Can we talk now?" she asks.

"Yes," he says, placing his hand over her fingers.

Jim looks out the window and takes a deep breath. He runs his free hand through his short blond hair. Finally he faces her.

"Kat," he says, squeezing her hand, "what really happened the other night, at my house?"

Kat doesn't see the connection between the other night and this evening's events. How can he still be harping on the party at his house when they're on the brink of death?

"You mean when you panicked in the den?" She pulls her hand away from his.

"Uh, no. I panicked?"

"Well, kind of. You were so stressed out, and when I—"

"Did you see me gamble online?"

Kat blinks hard. "Gamble online? What does that have to do with anything?" Suddenly the train feels like a spinning teacup at Disneyland. *Netscape, maximum 20,000 dollars, cheap game, Mafia, "Would you like to bet again?"*

"Just answer me Kat—yes or no? I have to know exactly what happened."

"Does this have something to do with those jalopies that were chasing us?"

"I think so." Jim's voice warbles.

Kat hangs her head. She rapidly scrolls through several scenarios. 1. She can deny the whole thing, tell him she doesn't know what he's talking about. 2. She can make him believe he was so drunk that he gambled uncontrollably and she and her friends had to pry him away from the keyboard. 3. Some random friend—a man who never gave his name—stopped by and must've used the computer when no one was around.

"You mean that gambling site is for real?" she asks, already certain of this but stalling for time.

"So you *do* know what I'm talking about."

"Jim, I'm sorry," she says. "I didn't know it was real. I mean, I didn't need a password or anything. How was I supposed to know?"

Jim tosses his head back and closes his eyes. "Oh God." He pauses, and Kat doesn't say a word. He then kicks the seat in front of him.

"*You* did this?"

A tight-lipped businesswoman whose seat Jim kicked turns around. Kat looks at the floor.

"Well, there's got to be something we can do," Kat says. "I mean, it's not your fault, and I didn't know it was a real casino. Can't you get a lawyer and fight this?"

Jim sits motionless, his head still tossed back, eyes still shut. He doesn't answer her. She doesn't know what else to say. She looks around at the crowd—mostly people with briefcases or backpacks—all going about their nightly routine. A loud-speaker announces that the Berkeley stop is coming up.

"Jim, the next stop is ours."

He doesn't budge. She taps him on the shoulder and he violently shrugs his arm.

"Aren't you getting off the train?"

He doesn't move.

The train stops and she stands up. "Jim, I'm getting off now."

Like a robot Jim flips his eyelids open, jerks his body to a standing position with one brusque movement, and stiffly marches out into the terminal.

25

As soon as they step outside Jim lights a match and takes a long drag off his cigarette. He still hasn't spoken to Kat. He watches her now as she tries to hail a cab, freaked at this seemingly guileless beauty who's just butchered his life. Everything he's worked for—money, marriage, strength, confidence, a future—has just been annihilated with a few simple keystrokes. Snuffed out by a she-devil wearing blue velvet pants and blood-red lipstick.

A taxi pulls up and Devil Girl jumps in. She holds the door open while giving *Zenith*'s address to the driver. She then looks at Jim and he quickly shifts his eyes but gets in the car. He still has his cigarette and doesn't bother to ask if he can smoke in the cab. He takes a hit and blows the smoke straight ahead. The driver unrolls his window but doesn't say anything. As Kat snaps on her seatbelt Jim feels her gaze on his cheek.

"So you're not even going to *look* at me?" she asks.

Crowds, traffic, sirens, lights, horns, voices, movement. Jim yowls like a madman but no one notices. His expression is stony, his mouth is shut, his vocal cords are still. Yet he screams and wails and struggles for air. He's a prisoner in his own flesh, being carried by the glamorous devil further down

120

to the unknown depths of depravity and destruction. He needs to be alone, in a place where he can see things clearly, talk to Mandy, maybe patch up one of the many fresh holes in his life before it sucks him into oblivion. And yet he can't leave Kat, somehow feels linked to her, protected and secure, in a sickening and deplorable kind of way.

Kat punches the vinyl seat. "Fine, when we get to the party you can go wherever the hell you want. Get as far away from me as you can. Get your head blown off for all I care."

"You've ruined me," Jim splutters, surprising himself. An avalanche of words tumbles out. "You've *ruined* me. I'm *fucked.* I might as well jump out of the car right now and hope to hell the traffic doesn't stop for me." The cab driver shoots a frantic look at Jim and slows the car down. "I'm penniless now, thank you very much, and I'm sure my fiancée is purchasing a 357 Magnum as we speak. I mean, it was bad enough hearing her phone messages the other night. We still haven't talked. By the way, what the hell happened that made her so upset? You never did tell me what happened after you drained my bank account." He stops for a moment to catch his train of thought. "But as if what happened at my house wasn't enough, you had to hurl us into CeCe James's garage, fuck up her car, then split without an explanation. Oh God, I just wonder if that fiasco has reached Mandy yet. Oh God—oh fucking God. Thanks for destroying my life."

The cab rolls up a long driveway to an old witchy Victorian house. The driver looks relieved when he stops the car.

"Fuck. You," Kat says, her eyes like glass. She runs out of the cab and up to the house, leaving Jim to pay the fare.

Jim extinguishes his stub of a Parliament and fumbles with his wallet, his hands shaking. It takes a few moments to register how much each bill is worth. Finally he gives the driver three fives. "Keep the change," he says.

Jim steps onto the lawn and the smell of crackling wood and toasty orange flames fills his lungs. The dusk-streaked air is damp and cool, and it's *real*. He breathes in the fresh tranquillity. An off-duty ice-cream truck putts up the road and Seven-Up Popsicles come to mind. Jim wonders if the tangy treat still exists.

The shock of his situation is slowly sinking in, turning into a nauseating actuality that won't go away until he fixes it. He sucks in the night and his head lightens up a bit. He can think more clearly out here. He didn't mean to rip into Kat, needs to apologize.

Maybe if he can talk her into letting him stay at her place, just for the night, he can devise a plan to wake up from this nightmare.

He knocks on the door and waits. The beating of a drum breaks out, rhythmic and full. No one comes to the door so Jim lets himself in. The small entry is dark and to his left a flickering light seeps between the door and the floor. He hears voices and clattering and pounding. A slender woman in her twenties with strawberry frizzed hair emerges from a bathroom and sees Jim. She's wearing a flowing sheer robe with only silver panties and a sparkling bra underneath.

"Hi, I'm Chantelle. Are you going to join us in the ritual?"

Chantelle's tongue is pierced, which distracts Jim from her soft-spoken words.

"Ritual?"

"Yeah, follow me," she says, giggling. She leads him into the candlelit room, which is filled with clusters of people who are either undulating to the beating pulse or sharing rapt emotion in intimate circles. Near the glowing fireplace is a 50ish woman wearing black leather pants with handcuffs dangling from her belt buckle. She's intertwined with a guy barely beyond his teenage years, and when he whispers in her ear she nuzzles into him and they fall onto a loveseat. Jim then spots the long silky hair and large gapped teeth of Sir Kengo and suddenly remembers Kengo at his house. Were they doing heroin in his living room? No, it was something else. Jim breathes through his tension. *Stay in the present.*

Kengo, who's wearing his black cape and dark eyeliner, is surrounded by *Zenith* devotees, but his wet pupils don't see them. He's nose-to-nose with a bald skinny girl whose sinewy legs wrap around his hips. Both are smiling but neither one talks.

Jim sees Chantelle lugging a toilet seat into the middle of the room, no one giving her a second look. Another heavier beat joins the first and the two rhythms seem to tease and flirt with each other. Bodies are now writhing and gyrating. Jim scans the room but can't find the drummers. Although he hasn't consumed anything but cigarettes, cranberry juice and caffeine since this morning his mind feels more disjointed than it did last night. These people don't seem real. The fiery light casts carnal shadows on everyone's faces. The toilet seat scares him. He wants to flee but doesn't know where to go.

Finally Jim spots Kat sitting in a corner, listening to a woman who keeps pointing her index finger as she talks. Jim wonders if this is the Empress. She looks around 45, with long wavy hair, thick bangs and round granny glasses. She's wearing a long red silk dress and a large shiny ankh pendant around her neck. Both she and Kat are drinking red wine out of large Mexican goblets and Kat keeps nodding in agreement. When Kat sees Jim her eyes widen.

Jim doesn't want to step forward into this alien atmosphere. He's still standing near the door, where he feels safe. He motions with his hand for Kat to come to him. She looks back at her host, ignoring Jim, and continues to nod at the woman's rant with a stiff smile.

Now Chantelle is circling the toilet seat, her arms stretched over her head, her sheer robe lifting and floating around her.

The percussion picks up and loud rhythmic cymbals come clanging into the room. DING-*du-dum* TING-*tu-tum* DING-*du-dum* TING-*tu-tum*. Jim turns to the right and sees a belly-dancer shimmying through the crowd. She shakes her way to the center of the room, and when the drums slow down she eases up on her finger-cymbals. While bending her knees and rotating her ribcage she lifts an edge of the black-and-gold veil that's skillfully woven under and over her undergarments. She masks her

123

face with it, exposing only her eyes. Then looking coyly at the people surrounding her she unhinges the veil from her bra strap. Her body billows and heaves. As she peels the veil from her chest and waist her beaded bra and full tummy come into view. The material still remains attached to the band of her panties, forming a skirt around her thighs. Her hips and breasts slither from side to side and as the drums accelerate into a wild frenzy, she throws back her head and her whole body vibrates, as if it's been charged with electricity. Jim heats up, can't take his eyes off her contorted movements. Each section of her body dances in isolation from the others. As she glides toward Kengo her arms reach out like young snakes, her stomach rolls like a series of waves, her breasts and pelvis jut alternately forward and backward. Jim is both excited and nervous that she may come over to him. Sparkles fly off her finger-cymbals and Jim tingles. DING-*du-dum* TING-*tu-tum* DING-*du-dum* TING-*tu-tum*.

The spell breaks when Chantelle grabs a wooden block and stick from the mantelpiece and bangs hard and out of tempo. Jim hates this and hopes the dancer ignores Chantelle. But it's some kind of signal, and the dancer disappears into the crowd while Chantelle tries to perform a tribal dance with her wooden block. She swings her head from side to side while circling the toilet seat and banging the block. Jim looks at the crowd, expecting to see disgusted expressions, but all eyes are entranced. Heads are bobbing, hips are rocking, toes are tapping. They're all phonies, Jim is sure. He looks for Kat, relieved to see her bent over, adjusting her boot. When she straightens up she eyes a platter of fruit and cheese and makes her way over to it. Jim rushes around the crowd and meets her at the food table.

"Hi," he says.

"Hi." She picks up a paper plate and brushes past him.

"Kat, I'm sorry. I didn't mean to be so harsh with you in the cab. It was just such a shock. I guess I was hoping that somehow those guys were wrong, that I wasn't really wiped out."

She shrugs her shoulders. "It's okay. I'm sorry too, even though I had no idea that game was real."

"I know you didn't." Jim is too freaked to eat but grabs a plate anyway.

Kat piles on the food. "What are you going to do?"

Jim realizes she considers this only *his* problem. He grabs two napkins.

"I need to find a phone," he says. He'd better call Mandy before she thinks he fell off the earth.

They sneak out of the room and into the lobby with plates in hand. The crowd starts chanting in the other room.

"Isn't this wild?" Kat says.

"It's weird," Jim says. "I wonder if there's a phone upstairs."

They climb to the top of a wrought-iron spiral staircase and find themselves surrounded by four closed doors. Jim taps on one and no one answers. He cracks it open and sees a purple bedroom with a large bay window looking out at the hills.

"We better not go in there," Kat says.

Jim closes the door and they slink across the landing to another door. Again Jim apprehensively knocks and then pokes his head into the large room. He imagines this to be one of the offices where *Zenith* is produced. It has three computers, a color scanner, a phone and a fax machine.

Jim steps in and places his fruit plate on a desk.

"Are you sure this is okay?" Kat hesitates before entering.

"That's funny, Kat. If only you'd asked that before touching my computer." Jim doesn't know why he said that. He's already forgiven her.

Kat flinches. "Fuck you. I said I was sorry, and *you're* the idiot who didn't put a password on his casino bookmark."

Jim panics. He doesn't want her to run away. "You're absolutely right. Forgive me. I'm just tired and stressed and on the verge of a breakdown." He takes her plate from her and places it next to his on the desk.

"I'm tired too." Kat sets her backpack on the floor and massages the back of her neck.

125

"Who are you going to call? Mandy?"

"Yeah." *Mandy.* Jim's stomach turns. He hasn't even thought of what he's going to say. He decides to tell her the truth—about the gambling, that is. She won't be happy, but once she hears the whole story it might not sound as horrifying as the scenarios that must be going through her head.

"Make your call. I'm going to the bathroom," Kat says. Then she brightens up. "Oh! I got a job here! I'm going to be assistant copyeditor."

"That's *great,* Kat." Jim hopes she doesn't start dancing around a toilet once she gets used to the place. "What was that lady in the red dress talking to you about?"

"That was the Empress," Kat says. "She's fascinating. She started off by talking about Micronesia and some omelettes she ate in a restaurant over there that made her see all sorts of visions. Then she segued into Greek art, and something about the art of sound, and she said that glamour can be traced back to the powerful sounds of Greek vowels, and—well, I couldn't keep up. But once she got it all out of her system she told me I had the job. They won't pay me right away, but she said after a few months we'll evaluate my work and then we'll talk salary." Kat beams at Jim. "I didn't even get a chance to talk to Sir Kengo. Well, I'll be back."

Jim crams a few slices of fruit in his mouth, making sure to stay away from the acidic pieces. He sits by the phone, calls New York information for the Parker Meridian, then dials up the hotel and asks for Mandy LeMattre.

"Her line is busy. Would you like to leave a message?"

"No, I'll call back." Jim hangs up, wonders if he can email Mandy from here. He knows that most people on the *Zenith* staff subscribe to The EGG, because he's noticed some of its editors online with an egg.com email address. He sits still for a moment, doesn't hear anyone outside the office. Quickly he rolls his chair over to a computer that's been left on and recognizes a program called Zterm, which he uses to modem into The EGG.

Name? jknight

Password?

Jim pauses. It's been a while since he's been on The EGG. Doesn't have time for it anymore, even though *Signal* has an active conference on the online service. Jim usually has an intern look at each topic and give him the highlights.

Password?

Jim types in !tESLA9.

The screen is stagnant for a few moments, then "Welcome to The EGG" rolls up. Jim is surprised to read "You have mail," since everyone knows to email him at signal.com. He types in "mail." Some recognizable junk-email addresses appear, then:

accounts@tropical.com

accounts@tropical.com

accounts@tropical.com

Jim winces. When *Signal* wrote the article on virtual gambling last summer they brushed off the rumors that El Tropical was run by a mob faction. Hell, that's what they say about *every* casino, on- or offline. And besides, the rumors never mentioned anything about primer-gray Mustangs.

Jim fantasizes about disconnecting himself from his present reality—email, technology, *Signal,* El Tropical—and living forever offline on a faraway island. The thought of Mandy ruins this scenario. He can't imagine her unplugged from anything.

Kat is taking a long time in the bathroom and Jim wonders if she's okay. He squeezes his achy eyes, then opens up accounts@tropical.com. He notices this message is a CC of an original sent to jim@signal.com.

Mr. Jim Knight,

We were appalled by the tone of your letter and will not tolerate the kind of delinquent and rude behavior that you have displayed to us so far. Watch your words, big guy.

If you have any questions regarding your debt, we can send someone to your place of work or residence tomorrow evening to discuss it with you. But we do expect an immediate response to this letter and some form of payment by midnight tonight.

Mr. Larry Goines
Casino Manager

We can send someone to your place of work or residence tomorrow evening to discuss it. They wrote this shortly after the sarcastic e-note he fired off yesterday, so *tomorrow* is really *today*—he's already missed the midnight deadline. The guys in the Mustang—and the Mercury—didn't look like conversational types. Jim's hands are clammy as he thinks about the stakeout at his house. Maybe he should have seen what they wanted. Maybe they came just to talk. Maybe Kat could have explained that it was she who unwittingly racked up the debt and that it was all an innocent mishap. If Goines could have forgiven Jim, it would have been because of an apology to the henchmen at his house. Jim's whole body quivers as he thinks of the mess he's in. He's sure that Mr. Anemic and his cohorts have already reported the chase and Goines must be madder than a hornet.

Jim's teeth start to chatter, more from nerves than the damp chill in the air. He opens the second message:

Mr. Jim Knight,

You missed the deadline of your first payment: midnight last night. This is a business that doesn't accept delinquent behavior from irresponsible gamblers such as yourself, so don't fool around. Meet us at your place of residence this evening at five o'clock so that we may collect on your debt. If you don't have the cash, we'll accept personal property that we deem a fair exchange.

128

Mr. Larry Goines
Casino Manager

Without digesting the e-note Jim dashes to the third message:

What the hell were you doing tonight with your scooter friend? You think this is a game? We've been polite and business-like up until now, but the party's just ended. Forget the payment plan, you blew it. We want it all—the whole $199,115—sent to us in the form of Digicash by 8:00 tonight. Don't play cat-and-mouse with us, Jim. Our claws are sharper than yours.

Jim pushes a window open and heaves, his abdomen violently contracting. With nothing much in his stomach his physical rebellion is fruitless. A fiery streak of pain rips through his chest.

Weakened, with teeth still chattering, Jim falls back into a chair. He spots a sweatshirt on a nearby stool and uses it to mop up his sweat-slicked face.

He looks at the scrap of paper with the Parker Meridian's number. It would be so much easier just to email Mandy, but she's expecting a call. He needs to hold it together with her, the one steady thing still going in his life. He lights a cigarette.

"Parker Meridian."

"Mandy LeMattre please." Jim bends forward in his chair and arches his back, trying to stop the quivering, but it's uncontrollable.

The phone is ringing in Mandy's room now. Jim's chest tightens.

Mandy picks up on the second ring. "Hello?"

"Hi Mandy, it's me."

Mandy is silent, forcing Jim to continue.

"Uh, how are you?"

"Cut the bullshit, Jim. Why haven't you been answering my calls? And who was that tart who answered the phone two nights ago?"

Jim launches into the story of how his car broke down, how he went to Danny's to meet Cooper, then how they all ended up at his house. He admits he was a fool to smoke the dope and explains that he was passed out when Kat answered the phone. He can't get himself to confess Kat's online catastrophe, waits to see if she brings up CeCe James's dented car.

Mandy laughs. *She laughs!* If Jim weren't so gutted he'd dance. This is the first good thing that's happened since he left her at the airport. Perhaps things aren't as serious as they seem. Perhaps he *should* tell her about the gambling incident.

Then she speaks. "God, are you a fool. Do you know how it looks, hanging out with those punks? I mean, going to Raymond's is one thing. He's a respectable *Signal* employee, and Darren Cooper was there. But hanging out and smoking marijuana with those, those *losers,* and then inviting them over to our home? What is *wrong* with you?"

Jim is at a loss for words. He's not sure where he erred in his story. After all, Cooper was supposed to meet him at Danny's, and then at his house.

"Mandy, they're nice people." Jim wants the shaking to stop. He puffs as hard as he can on his cigarette but his skin continues to tremble.

"How do you know they didn't steal anything? They could have taken a couple thousand dollars' worth of jewelry when you were passed out. Did you check my jewelry box?"

Jim feels like saying, "No, but I checked my email and we're wiped out, babe."

"God, this makes me angry," Mandy continues. "Use your thick head once in a while, would you?"

"I'm sorry," Jim says. Mandy apparently hasn't heard from CeCe James yet. He hopes CeCe dies before Mandy returns.

"And what about yesterday? Why didn't you call me like you promised in your email?"

"Mandy, I was playing at the Slow Club, remember? It was really late when I got home. I didn't want to wake you." He can't tell her the truth, that he forgot she existed, that his every molecule was throbbing for Kat.

"Well, from now on at least *email* me. God, you piss me off sometimes."

130

Mandy then proceeds to tell Jim about her success with today's meetings, how Absolut Vodka is about to sign a 12-issue back-cover contract. "I've got them by the balls," she says with a snicker. Their domestic spat is over, as far as Mandy is concerned.

Kat comes into the room, her hair wet and slicked back. She grabs her fruit plate and leaves again. Jim doesn't want her to go. He listens to the rest of Mandy's day, which includes a lunch at Tavern on the Green with a media buyer from Chiat/Day and two other meetings in the city. She then says she's tired, hopes his day was fine, turns on the baby voice to say she loves him.

"Love you too," he says.

"Now try not do anything else stupid while I'm gone. By the way, this trip isn't going to last as long as I'd expected. I'll probably be home by the end of this week."

26

When Kat hears Jim hang up the phone she gets up from the floor. She pokes her head in the office. Jim is slouched forward, his arms wrapped around his chest.

"Is everything okay?"

Jim straightens up. "Where were you?"

"Just sitting out in the hall." She tosses her empty plate into a trashcan.

Jim is staring at her hair and Kat touches it to see if it's dry. Still damp.

"I hate the way my hair looks after I've worn my helmet," Kat says, sheepish about her hang-up with appearance at a time like this. "I just wet it down a little."

"It looks good."

Kat wants to ask how the phone conversation went with his girlfriend but is distracted by movement on the computer screen.

She points at the Mac.

Jim looks at the screen. "Shit."

Kat gets closer and sees an instant message from accounts@tropical.com.

"*Shit!*" Jim looks at his watch, nervously blinks a few times, then looks at the screen.

Kat reads over Jim's shoulder.

It's after 8:00, Jim. I've tried to be cordial with you. I'm not an unfair man. This is not an unfair organization. But we also don't take any crap from assholes like you.

You've danced, my little man, and now it's time to pay the piper.

Make it easy on yourself and send us your debt in the form of Digicash immediately. This is our last correspondence over email. If you don't pay up *right now* you'll have to deal with us in person. We WILL collect our moneys. Don't forget, we know where you live. We know where you work.

Jim jumps away from the keyboard and hits his head against Kat's jaw. She bites her tongue and tears gush out of her eyes.

"I don't know what to do!" Jim wails. "He wants almost 200,000 bucks *right now.* I don't have that kind of money. What will they do to me?"

Kat has no choice now. She has to help him.

"Okay, this is what we're going to do," she says, grabbing the phone. "I'll call Danny and have him pick us up. They don't know who I am, so we'll stay at my house tonight."

Jim nods in agreement. He's rapidly blinking and Kat hopes he doesn't start crying the way he did the other night. She walks over to him, puts her hands on his shoulders.

"It's okay, Jim. We'll be okay. We'll straighten this out."

He pulls her down onto his lap and buries his head in her neck.

"Oh Kat, what am I going to do?"

"Why can't we call the police or the FBI?" she asks.

"And say what? Those greasers in the Mustang never really threatened us. They could say they just wanted to talk. And I don't think the casino manager's letters could get him into trouble either. I'm legally at fault here, I think. I need to see my attorney."

Kat doesn't argue. She smells a trace of aftershave on Jim's

133

neck and it again reminds her of her dad—her dad with his family on a Sunday drive.

Jim pulls away from her as the office door opens. A Louise Brooks–like woman wearing a short black wig and an eyebrow ring pops her head in, then quickly turns her gaze away from Kat and Jim. "Oh!" she says, then shuts the door behind her.

"Well," Jim says, "I guess calling Danny is our best option."

Kat agrees. She dials up her neighbor. The phone rings four times and Kat is about to hang up when Kimmy answers.

"H-hello," Kimmy stammers.

"Kimmy, it's me. Kat."

Kimmy is silent. Something's happened.

"Are you okay?" Kat asks.

Kimmy hesitates, then says, "Oh God. Kat, your apartment is on fire."

Kat's knees buckle and she grabs the edge of the desk.

"What?" she gasps.

Kat hears sirens from Kimmy's end.

"They just got here," Kimmy says, referring to the firetrucks.

Kat asks how much damage there's been and Kimmy says it's hard to tell, but it looks like the whole building is burning down.

"Does anyone know how it started?" Kat asks.

"Not yet."

Tears roll down Kat's face. She thinks of her expensive new computer, the boxes of scrapbooks she never unpacked when she moved into her apartment, the snow-dome collection she started in high school. She tells Kimmy she'll call her back later and hangs up. There's no use going over to Danny's house. That street doesn't need another disaster.

Kat crumples to the floor like a rag doll. She can't understand how they know who she is, let alone where she lives. Her head jerks when she hears Jim cough.

134

"They burned my apartment down," Kat says, her voice breaking. She doesn't want to cry in front of Jim and takes a moment before continuing. "How the hell did they know who I was? I don't have a license plate on my scooter, I've never seen them before, I didn't have to type in my name when I gambled."

She looks at Jim. His elbows are propped on his knees, his head buried in his hands. He lifts his head to look at her.

"It could be a horrible coincidence. That's what it's *got* to be. Just a horrible coincidence," he says.

Kat is silent and they leave it at that. A coincidence.

"Well, we've got to find a safe place to stay tonight," Jim says.

Kat's heart is heavy, she doesn't feel like thinking of another plan. It's his turn.

He continues, "I want to get over to *Signal*, look through my notes on El Tropical. When I was editing an article we ran about them I came across a clipping about an activist group opposed to online casinos. Said some of these casinos were underground and dangerous. The activists sounded like fanatics and didn't have any hard evidence to back up their words." Jim sighs. "I should've paid more attention to them."

A clock on the wall says 8:25. It's dark and they don't have a car. Kat feels raw, her nerves shrill, and she wants to cry. She couldn't possibly go across the bay and play detective right now. Her thoughts jump to Yoke. *Yoke.*

Kat stands up and reaches for the phone again, shaking her head at Jim. "It's too dangerous now. We shouldn't go back to the city till tomorrow, when it's light out. I'm calling Yoke, see if he can put us up for the night. He lives somewhere around here."

Jim spins his chair toward the computer and logs off The EGG without saying a word.

135

Kat squeezes toothpaste onto her finger and rubs it into her teeth. Jim is already tucked into the living room couch and Kat feels a little shy about sharing a room with Yoke's younger sister, who rents a small house with him. Someone taps lightly on the door and Kat rinses her mouth before opening it. It's Yoke.

Jim and Kat agreed not to tell any of their friends about their situation with El Tropical. That kind of knowledge can only get someone in trouble. Instead, they told Yoke the truth about the fire, which has left Kat temporarily homeless, then lied that Jim locked himself out of his house and has to wait until tomorrow for a locksmith. Yoke couldn't understand how Jim and Kat ever hooked up with each other, but didn't push the issue when his questions were sidetracked.

Now Yoke is standing only inches in front of Kat, in boxer shorts and a faded T-shirt. He asks if Kat is okay.

"Yeah, I'm fine," she says, wondering how Yoke could believe that.

He sets his jaw in a way Kat's never seen before, giving himself a hard-boiled look, and presses his lips into hers. His lips are spongy and she feels his tongue slip into her mouth. A couple of nights ago this would have sent her through the roof, she would have been all over him. But tonight all she can think about is her apartment and the horrible danger she's stepped into.

Yoke pushes forward, forcing Kat to step back. He shuts the door behind him and playfully pushes her against the sink, pinning her wrists behind her. He's breathing hard and kisses around her ear, then sucks on her neck. She tries to warm up, doesn't feel a thing.

"Stop it Yoke. I can't do this right now," she blurts.

Yoke steps away. He looks hurt, or embarrassed, Kat isn't sure which.

"Hey, I'm sorry. I thought you . . . I should have been more sensitive." His jaw is relaxed now. He nervously rubs his shoulders, looks at his toes, walks out of the bathroom without saying goodnight.

136

Shit, did she just blow something good?

27

Mandy steps into the back seat of the Mustang and sits on the henchman's lap. She spots Jim and flippantly waves goodbye, cackling at some remark the goateed driver just made. Jim tries to chase the car, but his lead-laden legs root him in the middle of the street as it speeds away.

Jim opens his eyes to see a cluttered coffee table. His consciousness is still detached from his brain as he tries to figure out where he is. He sees a copy of *Force* on the table and his thoughts begin to crystallize. He's at Yoke's. Last night he and Kat rushed into Yoke's Honda and Kat rattled off a quick explanation as to why she and Jim needed a place to stay. Yoke barely said two words to Jim, and now Jim wants to get out of here.

He sits up and sees his pants draped over the couch's armrest by his feet. His watch is glistening on the table and he grabs it. He angles its face so that it picks up a ray of light coming through the closed blinds. Just after 7 AM.

Pulling on his pants, Jim maps out his next moves. He decides to leave Kat a note telling her he's going to *Signal* by cab. She can get a ride to work with Yoke. Once he gets to *Signal* he'll look through his El Tropical notes, see if he can find

137

the clipping about the anti-online-gambling group. And he'll call his attorney. Maybe he and Kat can meet for lunch and he can make sure she has a place to stay. He'll check into a hotel until he can get some help.

Jim notices a credit-card bill on the coffee table and finds Yoke's address on it. He holds the bill as he tiptoes across the room to a beaten bookcase, where there's a portable phone. He dials 4-1-1, gets the number for Yellow Cab, quickly dials the taxi company before he forgets the number. In a whisper Jim gives a gruff woman Yoke's address.

Out in the crisp air Jim's head is clearer than it's been in the last three days. He savors the morning's perfume. Yoke's residential neighborhood is lined with trees, plastic lawn ornaments, wooden mailboxes, newspapers stuffed in waterproof baggies, and large green trashcans waiting to be emptied. Yoke's porch has a swinging bench and as soon as Jim falls into it the taxi pulls up.

The cab smells like fresh tobacco, which reminds Jim that he craves a cigarette. He lights up his last Parliament. He feels freer, more distant from yesterday's events now that he's away from Kat. Or is it just that he hasn't logged into his email yet? He stays away from the thought of tropical.com.

The driver—who introduced himself as Yorgos—is an older man with salt-and-pepper hair, rosy cheeks, weepy eyes, and an oversized head. He's babbling about his days as a racehorse owner, describing his thoroughbreds as though they were long-lost lovers. There was Annie-Go-Lucky, She's-a-Lady, and Cleopatra. They were beautiful animals with healthy teeth, strong legs, powerful lungs. He could have made it big, he says, his Adam's apple bobbing, "if it weren't for those sons of bitches who ruined me!" He explodes into volcanic anger now, pounding his fist into the wheel. "They broke me, goddamn it. I'm just a goddamn son-of-a-bitch taxi driver now."

138

"There's nothing wrong with being a taxi driver," Jim interjects, trying to include himself in the conversation.

"What the hell do you know about driving a cab? No one

knows what I've been through!" Yorgos says, waving a fist in the air.

Jim doesn't know who broke this man, nor does he care. He takes a long hit off his cigarette and meditates on the city skyline, which is capped with white fog.

Half an hour later Yorgos gets off the Bay Bridge, still carrying on about racetracks, his face now smeared with tears. He suddenly interrupts his own one-man show with a high-pitched "Ohhh!"

Yorgos swerves the cab over to the side of the road, nearly bashing the rear of a parked station wagon, and throws the gearshift into park. Jim looks for blood but doesn't see any. Yorgos hasn't been shot. Maybe it's a heart attack. But before Jim has a chance to ask what's wrong Yorgos hobbles out of the car and begins jiggling his leg, holding on to the hood of the car with one plump hand for balance.

The meter is still running and Jim wants to kick it through the windshield. Finally Yorgos finishes jiggling and calmly takes his seat behind the wheel.

"Sorry about that. I'm a man with poor circulation. I just have to revive it every hour or so. Now where was it that you were headed?"

The cab finally reaches the corner of South Park and Second Street. Jim pays and gets out, telling Yorgos to keep the change. The streets aren't yet fully awake and Jim feels exposed while he stands before the *Signal* building's massive front door, reaching in his pocket for his keys.

Someone appears from around the corner and Jim jerks forward. The ragged man roars with laughter at Jim's skittishness, showing two rows of broken teeth. He then sobers up.

"Can you spare a dollar so I can get something to warm up my stomach?" The homeless man holds out a gritty hand, his palm cupped upward.

"Go away," Jim says without looking at the man. He jams the key into the hole and quickly lets himself into the lobby, making sure to hear the door click shut behind him.

139

Chopin is playing over the speakers in *Signal*'s space. That means someone is here. Jim looks around but doesn't see anyone. He goes to the bathroom and washes up. A shower was just installed but Jim only splashes water onto his face from the sink. He shudders at the dirty hand-towel hanging on a hook for employee use. His face is rough and he looks for a razor, even snooping in someone's gym bag. He doesn't find one but does swipe a roll of toilet paper, some Kleenex, and a bar of used soap from the bag—items that *Signal* stocks only when expecting important clients or celebrity-type visitors.

With his new toiletries tucked inside his buttoned jacket Jim steps out of the men's room, passing a writer and an assistant editor hunched over some sheets of paper. They look up at him and say hello, then go back to their business.

Jim gets to his station, locks the bathroom supplies in his desk drawer, then unlocks a portable file cabinet that sits under his desk, pulling out a file headed "Sept/Research." He riffles through news clippings, notes from interviews he conducted, business cards giving phone numbers and email addresses, and other miscellaneous scraps. In his impatience to find the blurb about the activists he accidentally spills the bundle of documents onto the floor. Instead of picking them up he drops himself to the ground and, with legs spread apart, shuffles through the pulp, ripping and wrinkling the folder's contents, but to no avail. Thinking they were only technophobic radicals at the time, he must've thrown the piece about the anti-gambling activists away.

Ignoring the mess on the floor, Jim stands on his knees and leafs through the hanging folders again, this time lifting a file that says "*Signal*, Stock." Attached to the top inside corner of the folder is a business card that says BERNARD, BLACK & TRENT, ATTORNEYS AT LAW. He sighs deeply.

140   8:20 AM.

Probably too early to speak to Penny Bernard, the attorney who represented him and six other *Signal* employees, including Mandy, when they were negotiating with *Signal*'s owners for partnership shares. Ms. Bernard was good—got them what they deserved. Jim rips the card off the folder, props it above his keyboard and dials the number. He can at least leave a message.

After the third ring a recorded message tells Jim he's reached Bernard, Black & Trent and that no one is in at the moment, but if he leaves his number and a brief description of his situation they'll be happy to return his call immediately. *Beep.*

Jim's first instinct is to hang up. He doesn't want to explain his dilemma over the phone, doesn't think anyone besides Bernard should hear the details. But in his desperation to talk to his attorney he leaves a message, revealing only his name and number.

"It's extremely urgent," he quickly adds before hanging up.

The assistant editor he saw earlier walks by and grimaces at the pile of paper spread out on the floor. Jim bends down, not getting out of his chair this time, and scoops all of his notes and articles back into the first manila folder, which he shoves back into its hanging slot. His stomach growls and he remembers he hasn't had his coffee yet.

The building is filling up and the music has changed to something folksy. Two copyeditors are sitting in the communal kitchen when Jim gets there. One is stirring sugar and milk into her mug, the other is picking at a dark chunky muffin. Glad that someone else has already brewed a pot of coffee Jim pours himself a cup.

A cigarette would be nice right now, but Jim would have to go outside to buy a pack, and also to smoke it. He doesn't want to miss his attorney's phone call and decides to stay at his desk and tackle his ever-accumulating email messages.

He connects to his *Signal* account and looks at his list of messages. Nothing new from Mandy or El Tropical, which is a relief. He starts from the top. The first message, dated nine days ago, is from an unknown writer in Denver checking on a query he'd sent Jim over two months ago. Jim can't even remember what the writer's idea was about. He hits "delete" and moves on to the next message.

The phone startles Jim, and he grabs it on half a ring.

"Hello, this is Jim."

"Hello Jim. This is CeCe James."

Jim's chest caves in and he wishes he hadn't announced himself. There's no way out of this, so he forges ahead.

"Hello CeCe. Listen, I'm deeply sorry for what happened yesterday. You see, this nice girl from work offered to take me home yesterday because my car is in the shop . . . " *His car.* Shit, he should have taken a cab to the mechanic this morning from Berkeley. ". . . and on the way to my house these gang members tried to steal her scooter, and your garage was open, and—well, you know the rest of the story. I'll pay for whatever damages were incurred." Jim is pleased with his story and remembers how impressed he was when Kat gave Yoke such a smooth fabrication of why they needed a place to stay.

"Well, the older gentleman your little friend ripped off didn't look like a gang member to me," CeCe says.

Jim spills his coffee across his desk and picks up his keyboard just in time.

"Are you still there?" CeCe says. She sounds mighty smug.

"Wh-what gentleman?" Jim feels sick. He balances his keyboard on top of his monitor.

CeCe sounds a little confused, as if she's not sure whether or not Jim knows that his friend is a thief. She explains that the old gentleman was frantic because that horrible little punk stole his wallet at the Embarcadero Center. He was trying to buy presents for his goddaughter, who's getting married in two weeks.

"Jim, he was an older man. He had a Mustang. Why would he try to steal that broken-down scooter you were on?"

142

"What did you tell him?" Jim says, his throat dry and tight.

"Well, I told him that she'd said her name was Kat Astura and that I could call the police, but he said he'd call from his car phone."

Jim thinks about the fire in Kat's apartment and suddenly loathes this bitch, who's now saying that he owes her 4,750 dollars to repaint her car.

"I don't know what you were *really* doing with that girl, but if I don't get my money by this weekend I'll have to ask Mandy for it. And I'd just *hate* to add any stress to her busy life."

"Okay CeCe. I'll bring by the money tonight."

Jim hangs up and stares at the spilled coffee sliding off the table and onto his shoes. He does have the money socked away in his and Mandy's joint savings account. He'll just have to take it out and think up a good lie when Mandy eventually asks about it.

He unlocks his desk and takes out the tissues he just procured from the men's room, uses them to mop up the brown drippy mess. He calls his voicemail hoping Bernard called when he was talking to CeCe. No such luck. He ignores his other phone messages and goes back to his email.

The confidence he woke up with this morning has completely unraveled.

28

It's 10:00 by the time Yoke and Kat reach the lot off Market Street where her scooter is parked. They didn't exchange more than 10 words during their drive over the Bay Bridge. Kat now talks to Yoke as if nothing awkward has come between them.

"Thanks so much for letting us stay at your place. I guess I'll have to go to my apartment today and see the damage." Kat opens her door and steps out.

Yoke stays inside the car and fidgets with his radio. "See ya later," he says, turning to Kat. "Good luck with your apartment and all." He goes back to fidgeting and waits for her to shut the door before he takes off.

Kat can't seem to get it right with guys. Her life turns upside down when she fucks them, and everything's fucked when she doesn't. She gets on her scooter and sees the same parking attendant, Eileen, cleaning out a pie tin with a hose. Two cats are meowing at her feet. Kat straps on her helmet, starts her bike, slowly drives by Eileen, hoping not to disturb the cats. Jim paid for the parking last night so Kat doesn't stop, and Eileen never takes her eyes off the pie tin to acknowledge her.

Kat's afraid to see her apartment. It's not the mobsters she fears as much as her own emotions at the sight of her loss. Her loss of identity. That apartment and its contents were the only things in San Francisco that gave Kat a sense of belonging, a sense of self, a sense of someone with a past and perhaps a future. She weaves through traffic a little more recklessly than usual. She feels so puny and insignificant in this big city. The world of publishing, book deals, romance, success and Jann Wenner belongs to everyone else she knows, but she's an outsider, a perpetual intern working to make other people's dreams a reality. Now she's even blown it with Yoke. She'll be 25 this year. And still not accomplished.

Several blocks from her street she swerves to the side of the road to scope things out. Cars whiz by, dodging the double-parked vehicles that constantly obstruct the flow of traffic, and nothing looks out of the ordinary. She doesn't feel like anyone is watching her so she pulls back out into the street.

As if in a dream she seems to float down the last few blocks before her apartment. Sound is muffled, time is meaningless, images move in and out of her head without her awareness.

Then she sees it. Dismal and charred and unrecognizable. Just a heap of blackened wood, melted metal and wind-blown ashes. It's worse than Kat had imagined. *Much* worse. She gets off her bike and stands motionless. A yellow plastic strip surrounds the dead lot, warning people to stay away. A breeze lifts some of the ashes and gently drops them back to another spot on the ground. Tears well up and spill down Kat's face as she stares in disbelief, and she rips through the plastic strip, into the debris, hoping to find something that could connect her to yesterday. She throws down her backpack, falls to her knees, scoops up the powdery black flakes, letting them drop across her thighs. She spots a dull chain, maybe a necklace, and reaches for it. But she can't figure out what it used to be, realizes it probably wasn't even hers.

Her vision blurs and she wipes her eyes with her sleeve. She looks around to see if her landlord or any of her neighbors are here but sees nothing familiar. A van with television call letters painted on its side pulls up and two men hop out. The excited driver slides open the back door and takes out a video camera while the tall thin passenger, wearing a windbreaker and tan slacks, sizes up the destruction and scribbles away on a scratch pad. He notices Kat and perks up.

Kat looks away from him, doesn't want to talk to anyone right now except her parents. She misses her green-and-white bedroom in their North Hollywood ranch house.

The man in the windbreaker bares a set of large bleached teeth and trots over to Kat.

"Excuse me," he says. "Were you a tenant of this building?"

Kat grabs her backpack and jumps to her feet. "No, sorry, I can't help you." She runs past the man, mashing black cinders with her Doc Martens, and hears him calling to her from behind.

"But wait a minute! Did you *see* the fire? Did you know anyone who lived here?"

Kat again uses her sleeve to wipe her eyes before she hops on her bike and fishtails into the street. She's got to get out of this city. She's got to call her parents, tell them to meet her tonight at the Burbank Airport. She has a VISA card her dad gave her to use in case of an emergency. She'll use it to take out a cash advance, which will buy her a one-way ticket on Southwest. She doesn't want to leave any tracks by paying for the flight with her credit card.

She drives toward South Park. She'll go to Clare's office, use her phone to call her mom and to let the bar know she won't be coming back, that she'll have someone pick up her last paycheck in a few days. Then she'll see if Clare can watch her scooter until she can have it shipped to LA. She also wants to say goodbye to her friends.

29

TO DO:

1. Read email.
2. Call Bernard again.
3. Eat lunch.
4. Fire Mara.
5. Take cab to pick up car.
6. Go to bank.
7. Pay CeCe.
8. Copyfit upcoming features.
9. Check into hotel.

Jim scratches off task #1 with a red pen. *Why take a Valium when you can make a list?*

It dawns on him that today is Thursday, the day Darren Cooper goes back to Vancouver. He should have contacted him.

Next on his list: Make another call to Bernard. Jim's suddenly nervous about confiding in her since she knows Mandy and Jerry. But he doesn't know any other attorney in town, and of course he's protected by Bernard's ethical responsibility to keep his situation confidential.

Her phone number is still on his keyboard. He casually looks around, finds himself free from eavesdroppers. Quickly he calls.

"Bernard, Black & Trent," says a young female monotone.

"May I speak to Penny Bernard?"

"She's with a client. May I ask what this is regarding?"

As if he's going to explain his delicate situation to just any-body.

"This is Jim Knight—I left a message on your machine this morning. Tell her I have an extremely urgent problem and need to talk to her immediately."

"And may I tell her what it's about?"

"I'd really rather tell her myself. It's pretty involved."

The robotic receptionist is silent, temporarily stunned by the break in her normal phone routine. She finds a new path.

"Have you been a client of Bernard, Black & Trent before?"

"Yes. She knows me. If you could just give her my mes-sage."

"*What* message? You still haven't told me what this is regarding."

Jim snaps a pencil in half with one hand. "I told you it's urgent! Just give her the fucking message!" He screams his phone number and slams down the phone.

A couple of people have straightened up, craning over their computers at him.

His stomach growls and he can't concentrate on anything. He enters Bernard's info into his computer, then looks at his list and sees it's time to eat. He slips his PowerBook into its bag to take with him. Might as well tackle #8 and copyfit an article during lunch.

As he reaches the staircase he hears Jerry holler after him, barking something about the Bill Gates article. It doesn't work, they need another editorial meeting right now. Jim pretends not to hear and hurries, skipping two steps at a time. They're always shuffling editorial around at the last minute and work always comes before food. But not today. Jim needs fuel. The changes can wait for 20 minutes.

Jim looks through the glass window in the lobby and sees Kat talking to Clare. She looks small and her face is blotchy. He thinks up an excuse to go in and talk to her.

He walks up to Clare's desk.

"Hi, Jim, what's up?"

Kat barely smiles at him, her lips tightly shut. He notices a muscle spasm in her right eye.

Jim wonders what Clare knows, if anything. "I need to talk to you about last night, Kat," Jim says, examining Clare's expression. Her inquiring look remains casual. "It's about that *thing* we were talking about. I thought maybe you could run to Caffe Centro with me and we could continue that discussion."

Now Clare looks intrigued. Jim wishes he'd said something more intelligent.

Kat smooths it out. "Oh, you mean my dad's new project?" She looks at Clare. "My dad's working on a documentary about factory workers and might interview Jim's cousin."

Factory workers? Jim feels his cheeks burn. Clare goes along with the story and asks Kat when her shuttle is coming.

"Not for another hour and a half," Kat says.

"Shuttle?" Jim asks.

Kat tells him she's going to LA, says she'll explain at lunch. Clare looks sad.

On the way to Centro Jim considers telling Kat about CeCe James and her encounter with Goines's henchman but decides against it. Kat's going to LA where she should be out of danger. He'd do anything to go with her.

"I just wanted to see how you were doing. I guess it's good you're leaving," he says.

"Yeah, I guess. I'm really sorry about everything that's happened." Jim isn't sure if she means she's sorry about what's happened to him or to her.

"Me too," he says.

149

At Centro they both order bread salad—greens tossed with squares of bread and vinaigrette—and cappuccino. A lanky tattooed guy behind the counter hands them their drinks right away. They find a small table inside, by the window. Jim props his computer against the wall. Maybe he can still copyfit an article after he eats, before he fires Mara.

Kat asks Jim what he's going to do. She's lost the fresh energy that gushed out of her two nights ago at the club. He wants to help her out but doesn't know how—he has so many of his own problems to think about.

"I put in a couple of calls to my attorney," he says, "so hopefully I'll talk to her by this evening. Tonight I'm going to check into a hotel just to be safe."

"Make sure to pay cash," Kat says, explaining that the bad guys may be able to trace his credit card. "When I get to the airport I'm taking out a cash advance for my plane fare."

Jim looks out the window and grunts involuntarily. He can't believe what he sees. The primer-gray Mustang. It's slowly cruising around the park. Kat follows his gaze.

"Oh shit. Oh my God," she says. "What do we do? *What do we do?*"

Jim takes her hand and holds it tightly. He looks for the Mustang's sidekick but doesn't see the Mercury.

"Kat, we've got to remain calm."

"What do we do?" Kat repeats.

A burst of air rushes in from the door and Jim looks up to see Mandy. *Mandy!*

"Jerry said I'd probably find you here," she says, running toward him with open arms.

Jim tears his hand away from Kat's and Mandy notices, stopping three feet short of the table. Her whole body expands like an angry wasp ready to attack.

"Mandy. Heh. You're back early."

"And this must be the cunt who answered the phone the other night," she says. Jim wipes the perspiration off his neck with his palm. People in the cafe are staring at them.

150   Jim sees the Mustang park in an illegal spot a few doors down from Caffe Centro. "Oh boy!" he yelps, before he can get ahold of himself. His hands begin to shake and he sits on them.

He turns to Mandy and babbles, "This is Kat. It's her last day in San Francisco." In his peripheral vision he sizes up the open window next to him, wonders if he could squeeze through it.

Mandy stares at Jim, waiting for him to continue.

Jim sees the gray-haired emaciated man—who's wearing the same black velvet pantsuit—and his goateed partner step out of the car. The third person, their androgynous-looking friend, slides across the front seat and waits behind the wheel.

Kat follows Jim's gaze. "Uh, I better go," she says abruptly. Wet beads line her brows. Kat tries to stand but Mandy pushes her back down in the chair.

"I want to know what the hell is going on here," Mandy says. She clenches her fists and digs them into her hips.

The casino men walk into Pepito's, the Mexican lunch counter a few doors away.

"Honey," Jim says as he stumbles to his feet. "I've got to help Kat fix her bike. I'll meet you up at *Signal*." Kat takes his cue and successfully stands up.

"Fix her *what?*" Mandy knows that Jim would never help anyone fix a bike. He'd tell them to take it to the shop.

Jim looks out the window in time to see Mara, in the distance, pointing at Caffe Centro. She's talking to the triangular-headed feline man who'd been in the other car—the Mercury—which is parked on the opposite side of the park.

Jim loses his balance and grabs his chair.

"I want you to be honest with me," Mandy is saying. "Did you sleep with her?"

The cat from the Mercury is cutting across the park. He's wearing black sunglasses and a fishing hat.

"Kat, jump out of the window and run down the alley!"

"Don't you dare!" Mandy screams, grabbing Kat's arm. "You're not getting out of this that easy."

151

Kat wriggles out of Mandy's grip, causing her to crash into a busboy. He drops a tray of dirty dishes on the floor and looks at Mandy as if she were crazy, then storms off to get a broom.

Mandy squints and tells Jim she'd like to speak to him outside.

"We've got to *go!*" Kat screams.

Jim's eyes roll wildly in their sockets, then lock onto the first pair of thugs coming out of the burrito joint, neither one carrying a to-go bag. They're walking toward the cafe. It's too late now for Jim to escape out the window.

"There's got to be a back way out of here," Kat says, grabbing her backpack.

They're out of time. Jim has no choice but to follow Kat. He grabs his computer case.

"Jim?" Mandy is shaking her head in disbelief.

"I'm sorry. You just don't understand," Jim says, backing away. "It's not what you think." Suddenly he remembers these creeps had been at the house. "Don't go home!" Jim blurts. "It could be dangerous! Stay at a friend's tonight."

Kat grabs Jim's arm and yanks him toward the back hall of the cafe, passing the to-go window, kitchen and bathrooms. They run out the back door.

Once outside Kat runs across the street, down an alley. Jim follows without looking at anything but her. Like an ostrich, he hopes if he doesn't see them he'll be invisible.

"Where are we going?" Jim shouts, thinking their escape attempt is futile. They can't keep running. These guys obviously know where he works.

Kat stops behind the burrito shop. Panting, she quickly spins a combination lock.

"My God, Kat. You know someone who lives here?"

"Not exactly." The lock clicks open.

"Get in!" She holds the gate open, and as soon as Jim steps into the caged porch Kat relocks it. She rushes to a door and flings it open. "Hurry!"

152   They step inside and she slams the door, locking the deadbolt from the inside.

"Come on," she says, leading him up a flight of stairs.

30

Halfway up the staircase Kat pauses, causing Jim to bump into her. Every part of her body freezes except her heart, which seems to have bloated to 10 times its normal size. Someone's upstairs, listening to music.

"Stay right here," she whispers to Jim.

Kat carefully places her backpack next to Jim's feet and pads up the carpeted steps. She eases her head into the apartment, first examining each wall-less "bedroom," then the living room. No one's in sight. She notices the TV hutch with the stereo and it hits her. The radio's been on since her last visit.

"Jim, it's okay. Come on up! And grab my backpack."

She rushes to the side of the bay window and peeks out. The cars are still guarding each side of the park.

"Do you see them?" Jim asks. He falls to his knees and peers out the window.

"Just the cars. I think someone's still sitting in the Mustang."

The park is filled with a lunchtime crowd but Kat doesn't recognize anyone.

Jim moves away from the window. "Where's the phone?"

A few jacks line the bottom of the wall but Kat doesn't see

153

any phones. She runs to the back of the flat. More jacks, no phones.

"I don't think there is one," she says, returning to the living room.

"Whose place is this?" Jim faces her, sitting on a couch.

Kat sits across from him. "A friend of Yoke's owns it, but no one lives here."

Jim glances around, admiring the eighties decor. Then he slumps forward. "Oh God. I wonder what Mandy thinks."

Kat doesn't respond.

Jim turns to look out the window, though he can't see much from the couch. "I guess we'll have to wait here till they leave."

"I can only wait for an hour." Kat wonders if she should still catch the shuttle she ordered. She feels a little guilty leaving Jim behind.

"Kat, those guys aren't fooling around. You're not leaving this place while their cars are parked right in front of us."

"How else am I going to get out of this mess?"

Jim doesn't say anything. He's back to his forward-slump position. Shit, now she sounds selfish.

"Why don't you come with me?" she says. "They wouldn't look for you in LA."

"I can't do that, Kat. They'd still be after me, and besides, I have a job here." Jim kicks the coffee table so that it skips a few inches toward Kat. "I don't have the slack that you do. I need to talk to my attorney and face this thing. Running away won't help."

Running away, that's what she'd be doing. And not only from the jalopies in the park, who've supplied her with an excellent reason to bolt. Kat never faces *any* challenge. Her life *is* full of slack. Damn it, why'd he have to say that?

154

She tries to fight the ugly truth but it worms its way to the surface: hiding from these crooks would give her a great excuse to delay her life some more. If she moved to LA she wouldn't have to face the possibility of occupational defeat. She could take the easy road, get a job at her dad's school, forget writing and publishing. But hiding at her parents' house would be the ultimate failure.

Her mom wasn't home when Kat called today. She was just going to show up in LA, unannounced. Her folks would've been happy to see her, but she's not expected.

"You're right," Kat says. "It's too dangerous for me to leave with those guys out there." Now Kat hopes the thugs hang around for a while, till her shuttle leaves her behind. If she can help Jim get through this maybe it'll give her something— strength, or whatever it is she needs to make meaning of her life. At least she won't rot away in LaLa Land.

Jim gets up to open a window, then searches his pockets.

"I'm out of cigarettes, and I'm really hungry," he says.

Kat remembers the Coke and runs to the fridge. Three left. She tosses one to Jim and takes one for herself.

Jim sits on the edge of the couch with his soda, squeezing his eyes, and takes his computer out of its case. He tells Kat he needs to copyfit a few pieces, that it could take a few more hours.

"How the hell can you think about work with those creeps out there?" she exclaims.

"I don't know," Jim says. "I guess it's a way to keep from freaking out."

Maybe she just doesn't have what it takes to be a *Signal* editor, but it seems awfully weird that someone could concentrate on work at a time like this. She lies across her couch and grabs the remote, changing the radio station to something that sounds jazzy. Jim doesn't respond to it. He's already in geek-boy mode.

It's amazing how quickly his physical and emotional states can change. His typing is loud and staccato, his shoulders already fused into his neck. He guzzles the Coke without lifting his other hand from the keyboard.

155

"Damn it!" he shouts at his computer.

After a few more fierce staccato taps he grabs his computer case and desperately fishes through it.

"Is everything okay?" Kat asks.

Jim pulls out a phone cord, then scrambles to the wall. He sees a jack near the TV hutch and runs over, jamming the cord into it. He sprints back to the couch, connects the other end of the cord into his laptop.

"I can't find an article I downloaded earlier. The phone line better work," he says ominously, not looking up at Kat. His expression is stony, his lips deflated to the width of sewing threads.

"Shit," he mumbles, turning the computer around to mess with the phone cord.

Kat flips over so her back is toward him. The black cloth of the couch is in her face, but it's better than the uptight scene behind her. With the remote still in her hand she aims toward the stereo and hits the off button. She doesn't want her new-found taste for jazz to be tainted.

The sound of a modem pulls Kat out of a dream, and for a brief hazy moment she's clueless as to where she is. It's dark outside, and inside she sees only the blue glare of a computer screen and an illuminated body hunched over it. Jim. She's in the apartment. Now she remembers.

"Aren't there any lights in here?" Kat says.

"You're awake." Jim's mood is lighter than before. He stands up, stretches, flicks on a light, then quickly switches it back off. He inches near the window and glances down at the park.

"The Mustang is still there. I can't tell if anyone's in it or not. The Mercury's been gone for a while now." Jim moves away from the window and unplugs his modem line from the computer. "Let's go to the back of this place so we can turn on a light."

156

Jim tries to take Kat's hand as they head back, but she dodges his grip. She follows him past the kitchen and bath-room to an area with a double bed and a coat rack. From the bed she can see through rows of vertical posts to another so-called bedroom at the back of the flat. She also has a pretty good view of the living room, including its window. But she's too deep into the apartment to be seen from the park.

Jim flips on a light switch.

"I finished my work *and* emailed Mandy," he says brightly. "I explained the whole situation, told her to call the FBI. She *has* to forgive me now, and I'm sure someone will contact us by email soon." His chest puffs up, as if the whole world should praise him for his valiant effort. Then his peacock-like stance deflates as if someone's just popped his chest with a pin.

"I have to admit, I'm a little surprised that Mandy didn't email me back right away. I sent her the message almost three hours ago. I need to slip out of here tomorrow and talk to her, make her see that none of this was really my fault. We've been together too long to end it like this."

Kat wants to slip out of here too, tell Danny and Kimmy what's going on. Maybe they can put her up until she finds another place to live. She can't be doing this alone with Jim anymore. He obviously wants to burrow back into his safe existence with his rich yuppie girlfriend.

Before she knows what's happening he wraps his hand around hers. Simultaneously a sharp clanging erupts outside at the back. Someone is furiously banging on the locked gate. Kat clutches Jim's arm as he gasps and lurches forward. He grabs his chest, then breaks free of Kat, looks strangely relieved, tells her to wait here. He runs downstairs, toward the back door.

"Jim! What are you doing?" Kat races after him. They'll kill him for sure. "Stop!"

Jim doesn't respond. He opens the door, sticks his head out, then disappears. Kat wants to follow him but has no protection, no weapon. This is too real. Her teeth chatter as she stands a few steps away from the door. She crosses her arms tightly. A few audible sobs break out before she has a chance to swallow them. She strains her ears but doesn't hear anything. More sobs. *Help him!* Why can't she hear anything? Finally she forces herself to step down. Ready to slam the door and lock herself in the apartment if she has to, she cautiously cracks the door open, keeping a firm hand on the inside knob.

Jim is squatting on the ground, against the gate, facing a large black fellow who's also hunched down. Kat can't figure it out. The man is counting money. Could Jim be paying someone off to kill the Mustang guys? Now the man slides something under the gate. A large, flat white box followed by a brown bag that barely makes it through the gap between the gate and the cement floor. Jim grabs the stash and sprints toward Kat.

The realization hits as he comes through the door. *Pizza.* Kat chuckles uncontrollably, shaking loose the anxiety knots that had strangled her gut.

"Goddamn it, Jim. You're such a jerk. You fuckin' scared me to death."

Jim goes pale. "Kat, I'm sorry. I kind of forgot about it myself until the guy started rattling the gate." Still in the stairwell, Jim leans over his pizza box and tries to kiss Kat on the lips. She turns her face and he misses his mark, pecking her jawbone instead. *Save it for your socialite.*

"Come on, let's eat," she says, marching back up to the flat.

31

They sit on the bed, scarfing the pepperoni pie in silence. Jim also ordered two cans of Pepsi, two bottles of orange juice, and three packs of cigarettes. Paper napkins are spread over their laps. The food seems to mellow Kat, her jerky movements finally smoothing out.

"How did you order this stuff?" she says, opening the pizza box for another slice.

"Some service on the Net called ModemMeal. You can choose from a bunch of restaurants in your local area and these guys deliver your order. I use them all the time."

More silence. Jim wonders what Mandy's doing right now. Probably sharing a bottle of wine with CeCe James, planning Jim's punishment. Can he still smooth things over with his fiancée somehow? Does he *want* to? He just hopes she's okay, hopes the crooks don't get her involved. He should but doesn't feel guilty about CeCe's slashed car. If she only knew his circumstances . . .

Thank God he was able to copyfit all of his articles and email them to the office. He hopes he's still in good with Jerry, who sent him a message today explaining that the Gates article hadn't worked. They replaced it with the original junk-email

159

piece Rhiannon had written. Jim cringes. His boss never turns down his work. Shit, he *can't* get behind, *can't* lose control.

Tomorrow he'll slink out of here and show up at his attorney's office. She'll have to make time for him. Once he takes action against Goines, life will certainly be his friend again.

Kat balls up her napkin and sticks it in the paper bag. She gazes absently at the rug, sipping her orange juice through a straw, her legs tucked under her. Jim's been so worked up about Jerry and Goines that he'd momentarily forgotten she was there. He tries to stuff the horrific events of the past few days into a black crevice of his brain. He wants to turn off the light and abandon himself with Devil Girl like he did the other night.

He places the paper bag, half-empty pizza box, and two Pepsis on the floor. Kat still has the juice straw in her mouth but has stopped sipping. Jim inches closer to her, breaking her trancelike pose.

"Thanks for dinner," she says, finally setting the bottle down near the bed. "I feel a lot better."

Encouraged, Jim puts his hand on her waist and leans into her, sliding pursed lips across her neck. She pushes him away.

"Don't!" Kat squirms away and heads for the bathroom.

How can she still be mad about the pizza guy? Jim throws himself onto the bed, angry with himself. Nothing's working. It's like he's been cursed, stripped of his savvy command over people and his environment. Over himself. The quilt smells like smoked ham.

Jim gets up and reaches for a pack of cigarettes. He'd stacked all three against a leg of the bed. He walks to the window, opens it, then sits on the floor and lights up. The bathroom door opens.

160

Kat sits on the bed again, this time with a magazine in her hands. *Interview.* She must've found it in the bathroom. She's been wearing the same clothes since Jim met her at the bar yesterday evening: green pants and a short gray sweater. They're beginning to droop. Tomorrow Jim's clothes will be stale too.

"What's going on with you?" he asks.

"Nothing." She scoots to the head of the bed and props herself against the pillows and the low headboard.

"Why'd you push me away?" Jim hates his last sentence. It makes his desperation and her rejection so real.

She rolls her eyes like she doesn't want to talk about it. Jim doesn't break his stare, won't let her off the hook.

"I just didn't want to do that," she finally says.

"But what about the other night? In the club?" Again Jim scolds himself. He shouldn't have said that last bit. Maybe she would have clued him in on what happened the *other* night in his bedroom.

"It was different there," she says. "*Everything* was different."

Now it makes sense. Of *course* it was different. She had an apartment then. What a jerk he's being. How pushy and insensitive. She's mourning her loss. How can he expect her to be seductive after what's just happened? He puts out his cigarette and moves to the edge of her bed.

"I'm sorry, Kat. I wasn't—"

"What the *fuck* are you trying to do, Jim? You're engaged to Mandy—you want to be with her—so leave me alone."

You want to be with her. Jim replays the last few hours in his head, can't find the words he said that could've triggered this change in Kat.

"Is this because I emailed Mandy? I *had* to. I had no one else to turn to. *Someone's* got to help us."

Kat stares at the cover of her magazine, won't look up.

"Kat, you and I are in this together. And I don't know what it is, but I do feel an intensity with you that I've never felt with anyone before. Didn't you feel it, the other night at the club?"

Kat finally flings her magazine aside. "It's like there are two sides of you, and I only want to be with one," she explains, throwing him off-track. "The other night you were the passionate musician, the soulful artist. You were so *different.* Tonight you're back to your computer-boy self, so anxious to *work,* even when your life's at stake, and to weasel back in with a

161

woman you don't seem all that crazy about, and—" She shakes her head.

He doesn't want to hear this, yet he prods her to continue. "And *what?*"

Her eyes roll up to the ceiling as she continues to shake her head. "I could never live such a rigid life. You're so stiff and self-absorbed, way too strained and conservative, like you're constipated or something. It's, I don't know, a turnoff."

Jim grabs his cigarettes and leaves the room. He steps into the second bedroom, paces from one end of the futon to the other. His blood swirls through his body like waves driven by a hurricane.

Of *course* he's more conservative than she! He's a high-profile editor who makes good money. *Constipated?* Who does she think she is? An intern nobody ripping *him* to shreds. He can see the back of her pea-sized head, which is just inches from the invisible wall that separates his room from hers. He lights up again, blowing smoke in her direction.

She turns around, waving off the smoke. "Stop it! Sorry if I pissed you off. I didn't mean to."

"What the hell did you mean by all that? I have a fiancée who finds me *very* passionate." He can't think of the last time he and Mandy screwed. But it's not only his fault, she's busy too.

"Good. I'm glad you two are passionate with each other," she says.

Jim opens the window and stands near it.

She puts her pillow in her lap. "I shouldn't have said some of those things, it's not what I really meant. It's just, at the club you were like a poet, your energy was magnetic, your body language spontaneous and charismatic, like you were up for anything. I was attracted to that person." She hesitates before adding, "And you're not him."

162

"What do you mean I'm not him? I'm the same person! You're not making any sense."

Jim puts out his cigarette and lays it on the windowsill. He feels bruised and exhausted, as if someone's just beaten the pulp out of him. He flops on his bed, hiding his face from her stare. Just a homely, sexless oaf in Kat's eyes. She finally turns off the light, making it easier to breathe.

"Sorry, Jim. I don't think my words came out right. I mean, you're a great guy and all . . ." Her voice trails off.

Great guy, sure thing. No comment. He closes his eyes and tries to hold on to his anger but it keeps tugging away, revealing his shame at her perception. He understands what she meant.

32

The cold pizza is delicious. Kat nibbles as she scopes out the park. At first she thinks they're free, then notices the Mustang in another spot, closer to the *Signal* building. Two of the henchmen are sitting in the front seat, the third person is gone. The Mercury isn't around. The park is still this morning, except for the rain that slaps the grass and trees. Hooded people with laptops and to-go cups run in both directions on the sidewalk below the window.

Kat's outfit is starting to smell like it's been sitting at the bottom of a laundry basket. After the pizza she'll try to sneak out of the area unnoticed to buy some new clothes.

Her hair is almost dry. She's glad she jumped in the shower first, got the good towel—the one without Yoke's dried-up Coke stain.

A fizzing sound in the kitchen startles Kat. Jim is in there drinking soda and picking at the pizza.

"Hi," she says, still feeling bad about their conversation last night.

"Hi." He closes up the remaining pizza, wedging the side flaps of the top into the box, and shoves it in the fridge.

"Jim, I'm really sorry about last night. I didn't mean it."

He sits on a couch and props his computer on his lap. "It's okay. I don't care." He won't look at her.

"Sorry I'm opening up my computer," he says. "I know it bugs you. I just need to see if I got any important email regarding our situation. And I need to get my attorney's address."

"You're seeing the lawyer today?"

"Yeah."

She ducks slightly, suddenly spotting Yoke and Moony rushing through the rain toward their office. Yoke actually looks up at the apartment but nothing registers in his face. She kind of wishes he'd seen her.

"Yesterday I thought it'd be a good idea if you came with me to the attorney's office," Jim says, waiting for his modem to quiet down, "but it doesn't really matter."

"I'll go if you still want me to." Kat moves away from the window, ready to leave. She's never been to a lawyer's office before.

"Whatever," he says.

Kat peeks over Jim's shoulder as he scrolls down his new messages. Nothing from Mandy or anyone else she recognizes. Jim opens up an online address book and looks up Penny Bernard. Then he slams his laptop shut.

"If you want to go I'm leaving now," he says.

Kat tells him the lock combo, in case they get split up. They decide to sneak down the alley to Third Street, which is pretty busy. They can catch a cab from there.

The rain has slowed to a misty drizzle. Kat buttons up her sweater and tightens her backpack. The alley appears to be empty as Jim locks up, but as soon as they head away from the apartment they notice a thin, pink-lipped woman wearing a baseball hat and large sunglasses. She's walking toward them. Jim gasps, causing the woman to freeze. She takes a long look at their apartment, then does an about-face and runs in the opposite direction. The sudden sound of a hammer sends Kat into Jim's back. Some construction worker isn't letting the rain stop him.

Kat releases tension through giggles. They head toward Third, walking in the opposite direction from *Signal,* sticking close to the building walls.

Once in the cab, Kat relaxes. Jim unrolls his window and closes his eyes, letting the light rain hit his face. She does the same.

The waiting room of Bernard, Black & Trent is small but plush, a rube's vision of prosperity, with royal-red velvet chairs, heavy oak tables, gold picture frames, crystal vases filled with silk flowers, and deep-blue wall-to-wall carpeting.

"But you don't understand, it's an emergency. My life is in danger!" Jim's been arguing for several minutes with the receptionist, a young black woman with straight shoulder-length hair and a white silk blouse.

She doesn't buy his urgency. The phone rings and she answers it, turning her back on Jim. His head falls into his hands, his elbows planted on the check-in counter.

Kat wonders what this woman thinks of Jim, with his rain-soaked hair, wet wrinkled shirt and razor-stubbled face. All this because Kat pried into his Netscape bookmarks. Because she was stuck at Jim's. Because she was supposed to party with Darren Cooper that night but he canceled. This is all *Cooper's* fault.

"Okay," the receptionist says, swiveling to face Jim, "looks like you're in luck. Someone just canceled his 4:00 appointment for tomorrow. How does that work for you?"

Jim pounds his fist on the counter, causing the receptionist to flinch. "No! I need to see her *today!* I might not be alive tomorrow!"

The receptionist, who's been drinking coffee, slowly places her cup on a crocheted coaster. "I don't have time for this, Mr. Knight. Either you take tomorrow's slot or you take your business elsewhere."

"Fine. If I'm still alive I'll be here tomorrow at 4:00." Jim hands her a business card and leaves the office without saying another word. Kat follows him out. He speed-walks down the building's hall, through the exit door, down Divisadero Street. The rain has stopped.

"Jim, wait up," Kat says. He's headed toward Haight Street, a perfect place for her to buy a few things to wear. She catches up to Jim, grabs his arm. "What are you doing?"

"I don't know," Jim says, still walking at a fast clip. "I need to be in the office. This has got to end, but I don't know how to end it. I don't have more than 5,000 dollars to my name and half of that is Mandy's. My life is so fucked!"

Kat has to practically jog to keep up with him. "Can you call the office, tell them an emergency's come up and you'll be back in two days?"

He doesn't respond. They reach Haight Street and Kat turns onto it. Jim is right behind her. He stops to light a cigarette. "Where are we going?" he asks.

If she didn't know him she'd think he was cute just now, his wet disheveled hair hanging in his face, the 5:00 shadow, the slept-in clothes that give him an I-don't-give-a-shit look. He takes a drag off his cigarette, waiting for Kat to answer.

"I need to buy a few things, some shirts and stuff. And you can find a pay phone to call the office."

Jim nods, apparently agreeing to her plan. His arms are turning purple with goosebumps, reminding her how cold it is. They silently continue their walk toward the business section of Haight Street.

33

Jim finds a pay phone next to a huge used-clothing store and tells Kat to go on inside. The few times he's stepped into a used-clothing store he's noticed a depressing, musty odor. He hopes her new purchases don't kick up that stale stench.

A few young guys wearing dreadlocks and tie-dyed T-shirts are setting up percussions—a conga and some bongos—on the sidewalk across the street. He's seen them before, at the Slow Club. Jim quickly turns his back on them, tries to ignore the wrenching pangs lodged in his throat.

The sun is already breaking through the clouds and Jim squints as he drops a quarter into the battered phone. Maybe Mandy's read his email message by now, maybe she's ready to forgive him for yesterday's cafe scene. She'd be able to come up with a solution. He calls *Signal*, dialing her extension. As the phone rings he panics, wonders if he's put her in danger, prays that nothing happened at the house.

It's an eternity before she picks up. "Hello. This is Mandy."

"Mandy! It's me. I just wanted to make sure you were okay. You never emailed me back."

Silence.

"Mandy? You didn't go home last night, did you?"

"Oh, *did* I—and now I understand why you didn't want me there. You son of a bitch. What the hell is *wrong* with you? You didn't even have the decency to clean up the evidence. You slept with that scrawny cunt from the cafe, didn't you?"

"No!" Jim wonders if he's lying. "Mandy, you've got it all wrong. Didn't you get my email? You see, I'm in trouble. That's what I wanted to—"

"Fuck you, Jim." Her voice cracks but she holds it together. "I'm not going to read any of your bullshit e-letters. Chelsea told me you had the audacity to bring that girl to the club, that you two were all over each other like animals. And then CeCe called. Apparently you crashed into her car and owe her a lot of money. She said you were on that girl's *scooter!* Are you on drugs? I found some weird bottle at the house . . ." She's spiraling into hysteria.

"Mandy, stop. *Listen* to me."

"No, *you* listen to *me,* asshole. I want your stuff out of the house by tonight. I'll call the police if I find you there, so you'd better do it now. I'll burn anything you leave behind."

This is all moving too fast. Is this the woman he was going to *marry?* Jim grips the phone booth for balance.

"If you'd just hear me out for one minute, babe." Mandy doesn't respond so Jim continues. "It all started the night you left, when I was supposed to go to Raymond's . . . "

Jim hears a couple of voices on Mandy's end, realizes she's talking to someone in her office, not listening to what he's saying. He hears her tell the person what a prick Jim is.

"Hello, Jim? This is Chelsea. Where are you?"

Jim tightens his grip on the cold metal.

"Uh, hi Chelsea. I'm on Haight Street right now." *Don't say that!*

"I see. Well that makes perfect sense. May I just ask you a question?"

He sees Kat through the window of the store, talking to a young male clerk wearing a bright-orange frizzy wig. Jim wishes he were in there with her, that Chelsea and *Signal* didn't exist.

169

Chelsea doesn't wait for Jim to respond. "Who's Mr. Goines?" she asks.

Jim drops the phone and almost falls to the ground himself picking it up.

"What do you mean?" he babbles, adjusting the receiver.

"What do you *think* I mean? *Who is he?* A man came to the office four times yesterday and once this morning looking for you. Said he was a friend of Larry Goines. When Mara asked what he wanted he said she was 'acting out of line,' that it was none of her business. We don't want to see him here again."

Jim wants to throw up. He tries to sit on the little shelf in the booth and slips, banging his shoulder into something sharp.

"What did he look like?" he asks.

Chelsea speaks at the same time, not hearing Jim's question. "Anyway, Jerry and I are putting you on a one-week leave of absence—unpaid, of course. When you come back we can talk about your future at *Signal*. Get your shit together, Jim. We don't want it in the office."

"*What?* Chelsea, if you'd just let me explain. Can I talk to Jerry?"

"We don't have time for this. If you show up before next week is over we'll kick you out. Like I said, get your shit together. Bye, Jim."

The ground is dry against the clothing store's wall where Jim decides to fall. *One week.* He's never even taken a vacation for more than three days. Who's going to edit the features? Who's going to help with new ideas? What about the raise he was supposed to get next month? *When you come back we can talk about your future at* Signal.

He doesn't feel the pavement under his fingers, can't tell how warm the sun is on his face. Ashamed, he buries his head in his hands. It's a relief to cry. He cries about his implicit breakup with Mandy, the deep financial trouble he's in, his suspension from *Signal*. It's like he's been pushed down an icy slope, has no control over where he's going, blindly racing full speed ahead.

170

"Hey." Kat taps Jim with her foot, then sits on the sidewalk next to him.

When Jim looks at her she crinkles her brows. "Oh Jim, what happened?" She wraps her arms around him and he hugs her back. She's wearing a new vintage sweater with a slight mildewy scent, but he likes it. The material is soft and cuddly and safe. He holds her for a long time.

"I got you some presents," she says, pulling away. She opens a huge bag and pulls out a maroon sweater that zips up the front. "Here, I hope you like it."

Except for the small rip in the side seam it looks like something Jim's grandpa would wear.

"Thanks," Jim says, his eyes welling up again. Shit, he hopes she doesn't notice.

"And I got you something else." She pulls out a cheap pair of sunglasses. Jim thanks her again and tries them on. His eyes can finally relax from the glaring sun reflecting off the wet pavement.

"Let me pay you for these," he says, pulling out his wallet. His hands are shaking.

"Don't worry about it. Your stuff only came to a few bucks."

She shows him what she got for herself—a couple more sweaters like the one she's wearing in various colors, a brown pair of jeans, and an overcoat, which she says is big enough for them to share while they're together. She then surprises Jim by stroking his cheek with the back of her hand.

"Are you all right?" she asks, her face only inches from his.

Her red-lined lips turn down at the corners as she examines his face, looking for clues as to what happened while she was in the thrift store. She actually *cares* about how he feels. Jim swallows the new emotions that are trying to unravel him. Here's a woman who can tuck away her own problems to worry about him. He wants to confide in her, tell her about the wretched conversation he had with Mandy and Chelsea, but he's so overcome with Kat's selfless concern that he only nods his head, letting her think he's okay.

171

"Did you call *Signal,* tell them you'd be out for a few days?"

Jim closes his eyes and nods, then feels Kat's soft sweater around his body again. He doesn't hug her back this time but sits there limply in her arms, hopes she never lets go. But she does—and too abruptly.

"Hey Jim, let's get out of here."

He opens his eyes, tries to see what's distracting Kat. She's staring across the street.

"I don't like that guy over there. He's been sneaking stares in our direction ever since I came out of the store."

Jim notices a long-haired blond wearing a pinstripe vest over a white dress shirt, and a scarf wrapped pirate-style over his head. The guy is leaning against a telephone pole, gazing vacantly at the stream of traffic.

"He looks okay to me," Jim says, relieved to get off the subject of himself.

"Why don't we get something to eat?" she says, quickly gathering her bags. With her free hand she takes his hand and Jim reluctantly leaves his seat on the pavement.

She leads him down busy blocks of clothing, record and book stores. In their silence Jim's mind races back to Chelsea and he dissects their conversation, hoping to find a second interpretation, one that could put him at ease. First she asked about Goines—a fair question. But he can't be fired just because some weirdo was looking for him. For all Chelsea knows, Goines is some crackpot Luddite who just came to harass him. Then the part where she bans him from the office for one week. This *isn't* fair. What did he do, after all—besides piss off Mandy and play hooky from *Signal?* Oh, Gerald's going to *love* this. He's probably in Jerry's office right now, discussing the cover story for the next issue.

Suddenly Jim finds himself sitting in a colorful South American tapas bar with bright plastic tablecloths and loud music.

172

Kat talks with the waiter but the conversation doesn't make sense to Jim, their words bouncing off his brain like repelling magnets. As he stares at the menu his mind wanders to Jerry and what *he's* thinking. How could he be involved with Chelsea's capricious decision to suspend Jim from work? Sure, his Gates article was weak, and he's missed a day and a half at the office, but he worked from the apartment last night. He's really not behind.

Suddenly his shock turns to anger. After all the hours and overtime he's poured into *Signal,* all the days he dragged his ass to the office even when he was sick, all of his brilliant ideas that Jerry scooped up without so much as a thank-you. After all that, where are they when *he* needs *them?* They're on Mandy's side, of course. She's pulling in the big bucks for the company, keeping the magazine fat and healthy with dozens of 20,000-dollar ad-page sales each month. A good advertising sales exec can make more money than the president of a magazine. If Queen Mandy wants Jim out, he's out. He can be replaced.

A pitcher of sangria arrives at the table. Kat pours him a glass. She's his buoy in the middle of a piranha-infested sea. Her cheeks are flushed from their walk and she flaps her furry sweater to cool off. The more he's with her the less he understands what he saw in Mandy.

"What did they say when you told them you weren't coming in for a few days?" she asks, referring to his dreadful telephone conversation.

"You know, I don't want to even talk about it. Why don't we pretend that South Park doesn't exist?" Jim holds his glass up and they make a silent toast.

34

Jim pours the last of the sangria into their glasses, splashing the table a few times, trying to contain his laughter. They've managed to polish off seven tapas dishes and two sangria pitchers. Kat feels happy, energized, and she's relieved to see Jim in better spirits as well. She wants to continue in the hysterics but her abdomen muscles have given up on her. Exhausted, she only smiles.

That he had thought they'd slept together in his bedroom doesn't crack Kat up as much as the way she and her friends had made themselves at home while he was on the verge of passing out, never considering how Jim might later react to the disarranged sheets and pillows. And to think that their party clutter misled not only him but Mandy too, her suspicions aroused when she discovered a lipstick-stained wine glass on the floor near the bed.

"What an idiot I was that night. That goddamn *Signal*—I should've just relaxed and had fun with you guys," Jim says, slugging back the last of his drink.

Whatever his bosses said to him on the phone today must've been harsh.

"*I'm* the idiot," she says, her mood taking a more serious

turn. She remembers how crazy she was for Yoke that night. "You were just being responsible. I keep spinning my wheels, always starting articles and books and never getting past the first page. I don't even know if I can really write."

The waiter brings their check and Jim hands him a credit card.

"Of *course* you can write," Jim says.

"How do you know?"

"You're too dimensional, too sensitive not to be a good writer. Man, you're so perceptive. You *feel* things, empathize with others, which most people don't do really well. And you're smart. If you could just get past your insecurity—which we all have, believe me—and pour yourself onto paper . . . "

Like his music at the Slow Club, his words penetrate, move her to an unfamiliar place—this time an uncomfortable one. He's saying things no one else ever notices, seeing her as no one else does. She would've thought he was the blindest of everyone she knows in South Park. She tries to resist the under-tow that's drawing her toward him on a level much deeper than her usual surface lust.

"Thanks for the great lunch," she says nonchalantly, reaching under the table for her bags. "What's the game plan?"

Jim shakes his head hopelessly, endearingly. Kat wants him to kiss her. "I guess we just have to lie low until tomorrow, till we see my attorney," he says. "I don't know what else to do."

As Jim signs the VISA slip Kat stands up, looks around in a red wine–stupor at the layers of people standing near the bar, waiting for a seat. Then she sees him. The same man who was staring at them near the thrift store. He's standing a few people away from the bar, without a drink, and when Kat locks eyes with him he turns away, acts like he's trying to get the bar-tender's attention.

"Let's go!" Kat says, running from the table with Jim still in his seat.

"Wait up!" she hears Jim say.

When they get outside Kat sprints down the street. She

175

checks once to make sure Jim's behind her. He keeps telling her to slow down but she doesn't until she's several blocks away.

Jim finally catches up to her, grabs her by the wrist.

"What are you doing?" he asks, doubling over to catch his breath.

She pulls her wrist from his grip. "That creep from across the street was in there!"

Jim looks toward the restaurant. "Are you sure?"

"Yeah." Kat looks all around, expecting to see the Mustang.

"Come on," Jim says. "We'll catch a taxi and get out of here."

It's now gray outside and cooler, but dry. As they wait on the curb for a cab, Kat pulls out her new overcoat and offers it to Jim.

"What about you?" he asks, lighting a cigarette.

"I'm not cold."

The coat is so right, makes Jim look like someone she's always hung out with. She takes his hand and their fingers interlock. With his free hand he takes her bags from her.

"I don't want to go back yet," Kat says. The South Park flat with its austere decor and front-door hitmen reminds her of death.

"Where do you want to go?" Jim asks.

Kat thinks he'd buy two first-class tickets to Paris if she told him to.

"I don't know," she says. "We could get lost in Chinatown, look for weird toys and herbs. I know a—"

Jim isn't listening to her. His attention is fixed on a couple of guys pounding on drums.

"Jim?"

"I saw them setting up earlier," he says in a trance.

Kat looks at the bongoist, a thin hunched guy with long black dreadlocks and shut eyes. His head sways the way so many did at the Slow Club. His friend is dripping over the conga, involuntarily shouting between certain beats, staring at something no one else can see. Their rhythm is like a tonic that simultaneously mellows and arouses her. Wafts of patchouli oil weave through the air.

The pounding abruptly stops while the musicians squirt water into their mouths and wipe their faces with a shared red cloth. Kat takes a full breath, then expects to resume her conversation about Chinatown's demented toy stores with Jim. But he's still out, still transfixed by the musicians.

"Jim?"

He turns to Kat but doesn't say anything. His eyes are glassy, sad. Kat surprises herself when her own eyes tingle and threaten to make a mess. Jim reaches into his pocket, walks over to the drummers and drops some bills into their open conga case.

"How are you doing?" Kat asks when he comes back.

Jim takes a deep breath. "God, I don't know why I'm so emotional."

Kat buttons the top of his coat. "I like you like this. Emotions are good."

She's about to suggest they take a long walk through Golden Gate Park, which is just blocks away, when someone bumps into her backpack, knocking her forward into a bus stop.

"Shit!" Jim says, jerking Kat by the arm before she flips over the bench. As he pulls her to her feet she turns back and sees who ran into her: the freak with the pinstripe vest. He bends down to tie a high-top tennis shoe, pretending he doesn't notice Kat staring at him.

Signs and lights seem to jump out at her as Jim pulls her down a side street. A crowd of people are emptying out of a movie theater—its rear exit door. Jim is about to go in the opposite direction but Kat takes charge, steers him into the crowd. They sneak inside the dark building.

Kat's been here before—an old-film revival house whose traditional seats were long ago replaced with padded lawn chairs, loveseats, and old granny couches.

"Are you okay?" Jim asks.

"Uh-huh." Kat needs to sit down, stop the wobbling in her legs.

177

"Who the hell *is* that guy?" Jim asks, looking behind his shoulder.

"I don't know. Must be one of *them*. Let's go to the back where we can watch who comes in," Kat says.

They go to the back wall, a short row with only two chairs and a sofa that's missing an arm. Kat plops in the sofa and Jim sits next to her.

"He'll never know we're in here," Kat says, her adrenaline-enhanced jitters settling down a bit. "He'll eventually think we left the Haight."

"Yeah." Jim leans his head back to stare at the ceiling. "Kat, I think we should check into a hotel, at least until we get some advice from my attorney. It's crazy hanging out in that apartment with those cars parked right in front." He turns his head to look at Kat and she moves closer to him.

"That's a good idea," she says, timidly kissing him on the cheek. Without missing a beat he responds, his lips touching hers. She likes the tobacco-alcohol taste.

People start coming into the theater and as if on cue Kat and Jim break away from each other and stare at the blank movie screen. He puts his hand on hers and she stiffens. So different from the night in the club, when he was just a passion-release. Now he *sees* her and everything's changed. She's come to that line, the one that dares you to cross it, dares you to toss your heart into an impetuous vortex.

"Doesn't look very crowded," Kat says, her chest palpitating every time Jim rubs his fingers across her hand.

"Do you know what's playing?"

"I think it's a Russ Meyer film: *Faster, Pussycat! Kill! Kill!*" Her cheeks burn and she wishes she hadn't said the title. Sounds like a porno flick.

Now he's quiet. Kat wonders what he's thinking. She scans the faces in the theater even though she's quite sure their stalker won't show up.

Heat emanates from Jim's hand as his grip tightens over hers, and without warning he slides toward her, lightly pecks her neck with his lips. She squeezes his hand, each of his kisses chopping her breath, her light-headedness backed by a heated, sangria-intensified rush. She faces him, presses her lips into his forehead. Crossing the line, toward the vortex.

The lights dim, the previews start. No one else sits in their row. Kat straightens up, wanting to at least make an attempt at watching her first Meyer film. She watches the screen, not hearing a word being said. Except his.

"I'm glad we got into this mess," he whispers, his breath muffling her ear in a way that makes her whole body tingle, "or we wouldn't be here together. You're worth anything that those guys might do to me."

The Meyer film is history. Kat turns to Jim and, like the other night, loses her mouth in his, can't get enough. He lets his coat slip off as he leans into her. She resists lying down on the couch.

His coat is wedged between them and she yanks on it, draping it over his thighs. She takes a breath and slips her hand under the coat, sliding up a thigh.

"Oh God," he whispers when she reaches his cock, massaging the outside of his pants.

His breathing becomes audible and for a second she's conscious of where they are. But the theater isn't crowded, and no one can see them anyway. The audience cheers at something on the screen.

Not sure what to do next she backs off, wrapping her arms around his waist instead.

"Oh God, Kat," he whispers again. "I wish we were away from all of this. I don't want to know anything but you."

His hands tease, slowly sliding up from her waist and down again, his thumbs like electric wires every time they press into her breasts. She reaches for his thigh again, feels the muscles in his leg. Her tongue slips out of his mouth, makes its way to his ear. She wants to whisper the way he did with her but doesn't know what to say.

Whack! Something bashes against Kat's shoulder, then blinds her with bright light.

179

35

Kat quickly jumps away from Jim. It takes him a couple of seconds to remember where they are.

"What do you think this is, a motel?" says a gruff voice. "I'm going to have to ask you to leave."

"Sorry," Kat says.

The shriveled usher stands over them, his flashlight pointed to the floor.

Jim's never been kicked out of anywhere before, can't look at the man. He puts on his loaner overcoat, buttoning the front to hide any lingering hard-on.

Kat takes his hand. "Let's get out of here."

Once outside Kat quickly surveys the street and Jim glances through the nearest window—a skateboard shop—but they don't see the guy who bashed into Kat.

Then Kat busts up, imitating the old theater man's Midwest accent.

"What do you think this is, a *mo*tel?" she mocks. She doesn't reveal a trace of shame or embarrassment. Jim kisses her, coveting her childlike nature, craving it for himself.

She lets go of him, pokes him in the chest with her index

finger. "Now you stop that! What do you want to do, get us kicked off Haight Street too?"

He tries to grab her finger but she's too quick. He lunges forward and embraces her. "We need to go back to the apartment just to get my computer. Then I want to check into a hotel and be alone with you," he says.

"Me too." She takes his finger and sticks it into her mouth. He sucks in his next breath, makes sure his coat is still buttoned. No one's ever stirred him up like this. He sees a cab and reluctantly steps away from her, flagging it down.

Inside the cab he rolls down the window and smokes. Kat sits right up against him, holding his free hand. He hopes she does that thing with his finger again, but the driver asks if she works in South Park and she starts talking with him.

Jim doesn't like this break from Kat, needs to keep communicating with her or the rest of his world will come to life. One week off of *Signal*. His car, still in Berkeley. All his stuff at the house. Shit! Mandy wouldn't really *burn* it, she can't be that ruthless. Though she's already fanning the fire at work. Jim's heart skips, his breathing hurts. He turns to Kat, who's still politely chatting up the driver, and buries his face against her side. Her soft angora-covered tit cushions his nose and it takes all his willpower not to slurp it up with his tongue. She laughs, says he's tickling her.

"What are you doing?" She inches away from him, then smiles and throws her legs over his. He's relieved to have her attention again. Her green pants are starting to show dirt and he can't wait to take them off her.

"Do I make a right on South Park?" the driver asks.

"Actually no," Kat says. "Turn in the alley just before it . . . right here!"

The cab swerves to the right and stops behind the burrito joint.

"I'm just running in to get something," Jim says. "I'll be back in a minute. Then you can take us to the wharf."

"Not me," the driver says. "This was my last ride. I'm off now."

"What?" Kat exclaims. "That's crazy! The ride's not over yet."

The driver was about to light a pipe and it dangles from his mouth as he talks. "Oh yes it is. If you want me to call you another cab I'll be happy to."

Jim looks at his watch. "Can you have one pick us up right here in two hours, at 5:00?" He quickly looks at Kat, squeezing her calf, and she smiles.

"Yeah, sure," the driver says.

Jim pays the fare, anxious to shut himself off from the noise that comes between him and Kat. She's already spinning the dial on the lock pad. The gate opens and Jim waits for her to enter, then closes up, making sure the lock is securely clamped.

Once inside the building Jim presses against Kat's back, hugging her from behind at the bottom of the staircase. As they lumber up the steps together she takes his hands and places them over her breasts. He sucks on her neck and she squeezes his hands.

"No one's ever made me feel this way," he says at the top of the steps.

She blushes, looks at the floor. "I know."

Kat backs into the first bedroom while she takes off Jim's coat. As they fall onto the bed she traces his lips with her finger.

"I adore your teeth," she says. "They're so perfectly crooked, so real. They're your best feature."

Jim loves her for saying that. He's always hated his teeth, a blaring reminder of his parents' low-income status. Before he has a chance to return a compliment she sits on top of him and begins to slowly unbutton his pants. He watches her, trying to keep his breathing steady. Her slight overbite is *her* best feature, both girlish and erotic, organic. Already he feels himself getting hard. He reaches for her sweater, tugs on it.

Someone giggles from the far end of the apartment.

182

Kat leaps off the bed. Jim quickly buttons up, wired and alert.

"Oh, they stopped," a woman says, disappointed.

Kat gasps and grabs her backpack.

Jim looks through the gapped wall into the living room and sees a woman sitting on the futon, facing them. She smiles and waves. A man is facing her on the other couch.

"Who are you?" Jim shouts.

"Let's go," Kat says, picking up her other bag. She rushes past Jim, out the room, toward the stairs.

"Not so fast," a nearby voice says.

The hideous two-note clank of a cocking gun paralyzes Kat. Jim is still standing in the place she left him. A man in a black velvet pantsuit and purple ruffled blouse appears from behind one of the columns separating the bedroom from the living room—the sickly Mustang man they'd seen sneaking around Jim's house. Up close his face reveals thin spidery veins, accentuating the waxy sheen of his skin. His eyes are eerily oblong in shape, and a holographic pentagram hangs from a thin chain around his neck. His right hand cradles a gun.

"I want both of you to walk slowly into the living room," he says. "The girl first." He keeps the silencer-equipped gun pointed at Jim. Shit, they could be shot to death and no one nearby would hear a thing.

When Kat hesitates by the staircase the man rams the gun into the side of Jim's face. The loud clunk it makes hitting his head scares Jim more than the dizzying pain the blow causes, makes him wonder if his skull is cracked.

"Move it," the man says to his hostages, ordering Jim to sit next to "Cora."

Jim sees his laptop set up on the coffee table. Another laptop, zipped inside its case, leans against the side of the couch.

Cora pats the cushion next to her. She's the same woman they ran into this morning in the alley! Quite pretty, in her mid-30s, with baby-smooth skin, a Catholic-girl nose, short blond-streaked hair, and wide green eyes. Her body is slender and athletic, except for her tits, which look like pointy rocketships. Jim tries not to stare at them. He sits next to her and Kat takes his other side.

183

"Hi," Cora says, as if they're friends.

The guy across from them is the same person who was driving the Mustang in front of his house, the one sporting a goatee. His cheeks are a mass of craters yet his skin is taut, lustrous, obviously lifted by an overzealous surgeon. His eyes are small and intense, like glowing beads.

"My name is Vern," he says crisply, accentuating each syllable. "Time to step out of your rebellious child and face your debt like responsible adults. We will not be enablers to your dysfunctional behavior—"

"And we've already met," the gunman says, cutting off his partner. "I'm Larry Goines. *Mister* Goines to you, you disrespectful little fuck." He grins at Jim, massaging the tip of his gun. "You couldn't have picked a better hideaway. And with such an easy combination lock! I didn't even get to show off my skills."

So he's not just a henchman, he's the head honcho, the casino manager. He flew all the way from the Bahamas, or wherever El Tropical is based, just for Jim? Suddenly it's hard to breathe, the room is steamy-hot and Jim clenches the edge of the couch, willing himself not to faint. He has nothing to offer these people except half of his 5,000-dollar savings account.

"What were you thinking?" Goines says, still aiming his gun at Jim while taking a seat next to Vern. "You had the audacity to assume you could dodge us forever, get away without paying your debt?"

"I don't know," Jim says weakly. "I just don't have that kind of cash right now and I didn't know what to do."

"Well why the fuck did you play such high stakes if you didn't have the money?" The blue lines under his skin pop up and spread like lightning across his face, clashing with his puffy purple shirt collar.

"I, uh . . ." Jim's mind draws a blank. He wants Goines to repeat the question.

184

"*I* did it," Kat says. "*I* was the one who gambled that night. I didn't know it was a real casino." Her voice is strong, almost challenging.

Jim wouldn't have gotten Kat involved, but he's shamefully glad she piped in. They should know this important fact. Maybe it'll make them reconsider his fate.

"I'm not talking to you," Goines says, shifting dead-goat eyes in Kat's direction for a quick second, then settling them back on Jim. "I don't give a shit *who* gambled that night. The fact is, your account with us shows a negative balance of $199,115. It's all computerized, there's nothing to dispute. We're here to collect."

"You're a very repressed young man, Jim, and living in denial only worsens your condition," his sidekick Vern says, playing with the handle of a hunting knife that's tucked in his hip pocket. "If you want to become a whole man you need to be accountable for your actions." What's wrong with this creep? Isn't he listening? It wasn't *his* action that put him in debt.

Goines abruptly stands up, orders Jim and Kat to give him their wallets.

Jim thinks of all his credit cards, a couple of which belong to Mandy. Fighting his own resistance, he digs into his back pocket and hands the wallet over. Kat takes off her backpack, fishes through its side pocket, then through its main section.

"Shit," she mumbles, shaking the bag.

"Give that to me," Goines says, snatching the backpack from her.

Kat looks at Jim, her lips tightly pinched. "That blond guy today, he fuckin' took my wallet."

Jim remembers how the man fell over Kat, draping her body for a few seconds before stepping back. A goddamn pickpocket. He must have seen her coming out of the clothing store, displaying all her new buys, figured she had more money than most around there.

Jim doesn't know what to say to Kat. He wants to tell her he loves her but instead mouths, "Don't worry," as if that'll make her feel better.

After a thorough search Goines tosses Kat's bag aside and points at Jim's wrist. "And your watch," he says.

Jim shakes his head. His gold watch was a gift from Mandy, given to him on their first anniversary. It's worth thousands of dollars, she'd kill him if she found it missing.

Goines walks around the coffee table, touches Jim's collarbone with his gun. "Your watch!"

3:17. Just random numbers. Jim peels the precious metal off his wrist and hands it to the ghoul, who wads it up as if it were a piece of junk mail and shoves it into his pocket.

"One thing doesn't make sense," Goines says, tapping Jim on the head with his gun. "We couldn't log into your email, it said we needed a password. So why didn't you set up a password to enter El Tropical? Something's not consistent here."

Jim rubs his head, says he didn't think he needed a password for the casino since it was set up at his home. Another whack. Jim wishes the asshole wouldn't treat him like this in front of Kat.

"Well, we could've been through with business before you got here had you not been so paranoid about your email. Now I want you to send a message to your boss, Jerry Liebowitz. Cora's already typed a nice letter for you. Cora, where's the note?"

Cora leans over Jim, her tight gingham blouse revealing sharp shoulder bones. She opens up a Microsoft Word document on his desktop.

"Here it is," she says, standing up, her high, perfectly rounded bubble-ass almost kissing Jim's face. She eases past him. "Excuse me, I have to pee."

Vern points to the laptop. "Read the letter my wife wrote."

Jim looks at the screen.

Dear Jerry,

Help! This is Jim. I'm being forced at gunpoint to write this letter to you. Some men are holding me hostage in a basement and say they'll shoot me if they don't receive 200,000 dollars by noon tomorrow. They want you to wire it in the form of Digicash to this email account. They want me to warn you not to call the police and not to tell another soul about this, or I'm dead.

Please help me, Jerry. These guys are extremely hostile.

Jim Knight

Jim doesn't know if the e-letter will fly. What about the call he made this morning from Haight Street? He didn't mention any hostage crisis to Chelsea. He *did* tell Mandy he was in trouble . . . but was she listening? Jim decides not to say anything about his conversations with Mandy and Chelsea. Maybe Jerry will pay these guys and save the day.

36

Kat's mind scrambles for a way out of this. If she has to kill these people to get out of here she will, because there's no way Goines is going to let her and Jim go free even if he gets the money. He and his cohorts can be identified now. She's going to have to fight to save her life.

Cora comes back from the bathroom, asks if she's missed anything.

Vern asks her to sit on his lap but she says she'd rather sit next to Jim so she can see the computer screen.

Cora taps Kat on the nose. "Why don't you sit next to Vern so we can have more room?" Kat fumes at the way this pseudo-priss treats her. The woman's pink pedal pushers, matching pink beeper, frilly high-buttoned blouse and cone-shaped bra don't mask the cold-bitch essence that only another female would notice. Kat looks at Vern.

"I don't bite," he says.

"No," Goines barks from behind. "I want her to stay here. They shouldn't be separated, things would get too confused."

Cora sits where she was before and Goines orders Jim to send the letter, adding a subject line that says: HELP JIM KNIGHT. The room is silent, except for the modem tones and the sharp clicks of the keyboard as Jim enters his email password, and all but Vern witness the ransom note as it launches into cyber-space, on its way to signal.com.

"That ought to do it," Goines says, slowly making his way back to Vern's couch, keeping a sharp eye on his hostages. He digs his nails into his sparse gray hair and scratches like a dog with fleas. "Now we just have to wait."

Jim touches Kat's fingertips with his and she whisks her hand away. How could he have ever gotten involved with people like this? He may be savvy in the media market but he sure doesn't have any street smarts. She wonders how badly hurt she'd be if she jumped out the bay window. It's only one story up.

"Baby, get me my medicine box," Vern says, looking faint.

Cora bends over the back of the couch so that her ass is in the air. Kat hopes she falls on her head. But the woman is nimble and bounces back up with a brown leather doctor's bag.

Vern reaches over the coffee table and takes it. He pulls out a few dark bottles and a needle. Goines asks Cora to grab him a beer and she obediently sashays to the kitchen.

Reminding Kat of the ketamine session with Kengo, Vern flicks the needle, filled with the liquid he extracted from one of the bottles. With one swift movement he stabs it into his arm. Goines ignores the whole process, staring at Jim like a watchdog.

"Would anyone like a vitamin B12 shot?" Vern asks.

"I'll take one," Cora says, handing Goines his beer.

Vern fills the same needle with a second bottle's worth of contents.

Appalled, Kat holds her breath as Cora bends forward, facing her and Jim, and unzips the back of her pants. She bares her round rump to the men and Kat's relieved that her skanky snatch isn't exposed. Vern injects his wife. Goines smiles but doesn't leer.

"Thank you," she says primly, zipping her pants back up. Vern pulls her into his lap and she squeals, wrapping her arms around his neck.

Kat wants to barf.

"Let's turn on the stereo," Cora says, reaching for the remote. She scans the stations, blasting the sound when she hears Nine Inch Nails.

"Turn it down," Goines says.

A sick, claustrophobic dread creeps through Kat's skin. She needs a breather, says she has to pee.

Goines stiffens, then asks Cora to escort Kat to the bathroom.

"I can go by myself," Kat says, her dread turning to panic. "There's no way to escape from the bathroom." She desperately needs to get away from these people.

Jim is mute.

"Vern, give Cora your knife," Goines says. He never directly acknowledges Kat. "Go with her," he repeats to Cora.

Kat eyes the staircase, which is just beyond the bathroom, and wonders if she could make a run for it. Then she remembers the goddamn gate. It's locked. They'd catch up to her by the time she opened it.

Cora follows her into the small red-and-black bathroom. She sits on the edge of the Jacuzzi tub, holding the knife, staring at Kat.

"I can't go if you stare at me like that. Can you turn around?"

"No, I can't. But I won't look." Cora looks down at her shoes and shuts her eyes.

If Kat could just swipe the knife from the priss, she'd be able to hold *her* hostage, force Goines to drop the gun, threaten to kill the little lady if the guys didn't set her and Jim free.

A barbaric survival instinct takes over and as soon as Kat flushes she charges into Cora, who had relaxed her grip on the knife. Kat grabs it, twisting Cora's wrist, but the skinny bitch doesn't let go. She screams like Little Bo Peep and Kat slugs her in the jaw with her free hand, still trying to wrench the knife away. Kat's surprised at the woman's tenacity.

Cora's B-injected knight comes to the rescue, shouting,

banging the door open. He lifts Kat out of the bathroom and slams her into the hall. Kat's arm hits a metal column as she falls to the floor. Cora scurries toward her with the knife, but Vern blocks his wife and takes the weapon away from her. He waves it at Kat. "That was *not* okay behavior!"

As one last act of retaliation Cora kicks Kat several times in the legs and stomach.

Jim shouts and tries to rise from his chair but Goines pushes him down. "Sit!" Goines says to Jim. "We need to answer the message!"

Vern and Cora pivot toward the computer.

"What's going on? They already wrote back?" Vern asks, hurrying toward the laptop. Cora runs over to Jim and sits on his lap. Kat looks at the staircase. *Run!*

She steadies herself on her feet, wonders how fast she could open the padlock.

"Get over here!" Goines yells, obviously to Kat, though he doesn't waver his aim at Jim. Vern looks at her, placing his hand over his knife.

Jim nods slightly and gives her a half-smile, as if to say it's all going to work out. Yeah, and the Easter bunny will bring them chocolate eggs. It's obviously up to Kat to get them out of this.

37

Jim wishes Cora would get off his lap so Kat could sit closer to him. He tries to focus on the message in front of him:

> Jim, is this for real!? Who *are* these people? Does that girl you've been hanging around with have something to do with this? I don't understand why they kidnapped you. My head is spinning. You told me not to tell another soul about this, but I can't get the money without discussing it with Chelsea. Tell me what to do.
>
> Jerry

Jim swells, emotional over Jerry's loyalty. He tries to reach the keyboard to answer the message, not sure what to say, but Cora blocks him.

"I don't trust this Jerry fuck. He's just trying to buy time!" Goines says.

"We can trust him," Vern says calmly. "Jerry is in emotional shock over this. I get the feeling he's a rescuer, has probably played this role with Jim before . . . "

"*What?*" Jim exclaims.

"But the man is also trapped in a co-dependent relationship with Chelsea, so his hands are tied."

"Who's Chelsea?" Goines asks.

"The president of *Signal*," Jim says, eager to veer away from Vern's psychic X-ray.

"Shit, another fucking obstacle," Goines snarls. "Cora, write him back, tell him he can ask Chelsea for the money but no one else can know about this. Ignore the rest of his questions."

Her padded ass rolls upward as she leans forward to type, reminding Jim of the erotic way she received the vitamin B12 shot. He takes a deep breath and cranes his neck, switching his attention to the screen. She reads aloud as she writes to clue in Goines.

Jerry:

The only question I can answer is your last one. Yes, you can tell Chelsea—but *only* Chelsea—about my situation. Anyone else and they'll shoot me.

Cora looks up at Goines to see if she's on the right track. He gives her a nod to continue.

Please be careful, Jerry. You're my only hope.

Jim

She keeps HELP JIM KNIGHT as the subject line and, with Goines's okay, sends the message.

Vern gets up and takes three beers out of the fridge, passing the extra two to his friends. Cora tells him to turn up the stereo and he does. Angry rock. When will this end? *Pay up, Jerry.*

Cora moves to the music, still sitting on Jim. If only she were Kat. He plays connect-the-dots with the ugly blue veins in Goines's face, trying to distract himself from the bobbing flesh on his lap.

Kat sits at the very edge of the couch. Her eyes are set on the staircase. She's too rebellious for her own good. There's no way she could have taken this crew on with a knife. Why can't she just be a little patient? She unconsciously massages her

193

knee, triggering in Jim a breath-shortening flow of adrenaline. He looks away, tries to forget her rhythm in the theater, zeroes in on Vern's tasteless hair and goatee tint, an odious coral-brown.

"Oh my God!" Cora chirps, pointing at the screen. She's still grinding to the music.

An instant message from Jerry. Goines moves forward, then excitedly gets up, steps in back of Jim again so he can read the screen. "Turn down the goddamn music," he screams at Vern.

Jim looks at the monitor.

Jim:

I just caught Chelsea on her way out to do an errand. We'll send you the money, but she says it may be impossible before tomorrow evening. Tell your captors we're earnestly working on it as fast as we can, and to please be patient. No one else is involved. You have my word.

Jerry

Jim can't believe his luck. By tomorrow night these felons will be out of his life. He'll close his account with El Tropical and never make another bet as long as he lives. He'll have to tell Jerry the truth, of course, and he'll pay back every cent as soon as he can. He hopes Jerry is as understanding as he was about his previous gambling debt. He also hopes he'll still have a job at *Signal.* Mandy is over, that's clear, but Jim will be able to handle that. He'd never be able to marry her now anyway, not after meeting Kat.

Goines dictates Cora's response to Jerry:

Thank you, Jerry. You're saving my life. They say they'll wait until tomorrow evening, 6:00.

194

Jim

Cora finally gets off of Jim and moves to the kitchen. "I'm hungry," she says.

Jim smells chicken and craves a burrito.

"Excuse me," he says. Goines is still behind him. "Would it be all right if I had a cigarette?"

Goines slowly moves back to his couch and gives Jim permission to smoke. After Jim lights up Goines asks for the pack and takes a cigarette for himself.

"Phew! We need some air in here." Cora starts banging on the bay window, trying to open it up. Vern helps her.

Cora points at something out the window and hisses, "Who are they?"

Goines jumps and Jim ducks, worried the gun might go off. The front door jiggles.

"What's going on?" Goines rasps, shoving Jim in the chest with the gun. The blue facial lines are back, and Jim notices for the first time the stains, the brown-and-yellow textured streaks discoloring every tooth in the ghoul's mouth.

"I don't know," Jim says. "It might be the guy who owns this place." His hands shake the way they did in Caffe Centro and he tucks one under his thigh, uses the other to manage his cigarette. The floor is his ashtray.

"I jammed a toothpick into the lock on that door," Goines says. "They can't get in from the front."

"I think they're going around to the back," Vern says. "There are three of them."

"Shit!" Goines screams. The barrel of his gun is between Jim's eyes. Body spasms make it hard for Jim to sit still. It's as if he were being jerked apart from the inside.

"I'm going to hide, but this gun will be aimed right here the whole time," Goines says, touching Jim on the bridge of his nose with the gun. "Cora, turn on the stereo and sit on Jim's lap again! Vern, sit on the other couch with a beer and keep an eye on the girl. If the visitors suspect a thing, they'll all go down. And so will you," he says to Jim.

Goines disappears between two vertical beams in a corner of the room but Jim sees the metallic shine of his weapon. Hugging herself tightly, Kat looks whiter than Goines.

Cora jumps onto Jim's lap, singing to the loud music, and grabs a beer from the table. Vern sits back across from them and smiles at his wife. He spreads his thin legs over the coffee table.

The back door opens. With the stereo turned up so loud, Jim can't hear what the strangers are saying.

"Fuck!" Jim says before he can stop himself. Chelsea Simmons and Mandy walk briskly behind a stranger. They're headed toward the living room but don't seem to notice him yet. The stranger is a short young guy with bushy dark hair and sideburns, and his face reddens with each step.

Jim grabs Cora under her arms and moves her so that she blocks his face. Confused, she giggles and turns to peck him on the lips. Jim pushes her away, nervously glances at Vern, surprised to find the man smiling at his wife, massaging his goatee with his thumb and index finger.

From the periphery Jim sees something flying toward him but doesn't have time—or the physical ability with Cora on his lap—to dodge the object. Something large and blue bashes into his face, and then through blurry eyes he sees Mandy standing over him, ready to swing her purse again.

The music stops and the short fellow stands in front of Vern.

"What the hell are you all doing in my place?" The guy shakes his head when he notices the table, with its open beer cans, wet smeared ashes, and used B12 syringe.

Vern points to Jim. "Ask *him*. He's the one who invited us."

"You fucking bastard!" Mandy says, battering him with her purse again.

"You *know* these people?" the guy shrieks at Mandy. "How'd they get in here?"

"This is unbelievable," Chelsea says. "How *dare* you try to con us! How could you do this to us? Jerry was sick when he got your messages. We were about to borrow against the business for you! God Jim, we *trusted* you."

Jim can barely hear what Chelsea is saying between the

swats of the blue purse. He finally snatches the bag away from Mandy and flings it across the room. His face stings and Jim is sure his skin is torn up.

"How did you know I was here?" Jim says, closing his eyes. At least the painful beating stopped his uncontrollable twitches.

"We didn't," Chelsea says. "We were looking at this space as a place to board out-of-town clients. I just can't believe this. What were you going to do once you got the money? And who are these people?" She does a double-take when she spots Kat, as if she recognizes her but doesn't know from where.

Mandy, Chelsea and the landlord all stand around Jim, waiting for him to speak. He puffs his cigarette in silence. To hell with it all. He doesn't owe them an explanation. He's tried to do the right thing, to get help from his attorney, to warn Mandy this morning on the phone. Now he's got a gun pointed at his head by a madman whose plans have just been botched. There's nothing he can say to smooth this out, so why open his mouth?

Mandy bursts into tears. "This is so humiliating! Why are you doing this to me?" To *her*. Like he devised this elaborate life-threatening crisis just to hurt her.

Jim keeps his eyes on Cora's back. He finishes his smoke and hands Cora the butt, which she tosses on the table.

"Assholes!" shouts the young guy, stomping his foot. "You're going to pay to have this place cleaned." He points to the back door. "Get out of here! Right now!"

No one in Jim's party moves except Cora, who's bopping as if the music were still on.

"Come on," Chelsea says to her crew. She walks dangerously close to the poles that conceal Goines to pick up Mandy's purse. "The authorities will handle this."

Jim leans his forehead against Cora's spine, resting there until he hears a slam from the door downstairs.

38

"Shit!" Goines says, jumping out of his hiding place. "Why didn't you tell me this place wasn't safe?"

Cora hops out of Jim's lap and Goines repeatedly slaps him in the neck with his gun. "Everything's fucked up now, and *you* fucked it up!" Jim reaches out, blindly tries to stop the hits.

Kat catches Vern's attention, pleads with her eyes for him to show some humanity. He cracks his fingers, then stands up.

"Okay Larry, that's enough. It would be fruitless to kill the young man before we get the money." Vern picks up a jacket from the side of the couch and takes a cell phone out of its pocket. "Here, why don't you call Manny?"

Suddenly Goines looks nervous, the angry blood in his face instantly draining. The gaunt vampire is back. "What do I tell him?"

"He's *your* nephew," Vern says. "You need to learn how to stand up to him."

"Don't tell me what I need to learn," Goines snaps.

"Just hurry and call before the cops show up!" Vern says.

Blood is dripping from Jim's temple. He touches it with his finger. Kat reaches for a beer can, feels that it's still cool, and places it against Jim's head.

"Thanks," he whispers.

Goines tells Vern to handle the gun while he makes the call. Like a statue, Vern stands stiffly in front of Jim, pointing the gun at him. Cora comes over with a damp napkin and tells Kat to move over, but Kat doesn't budge until Vern shouts at her to follow orders.

Kat slams the can on the table and slides over. Out of the corner of her eye she sees something appear on the laptop's screen. Another instant message—but this time it isn't from Jerry. Cora's so eager to play nurse she doesn't see the new e-note, and Jim's eyes are closed. Kat strains to read it.

> Jim, are you okay? Don't fear the Mercury—it belongs to the FBI. We've been trying to contact you for days now but you and your friend are too evasive for your own good.
>
> This is probably obvious, but El Tropical is on your tail and they're very dangerous people. We've been trying to bust them for a year but can never locate their real whereabouts. We'd like to talk to you about setting up a sting.
>
> One of our agents has seen the Mustang, says he's parked next to it now, in South Park. Sit tight, Jim. If you can see the agent in the park, let him know who you are!
>
> Tommy Smith
>
> Agent, Federal Bureau of Investigation
>
> 415/555-3902

Kat can barely breathe, terrified that any movement from her will cause Cora to notice the new message. She memorizes Smith's phone number, then stealthily wraps her ankle around the computer cord. No one pays any attention to her. Goines is trying to make his call, cussing at the phone for not getting him through. Vern's eyes are locked on his wife, who's daintily

199

stroking Jim's skin with the napkin, going way beyond tending to his cuts. Jim remains motionless, looks like he's sleeping, though he's sitting straight up.

One, two, three! With one swift motion Kat swings her leg up onto the couch, dragging the computer off the table. It hits the carpet with a chilling clunk.

Jim gasps, tries to pick it up, but Kat swipes it from the floor, surreptitiously hitting the power button to complete the damage.

"Oh my God," she says. "I'm so sorry!"

Vern pivots with the gun, not sure who to point it at. Kat turns the computer back on, makes sure it's not broken.

"Leave it alone!" Goines shouts. "Put it back on the table." He licks his lips with a scaly gray tongue.

Jim frowns at Kat. Some survivor he is.

"Shhh!" Goines hisses, though no one is speaking. He steps into the bedroom and sits on the bed, phone to his ear.

Finally connected, he tells someone on the phone he needs to speak to Manny.

A jackhammer from the construction site next door interrupts the conversation, making Cora jump. Kat softly snorts to let Cora know what a wimp she is. The wimp struts into the kitchen and starts to put all the beers into a paper bag, preparing for departure.

Goines marches huffily to the bottom of the staircase to get away from the noise. Kat hears bits of his conversation but can't make out the words. Luckily the laptop seems to have rebooted without any problem. Kat peeks at Jim. He's tracing small welts that have flared up on the side of his face and neck. Cora comes to his rescue, placing her beer can against his cheek. Fuckin' copycat.

200

"Manny wants us to bring them to the center," Goines says, taking the gun away from Vern. His scalp glistens with perspiration. "He says we have to get the hell out of here, now."

Goines motions with his gun for everyone to get up from the couch. "Come on, let's move it."

Cora scoops up the B12 kit and puts it in the medicine bag while Vern packs up the computer.

Jim clears his throat. "Was that the guy from the Mercury?"

"What?" Goines asks, pocketing Jim's cigarettes from the table.

"The man from the Mercury. Was that him on the phone?"

Kat freezes. *You idiot!* Even in his beaten, deflated state Jim has to burn their bridge to safety. Kat kicks him in the ankle, motions with her hand to shut up. Goines notices the exchange. He pushes Jim in the collarbone with his gun. "What the fuck are you talking about?"

"I, uh—nothing. We saw a Mercury out there, thought the guy was with you. I guess we were wrong."

Goines pinches the back of Jim's neck, puts the gun to his head and pushes him to the window. Kat takes a few steps toward them, but not close enough to spot the FBI agent.

"Fuck! There *is* a Mercury," Goines says to Vern. "Think it's a Fed?"

Vern peers out the window. "Could be."

Goines yanks a handful of Jim's hair. "I told you not to call the Feds!"

Kat opens her mouth, ready to tell Goines not to be so abusive, but instinct bullies her into silence.

"I *didn't* call them!" Jim protests.

Goines lets go. His eyes dart around like a rat's, trying to figure a way around the new obstacle.

"We've got to distract that pig-fucker," he says. His eyes flash for a brief moment and he grins, asks Cora to put on her glasses and hat.

39

What an ass he is. If he'd just kept his trap shut he and Kat would be driving to some FBI headquarters with the feline-faced agent, returning to their pre-Goines existence. Of course Jim would now be homeless, but that would be only temporary. Anyway, after these last few days with Kat he'd live under a bridge before going back to life with Mandy. As for his job, he would've been on the phone with Jerry by this afternoon, would've cleared up the misunderstandings. But no, he had to try to show off, let Goines know that he was onto them and the imagined planted sidekick. He had to land them in the get-away Mustang. The car idles by the park waiting for Cora, who's luring the agent away.

The worst part of it all for Jim is discovering his inability to act as protector. Kat would've been much safer on her own. She's got some kind of sixth sense that he lost long ago. This lack of survival instinct makes him feel ineffective, small, ugly.

Vern stirs in the driver's seat, staring out the window for any sign of his wife. His goggle mirrorshades dominate his narrow face, make him look like a human fly. Jim and Kat are slouched in the back, their heads too low for anyone to see them. Goines keeps twisting around to make sure they're not trying to pull any "funny stuff."

Jim turns to Kat when she taps him lightly on the arm. She asks how he's doing, mouthing the words quietly. He nods that he's okay, though his gun-battered neck and temple feel as if they've been through a garbage disposal. She reaches out to touch a bruised welt near his eye, then drops her hand, petting his whiskered chin instead.

"I'm sorry," he whispers to her.

A saxophone sings to them from the park and Kat closes her eyes. Jim leans back, looking at the treetops. He's never noticed how dense they are before, never even thought of South Park as a place where nature exists.

"There she is!" Vern shouts. He honks the horn and revs the engine. Within seconds he opens his door and Cora squeezes into the back. She climbs over Jim, sitting between him and Kat.

"Step on it!" she says to Vern. "I don't want him to see me!"

Cora kicks off her pumps and props her feet on the bucket seats before her. Her toenails are perfectly manicured, the color of pink cotton candy. She laughs, tells Jim he can get up now. He and Kat both sit up.

Vern adjusts a book-sized video monitor that displays the precise location of the Mustang on a digital map. As he speeds toward the highway the car's electronic image makes its way across the screen. A few weeks ago Jim received one of these satellite navigational systems in the mail from a PR firm but he hasn't had the time to install it in his car.

"Hey, where's my cushion?" Cora asks, as if her ass weren't padded enough.

Goines grumbles and reaches under his seat, pulling out an overstuffed pillow shaped like Hello Kitty. She grabs it. The back-seat center hump already elevates her above everyone else. With the pillow's added height her head almost touches the ceiling.

203

The next hour is spent on the highway headed northeast, with Cora rambling on about her heroic deed. She explains how she'd approached the FBI agent acting as if she'd thought he was a regular guy who might be able to help. She'd had him on his feet in seconds. Cora had told him she'd seen some hoodlums roughhousing a young couple, that her name was Betsey Carlyle, that she worked at the Hyatt Regency but had the day off. After sending the plainclothed dupe on a frenzied search down some desolate street, heading away from the park, she'd bolted back to the car.

"He bought it all!" she squeals. "Did I do good?"

"You did *real* good," Vern says, reaching back to give her thigh a squeeze.

Jim gasps. Through the rearview mirror he notices a string of thick red goop hanging from Vern's nose. Cora laughs. "Sweetie, you've got Ener-B all over your lip!"

"Do you need a fix?" he asks Cora, offering her a small plastic tube of nasal vitamin B.

"No, the B12 shot was enough," she says.

Vern asks Goines for a Kleenex.

Cora stretches her legs across Jim's and asks him to massage them. When he hesitates, Vern looks at him in the rearview mirror and says, "Only an insecure husband with a small-penis complex would object to another man giving his wife a simple massage. When a woman requests assistance, a whole man obliges."

Cora's legs are cute in their tight pink pants, her knees a bit knobby in an adolescent way. Jim's hands soon get tired, but every time he stops she moans and jiggles her thighs, forcing him to continue. He notices that Kat's dropped off. He's glad she's asleep and doesn't have to watch.

Somewhere near Sacramento, Goines, who's been leering at Jim through the car's vanity mirror, tells Vern to stop for food. They swerve off the highway, head for a McDonald's.

In the parking lot Goines orders Jim to sit in the car with

him while the other three take a bathroom break and order the food. He says they should do this in shifts to keep better tabs on Jim and Kat. Vern protests, says they should all go in together, but Goines wins out.

"All right," Vern says, sighing. He takes the gun and wraps his arm around Kat as if they're lovers, keeping the weapon plunged into her side. Goines moves to the back seat and wraps his arm tightly around Jim's waist, poking the knife against his belly button.

"What's wrong with you?" Goines says as soon as the others are out of earshot, his sour cigarette-beer breath poisoning Jim's nasal passages. "Why didn't you want to massage her legs? You a fuckin' queer or something?"

Jim doesn't think the ghoul will kill him for taking the fifth so he keeps his mouth shut. Goines doesn't like it. The tip of the knife pricks Jim's stomach like a beesting.

"Your girlfriend is tougher than you. At least the dumb bitch tried to take out Cora. I bet you've never even killed a gnat," Goines says.

Jim tries to think of the right response to avoid another jab, but Goines isn't quite finished. "Me, I enjoy a good kill. One time I caught some son of a bitch in bed with my ex-girlfriend and blew his brains out. Didn't think twice about it. And I didn't even spend much time in the slammer. Pleaded temporary insanity and got out on parole."

A woman drives up and parks her car next to the Mustang. She gives Jim and Goines a double-take. Hasn't she ever seen a gussied-up corpse and a young broken professional sitting arm in arm in the back seat of a car before? Jim closes his eyes, trying to will this nightmare away, but it only gets worse. Goines's mouth is suddenly sucking on his.

Jim squirms, involuntarily releases a muffled yelp, and this time the knife punctures him. At the same time Goines shoves his fat tongue to the back of Jim's throat and Jim feels like he's giving the guy head. Sobs roll out of him, which only seems to excite the madman, kick-starting his tongue into a furious palpitation. Saliva drenches the outside of Jim's mouth.

Finally Goines pulls away, snickering. "Didn't want that lady next to us to think I was holding you hostage or anything."

Jim gags several times, expecting all of his organs to eject themselves from his body. Tears roll down his face.

"Don't act like such a goddamn woman," Goines says, plucking two of Jim's cigarettes from his pocket. He lights them both, hands one to Jim. "Now get yourself together, asshole. You tell anyone what just happened and I won't just kill you, I'll sacrifice you to Satan."

Jim puts the cigarette to his lips but can't inhale properly, starts choking on the smoke. He notices his Rolex wrapped over Goines's long silky sleeve.

Vern and the women come out of the restaurant and Cora runs ahead of the others. "Your turn," she says, climbing into the back seat. She looks at Jim and freezes in mid-climb, one knee on the hump, her ass pushed against the front seat. "What happened to you?"

Jim feels the knife twist slightly. He shakes his head. "Nothing. I was just thinking about my fiancée, that's all."

When Vern and Kat reach the car Goines slaps Jim on the shoulder, says it's time for them to hit the john. Jim would rather have his bladder rupture than be alone again with this perverted freak. He says he doesn't have to go.

Goines grunts. "It's up to you, but it's going to be a long time before we stop again."

40

Kat opens her eyes to a black sky and dryer, warmer air, sees on the computerized map that they're headed for Reno. Goines is driving now and Vern is telling him about a new hot tub he just ordered. It comes with adjustable seating and a supply of Bach flower remedies to mix in the water that should help his "condition."

"And with the remote control you can heat it up while you're still in bed," he boasts.

Cora is asleep, clinging to Jim's arm like a sickly koala bear, resting her head on his shoulder. It's disgusting, the way Jim kept massaging her spindly legs earlier, the way he doesn't shrug her off now. He could say no—if he really wanted to. Kat makes a fist and socks Cora's bony heel away, which was digging into her hip.

"When is Reba coming into town?" Vern asks.

"Sunday, I think. I've been trying to get the bitch to marry me. That would be my ticket out of here. You should see her house!" Goines whistles. "A beautiful two-story number in Encino."

"Hell, that's where I want to be."

"A couple more gigs like this one and you'll have enough

dough to go wherever you want," Goines says. "Just follow my lead."

"Will do," Vern says.

Kat can't imagine *any* woman who would sleep with Goines, let alone marry him. The car's map says 10 more miles to Reno. Reno might be good. With all the crowds and hubbub it might be easy to duck out. The thugs probably wouldn't even notice her disappearance right away. Goines concentrates on Jim, Vern on his wife, and bubble-ass Cora on herself. That leaves no one but her own team to watch over her.

"Not too much traffic tonight," Goines says to Vern as he turns off the main highway before they hit Reno, onto a small unlit lane that pummels the bottom of the Mustang with thudding rocks and other debris.

Kat looks at the satellite display and sees that the car has left the highway and is moving across a blank portion of the screen. Apparently the road they're on is too obscure to be listed on the digital map.

The landscape outside is barren, remote, nothing at all—the kind of backdrop where decomposed bodies are found by desert rats 23 months after the victims were murdered. Reno is no longer on their route. So much for disappearing into a sea of anonymous flesh.

Kat wonders who has the gun now, figures it must be Vern since Goines is taking a stint behind the wheel. Shit, she's sitting on Vern's side. She ignores the jittery bug whipping through her gut.

Stay alert.

Plan A: With eyes shut to feign sleep, she carefully places a hand over Cora's pants, then sweater, to see if she's carrying a weapon that could be snatched. No luck. Cora twists slightly and Kat pulls her hand away. She quickly devises Plan B: When Goines stops the car and orders Kat and Jim to step out, she'll take the only chance she's got left and run heedlessly into the endless black space. Hopefully Jim will do the same, though he's not as spontaneous as she. They'll most likely kill him, a reality that numbs her energy, would make her vomit if she

208

dwelled on it. *Don't think.* She has to turn off the noise, think only of herself. There's no other way out.

Vern turns around and rubs Cora's arm. "Baby, wake up. We're almost home."

Home? His statement envelops Kat like a warm bath. Home sounds safer than nowhere, gives her hope that they're not yet ready to murder. Kat looks ahead but sees only the impenetrable darkness. Do they live in a cave?

Cora stretches and yawns, slowly props herself back on the cushioned hump. "What time is it?" she asks.

"Around 10:00," Vern says.

Jim hunches over, his head dropped into his chest, and Kat can't tell if he's awake or not.

They make a sharp turn around a hill that takes them toward a short string of lights—some sort of civilization, sparse as it is. As they near the yellow-and-white glowing cluster, Kat makes out a mobile home, realizes they're headed for a trailer park—over a dozen scattered homes in all.

"That wasn't so bad, was it?" Goines asks Vern. "Once we hand them over to Manny you and Cora can clock out. Your pay will depend, of course, on how much we can squeeze from these two little fuckers."

Once inside the park they pull up to the stretch limo of the bunch, an extra-long double-wide unit that sags slightly in the middle. Kat notices a couple of video cameras near the front steps, slowly pivoting from side to side. Other than that, the trailer is pretty nondescript, doesn't have tinny *faux*-French doors or an Astroturf garden like some of its neighbors.

Goines stops the car, his eyes locked on the rearview mirror.

"What the hell?" He frantically shifts into reverse and floors it, almost bashing into another trailer. He slams on the brakes.

"The son of a bitch," he says.

Kat is completely lost. Jim looks up to see what the commotion is about.

"Looks like someone ran into your bike," Vern says calmly.

"Someone fuckin' *totaled* my bike!" Goines jumps out of

209

the car and inspects a pile of bike parts, what apparently was a fairly decent motorcycle at one time. He kicks one of its flattened wheels into the front of the car.

"Oh Lord," Vern says under his breath.

"Fritz!" Goines yells, banging on someone's front door. The car's headlights are still on, revealing a pink-and-white aluminum home surrounded by small statues of deer, squirrels, raccoons, and birds.

A squat blond man opens the door, then tries to shut it when he sees who knocked, but Goines throws his body into it and pulls the man out. The man can't keep his balance, keeps trying to hold on to the side of his trailer.

"What the hell happened?" Goines shouts, pointing to the heap of metal.

The man mumbles, his words too low to be heard from the car.

"Goddamn it Fritz! You drunk!" Goines jerks the man to the ground, kicks him hard.

A woman in a robe runs out of the trailer. "Leave him alone!" she screams. "Leave him alone, or I'll call the police!" A couple of unseen dogs react to the disturbance, howling along with the humans.

"You were supposed to *sell* my bike, not *destroy* it!" Goines shouts, continuing to kick Fritz on the ground. The woman pounds on Goines's back, crying that he's going to kill her boyfriend.

"Shut up!" someone yells from a distance.

Finally Vern sticks his head out the car window, reminds Goines that they still have business to take care of. Kat sees blood coming from the man's mouth, his girlfriend using her robe to clean it up.

Goines says something, pointing his finger at the woman, then hurls himself into the car.

"Goddamn it," he says, speeding forward. "He just lost me three grand."

They stop in front of the double-wide trailer. Vern turns to

210

Goines. "That was not okay behavior. What's Manny going to say when he finds out what you did to Fritz?"

"If Fritz is smart he'll keep his mouth shut," Goines grumbles. "Come on, let's all get out."

Goines shoves Jim in front of him and Vern steers Kat by holding on to the back of her head. She's clutching her backpack and bag of used clothes with one hand. A wiry guy in his 20s wearing a tank top and dusty jeans opens the door before anyone knocks. His head sways back and forth with half-shut eyes.

"Everything's fucked up," he says to Goines and Vern, running nervous fingers through the long part of his mullet hairdo. Suddenly his sleepy lids flip wide open, exposing bewildered green eyes, then just as quickly they droop back to their strung-out half-mast. As soon as they all step inside, he runs to a table and snorts a thick line laid out on the surface of a CD-ROM.

Kat is surprised at how impeccably mod this trailer looks on the inside, so ultra-chic, like a retro-futuristic pad you'd find in *Barbarella* or *2001: A Space Odyssey*. They're standing in a white-and-silver modular living room with globular lamps hanging from the ceiling and streamlined plastic couches covered with inflated Mylar pillows. A wide-screen television set with a WebTV box sits against one wall, underneath a separate hanging monitor that displays live surveillance shots from various areas of the park.

Goines pushes the guy away from his mound of powder. "What do you mean everything's fucked up? Where's Manny?"

"Want a line?" the guy says, sniffling. He's amped and Kat can smell him from across the room.

"No Johnny, we're here to see Manny. These two are the delinquents he asked us to bring up from San Francisco," Goines says.

"Excuse me," Jim interrupts. Kat holds her breath. "Is there a bathroom I can use?"

"Yeah," Johnny says. "Down the hall, first door on the right."

211

Goines tells Vern to escort him.

"Everything went haywire a couple of hours ago," Johnny says. "Manny's not here, something's happened. You better talk to Curtis. He's in the office."

Goines quickly steers Kat down a narrow hall. Another camera hangs from the ceiling. They pass the bathroom, heading for the last door. Cora lags behind.

The office is a stark, spacious room with rows of computers against the walls, some sporting two monitors, one stacked above the other. Cold air blasts through the room and Kat is thankful she's wearing a sweater. All of the monitors are on, most hiding their data behind screensavers. The exposed screens display either charts, graphs, and rows of numbers or video shots of locations that don't look like the nearby vicinity.

A large bearded man who could pass as an out-of-work lumberjack sits in front of one of the computers, frantically clicking through pages of a database, apparently unaware of their arrival. He's got a deep shiny tan and a faded tattoo of Darth Vader on his arm. Two open beer cans sit on the desk, one on each side of his keyboard.

El Tropical: This is it! Not that Kat was expecting headquarters to look like the MGM Grand, but casinos, even virtual ones, should at least have some chandeliers, a couple of gaudy suits, maybe some ringing bells for ambience.

As Cora joins them, closing the door and moving to stand beside Goines, Kat senses motion behind her. She spins around, gasping in surprise. A plump boy not more than eleven years old is hunched in a swivel chair in the corner. One hand in a bag of potato chips, he eyes Kat with a freckle-faced stare. She smiles at him but his curious expression doesn't change.

"Curtis!" Goines stomps his foot and the computer man spins around, knocking over one of the empty beer cans. "Where's Manny? I've got his delinquents from San Francisco with me."

"Manny ain't here," Curtis says, his face dripping with

sweat despite the frigid temperature. "Something blew up at the meth lab in Fresno—huge explosion! Nick and Ronnie died, and now some fat-ass narc is poking around. So Manny and the whole crew flew out of here a few hours ago to relocate the lab, leaving me in charge of everything. Fritz was supposed to be here fifteen minutes ago to monitor play activity but I don't know where the fuck he is, and I'm going nuts." He swivels his chair, rolling it down to another computer.

Goines doesn't tell Curtis that Fritz is now out of commission. He cracks his neck, snapping it toward a shoulder.

"Shit!" His elbows lash out like spastic chicken wings. He unbuttons the top of his purple shirt, lights a cigarette. Jim—along with his escort—comes into the room, brushing his hand against Kat's. Kat steps away from him.

Vern asks from the doorway if anyone needs a drink. No one responds. Kat's too tense—and morbidly curious about where this night is going—to think about her thirst. Cora silently follows Vern out of the room.

"What the fuck did Manny say before he left? What did he want me to do with them?" Goines asks, pointing at Jim.

"Beats my ass," Curtis says, trying to keep up with the action on his screen. "It all happened too fast. Hell, you're the *casino manager,* not me."

Goines reaches into his velvet coat pocket and pulls out his cell phone. "What's his number in Fresno?"

Curtis grinds his teeth, then explodes. "What do I look like, a fuckin' operator? Check the 'Rollerdex.'"

While Goines makes his call, Jim steps daringly close to the Sun workstation. He glances at Kat and she tries to motion with her head to step away but he ignores her. At the same time, Goines shouts, "Curtis, the number's out of order. What's going on? You think the lines burned in the explosion?"

"You're calling another cell phone, you idiot." Curtis jumps out of his chair and grabs Goines by the collar. "If you weren't Manny's uncle I'd kick your head in for distracting me at a time like this."

213

The boy in the corner hops to his feet, causing both Kat and Jim to flinch. "Know something 'bout computers?" he asks Jim.

"Yeah."

Curtis is now shouting at Goines, ordering him to hand over the phone so *he* can make the call.

The boy grabs the mouse that Curtis had just been using. He opens up a window. "This computer has 128 megabytes of RAM and runs on a T-1 line," the kid says, showing off. The screen suddenly displays a complex maze of slider bars, check boxes, radio buttons and other various controls.

Kat glances at Goines, who's nervously trying to light another cigarette from his half-smoked first. Curtis is punching numbers on the phone. "Hey, this is Curtis. Manny around?" Curtis shakes his head, glaring at Goines.

"Everything is controlled from here," the boy says, opening up another window and scrolling through a list of names. His sticky fingers touch the screen, leaving smudges on the glass. "These are the people who are playing right now."

A few of the names are highlighted in either gray or red. The boy clicks on one of the gray names and a vertical bar appears next to it. He slides a knob toward the bottom of the bar. In seconds the gray behind the name disappears.

"Now they're going to lose," the boy says, playing with the mouse.

"Hey, get out of here!" Curtis says to the boy, shoving the phone into Goines's chest. "It's past your bedtime."

The boy grabs a Walkman sitting near the computer and runs out, ducking when he passes Curtis.

Kat looks for a chair, sits in the boy's empty seat. This is too much. She remembers winning the first few rounds that night at Jim's. Then his name must've gone to gray. The boy probably spotted it, excitedly hollered for Curtis to check it out. Suddenly Kat's odds dramatically changed and Jim's name was soon highlighted in red.

Jim glances at Kat, his lips as pale as his skin. He then looks back at the screen.

"I need to talk to him now. . . . Yes, I'll hold on," Goines says into the phone, scratching a fresh patch of pink welts on his neck.

"Where's Vern?" Goines shouts, the phone still up to his ear.

"I'm right here," Vern says, coming in from the hall with a glass of mineral water.

"Well watch our hostages, for Christ's sake. I'm not the only—" Goines stands to attention like a trained Doberman. "Manny?" he says.

Then he slouches. "Well tell him to call me tonight. It's extremely urgent! I need to know what to do with the delinquents!" He folds up the phone and slips it into his coat pocket.

"What's the status?" Vern asks as they all move to the living room.

"There was an explosion," Goines says. "Manny's running around, trying to salvage what he can, completely forgetting about *us*. Shit, how could he do this to me? What do I *do*? He's never left without clear instructions before."

"Did they say when he was coming back?" Vern asks.

"Supposedly tomorrow. We'll know more when he calls me back." Goines looks at Jim and Kat, shakes his head. "I guess I'll have to lock you two up in my bathroom for now."

41

El Tropical is rigged.

Underneath the layers of rage and shame at being so fool-ishly gullible, so *Signal*-impaired, shines a tiny flicker of excite-ment over the hot feature Jim has in his hands. If he can get out of here alive, his story will make news around the world—and *Signal* will get it first. They'll definitely take him back.

He and Kat are forced outside, escorted by the ol' Mustang trio. They walk past the car, down a gravel path. Behind Fritz's home are two others. One is small and dark, the wheels still exposed. The other, much larger, is lit up. It looks much more welcoming, with potted plants, lounge chairs, a couple of shade umbrellas, and Astroturf surrounded by a brown wood fence. At the far end of the nicer trailer, a discarded hot tub lies on its side.

Goines leads them to the dingy unadorned home, taking out his keys. Jim wonders how they're going to sleep in a bath-room. Even under these vile conditions he can't stop the ner-vous flutters he feels when he thinks about spending a whole night in a small room with Kat.

"Well, our commitment to this job has been carried out, so

we'll say our goodbyes here," Vern says to Goines. "But don't neglect to call me as soon as Manny returns. I would like to witness any financial transactions that are made between Mr. Knight and the casino. That was part of our agreement, after all."

"Yeah, yeah," Goines says, waving his gun at Jim and Kat, his way of telling them to step toward the front door. His partners head for the fancier trailer across the street.

At the faint sound of an engine they all turn to see a car in the distance, racing toward them. Goines freezes, squinting.

"Oh no," he says, anxiously dancing from one foot to the other. No one pays attention to him.

"Vern, Cora! I think it's Reba! She wasn't supposed to come to town for two more days."

Vern turns around, shrugs like he doesn't know what the big deal is.

"She can't find out about these assholes. She doesn't know anything about this. I told her I was through with Manny's gigs. You've got to hold them at your place."

This is the first time Jim's seen Goines look vulnerable. His hands are twitchy, his posture suddenly drooped.

Vern lets go of Cora, crosses his arms tightly. "Oh Larry, I don't know. This wasn't part of our verbal contract."

"No way, Larry," Cora says, "Why should we take them when you're getting a bigger percentage than us?"

The vehicle is distinguishable now, a white luxury car of some sort.

"Damn it, it's not an option. She can't know about this! You can have another percent. Now take my pistol!"

Vern hops to attention, takes the gun. He shakes his head, says this isn't right, it's out of his league. Goines shoos him away with his hand.

"This will all be settled tomorrow," he hisses. "Go!"

217

Vern takes Kat's wrist, tells Jim to step ahead of him, to follow Cora. She leads them into the fenced area, then across the yard to the front door.

Jim hears the car pull in beside Goines's trailer. He quickly peeks, sees it's a Cadillac.

Silently they enter a kitchen cluttered with pill and vitamin bottles, end up in an earth-colored living room. A WebTV box is the only object Jim notices.

Vern's forehead glistens. "Keep on walking," he says, pointing the gun at them. "Cora, make some food while I escort them to the den. I'll need to take the computer out of there."

Computer. Jim's is still in the trunk of the Mustang. He tries not to think about it as he follows Kat into a humid, windowless room. Everything looks yellow, tinted by fluorescent lighting. The computer is on a clean desk with not a scrap of paper in sight. Just a photo of Vern and an olive-skinned guy with short greased platinum hair, radiant cheeks and round wire-rimmed glasses. The stranger's eyes lock onto Jim's, shiny brown magnets that dominate the picture, cruel yet charismatic. The two men are standing in front of a black Range Rover.

"When you're through admiring me and Manny, pull out the couch," Vern says to Jim. "It turns into a bed."

Manny. Not what Jim had expected. This new image is even more frightening than the one he'd imagined. The casino owner looks so young, attractive, determined, fearless, what Jim would expect a sociopath to look like. Now Kat is staring at the photo.

Jim tugs on the base of the couch, unhinging it. It stretches out into a wavy double mattress.

"I want both of you to sit down and keep perfectly still," Vern says, his gun never off Jim. "You can use this time to meditate on the road that led you here. Especially you, Jim. Your infantile soul is crying for some self-examination."

Jim is about to protest but stops himself. This man is crazy, just trying to trip him up with nonsense.

218

Jim and Kat sit on the side of the bed. The walls are blank except for a diploma announcing a master's degree in psychology from Cal State Northridge, awarded to a Vern Loomis. The man could easily pass for a psychologist, with his goatee, angular jaw and trim physique. How did he end up with Goines, in the middle of the desert, caught up in a casino racket?

The gun is aimed at Jim's forehead but he barely notices it, overstimulated, numb. How strange. The gut-wrenching anxieties that have kept him awake every night for the past 18 months since he began working at *Signal* have finally disappeared, the gun is just a nuisance. He only feels depleted, exhausted.

Cora comes in with a tray of peanut butter sandwiches on wheat bread. She's also carrying a carton of chocolate milk, plastic cups tucked under her arm. She places everything on the foot of the bed.

Vern hands her the gun. "Baby, monitor them while they eat. I'm going to remove the computer."

While Vern starts plucking cords from the back of his computer Cora stands over the bed, eating, one arm jutting out with the gun as if she's ready to fire. Jim can't believe she'd really shoot him but goes along with the plan.

Cora reminds Jim of a cheerleader he used to date in college. The cheerleader had the same lean form and prim-retro style as Cora, the same Christian athlete personality. After five months she confessed to Jim that she had a husband overseas who was studying for a year at the Sorbonne.

Kat doesn't look at anyone while she eats, hasn't connected with Jim in any way since they left South Park.

"Are you almost finished?" Cora asks her husband. Her arm is beginning to tremble and she takes the gun with her other hand.

"Yes, I'll return in a moment," Vern says, carrying the computer out of the room.

Cora winks at Jim, tells him he can find blankets and pillows in the closet.

"I don't like this any more than you do," Vern says to his hostages as he reenters the room. He takes the gun from Cora. "If you just cooperate with us there shouldn't be any trouble."

He and Cora leave, locking the door behind them.

Ways to escape this place immediately come to mind: try to pick the lock and run until they hit the main road; find a way to get online—perhaps via WebTV—and email an SOS to someone, probably a friend of Kat's since Jim has burned all his connections; sweet-talk Cora into helping them out; swipe the cell phone and call the police. . . .

Before Jim has a chance to talk these schemes out with Kat she's on her feet, checking out a small adjoining bathroom. She immediately reappears, paces near the bed.

"There's a window in there, but of course it's too small to climb out of," she says curtly. She won't stop moving.

"I thought we might be able to pick the lock," Jim says, "or maybe I can somehow get Cora to help us. She doesn't seem like the others."

Kat stops in mid-pace. "That's the stupidest thing I've ever heard," she says, her caustic tone catching Jim off guard. "Of *course* she's not like the others, she's *worse*. She's a tease, Jim, she's just fucking with you. As if that wench would ever care about anyone but herself. God, she's disgusting."

"Kat—" Jim doesn't know how to respond. Her anger stuns him. He doesn't dare tell her he kind of likes Cora, a wild spirit mixed up with the wrong crowd. After the way Kat tried to kill her in the bathroom he's surprised Cora's as nice as she is. Kat should hate Goines and Vern, not Cora.

"Well, you can't hate her as much as I hate *Mister* Goines," he says, almost gagging when he thinks of the back seat of the Mustang.

"We've just got to bust out of here tomorrow," Kat says. "I'll kill that bitch if I have to."

Jim wishes she wouldn't talk like that, doesn't understand this harder side of Kat. He saw a flash of it last night, in the apartment, when she accused him of being strained, conservative, constipated. Now she's lashing out at Cora, the only person here who could possibly save them. He needs to get off this topic.

220

"Did you see how the whole operation is rigged? God, how could I have been so ignorant?" Jim whispers, remembering the horrifying red and gray slider bars on Manny's computer. He's never heard of anyone else using the Web to gamble. How could he have been such an idiot?

"Well, these crooks seem lost now that Manny's away," Kat says. "You should have seen Goines and that fat computer guy when you were in the bathroom. They were totally freaked. As long as Manny doesn't show up we might have a chance. These guys might be techno-savvy, but as kidnappers they're not as professional as they like to pretend." Kat picks up the photo of Manny and Vern, scowls, lays it back on the desk face down.

"You're right," Jim says. "See, that's what I mean by you being so perceptive."

Kat doesn't respond the way she did when he told her the same thing in the South American cafe. She's now standing over the bed with her arms crossed.

"Think we could pick that lock?" Jim says, gesturing toward the door.

"Right. And how do we do that?" Kat asks. "The keyhole is on the other side. And they took your wallet, so we wouldn't be able to unlock it with a credit card either."

Jim can't believe Kat's negative attitude. It's like some hateful teenager has taken over her body. He extends his arm, silently asking her to hold his hand, to sit next to him, to be real again.

"I think I'll take a shower," she says, ignoring his invitation. She disappears into the bathroom, locking the door. Jim has a sick feeling that she's turned off, isn't drawn to him the way she was on Haight. And after the way he blew it today with the FBI character he can't blame her.

Jim's neck and face burn, still raw from the pistol-hits he took earlier today. They need to brainstorm their way out of this, but with Kat's dark mood and his dizzying exhaustion maybe escaping is impossible until tomorrow. He checks the closet, finds a couple of pillows, sheets and blankets that he spreads across the bed. Immediately he's under the covers, flinging his shoes, shirt and pants toward the desk. His thoughts blur the instant he shuts his eyes. But he doesn't make it to the dream side. Like a tray of ice spilling onto his face, Cora's muffled voice awakens every cell in his body. She's in the next room, arguing with Vern.

"I don't care! This wasn't the plan!" she screeches.

"Shhh!" After that admonition Vern's words are too soft to be heard through the wall, but Cora soon interrupts him.

"Larry doesn't know what he's doing without Manny's crew. I don't know why you listen to him. This should be *his* problem, not ours. It's a hell of a lot more than we bargained for."

"Keep it down," Vern says. Again his voice drops, as does Cora's, but their bickering tones pull Jim out of bed. He tiptoes to the other side of the room near the desk, puts his ear against the wall. His heart beats too loudly and he hopes no one's returning to check on him.

Vern is barely audible: ". . . Just until tomorrow, I promise. I'll tell Larry he has to bring them to his place. . . . Just another couple of jobs like this one, and . . . back in LA. I'm committed, baby, I—"

"You've said that before," Cora says. Jim holds his breath, straining to hear her waning voice, but nothing else rings clear. She's whining now, and Vern seems to be lecturing her, probably psyching her out the way he tried to do with Jim.

Jim doesn't care what Kat says, he was obviously right. Cora's not like the others. She doesn't want to be here. If only Jim could figure out a way to have a few words alone with her, see if he could enlist her as an ally.

Now the couple is quiet. Something falls over, probably a chair. Jim cups his hands around his ear, pressing harder against the wall.

After a few muffled thuds Cora squeals, "Come to Mama!"

She's cooing now, her words turning to murmurs, giggles,

moans. Something thumps against the wall, causing Jim to hop. The banging continues, in conjunction with crooning bedsprings and a rhythmic yelp.

Jim realizes the shower isn't running anymore. Soon the swishing sound of a faucet in the bathroom stops too. He leaps across the room, turns off the light, dives under the sheets before Kat swings the bathroom door open.

Jim keeps his eyes shut, his back toward Kat. She crawls in next to him, the smooth skin of her back against his. She's not wearing a shirt.

The pace picks up in the other room and Jim's heart accelerates. He's wide awake now, peels himself away from Kat's skin, mortified that she might hear his breathing. He tries to slow it down. What kind of pervert is he, getting so heated over trailer sex at a time like this? Jim scrunches up his face, wishes he were someone else.

42

Kat pulls on a cream-colored sweater and the brown jeans she bought on Haight Street. Too much clothing for this climate but she's got no choice.

Her instincts tell her it's later than morning. Kat rubs her aching skull, hasn't felt this groggy since her last hangover. She doesn't remember dreaming last night, wonders if Cora spiked their chocolate milk. Jim is still out, stone cold. Yes, the bitch must have slipped them some sort of tranquilizer so they wouldn't try to escape.

Since Kat woke up her muddled mind's been ricocheting between scenarios of how they might escape the desert and scenarios of the countless relationships she's crushed. Every time her heart charges out of control she quickly pulls in the reins, evades the unknown before it swallows her whole. Now she feels like a jerk about her catty rage last night. To hell with Cora, jealousy, irrational insecurities . . .

Kat runs to the bathroom, looks out the small window. The so-called trailer park is whitewashed by intense sun. Could it be afternoon already? The window's not large enough to give her a sense of direction, allow her to map an escape route. No bikes in sight, just a couple of cars and a truck whose keys are undoubtedly tucked in their owners' pockets.

A large animal stirs near the front-yard fence. Kat presses her nose against the window to get a better view, realizes it's the boy from last night, on all fours, staring like a pointer at Larry Goines's trailer. Kat looks over at the tin hovel across the way and sees what must be entertaining the kid: a buxom blond woman pouring herself a drink in the kitchen, naked. The woman moves to another room and the boy sprints out of Kat's view.

The rusted medicine cabinet contains only a bottle of aspirin and an old toothbrush. Inside the shower is a plastic bottle of generic shampoo.

Back in the den with Jim still asleep, Kat rummages through the desk, looking for anything with a cutting edge or tip. She finds a box of staples, some creased stationery, duct tape, a black T-shirt that says "I'm Okay, You're Okay" on the back, another that says "Hugs Not Drugs," and a yellowing stack of VERN BEAZEL: INDIVIDUAL/GROUP THERAPIST business cards that sport a Tarzana address. All junk—nothing barbed or razor-sharp.

"What's going on?" Jim asks, slowly sitting up. He reaches for his pants.

"Did you sleep well?" Kat asks sweetly, wanting him to know last night's mood has passed.

She touches the protected diploma on the wall. Glass. She pulls it down. Jim rubs his temples, then stumbles to his feet and leans on the desk in front of her.

"What are you doing?" he whispers.

"I thought maybe we could make some sort of weapon," she says. "We *need* to get out of here, Jim. They'll kill us otherwise. Even if you had the money they'd kill us now that we know who and where they are."

The acrylic frame is cheap, falls apart when she tugs on one of its sides. She wraps the glass in a sheet, then sets it on the bed, pressing down on the bundle with one of her boots until it cracks.

225

"Careful," Jim says softly.

She opens the sheet, relieved to find a knife-sized chunk of glass.

"Can you hand me the duct tape?" she asks.

Jim gives it to her, asks if he can help. But Kat wants to do this herself. She starts bandaging half of the glass blade, creating a handle.

"This might come in handy," she says, tearing the tape with her teeth. She hands the homemade weapon to Jim.

He finally snaps into survivor mode, hurries to get dressed. He notices the "I'm Okay, You're Okay" T-shirt in the open desk drawer, puts it on, then tucks the glass knife under the waistband of his pants.

"You're incredible," he says, sitting on the desk.

Kat can't suppress her smile. She folds the diploma, busted frame, and remaining glass fragments into the sheet and hides the bundle between a couple of blankets in the closet.

"I wonder what time it is," Jim says.

"I think it's late already—at least that's how it looks from the bathroom window. Cora spiked our milk, I'm pretty sure," Kat says.

Jim moans and Kat's glad he doesn't come to Cora's defense.

Not a peep from the neighboring room. Kat takes a deep breath and makes her way to the door, slowly turning its handle in case by some miracle it's unlocked. No such luck.

"Come here," Jim says.

Kat walks over to him, suddenly shy.

"Is everything still okay between us?" he asks.

Her natural reaction is to bristle. Talking about one's relationship is like revealing the secret to a magic trick. Once it's exposed the magic disappears. But Kat doesn't want to blow this. She's surprised she cares as much about Jim as about the imminent danger they face.

"Yeah. I'm sorry if I was distant last night. I don't know why I was like that. Just tired, I guess."

226

"I thought you hated me for blowing the FBI agent's cover."

Kat turns toward him, amazed at how off the mark he was. Could he be so clueless about Cora's overt advances? Impulsively she straddles her legs around him, wraps her arms around his neck, her breath merging with his. Now Jim's the one who seems surprised.

"Of *course* I don't hate you. I was just really riled yesterday, not only from everything that's happened, but it seemed like you and—" Kat shouldn't be telling him this, showing him all her cards like an amateur. Anyway, Cora doesn't deserve any attention.

"Go on. Me and who?" Jim asks.

"Nothing."

"Kat, I'm totally over Mandy. You've got to believe me," he says, misinterpreting her incomplete confession. "That woman is poison, would like to see me on the streets. Shit, I don't even want to *know* what she's telling Chelsea right now."

"What'll you do if they fire you?"

Jim shakes his head. "I don't know. That just can't happen. I *can't* lose that job." His voice rises and Kat motions for him to keep it down.

After the scene with Chelsea and Mandy in the South Park apartment she thought it was obvious that Jim was canned. But then, everyone deserves to be heard. Maybe they'll believe him.

"I don't want to talk about my job." Jim shifts the knife in his pants, makes sure his shirt conceals it. "I can't believe how resourceful you are, making a weapon out of someone's diploma. That's what I love about you."

Love. Kat releases her arms from his neck, needs more air.

"I don't think you realize how smart you are," he says. "You're more clever than these guys, more clever than most people. But sometimes you take a defeatist attitude. If only you'd believe in yourself."

He hits a chord, as usual. Her bad attitude fucks everything up. She plays with his long nail-bitten fingers, braiding them together until his knuckles turn red.

227

"Well, it's hard to believe in myself when I've got nothing," Kat says, hating the stale self-pity reruns that discount everything he just said to her. "No apartment, no job, no money. And no one." Why is she saying this? She knows that last part isn't true. Even if Jim weren't around she'd have Clare and Kimmy and Danny.

"What do you mean, you have no one? I'm here, Kat. And I really care for you. A lot. God, I hope this is just the beginning for us. You're everything I could ever want in a woman."

His words intoxicate Kat, she wants to hear more, hear what that "everything" is that she possesses. Not that she wants to marry him or anything. His conservative dork-boy side is hovering somewhere nearby. But guys never talk to her the way he does, at least not with their clothes on. She squeezes her legs around him and his lips touch the corner of her mouth.

"I'd rather die than leave here without you," he says, pressing his face into the side of hers.

A bit dramatic but Kat lets herself believe him, and this vulnerable trust lifts her. She'd do anything for him right now.

The doorknob rattles and Vern is suddenly standing in front of the desk, his ear plastered to a cell phone. He aims the gun at them. Kat dismantles herself from Jim.

"Good afternoon," he says. *Afternoon.* Kat knew it.

"Larry will be here in just a few minutes," Vern says, covering the mouthpiece of his phone. "And Manny's returning tonight. We suggest you quickly come up with a solid plan to pay your debt, if you want to stay alive."

43

"Both of you, sit over there," Vern says, pointing to a beanbag chair near the coffee table. The room is dim though the curtains are open. Through the window Jim notices a blond cube-shaped woman leaving Goines's trailer.

Goines. Just his name triggers a hot flash.

Jim sinks into the squishy vinyl blob, feels Kat's legs press against his. Her new used jeans are baggy and short, pants a fisherman would wear. If only they were in a boat together, drifting in some foreign green sea, far far away from anything associated with wired life.

In his periphery the television glows without movement or sound and Jim glances at it. His heart stops. *Mandy!* She's on the screen. A photograph of her with pursed lips, crossed arms, wicked brows.

Jim leaps to his knees, leans toward the WebTV image. He sees the headline "Transmitter" and realizes this is *Signal's* Website, its table of contents. Alongside Mandy's photo a high-lighted caption reads "A Tale of Drugs and Digital Deception." In his desperation to read the article Jim's arm extends in mouse-clicking reflex. Then he remembers where he is.

Vern clears his throat. "It was a very interesting article," he says, turning the television off from the couch. "They made you out to be quite a fascinating character."

"Fuck you!" Jim says before he can control himself. He feels the glass blade Kat made digging slightly into his skin, is ready to whip it out, slice this man's shiny head off in exchange for the remote control.

Mandy's never posed for an article before. *Drugs and Digital Deception*—obviously about him. *Jerry. Chelsea.* Do they think he's a con? Are the police after him? Will they believe him?

Vern stands up. "Game's over, big fellow. Sit back down before I blow a hole through your heart."

Kat gasps, her face bleached and small. She nervously leans over and Jim sits next to her, his chest dripping, pounding.

The phone rings and Vern answers, starts talking to someone about a hot tub, his eyes steady on Jim.

"I'm going out of my mind," Jim mumbles. He doesn't respond when Kat places her hand over his wrist.

"Look at that house on the hill," she whispers. "It's got a ham-radio antenna."

Jim glares out the window, sees a small house perched about a mile up the side of an arid brown hill. Jim doesn't know how to respond—what does he care about some seedy hobbyist's antenna? Didn't she see the image of Mandy? And its caption? She should be thinking like him—about destroying this place, getting the hell out of here. But the fact that it interests Kat makes him crane his neck to get a full view of the spindly metal tower.

"Uh-huh," he says.

"Listen, I have an idea," she whispers almost inaudibly. "I know—"

Vern reaches over and shoves Kat, causing her to slam into Jim. He cups his hand over the phone and tells her to keep quiet. Her eyes immediately water.

230

Losing his sense of reason Jim pounces on Vern, trying to reach for the sharp object tucked into the side of his pants. *Draw blood, gouge an artery, kill!!* Vern, in the middle of asking his caller about Jacuzzi jets, kangaroo-kicks Jim in the gut. Jim tumbles over the coffee table, hitting his head on one of its legs. The room somersaults.

Vern hangs up the phone without saying goodbye and trains the gun at Jim.

"That was not okay!" he says to Jim. "You're pushing me too far."

Jim is on fire, his throbbing head splitting with pain. Before he has a chance to orient himself Goines rushes in, says Reba just left to spend the day in Reno. He needs to see Jim, to interrogate him at his house alone. Manny's orders. His oblong eyes scan the room, glimmer when they spot Jim on the floor.

When Vern informs him how unruly Jim's been, Goines shakes his head. "Manny will love to hear this when he gets back tonight. Now get up," he says to Jim. "You're coming with me."

"I thought you didn't want to separate us!" Jim cries, petrified at the thought of being alone with Goines again. No one acknowledges him except Kat, whose expression begs him to keep quiet. He notices a fresh sore on Goines's bottom lip and gags.

"Good," Vern says. "Take him off my hands. I guess I can accept responsibility for the girl for a *little* while longer."

Jim shakes his head, tries to cling to the rug, but already he's in the kitchen, everything moving quickly, in slow motion, with the so-called casino manager digging an ornate dagger into his ribs. Jim weaves through the front yard, his head still whirling like a lopsided top, but Goines steadies him with a firm grip.

Jim sees the boy from yesterday popping a wheelie on his bike between the trailers. The sun beats on Jim's face, a brief reminder of real life. The next second he's tripping over metal steps, shuffling across a dingy living room with an avocado linoleum–tiled floor. Dozens of unassembled cardboard boxes are stacked against the walls, and a small table sits in a corner, covered with a pile of wires, a disheveled mound of paper, and a paperback book called *The Satanic Bible* by Anton Szandor LaVey.

Goines clears his throat, fidgets with a pack of cigarettes. "Sit down," he says.

Jim sits on the edge of a black high-backed booth-style couch, the only seat in the room. A large piece of fiber glass stacked on cinder blocks serves as the coffee table. Goines sits next to him.

"What did you do to piss off Vern?" he asks, lighting a cigarette. He places a strong hand—the same one that holds his weapon—on Jim's thigh, caressing the trousered leg with the dull edge of his knife.

The room is dark, its blinds morbidly shut, and the stench of stale liquor emanating from Goines's mouth triggers another gag. Jim turns his head, wonders if he could successfully make a grab for the dagger. Goines is decrepitly pale, intoxicated, and strangely uncomfortable. With his free hand the old man unbuttons the top of his shimmering gold polyester shirt, revealing the same holographic pentagram he wore the other day.

"Cat got your tongue?" Goines asks, extinguishing his half-smoked cigarette. Shifting the dagger to his other hand, he slides his fingers along Jim's thigh. As Jim reflexively stands up Goines jumps on him, presses the tip of the knife into his groin. A sick gush of adrenaline shoots up Jim's colon and spine. The decadent man leans into Jim, forcing him back to the couch.

It's even worse this time when Jim is forced to open his mouth. He's alone with Goines, trapped in the cadaverous man's own stifling lair, no one else expected for hours. Goines lies on top of him, wrapping his tongue around Jim's, the knife now at his throat. Again Jim's eyes pool up. His throat contracts, guttural retching sounds erupting from his throat. He struggles to wriggle free but Goines keeps him in place, knocking him in the head with the thick steel handle of his sword-like blade. Bullets of pain splatter across Jim's skull, all he sees is red static. Their teeth gnash together as Goines excitedly bucks his jaw. Jim tries to shut his mouth but it's as if Goines has it clamped open with a car jack.

"Take them off," Goines says, coming up for air. He tugs on Jim's pants.

"Please," Jim whimpers. "Don't do this."

"Don't do what?" Goines says through heavy breaths. His body is trembling as much as Jim's. The madman humps Jim over his pants, then fumbles with Jim's fly, manages to unzip it.

"Take them off." Goines snickers and bites Jim's neck.

No! Jim shakes his head, challenging Goines's threat to kill. He'd rather be stabbed to death than strip down for this monster. Goines raises his arm, ready to strike Jim's skull again.

No more pain! Jim abruptly changes his tactic, reaches for his pants, brushes his own handcrafted dagger with his pinkie. He whispers, "Don't hurt me. I'll do what you want." If he can just keep control of his mind and wait patiently for *the right moment.*

Goines smiles, starts undoing his own slacks. His skeletal body hardens, still trembling, his small bulge mashing into Jim's hip. Again Jim whimpers, barely able to maintain his cool facade. He concentrates on his breathing, tries not to panic. Goines grunts, attempting to kick off his own pants without interrupting his grinding motion. He savagely twists and kicks his legs, suffocating Jim with another slug-tongued French kiss. Then he tries to get into Jim's boxer shorts.

Jim feels on the brink of emotional explosion. *Hold it together!* He reminds himself of who he is: a college graduate from Orange County, a successful editor at *Signal,* a man of intelligence and power, a survivor.

"I'll do what you want," he repeats to Goines, who keeps reaching into Jim's pants, losing his balance each time he tries to feel some skin.

Jim tells Goines he can't take off his pants with so much weight on him. Goines slides to one side, the hand with the knife limply hanging off the couch. A small window of opportunity, perhaps Jim's only chance.

Slightly lowering his pants to appease his attacker, Jim

casually reaches for his hip, pinching the taped end of his blade.

"Turn over, you fuckin' whore," Goines says, beating his own cock.

Jim lifts his waist as if he's about to flip, then plunges his hand with the glass scalpel into Goines's neck. He hits his mark, but the weapon glances off the older man's skin.

"What the—?" Goines's face blisters with veins as he realizes what's just happened. "I don't care *what* Manny wants us to do with you. I'm sending you to hell!" Goines says, raising his knife over Jim's head. "No one fucks with me. Hail Satan!"

Jim abruptly bends his leg, kneeing Goines between his thighs. At the same time he twists his torso and with one swift fluid motion slits Goines's neck with the glass weapon. Blood squirts onto Jim's shirt, splashing all over his face and neck. He waits for Goines to fight back, expects his own head to roll off the couch. But Goines drops his weapon on the floor and collapses over Jim, struggling with his arms to pull himself up. Jim reaches for the heavy dagger, hurls it across the room. It crashes into a mirror, causing Goines to flinch. The man's body is heavier than before, pinning Jim to the couch. Blood keeps pouring out.

"Oh God," Jim moans. He grabs a clump of hair to lift the man's head off his chest. Goines's mouth drops open, more blood spurting from his neck. The man tries to speak but his voice box gives out.

Jim involuntarily barks, frantically flaps his arms, uses all his strength to roll the body off him. Goines thuds to the floor. Bursts of guttural noise explode out of Jim's nose and mouth. With unsteady hands he zips up his pants, then leaps over the man, knocking his knee into the fiberglass tabletop. He ignores the pain.

234

"A phone!" he shouts at the gasping Goines. "Where's a phone? We've got to call 9-1-1!"

Jim rotates in place, searching desperately for a phone. He notices a cell phone on the floor, on the other side of the table.

Jim hits the buttons quickly, aware that Goines is fighting for each breath.

"Your fraud-prevention feature has been activated," Jim hears. *"To make a call you must first deactivate this feature. This message—"*

"It's blocked!" Jim screams. "What's the code?"

One of Goines's hands drops to the floor, the other relaxes on his red-puddled chest. His eyeballs roll to one side.

Aargh! Jim's teeth chatter, though the temperature must be well over 85 degrees. He moves onto a dry spot of the couch and bends over the body, checking for a pulse, verifying that Goines is dead. *Dead!*

Jim wobbles to his feet, his hands soaked with blood, and runs frenetically around the living room, not sure what to do next. He looks for another phone, doesn't find even a jack. He tries the cell phone again, smearing it with a red handprint, then drops it to the floor.

Jim Knight, murderer. Manslaughter, trial, prison. He knows he acted in self-defense and most likely wouldn't do time for this, yet he's filled with a sick panic. The lies the Loomises will certainly tell, combined with the false impression Mandy and Chelsea have of him now—couldn't those things convict him? And Manny! What will the mobster do if he finds out Jim killed his uncle? He runs to the window, peeks out, doesn't see anyone.

A growing pool of blood surrounds the corpse, whose pants are still tangled around its ankles. Reaching across the coffee table from the far side of the body, he pulls Goines's pants up a ways, then searches his pockets for the car keys. They're empty. Jim tries to think clearly, keeps blanking out, finds himself hyperventilating.

Lighting a cigarette, he tries to make a mental flowchart of his next moves.

235

The first logical step is to clean up—the floor, the couch, the phone, himself. After that, he's got a couple of options. He can:

A. Find the car keys, return to the Loomises as if Goines sent him, wait for the right moment to take Cora hostage with the knife, then rush Kat—and Cora if need be—to the car. From there:

   1. Drive to some unknown destination

       1a. where they can live on the lam happily ever after.

       1b. where Kat can separate and go home if that's what she wants, he remaining forever a fugitive.

   2. Take Kat back to San Francisco, try to clean his hands of this mess and somehow avoid going to jail.

Or:

B. Hide the body first, then attempt plan A, leaving him with less to explain to the authorities if he opts for the San Francisco route but more chance of fouling up his escape from this rat hole.

Or should he pack the body in the trunk of the car, then go to plan A, which was . . . ?

Jim loses his flow of thought, doesn't even remember the first step anymore. He takes another cigarette, lights it with his first one. The lifeless flesh in front of him makes it hard to focus. He walks away from the body, paces from the living room to the bedroom—a stark, cavelike area with only a candle-encircled mattress on the floor, buried beneath twisted bedding, a woman's floral suitcase, heaps of mostly leather, vinyl and velvet clothing, a black cape, a pair of handcuffs, and a bottle of whiskey.

Jim gasps for air. *Blood stains, the body, Lysol,* DNA, *cops, Kat, fugitive, Mandy,* Signal, *death row* . . . His thoughts pulse like a strobe light, flashing too quickly, giving him no cues as to what to do next. He hugs himself, stepping from side to side. This can't be his end, he repeats to himself. This *can't* be what he's all about, his life's sum total.

44

This isn't right. Here she is, still sitting in the beanbag chair, drinking a cup of half-decent coffee that Vern finally gave her, while Jim is probably sitting under a hot spotlight getting the third degree.

Kat just hopes Jim is feeding Goines's hope. If these crooks think there's a way to collect on Jim's supposed debt, *maybe* they'll set her and Jim free. She wishes she could be there to help Jim with some fast-talk.

She remembers what he told her this morning, about wanting to be with her when this is over, about her being "everything" to him. He says she's perceptive, but *he's* the one who knows how to wrap her heart with words. It's hit and miss with him, but there are dizzying moments when he's everything to *her*. But then Kat wonders if she could seriously date him if they were immersed in their South Park routines again. What with his *Signal* attitude, *Signal* friends, and all.

South Park routines. She's never realized how much she hates being an intern, working for free, degrading her self-worth, self-confidence. Even here she's not important, practically invisible in her captors' eyes, just extra noise to watch out for. *She* was the one who racked up the blackjack debt, but Jim's the center of their focus. Funny how it takes hundreds of miles from real life to figure out what's really going on. Power and stability would be a pleasant change. She needs a bona-fide job.

Vern is standing by the window, trying to keep an eye on Kat while he spies on his wife, who's talking to someone out front. His fists are clenched, his face red. He whips out a small brown bottle with a rubber bulb dropper and squirts some fluid into his mouth, grimacing at the taste.

"It's funny how we forsake our own instinctual strength for the false security of another's program," Vern blurts. He spins around, stunning Kat. This is the first time anyone but Jim has directly addressed her since they stepped into the Mustang yesterday. She doesn't respond, not understanding what was just said.

"Even if you weren't here you'd be dying. Why do you spend your life following men who think nothing of you?"

Kat can't believe what she's hearing. *Go to hell.* This psycho doesn't know anything about her. She looks out the window, notices Cora throwing her head back in laughter. Kat can't see who she's talking to. Vern glances at his wife, clenches his jaw.

"Your boyfriend's psyche is trapped in the id. He's stuck in his first and second circuits, if you will, never quite progressed past those rudimentary stages of development." Vern unconsciously begins to slap his thigh with the side of the gun. "So how can you expect him to care for you? He's only out for number one: himself. His biggest concern is his penis, an extension of his ego, and he'd love to stick it in my wife. Hell, he'd leave you here to fend for yourself if it meant saving his own ass."

Not true. She tries to mute his toxic words before they taint her. This quack doesn't know anything. Kat steadies herself, won't let him brainwash her.

238   "Jim's not my boyfriend," Kat manages to say. The coffee suddenly tastes like dirty water.

Vern's head bobs a few times, following some movement outside. Then without warning he bolts back to the couch, propping his legs on the coffee table. His short breaths fill the room.

Cora walks in with a small package wrapped in aluminum foil, beaming at no one. Mullet-boy—the one who answered Manny's door last night—follows her in. He reminds Kat of an underfed rooster, his narrow face framed at the top with short spiked bangs, the rest of his longer tresses pulled back by a rubberband. His glassy eyes don't focus on anything in particular.

"Hey," the rooster says. He looks in Kat's direction.

"Johnny just talked to Manny on the phone," Cora says to Vern.

"And why do you think you should deliver the message to my wife ahead of me?" Vern asks, frowning.

"Well I—"

"What did Manny say?" Vern interrupts, scooting to the edge of the couch.

Cora goes to her purse, which is near a video rack, starts rummaging through it. Her tits are pointier than ever in her spandex leotard. How could Jim find her appealing?

"He'll be rolling in at 8:00 tonight. Says while he interrogates the delinquents he wants you to prearrange a pickup at the bump. For midnight." Johnny quickly looks at Kat, as if signaling that she's somehow involved with their pickup.

8:00. Kat scans the room for a clock, can't find one. Not more than half a day left and still no plan, no escape. At midnight she'll be waiting at some meeting place called the "bump." Where will they take her from there?

Cora finds what she was looking for: a plastic drinking straw cut to one-third its size. She grins and winks at her friend.

Vern frantically shakes his head, springs to his feet. "What are you doing?"

Cora laughs at him. "It's just a little present Johnny brought me. I don't want to get into it with you right now." She tells Johnny they can sample "it" in the den.

Every muscle in Kat's body stands alert, waiting for their cue. If only she knew the command. Time is gaining on her, paralyzing her ability to think this out. She knows one thing for sure: she can't slip away as long as Vern holds the gun.

239

"Cora, if that's what I think it is, this is not okay. Hand the present over." Vern holds his palm out.

Cora's face hardens. She turns away from her husband, marches into the kitchen, out of Kat's line of vision. Vern follows her, then whips around to look at Kat, remembers his duty.

"Stop treating me like a child," Cora snaps.

"Damn it, Cora. You know the cycle will just repeat itself again. You can't handle methamphetamine." Vern keeps one foot in the living room, one in the kitchen.

"And you can't handle the simple responsibility of getting me out of this goddamn park," she says. "Manny doesn't trust women with his computers, so what else am I supposed to do with my time?"

Vern raises his voice. "Don't talk to me in that tone, Cora. I know you're not happy here, I *got* that. What I don't get is your hurry-up driver. Why can't you be patient? Only another gig or two with Larry before we've saved enough to go back to the Valley, and with my Epstein-Barr coming to a closure . . . "

Kat's attention is diverted from this litany by the sight of someone peering out the window across the way, at Goines's trailer. It's odd how the blinds are all shut in the middle of the day. Jim's been gone too long. She plants her feet firmly on the ground.

Seeing that Johnny intends to stay in the living room, Vern relaxes his guard, joining Cora in the kitchen. Kat dares herself to escape through the living room window, wonders if Johnny will holler if she stands up. But she doesn't know what she'd do, where she'd go, especially with Jim still stuck in Goines's trailer. Maybe she could distract Goines somehow, throw a rock in his window or something, then make a run for it with Jim. She feels the floor underneath her feet.

240 "Got her covered there, Johnny?" Vern calls from the kitchen.

"Yeah, she's not going anywhere." Johnny takes a seat on the couch, pulls a clear plastic bullet of white powder out of his shirt pocket and sticks it up his nose. After a drawn-out snort he offers some to Kat.

"No thanks."

"Where you from?" he asks, shoving the bullet up his other nostril.

"Chicago," she lies. As if she'd give this derelict any personal information. She steers the conversation away from her.

"Who lives in that house on the hill?"

Johnny wipes his nose and stashes the drug back in his shirt pocket. He looks at Kat.

"That old geezer isn't anybody. Just some antisocial kook who keeps to himself."

Johnny keeps pinching the bullet from the outside of his shirt, as if afraid it'll disappear on him.

"You work for Manny too?" Kat asks.

"Yep. Almost everyone around here does. Once you hook up with him you can never leave. Those two"—Johnny points to the kitchen—"they'll never make it back to LA. Not unless Manny can use them down there." Johnny starts tapping his feet. "Yeah," he says, his eyes losing focus. "This place is funded by the mob. That Manny, he's a real son of a bitch. But then life sucks, so what?"

Cora wails from the kitchen. "I *hate* you!" she screams. "I really *hate* you!" A glass shatters.

Vern moves out of striking range, resuming his post between the kitchen and the living room. "Shhh," he says to Cora, trying to calm her down. "Come on, baby. Stop with the cold pricklies." He lowers his voice. "I'm sorry, it's my fault. I was in my pig-parent again, trying to control you. Please, be a good girl." Vern's eyes keep shifting from his wife to Kat.

Cora is silent.

"I trust you know your limits. Just don't ever use that stuff around me, that's all I ask. Do it when I leave for Yosemite next month."

He disappears into the kitchen again for a moment, perhaps embracing Cora. Then they both come back to the living room together, Vern's arm around his wife. She's dabbing her eyes, her face a bloated cranberry.

Vern plops down on a torn rocking loveseat on the other side of the room. He sets the gun in his lap and clasps his fingers together, stretching, then cracking them.

Cora plants herself on Johnny's lap, cuddles up.

"I need to get some fresh air," Vern says, scowling at Johnny and Cora. He obviously doesn't enjoy his wife's ass on Johnny's crotch, though it was fine, even intriguing, when it was nestled on Jim's.

Vern takes a corner of his shirt and wipes his forehead with it. "Cora, would you call Larry, see if he's almost finished with Jim, see if we could drop the girl off at his place? I've got to get out of here."

Cora gets off Johnny's lap, leaves the room for a moment, returns with a phone.

Johnny stands up. "I really better go," he says, tapping his teeth together after he speaks.

"Oh, okay," Cora says. "Thanks again for, you know."

"No problem." Johnny leaves without acknowledging Vern.

Cora hits a button on the phone, squishing into the same chair as Vern. He puts his arm around her.

"His phone isn't on," she says.

Sharp hunger pangs shoot through Kat's gut and she timidly asks if she could have something to eat. Both Cora and Vern compose themselves—he grabbing the gun from his lap, she jumping to her feet, standing erect.

Cora looks questioningly at Vern and he tells her to make Kat a sandwich, says he'd like one too, with some sparkling apple cider.

"Let's make it snappy," he says to his wife. "After we eat we'll go to Larry's and drop her off. It's *his* turn to babysit."

242

45

Jim heaves repeatedly, bent over a small leaking toilet, then puts the seat down and sits to think.

He hasn't been able to find the goddamn car keys, has to plan a whole new strategy. Maybe hide the body from Manny's brood as best he can to buy time, try to find someone who'll let him use a phone, call the FBI. Perhaps the man who was beaten up by Goines for wrecking his motorcycle would help him out. Fritz. He might relish the chance to bust his neighbor.

If only he could discuss this with Kat, she'd probably think of something he's forgetting. He never wants to be away from her again, wants to patch this catastrophe for her. *She's the one.*

Jim splashes cold water on his face and over his bare chest, sponges himself down with a brown frayed towel, using a bar of soap to help rub off the blood. The small mildewy bathroom has no ventilation, smothering Jim's every breath. He opens the cabinet under the sink to see if a body would fit. Way too small, especially with large dripping pipes in the way.

The bedroom has only a chest of metal drawers and a narrow closet that's already jammed with bright, costume-like clothing, an old computer, a box of tools, and other junk. On the off-chance the car keys are in the flimsy dresser, Jim rummages through each drawer. They're filled mostly with women's lingerie and blouses, hair products, and strange metal cups and gargoyles. Jim shudders. He finds a black T-shirt and puts it on, hoping Vern and Cora don't notice the missing "I'm Okay, You're Okay" psychobabble on the back. The car keys don't turn up, but underneath a pile of men's socks and briefs he finds his wallet, his Rolex, and an overstuffed money clip— could be hundreds of bucks in cash. He stuffs the booty in his front pocket. Time is running out. When is Manny coming?

Jim runs to the living room with another damp brown towel, stumbling over his own feet. *What?* He freezes a few feet from the couch. The boy from Manny's office is squatting next to the corpse, his shoes right in the blood. He's cautiously touching a lifeless eyeball with his index finger. The boy looks up, jumps away from Goines when he sees Jim. A spot of blood stains his striped T-shirt.

No one should see death at such a young age, and Jim feels responsible for gouging a piece of the boy's youth. Not that this kid's innocence hasn't already been desecrated by his depraved community. But seeing him here makes it all too gruesome and Jim is flooded with shame and self-disgust. He catches his warped reflection in the metal trim of the couch and gasps.

Jim and the boy stand motionless, each waiting for the other to make the first move. Jim expects the kid to run out, announce to the entire aluminum village that Goines is dead. That Jim is the murderer. *Murderer!* Jim tries to shake the title from his head.

"Where's the knife?" the boy finally says, throwing Jim with his calm demeanor.

Jim points across the room. "It was in self-defense," he says, as if pleading to a jury. "He was trying to kill me."

244

Seeing that the boy isn't about to run out, Jim sits on an arm of the blood-splattered couch, tries to gain composure. What's he supposed to tell this kid? Jim has no choice but to trust the boy, try to enlist him as an ally.

"Listen, you can't tell anyone you saw me in here, okay?

They'll kill me if they find out, and it really was an accident."
Jim presses his hands together as if in prayer.

"I know," the boy says, "he was trying to kiss you. He
deserved it."

Jim nearly falls off the couch. He takes a few steps back,
away from the kid.

"How—?" Jim looks around, wonders where the kid
could've been hiding.

"I saw the whole thing," the boy says. "On the computer
screen. See that light?"

Jim looks up at a dim track light on the ceiling, his mind
reeling with the lurid scenes this kid just witnessed. "Yeah."

The boy flicks the light off. "It has a hidden camera in it.
Manny put one in everybody's living room. Only me and
Curtis—my uncle—know about them."

"Oh God," Jim squawks. *The kissing, the humping, the glass
blade, the corpse . . .*

Manny will know what Jim did to his casino manager, will
severely punish him. To death. He runs to the window, peeks
through the blinds, sees no movement. The view looks like a
bad two-dimensional photograph.

"I won't tell on you," the boy says. "I *hate* Mr. Goines. He's
mean."

"But the tape! Where is it? Who else saw it?"

"Don't worry, with Manny gone only my uncle Curtis
would have seen it. But he's crazy right now 'cause of the disaster in Fresno. A man named Fritz was supposed to help him
with the casino but he's in the hospital, got beat up the other
night." The boy looks up at the light. "I already erased the
tape. How else could I have come over to inspect the body?
They'd kill me if they knew I was here."

Jim's too panicked to realize how fortunate he is to have
found a lonely, curious boy in the trailer park. "I've got to get
out of here! What do I do now? What do I *do?*" He steps
toward the near-translucent corpse, knowing he somehow
must make it disappear.

"Why don't you take him to the bump?" Roddy says.

245

"Bump?" Jim asks, the walls beginning to pulsate, time reaching its limit. He'll take the dead man *anywhere* away from here.

"Yeah," the boy says, moving toward the kitchen. Jim hears the refrigerator door open. "The place where they drop off dead bodies. If you stick him by the edge of the stream, someone will pick him up and dump him somewhere in the middle of the desert. I tried to follow them once, but they went too far."

The boy comes back into the living room with a can of soda. His eyes are sparkling. "Want me to get my wagon? We can take him there."

"Okay," Jim says quickly, knowing it's wrong to involve the boy but too desperate not to take him up on his offer. "Just *hurry,* and don't let anyone see you."

As soon as the boy leaves Jim assembles one of the large boxes, hating himself more and more. He's too tired and repulsed by the situation to cry, feels empty, void of humanity. He lays the box on its side, then notices a plastic tarp wedged behind the stack of cardboard against the wall. He opens up the plastic, realizes it's a motorcycle cover, the perfect size to wrap up Goines.

The corpse is heavier than he'd imagined and he uses all his strength to drag the body out from between the table and the couch, rolling it onto the tarp. He grabs both the hunting knife and Kat's homemade scalpel, along with the dirty cell phone, and piles them on top of Goines.

An oblong pool of blood is coagulating on the linoleum floor. Jim drapes his towel over it, sees that it's drenched in seconds. He runs into the bedroom and grabs the bedspread, uses it to mop up the vinyl couch and the rest of the floor, eliminating the bloody shoeprints left by the boy. Jim spins around, making sure every drop has been sponged before he spreads the bedspread, along with the bloody T-shirt and towels, over Goines's body. Woozy and drenched with perspiration, he wraps the whole mess up inside the tarp.

"Ready?" the boy says, panting by the door.

246

"In a minute." Jim runs to the kitchen and washes his hands and arms again. Then he drags the human burrito toward the front door, shudders when he sees Vern's trailer across the way. The boy tells Jim to roll the body down the stairs, let it fall into the wagon. Jim follows the order, then jumps to the ground. He grabs the wagon handle. It's a heavy load and he feels naked until they round the trailer, out of Vern's line of sight.

"Follow me," the boy says. "I know how to dodge all the cameras."

The wagon catches on every little scrap of debris, making it hard to pull.

They pass Fritz's pink-and-white trailer and Jim is tempted to just dump the body in the middle of the road and knock on the drunk's door for the phone. But the boy said Fritz is in the hospital.

"How far is this place?" he asks his young friend.

"The way we're going, about a 15-minute walk. It goes a lot faster when you don't have to worry about being seen."

The trailer park is even more dismal in the daylight than it was last night. A faded sign with cracked letters looms over Jim: WELCOME TO LOVE PARK. He discovers that at least half the mobile homes are abandoned. Could be only eight or nine out of around 18 that are actually in use. Jim sees one adult—a middle-aged woman in an electric go-cart trying to catch a dog—but she doesn't look his way.

Jim asks the kid what his name is.

"Roddy," he says.

They walk in silence for most of the way, Roddy huffing more than Jim. They're now too far to be seen from Vern's vicinity. The oppressive sun sears Jim's scalp and he wonders if it's damaging his brain. Can't stop the flashbacks: *sluglike tongue, bucking jaws, tenacious hands, oozing neck, wrapped corpse.* He's stuck in a continuous loop, replaying the same scene with Goines over and over and over. Then the boy, touching the eyeball.

247

"See that shed?" Roddy asks, startling Jim. "That's where the bump is."

When they reach the wooden shed, perched above a dried-up stream, Roddy disappears inside. He steps out with a U.S. flag and places its long pole in a slot carved into the outside of the hut. He tells Jim to lay the body in back of the shed, says it'll be gone by tomorrow.

"They usually *schedule* for a pick-up," he says, "but when the men see this flag they'll know there's a body for them."

"What men? What do they do with the bodies?" Jim asks, not sure if the boy already explained.

Roddy shrugs.

The walk back is faster—*too* fast. He still hasn't got a plan to save Kat and himself. Manny's coming back sometime tonight. The Mustang keys are nowhere to be found. If he goes back to Vern's, they'll be at square one, with only one of the players 86'd. And there's no way he could hike to the highway in this heat.

He simply can't go any further without a plan. Spotting a large boulder slightly shaded by a scrubby desert tree, he veers away.

"What are you doing?" Roddy asks.

"I need to think," he says.

Slumping down on the boulder he reviews the situation. The most important step is finding a phone. No one knows where he and Kat are and that needs to change. If they're killed and taken to the bump they'll never be found, will end up another statistic on *Unsolved Mysteries*.

"Do you know if anyone's at Manny's place today?" Jim asks.

Roddy is throwing stones at a distant cactus.

"My uncle is in charge of the casino while Manny's gone. The only time he'll leave is to eat, shit and sleep."

248

Jim is sure he didn't speak like that at Roddy's age.

"Your uncle Curtis?" he asks.

Roddy nods.

Jim digs into his pocket, pulls out the money clip. Roddy perks up, his Frisbee-eyes spinning over the cash.

"Listen," Jim says. "How would you like to be my secret agent? I'll pay you 30 dollars."

The boy claps his hands and squeals.

"Here's the plan. I'll hide out and wait for you here behind this rock. I want you to find me a cell phone that works. If you can't get me one, keep a close eye on Manny's place. As soon as your uncle leaves there, I want you to report back to me. Is that a deal?"

"Yes! Are you going to pay me now?"

Jim hands him 10 dollars, tells him he gets the rest when the mission is accomplished.

"Oh, and if you can see what's going on at Vern's place—you know, from the videotape—please check on my girlfriend, Kat. Let me know what's going on over there."

Roddy swiftly nods once, as a soldier taking orders might do.

Even with the slight protection of the tree, the sun-drenched boulder burns Jim's skin through his T-shirt. His head is a sphere of fire. In a dizzy stupor he remains on his uncomfortable perch, his ravished stomach folding in on itself. Why didn't he think to have Roddy bring him a snack? He watches the shrinking red wagon as his prepubescent savior goes back to Love Park.

46

Cora knocks on Goines's trailer but no one answers. She tries the handle and finds the door unlocked.

"Let's go in," Vern says, prodding Kat in the back with his gun.

Obviously Goines isn't home, his trailer so dark that Cora, scouting ahead, bashes into a kitchen chair, scattering a bunch of coins across the floor.

Vern moves slowly until he lifts the blinds, the sun streaming in.

"You don't think he would've taken off to sell blood at the plasma center, do you?" Cora asks, getting on her knobby knees to collect the money she knocked over. "He buys these stupid silver ingots with the cash they pay him."

"Don't be ridiculous," Vern says from the living room. "As if he'd be thinking about his ingots with a hostage on his hands."

Cora slams the ingots on the chair. "Maybe he wanted to sell Jim's blood too," she says.

Vern comes into the kitchen, tells Cora to check the bedroom. He sits on the edge of the chair, flips his bug-eyed mirrorshades to the top of his head. His posture is wilted, his goatee limp with moisture. Something's rotting in the trashcan and Kat breathes through her mouth to avoid gagging. Vern looks at her, tells her again that he doesn't like this any more than she does.

"No one's back there," Cora says. "Maybe they're at Manny's."

Something isn't right. The place is too quiet, was too dark when they first stepped in. Kat smells death in the air but tries to combat her instinct with positive images. She visualizes Jim happily typing at his computer in the grass of South Park. *Please don't be dead.*

She doesn't remember leaving Goines's trailer, suddenly finds herself walking toward Manny's, sandwiched between the Loomises. Every hair follicle on her body tingles. If they killed or mangled Jim she'll never forgive herself. Her life will be ruined. What a fool she was at his house that night with Yoke and her friends. She remembers mocking Jim's stiff walk, imitating him on the clarinet, playing with his Website like she owned the place. Just an ignorant intern trying to earn some guffaws at his expense.

A trumpeting car horn snaps Kat into the present. A white Cadillac pulls up and the buxom woman who was naked this morning unrolls the window. She's wearing large boxy glasses with a rhinestone R set into the corner of one of the lenses.

"Hi there!" she says to Cora and Vern. Her voice is thunderous.

Cora waves. "Reba! How are you doing?"

"Have you seen Larry?" Vern asks before Cora and Reba have a chance at chitchat.

"No, I've been in Reno all day. Had a couple of tax clients I had to see, and then I scored myself a bottle of Rohypnol. Here," the heavyset woman says, digging into a worn leather purse the size of a beach bag. She pulls out a plastic bottle and taps two white pills into her hand. Vern smiles, welcomes the barbiturate with an open palm. The smuggled drug from Mexico doesn't rile him like meth does. Cora immediately takes the pills from Vern and slips them into her skirt pocket.

"Boy is the sex gonna be hot tonight!" Reba says with a

251

laugh, exposing a large purple tongue and bridge-lined teeth. Kat notices a deck of tarot cards on her dashboard.

"How long are you going to be in town?" Cora asks.

"Just a few nights. Who's your little friend?"

"Uh, just a customer. In fact, we'd better split," Vern says. "Thanks for the gift."

Reba says goodbye and rolls up her window before churning a cloud of dust in the air.

"What a dysfunctional pair she and Larry are," Vern says.

They walk by the Mustang, approaching Manny's front door.

"Give me that!" a man shouts from Manny's living room.

Cora runs up a couple of steps and peers through the screen door.

"Ouch!" a young voice says.

"The phone is *not* for you to play with!"

Cora raps on the screen. "Curtis?"

The screen door flings open, hitting Cora in the hip. The peeping boy from this morning shoots out, runs off. Curtis steps out, holding a cellular phone.

"Is Larry here?" Vern asks.

"No, haven't seen him around," Curtis says. "Why the fuck isn't he pulling his weight around here? It's disrespectful to Manny."

Kat notices the boy peeking at them from a distant tree, wonders how corrupt the files are in his small developing brain.

"Larry's disappearance is unacceptable," Vern says with a few nervous blinks. "Get in the car," he orders Kat and Cora.

"Don't treat me like *I'm* the bad guy," Cora says.

Vern apologizes, says he can't handle Larry's games much longer, doesn't have the constitution for such ceaseless chaos, wouldn't have taken the job if Larry hadn't promised it would be over after the trip to San Francisco. He hands the gun to Cora, tells her to pay attention to the girl while he drives.

Kat slides into the back seat and rolls down a window. She spots the keys sitting in the ignition and perks up. Do the keys

252

stay in the Mustang at all times? *The perfect getaway car.* Her wardens are beginning to weaken, their emotional and physical frailties threatening to split them apart like a tight pair of jeans that can no longer support an expanded rump. If she can stick with the Loomises for a couple more hours, she'll find a tear large enough to slip through, and the car will be her ticket to freedom. But if they pass her off to Goines or Manny she may not be so lucky.

Vern starts the ignition and cruises around the spiritless park, his head whipping from side to side in search of Goines. Kat imagines the ashen monster burying Jim in some far-off corner of the desert. She shakes her head, tries not to think.

"Damn it," Vern says. "It was very manipulative, sticking me with his hostage, then leaving without informing me. He's always got a hidden agenda."

Cora suggests they wait for Larry at home but Vern accelerates in the opposite direction. He says they couldn't have gone too far or Larry would've taken the Mustang.

After half an hour of circling the park several times, popping into a vacant trailer that Larry occasionally uses for extracurricular affairs, then touring the outlying dirt roads of the mobile neighborhood, Cora leans into the dashboard, shouts for Vern to stop.

Kat sees him too. Jim, springing from the side of a rock and running toward the mountains, away from the car. It's easier to breathe now and Kat forces her bunched shoulder muscles to relax. He's alive!

"What's he doing?" Vern shouts, speeding up, honking. "And where's Larry?"

"Careful Vern!" Cora yells.

The car is off the dirt road now, bulldozing small desert weeds that cover the vast dry terrain. More honks. Jim slides, almost falls, turns around to glance at his pursuers, then slows his pace. He turns around again, looks directly at Kat. He stops moving.

Vern catches up to Jim, opens his door before he brakes the car. A shower of dust sprays Kat in the face.

253

"What the hell are you *doing* out here?" Vern asks. "Get in!"

Jim takes another look at Kat. His face is sunburned, his eyes hard and crazed. He doesn't budge until Vern reminds him that they could easily shoot his girlfriend out here without anyone finding out. Finally Jim crumples into the back seat, slouching like a blow-up doll that's sprung a leak.

Vern has a hard time turning around the car, surrounded by too many boulders and dried-up stubby bushes. He throws the gear into reverse and floors it.

"Where the hell is Larry?" Vern asks, his wet red face turned toward the back window. When they reach the road he slams the car to a skidding halt, fiercely shifts it into forward.

Jim closes his eyes. "I don't know. Some guy came by when we were at his place and whispered something. The next thing I knew Goines took off with him. When I realized he was gone I made a run for it. Sorry."

Made a run for it. Kat grabs her chest. What did it all mean this morning? Didn't he say he'd rather die than leave this place without her? Didn't she mean "everything" to him?

She catches Vern grinning into the rearview mirror, gloating over his earlier words—*He's only out for number one: himself.* He lifts his sunglasses, shoots a sinister I-told-you-so look at Kat.

"Who was the guy Larry took off with?" Vern asks Jim, his frantic voice incongruous with the silent communication he just directed at Kat. "Was it Johnny, the fellow who answered the door last night at Manny's?"

"Y-yeah, I think that's who it was. They were standing by the front door and I couldn't see him too well."

Kat tries to stay focused on the precarious situation at hand. But she can't stop thinking about Vern's biting analysis. *He'd leave you here to fend for yourself if it meant saving his own ass.* Jim opens his eyes and flops his head toward her, mouths out "Hi."

Fuck off. Kat glares, then turns before her eyes pool up. All men suck.

47

Vern pulls the car up to his house and slams on the brakes. He's been silent for the last couple of minutes, now he explodes at his wife.

"I'm going to *kill* that Larry when I see him! How could he be so irresponsible? I can't *do* this anymore. I haven't had any of my treatments for the last two days, I'm going way beyond the call of duty, yet Manny's paying *him* more than *me*."

Jim shuts his eyes again, finds a dark spot deep inside that shields him from the horror of what he's done. From Vern's eruption. From Kat's unexpected glower. From the ominous caption he read on *Signal*'s site. From himself.

Vern tells Cora they need to lock Jim and the girl in the den, then he'll go see Reba, see if she's heard from Larry since they saw her.

The thought of running away at this point seems futile to Jim. His head is heavy, his mind flighty, his body simultaneously aching and queasy and numb. His empty stomach seems to be feeding on itself.

"Baby, prepare a shot for me," Vern says as he pushes Jim and Kat down the short dark hall into the den.

Nothing has changed. The bed is still open, still sheetless. Jim is sure the broken glass is still under the mattress.

Vern shuts—and locks—the door, leaving without saying a word.

Kat's back is toward Jim, her arms are crossed. She's pissed at something.

"Kat, talk to me," Jim says. "They didn't hurt you or anything, did they?"

"I can't believe you," she hisses, abruptly spinning around to face him.

He sits on the bed, takes a few deep breaths, thinks the sun really may've fried his brain. He tries to concentrate on the conversation.

"Why? What did I do?" Each word floats separately, unhinging itself from the rest of his sentence.

Kat slides forward, pushes Jim onto his back, socks him in the chest. "*You're* my problem, you fuckin' asshole. How could you have tried leaving without me? I never would have deserted you." She's crying.

Jim sits up, tries to hold her but she wriggles away with sharp elbows. He should tell her what he did to Goines but can't, can't make it real.

"Kat, please, I wasn't deserting you. I would never leave you. God . . ." His voice echoes in his head, black splotches obstructing his view. Kat splits into two, like Siamese twins connected at the ankles. He pinches himself, makes sure he's awake.

"I was waiting for little Roddy . . . " *Roddy, rock.* What's his point? He's too fatigued to finish, closes his eyes, feels his head sinking into the mattress.

He hears Kat step around the bed, senses her bending over him.

"Are you okay?" she asks, her hands on his cheeks. She shifts his heavy legs, aligning them with his body, then pats his pants. He's not sure what's going on, feels her hand in his pockets. Is she trying to take off his clothes?

She gasps. "You jerk! You *were* on the run. How'd you get your stuff back? And all this money?"

256

Her voice spins with the room, the bed rocks like a ship. His T-shirt, stuck to his skin perhaps by dried blood, pulls on the hairs of his chest.

"I feel really weird." Jim's not sure if he said that out loud.

Then he finds himself floating around the room. He settles back down on the bed when he hears Kat shouting his name. She's banging at the door, screaming for someone to help him. Why? Did he black out? He manages to prop himself up, leans against the headboard. He can think a little clearer with his eyes open.

Cora comes in with the gun in her hand. She asks what's going on.

"I don't know," Kat says. "He's sick, feverish."

Cora tells Kat to stand at the far side of the room. She then slowly approaches Jim, wearing a cute yellow tennis skirt and a white leotard. Jim expects her to toss pompoms in the air. Instead she places a cool hand on his forehead.

"Wow, you're boiling, and your skin is pretty burned. You might have a little sunstroke."

Kat points toward the door. "Call a doctor!"

"Shut your fat trap," Cora says. "He's just dehydrated. No one's calling a goddamn doctor."

She juts her arms out, firmly holding her weapon while she tells Jim to get off the bed. She then orders him to slowly walk to the hall. Things seem more normal to him when he's moving, though he stumbles into the door jamb on his way out. Cora shuts and locks the door before Kat can leave the room.

"Bitch!" Kat screams as Cora leads Jim to the kitchen.

"Sit down," Cora says, pointing to a glass table.

The tabletop is cool and Jim lays his head on it. He watches Cora as she pulls a frozen dinner out of the freezer and pops it into the microwave.

Alone with Cora. Jim pants. This is the moment he's been waiting for, his one chance to get help. If his brain would only cooperate.

Cora then opens a bottle of sparkling apple cider, adds a

small vial of brown liquid that she calls Royal Jelly to the juice and hands it to him with a straw.

"This ought to help you," she says.

And it does. Once he takes a sip of the sweet fizzing elixir he can't stop. He guzzles until the bottle is empty.

Cora smiles, refills his glass with water, stirs in a packet of ground-up vitamin C. "Your chicken enchilada will be ready in six minutes," she says, handing him his drink.

The cloudy C-fortified water isn't as satisfying as the juice and he drinks it slowly. Cora takes two white tablets from her skirt pocket and slugs them down with a bottle of juice, then pulls a folded piece of aluminum foil from the same pocket and sets it on the table.

"Listen," she says, sitting down across from him. "Vern is out for at least an hour. He couldn't find Larry and drove into town with Reba. She thinks she knows where he might be."

Jim's heart revs, kick-starting a bout of hysteria. They're looking for Larry Goines! They'll find the dead body and know he did it! *No. They don't know anything.* He counts to five with each inhalation, making sure he doesn't give himself away.

"Sooo," Cora says with a mischievous grin, "now is my chance to sample this batch of meth. Vern didn't want me to snort it around him."

Putting the gun in her lap, she opens up the shiny package, revealing a small white lump of powder. A memory-balloon bursts: Jim flashes back on the hideous fool he made of himself when he screamed at Sir Kengo, forbidding him to do heroin in his house. Danny snapped at him, calling him a jerk or a geek. He must've been the laughingstock of the party. He tries to remember what happened next, but the past is as warped as the present.

258

Cora sprinkles some of the meth onto the table, then reaches into her pocket for a shortened straw. Without taking time to organize the powder into lines, she vacuums part of it up with her nose.

"Want to try some?" she says, wiping her upper lip.

Jim stares at the drug. "No thanks."

A stream of enchilada fumes wafts around the table and Jim's stomach growls.

"It'll make you feel better," Cora pressures, like the sexy sorority girls used to do when he tried to turn down pot or coke.

"Well, maybe after I eat," Jim lies. "But you go ahead, it doesn't bother me." Maybe if she trips out he'll be able to grab the gun from her, or at least con her into letting him go.

She laughs, moves over and hops onto his lap, wraps an arm around his neck—the same arm that's attached to the gun.

"You're a good guy. I like you," she says, her lips dangerously close to his. Jim reaches for his water and Cora twists away from him, spreading the rest of the powder across the table. Arching her back like a cat, she inhales loudly.

"Come on," she pleads, handing him the straw.

"I don't know. I uh—"

The microwave dings and he jumps, his hand accidentally sweeping a bit of the powder off the table.

"Oh God, sorry," he says.

Oblivious to his clumsiness Cora heads for the microwave and begins to babble. She says Reba used to be their tax consultant when they lived in Los Angeles.

"Then, when we got in financial trouble, she fixed us up with her boyfriend—Larry, of course. She told us he could get us work up here with one of the casinos. I didn't want to come, but Vern didn't know what else to do. This place is a prison, it's hell."

She's repeating what Jim heard through the wall last night. This woman is crying for freedom. Does he dare suggest she leave with him? That they all run off before Vern gets back? If only his head weren't so discombobulated, he'd be more sure of himself.

"Let's go in the other room, where you'll be more comfortable," she says, flopping her gun in the direction of the living room.

Please God please God please God . . . In his panic to smooth-talk Cora before Vern returns he speaks without a private

259

rehearsal. "Cora, if you're not happy here why don't you let me and Kat go, and you can come with us."

"Huh?" Cora takes a step back, her eyes dilating though the lighting hasn't changed. She glances at the small amount of powder left on the table, unconsciously wipes her nose.

Jim smiles, extends a shaky hand. "You don't need that gun. Why don't you put it down?"

"Stop it! Step back!" Cora scrunches her face, curls her lip and unexpectedly fires the muted gun. Glass shatters in the living room.

Jim dives under the table, his pulse pounding into the linoleum as he jiggles his arms and legs to make sure he's still alive. She actually pulled the trigger!

After a moment of stunned silence Cora titters. "Oops. Look what you made me do."

Jim holds his breath.

"Come on, get up. Your meal is getting cold." More titters.

Fear causes a putrid chemical tang to explode in Jim's mouth. He almost loses his bladder as he slowly gets to his feet, doesn't dare look Cora in the eye.

Reaching for his Styrofoam tray with a potholder Cora tells him to walk in front of her. "And take your water," she says.

Like a magnet she follows him into the living room, bumps against his heels. He places the cold glass of water on his throbbing forehead. A blast from the stereo startles him, and suddenly Cora's arm is linked with his. She shimmies her pointed tits to the music as if the gunshot never happened, whisking him past the couch, down the hall. Loud steel and metal bounce off the walls, rattle the floor, wrap around his bones.

She stops at her bedroom, a dim lacy cubicle with a floor that seems to slope dramatically toward the far wall. He hesitates but she pushes him in with the tip of her gun, tells him he should eat if he wants to feel better.

260

As he puts his weight on the bed he gasps, didn't expect the mattress to be filled with water. At first there seems to be a leak, then Jim grabs on to the thin bedspread as he tries to steady his water glass. Half its contents have already splashed onto his pants. He leans against the headboard, huffing like an old man. The music makes him feel old too—so alien to his nervous system.

"Put your left arm behind your head," she says, reaching into the drawer of her night table.

Jim doesn't understand. He lifts up one arm. "What do you mean?"

"I mean I can't completely trust you," she says, pulling out a set of handcuffs. "Wrap your fingers around the bedpost."

"You can trust me." Jim smiles. His lips quiver with the rest of his high-amped body and he wonders if she notices.

Cora points the gun at him. "Jim, I like you. But I like myself better. Now put your damn hand behind your head. I'm not going to hurt you unless I have to."

Jim's arm flies behind his head and in a second it's shackled to the bedpost.

Cora shoves some pillows behind his head, tells him she used to be a nurse.

"Just relax," she says. "Let me feed you." She plops down beside him, creating a minor tsunami.

"Can you bring Kat in here?" he asks.

"No." Her head briefly nods as if she's about to pass out. Then she brightens, grabs his tray of food.

She blows on a forkful of dripping enchilada, then slides it into his mouth. It's still too hot and he spits it back onto the tray.

"Water!" he cries, the skin of his tongue smoldering into fuzzy flames.

"Sorry," she says, laughing. Once she laughs she can't stop, her button nose swelling into a red bulb. He doesn't know what the joke is but laughs as well. This is the part where they bond, a necessary step before he makes another attempt at befriending her. His stomach seems to split down the center and he's hungry enough to eat his own hand. But Cora's clownish cackle comes first. Something must be funny. Jim roars with her, careful not to make another mistake.

48

She's been in the den long enough—Cora's clearly not coming back to check on her. She tucks Jim's wad of money into her pocket. The keys should be in the Mustang, it's time to run. Kat takes a credit card from Jim's wallet and slides it into the seam of the doorway, working the handle at the same time.

She furiously twists the doorknob, not worried about the noise. She can't even hear herself think over the obnoxious stale rock blaring through the walls. Is that Miss Priss's way of nursing Jim back to health? A charlatan in every sense.

Jim. She still wants to save him, even if he did try to fuck her over. But she can't afford to mess up, has to split when she has the chance. She'll have to slip out of here unnoticed, take the Mustang to Reno, call the police, FBI, whoever else she can think of from there. They'll be able to come back and rescue Jim.

Just as the door snaps open, the screeching guitars are cut off by a DJ advertising some nightclub in Reno. Kat pokes her head out of the room, sees that the coast is clear. But as soon as she steps into the hall she freezes. She hears laughter in the bedroom. *Jim and Cora.* Fear turns to disbelief.

Her first reaction is to barge in, break a lamp over Jim's

head, punch Cora till her teeth fall out. That evil wench finally got the lying prick all to herself! The two impostors belong with each other and Kat wants to kill them both. But before she charges for the bedroom door her instinct for self-preservation kicks in.

Taking a deep breath she tiptoes down the hall and cuts across the living room, expecting to take a gunshot in the back. Fueled to high speed with an adrenaline head rush, she's suddenly in the kitchen. She sees aluminum foil and traces of what looks like cocaine or speed on the table.

Vern could barge in at any minute, time is scarce. Kat peeks out the window before opening the front door. A go-cart flies by but its driver doesn't see her. She steps out and runs across the synthetic lawn, her eyes scanning the area for parked cars. *Where's the Mustang?* Frantically she scuttles across the road, crouched low, passing Goines's dump to get to Manny's. She runs around the trailer-deluxe, trying to dodge the cameras that loom above. The Mustang isn't there either.

With the sun setting maybe she could escape by foot without being noticed. She tries to shake the lurid scene she imagines going on in the Loomis trailer, can't even attempt to figure out Jim and his true motives, keeps swallowing to cork her emotions. She makes herself focus on the escape plan. It could take half the night before she makes it to Reno, but a lone hike will do her good. She'll be able to think, purge the latest data from her system. Once she's back in San Francisco Jim will be history.

"Pssst!"

Kat spins around, ready to flee. She sees the boy a few yards away, crouched under Manny's stairwell. He motions for her to meet him at the back of the trailer, then crawls back into darkness.

What the hell does he want? She follows the road they arrived by as far as she can with her eyes, knows she should take off now, but the boy intrigues her. And if she doesn't meet him, maybe he'll rat on her.

Kat sticks to the walls, circling the huge mobile beast until she reaches its rear. With no other trailers in back of this one she feels safer.

In a moment the boy is at her feet. He's coated with a layer of dirt, holding a powerful flashlight and a key. He turns off the light.

"I couldn't get the phone, my uncle's been on it almost all day. But the key will get you into this door." He points at a small door a few feet away from her. "This is the office. Maybe you can call someone from a computer."

The boy hands her the key and flashlight, tells her to use the light if she needs to see anything. He warns her that if she turns on a room light his uncle will probably notice.

"He's not in there now, so you should hurry. I'll go around, hang out by the hall. If you hear me cough, you'll know someone's coming."

Where did this incredible angel come from? Kat asks the boy for the name of the trailer park.

"Love Park."

She thanks the boy, asks him why he's doing this for her.

"For my 20 dollars! I was hoping you'd give me an extra 10 for the flashlight."

Kat nervously snickers, not sure why his entrepreneurial spirit sickens her a bit. Pretty presumptuous to think she'd have that much cash on her. But she does. She pulls out the bills she found on Jim and hands the ballsy kid his fee.

For a nanosecond Kat ponders the 400-and-some-odd dollars, can't imagine how Jim got it. But then she feels the weight of the key in her hand. It slides easily into the door, clicks when she turns it, gets her into the office. A man's voice drones in the other room, a one-sided conversation. Must be Curtis on the phone.

264

She plants herself in front of the Sun workstation. The room is dark but she doesn't need the 10-dollar flashlight to see what's on the screen. She opens an email program and enters as many of her friends' addresses as she can think of—

about 10 in all. Her list includes Clare, Danny, Yoke, Mary, and some virtual friends she's met on The EGG.

Subject: EMERGENCY/KAT ASTURA

This is Kat Astura and I'm in huge danger. I'm being held hostage with Jim Knight from *Signal* at some little trailer town called Love Park, maybe 10 miles from Reno. These people run an online casino called El Tropical and they're very dangerous. PLEASE someone call the FBI!

Curtis's voice gets louder and the boy coughs. Kat quickly types the FBI phone number that was emailed to Jim yesterday when they were in the apartment. She hits "send" without reading over her note, already on her feet, ready to flee.

But her e-note doesn't disappear. A box pops over her message asking for a password.

Shit!

The kid pops his head in the office, sending Kat to the back door.

"It's just me. Hurry up!" he whispers.

"What's the password to send email?"

The boy shrugs. "They don't let me use the Internet."

Kat looks for another email program, doesn't see one.

"Is there a phone I can use?" She'd call 9-1-1, the FBI, her parents . . .

"No!" the kid says, immediately disappearing.

How ironic, Kat thinks. All this technology and no goddamn way to reach the outside world. She deletes her message and grabs the flashlight, ready to make her trek to Reno. But with Curtis at the other end of the trailer she acts on an impulse.

Back at the computer she calls up the gaming program and scrolls through the list of active players. Around two-thirds of the names are highlighted in red: their odds are rigged against them. The rest are either gray or not highlighted at all. It's the gray ones who are winning. If Curtis were in here he'd probably zap most of the grays with a simple shift of the slider bar,

265

and the winning streaks would suddenly break up. He also might change a few reds back to neutral, give the losers some hope.

Kat quickly resets a master control at the top of the list so that every player has a 100 percent chance of winning. The whole list turns to gray. She closes the window, hopes these people wipe out El Tropical before Curtis returns to his post.

She hears Curtis yell from the living room, telling Roddy—must be the boy—to go home and make some sandwiches for dinner. The boy coughs dramatically before stomping out the front door.

She's been lucky so far but if she doesn't leave now she's sure *her* name will turn to red. Grabbing the flashlight she slips out the back door. For a moment she simply leans against the trailer, watching as the star-splattered sky intensifies, the sun's last rays fading behind the mountain. She spots the wide tree the boy was hiding behind earlier today and runs over to it.

Something rustles in a nearby bush. Probably a rodent, but just to make sure she turns her flashlight on for a second. The tightly focused beam penetrates the desert's dusk, begging for someone to take notice of her. *Fuck!* Her thumb stumbles, flicking the light off and then immediately on. She takes a deep breath and turns the light off again.

As she hunkers down by the tree she notices the figure of a man puttering around underneath the looming silhouette of the ham-radio antenna up on the hill. Squeezing her 10-dollar flashlight she tells herself it's a bad idea but can't help herself: going against the odds, she aims the flashlight at him, turns it on.

49

Like anchors, the heavy Mexican food and vitamin-enriched liquids have secured Jim's mind. His body feels familiar again.

"You look a lot better," Cora says in a monotone. She slides his empty tray under the bed. She hasn't said more than a few sentences since her manic outburst, has fallen into a melancholy stupor, nodding into brief unconsciousness every five minutes or so.

"Thanks Cora. I bet you were a great nurse." Jim wonders how Kat's doing, wants to get her out of the den, wonders where Cora's gun is.

Cora folds her mouth over to one side, something she's been doing since the meth fest, then shuts her eyes.

"Oh Jim," she slurs. "I've made such a mess of my life. I should never have come here."

Jim gently strokes her hair with his free hand, gearing up for his second chance, waiting for a cue.

"I could've been with a rich stable engineer who really loved me, but this was in the '70s when it was uncool to be straight. So I chose Vern." Cora opens her drugged lids, looks at Jim. "He was wild, would invite 20 people over at a time to get naked in the hot tub after a heavy group-therapy session. We'd smoke dope and screw each other's partners all night long."

"And you became unhappy?" Jim asks.

"No! Not then. We had a blast. He had this huge funky farmhouse in the San Fernando Valley, and every day was like a retreat from life. It was *great*."

Cora nuzzles into him, buries her head in his thigh. If only he could grab the gun he'd be able to threaten her, force her to let him go. But the weapon isn't on her. He eyeballs the room, tries to see where she put it, is horrified by what he spots through the window: a group of young characters stepping out of a black Range Rover. The Mustang parks alongside it, its headlights illuminating a bespectacled young sharpie combing back his platinum hair. *Manny*.

Immediately Jim turns off the bedside lamp with his free hand, tells Cora it's nicer in the dark.

"But then everything fell apart," she moans, not reacting to the change in lighting. "Vern got involved with multilevel marketing, seduced all his patients into becoming colloidal silver salesmen for him . . . "

The group moves toward Manny's headquarters and Jim sees Vern sprinting away from the crowd, but away from his home as well. Only minutes left.

"We were climbing fast on the pyramid ladder, making loads of money, until a few of his so-called friends sued us, said the silver had caused their skin to turn permanently blue. We lost *everything*—the house, our business . . ." Cora dramatically wails. "I wish someone would take me away from this dump!"

She's handed Jim his ticket.

Jim places his free palm on Cora's back and massages her. She responds beautifully, wrapping her arms tightly around him, pecking him on the chest. He takes a deep breath and puts his mouth to her ear. He pretends he's talking to Kat.

268

"Cora, let *me* take you away from here. You'd be saving both of us, and I know I could make you happy."

She's silent. Maybe calculating his offer, maybe tripping on a new thought that has nothing to do with their conversation. He can't tell. Her body doesn't move. He keeps massaging her back with the same wide circular motion, afraid any change in rhythm will set her off, remind her why he's here and what her real duty is.

Finally she moves her mouth to his ear, as if she needs to communicate in the same way that Jim did in order for him to understand.

"Just you and me?" she asks.

"Yeah, sure."

"What about *her?*" Cora asks, pointing to the adjoining room.

Jim swallows, never had an easy time with lying. "What *about* her? We were together only because she got me into this mess."

Cora covers her mouth with her hand as if she's about to giggle. "You mean we'd leave right now? Just like that?"

"Yes!" he says, suddenly catching Reba near the Mustang. Who is she waiting for? "Come on Cora, let's go."

"Oh my God," Cora says, her eyes widening. She crawls backward on the bed and with a shaky hand reaches for the handcuff key in her nightstand drawer. She crawls back over to him, licking her dry lips.

"I guess we could take Johnny's extra car. It's a wreck but it'll get us out of here." Her legs straddle his hips. "I can't believe we're going to do this!"

Jim can't lift his eyes to meet hers.

She gets on all fours so that her head is directly above his and, while blindly poking her key at the handcuff with one hand, dips her head so that her lips are only inches from his.

"I knew the first second we met that there was something special about you," she says. "You're like the stable engineer I should've married."

Any second now. Jim doesn't relax his stiff smile. Her movements are slowing down. *Unlock the fucking metal.* He glimpses Reba walking toward the front door.

269

"Damn it Cora!" Jim snaps. He tries to gain control of himself. "Baby, you have to unlock me *now* or it'll be too late for us."

Her left eye begins to spastically twitch as she jiggles the key in his cuff.

Click. For some reason he's shocked when his wrist falls out of the cuff. He's free! She collapses onto him, her tits crushing into his chest. She giggles, says she can't believe she's going to do this.

"We have to do it *now!*" he says. He forces himself to sit up, lifting her dead weight with his stomach muscles. Her legs wrap around his waist as he scans the dim room for the gun.

"Damn it Cora, get off of me!" He tries to get up but she bounces and clings to him like a monkey. The bed jiggles and gurgles and Jim falls on top of her. More screeching.

The hard music suddenly becomes even louder, flooding the bedroom. Jim rolls sideways and looks up.

"You're my engineer stud," Cora says, laughing, bouncing harder, oblivious to Vern, who's entered the room with Reba, who's got Kat in a chokehold. *Kat?*

Reba flicks on a light. "Hey, she's swingin' without you!" she says to Vern, pointing to the scene on the bed with an incredulous smile.

Cora pushes away from Jim. She rolls off the bed, then crab-walks backward until her back is against a wall, below the window.

The psychologist is speechless, nervously picking at old facelift scars.

Jim looks at Kat, whose head is pushed slightly forward by Reba's thick arms. She deliberately avoids eye contact with him.

Reba drags Kat across the room, picks the gun up from the floor.

270

"This is too much to process," Vern finally says to his wife. "Why . . . what were you *thinking?*"

"It's not my fault," she cries into her arms. "It's the meth and the roofies. And—and he was trying to *seduce* me!" she hollers, pointing at Jim.

Jim chokes on his breath. *"What?"*

"It's never her fault!" Vern shouts, suddenly losing all composure. He picks up one of her pink pumps and hurls it across the room, knocking over a framed photo of himself. "She didn't mean to take the Rohypnol without me! She didn't mean to make love to this moron in my absence! Well you know what? I've had it with your bad script!"

"We didn't make love," Jim says, glancing at Kat.

"Shut the fuck up," Vern says, blinking hard. "Reba, give me the gun."

Reba stares at Vern. "You're crazy!"

"Give it to me!" He rams his head into Reba, grabs her wrist. Kat gets caught in the tussle, tries to squirm free of the woman's grip.

Jim jumps off the bed and tries to pry Kat from the madness but is yanked away by a sharp-nailed hand—Manny's. The tanned youth smiles warmly at Jim, then punches him in the stomach with brass knuckles. Jim doubles over, falls back onto the bed.

At the same time the room explodes, gunpowder filling the air. Kat screams. Cora dives under the bed. A fluorescent lightbulb falls from the ceiling, crashing by Jim's feet. Another explosion, this time shattering the window, causing Reba's meaty arm to reflexively extend. Kat breaks free.

She scurries toward the door, blindly running straight into Manny's grasp, and as he raises his brass hand high in the air a line of blue uniforms storms in. Four men altogether.

"FREEZE!"

Jim doesn't think he's hungry, but when Officer Rodriguez hands him a Twinkie from the vending machine he downs it in seconds. They've interrogated him and Kat separately for two hours, will set them up with the FBI for more questioning tomorrow. He's now waiting for Kat in the lunchroom.

Several officers had stayed behind at Love Park, arresting the Loomises and searching most of the trailers and the surrounding area. Jim keeps praying to a god he's never believed in that no one will discover and connect him with the bump.

"Thank God Kat was able to get to a phone," Jim says to the officer who gave him the food.

"She wasn't the one who called us," the officer says, adjusting a clip around her short ponytail.

"But I thought . . . "

"The old man on the hill called us after receiving a frantic message from Miss Astura. She'd used Morse code with a flashlight! Told the man to call the police."

Jim's heart rushes. *The ham-radio antenna.* That's why she was so excited about it this morning. What a dope he was, thinking she was just making small talk. She never does anything small. He's asked to see her, wants to hear her version of events. Then later, when they get back to San Francisco, he wants to tell her he loves her.

An older cop swaggers down the hall, comes into the lunchroom. "Miss Astura doesn't want to see you right now."

Jim stands up. "Where is she? I *have* to talk to her."

"Simmer down," the officer says. "We'll escort you to a nearby motel for the night. But not the same place as your friend. Miss Astura has made it clear she doesn't want to have any contact with you."

Jim shakes his head, the horrible sun-induced blotches plaguing his vision again. He pleads with the man, tells him it's urgent that he speak to her, but it's like talking into a dead phone.

Jim counts the hours till tomorrow, till he has a chance to be with Kat again. As soon as they're alone he'll tell her *everything,* the whole ugly truth about Goines, make her understand that he wasn't running away from her, that the thing with Cora was completely misinterpreted by her demented husband, that Kat has changed his life, he can't live without her.

272

50

The phone rings again.

"Screen it," Kat says to Kimmy. "It's probably him."

It's been three days since she returned to San Francisco. Danny and Kimmy have been the perfect hosts, giving her a place to crash until she finds an apartment of her own. Without any possessions she doesn't take up much room, but still, guests—no matter who they are—go stale quickly.

Kimmy picks up the phone when she hears Danny's voice on the answering machine.

Jim has called four to five times each day. He tricked her parents into giving him the number, saying he was her old boss from the bar. Kat managed to avoid him in Reno, wonders how long he's going to keep hounding her.

What does he want? The El Tropical disaster is over. Manny was arrested two days ago, charged not only for all of the felonies associated with his corrupt Website in Love Park, but also for his methamphetamine lab in Fresno. Kat's sure they'll dig up more on the hood before they're through with him. Larry Goines is still missing, but the FBI has said they'll scour the state—even the country—until they find him. The

273

Loomises are in the Nevada County jail, will be there until they get a hearing. Reba got off scot-free, at least for now, insists she has no knowledge of El Tropical, the hostages, or the meth lab. The cops must've missed the bottle of Rohypnol in her purse. Kat has no idea what happened to Curtis and the boy.

So why doesn't Jim leave her alone? *It's over.* Kat doesn't care what his lame excuses are, his behavior throughout the kidnapping was heartless and disgusting. She can't imagine what kind of explanation the stupid dork could come up with for hiding out so far from the mobile-home park. Obviously he was running without her, had retrieved his wallet and gotten his hands on a wad of cash. And then the icing on the cake: the slimy scene with Cora, as if *any* hunk of meat would do. He's clearly just a weak, shallow, desperate loser.

Kat's throat flutters, she tries to redirect her thought processes, looks at the newspaper in front of her. She never wants to think about him again. Needs to take a sabbatical from *all* guys for a while, just focus on her career—for real this time. While she—ugh!—interns for *Zenith,* she'll knock on every door in South Park, seriously search until she finds a *real* job that excites—and pays—her. And she'll spend her nights writing instead of partying.

Three apartments near lower Haight Street, within walking distance of her old place, look promising. Kat circles them with a red ballpoint pen, keeps scanning the classifieds. She doesn't know where she'll come up with $975 a month, the typical rate for a one-bedroom apartment in a semidecent neighborhood. Perhaps her parents will give her a loan.

"Oh Danny, you're so *cute!* How did you know it's my favorite?" Kimmy says, hunched over the phone.

Kat needs to move soon, can't hang in such a happy Nick at Nite environment much longer, at least not during her hiatus from the XY species. She takes a sip of coffee, turns another page of the paper.

"Kat, can you get that? I think it's the UPS guy." Kimmy continues talking to Danny.

Kat didn't hear anyone knock. She tightens the bathrobe

Danny lent her, then opens the door. She gasps, not ready for Jim. It's too late to slam him out. He's already wedged himself between her and the door jamb, his cigarette smoke rudely snaking its way into the apartment. With each movement he emits a sweet pungent stench and Kat backs away. She hardly recognizes his face—a patchy drinker's bloat.

"What the hell are you doing here?" Kat tries to push him away from the door but his feet are like blocks of cement.

"Haven't you gotten my messages?" he says. "I really need to talk to you."

Seeing him is like stepping dangerously near a bed of quicksand. She doesn't want to get pulled down with him the way she did last week.

"I have nothing to say to you," Kat snarls. "Get away from here and don't come back."

Jim shakes his head, doesn't budge. "If you'll just give me five minutes I have something important to tell you, something no one else can know, and it'll explain why—"

"I don't *care!* I don't want you around me!" Kat tries to tone down the shrillness in her voice, but she's feeling desperate. "You're drunk and you're nothing but bad luck. Now please leave before I have to call the cops."

"Is everything okay?" Kimmy shouts from the other room.

"Everything's fine," Kat replies.

Jim drops to his knees, an inch-long ash chunk breaking off his dangling cigarette.

"You're not being fair," he says, choking on his words. "Kat, I *love* you. You're the only thing in the world that matters to me. I *never* would've—"

"Oh please," Kat says. "Is that why you were all over that skanky bitch? 'Cause you *love* me?" She inhales fiercely, trying to stop her eyes from welling up. He notices, seems to brighten at the sign of tears. He jumps back to his feet.

275

"I wasn't all over her, Kat. She *handcuffed* me. God, just hear me out. When Goines took me to his place, it wasn't to ask me questions. He was after—" He cuts himself off, looks over Kat's shoulder.

Kat turns her head, is relieved to see Kimmy coming to join them.

"What's going on?" Kimmy asks.

"Call the police," Kat says, humiliated by the pathetic spectacle on the porch. "He's harassing me and he won't leave."

Kimmy runs for the phone.

"Kat!" Jim pleads, throwing himself at her feet, *"please* don't shut me out. I need you! Don't you understand? I *need* you. I *love* you!" He keeps repeating himself, winding up into a delirious tantrum. The next-door neighbors peek out a window, commenting to each other. Kat tells Jim that he's making a fool of himself, that people are staring, but he's out of his head, doesn't hear a word.

"I *love* you!" he shrieks, tottering to his feet. He bumps into a rail, almost topples off the porch.

Kat turns her head, can't stand to look at this ravaged stranger, doesn't want to hear him say that word anymore. With Jim's weight out of the way, she's able to shut and lock the door, sliding downward with her back against it till she's sitting on the hardwood floor.

"Kat!" he shouts.

A moment later Kimmy hangs up the phone, says the police are on their way.

51

Dreams can sometimes turn murky, manipulative, tricking the dreamer into thinking a fictional thread is finished when in truth the dreamer is still on the other side of reality. Jim usually doesn't remember these infrequent episodes of false awakenings; once he's fully aware his mind zeroes in on his mental to-do list and the myriad details of his daily scheduled program.

But for the past few days his teasing dreams have been too intense to ignore. Every morning he's had to struggle and claw his way out of subconsciousness, breaking through only after many false starts. The line between fact and fiction keeps blurring and Jim has started a journal to hold the truth in place. But his efforts are only marginally effective. Even now, after shaving and showering, he looks in the motel's warped mirror and prays that this is real, that he won't wake up yet again.

The liquor is partly to blame. Ever since the morning after his first visit to the police station he's woken up to nail-pounding headaches, the kind that are best numbed by alcohol. But the hangovers keep getting worse, and he vows not to indulge himself today. He takes a few aspirin and hopes the pain goes away soon.

The cops never found his laptop, said it wasn't in the trunk of the Mustang where Jim had last seen it. Fortunately most of his work is backed up at the office. But without his computer it's been impossible to contact Chelsea and Jerry. He's phoned them at *Signal* every other hour like clockwork for the last three days, but they, like Kat, have chosen not to return his calls. The world is stonewalling him.

According to the demand Chelsea made six days ago, he's not supposed to show up at the office till tomorrow, which will be a full week. But he can't wait any longer. He needs to be back in South Park, is desperate to walk in his old shoes, to identify with Jim Knight, features editor of *Signal,* again. He wants to feel the familiar hunger, the passionate drive for dollars, the me-for-me mentality that propels people to the top— qualities he can't find within himself at the moment.

The bus ride from his downtown motel to work isn't as bad as he'd expected. The commuters don't look much different from him, normal-looking people carrying old-lady purses, university backpacks, leather briefcases, and the occasional laptop. Every time Kat pops into his mind he forces himself to come up with a new article idea. By the time his 10-minute trip is over he has three pretty strong concepts lined up.

Before entering the *Signal* building Jim steps into a corner market to purchase a pack of cigarettes. He wonders if the cheerful Asian man who knows his customers by name can tell that Jim has switched channels, that he's been branded for life as a murderer. It's agonizing to know something so atrocious, to have *done* something so atrocious, and have to forever keep it a secret. The owner smiles when he hands Jim his change, but something about the way he says, "Thank you, Jim," is disturbing. *Keep it together.*

Jim doesn't know what happened to his office key, has to buzz to get into the building. An unfamiliar voice asks who it is and Jim figures it's the new receptionist. He wonders if anyone fired Mara.

"Jim Knight," he says into the intercom.

A long pause. Jim buzzes again.

"Hold on a minute," the girl says, still not releasing the door.

A woebegone slacker from the first floor walks through the lobby, steps outside. Jim catches the door with his foot, lets himself in. As he passes Clare's office his bowels shudder. He can't help but scan the room for Kat through the large window, can't repress a groan when he doesn't see her. He looks over his shoulder, relieved to see no one behind him.

On his way up to the second floor Rhiannon passes him with a bicycle over her shoulder.

"Hi Rhiannon," Jim says as if he'd seen her just yesterday.

"Jim!" For a second she freezes, then casts her eyes to the ground, says she's in a hurry and skips past him, bumping his ear with a tire.

The last time he was here—the day he pretended not to hear Jerry in order to run off for lunch, only to be confronted by Mandy at Caffe Centro—seems like a year ago.

Mandy. He doesn't know what he'll do when he sees her.

Sure enough, a new receptionist. She's wearing glittery cat-eye glasses and bright-red lipstick. She stops typing when Jim walks by, asks in an irritated tone who he's here to see.

"I *work* here. My name is Jim Knight."

The girl eyes him suspiciously, then grabs a phone, turning her back on him. Jim hangs around, tries to decipher her whispery tones, but with the loud Japanese pop ricocheting against the walls he doesn't catch a word.

He walks past the rows of pedestrian desks that lead to Chelsea's office, knocks on her door. Chelsea's assistant jumps up from a nearby computer, tells Jim that Chelsea and Jerry are in a meeting and can't be disturbed.

"When will they be finished?" Jim asks.

The assistant shrugs, says the meeting might last all day, suggests that he go home and try calling tomorrow.

"I've tried calling all week!" Jim explodes, wanting to strangle this fresh-scrubbed MBA. He tries to open Chelsea's door but it's locked. It feels like the whole room is staring at him, though every time he glances at an individual he can't make eye contact. *Keep cool.* He clamps a lid on his cauldron of emotions.

279

"Who are they in a meeting with?" he asks calmly.

The assistant looks away. "Jim, why don't you call tomorrow? I'm sure Chelsea will speak to you then."

Before his lid blows Jim storms off, but not toward the exit door. He'll sit at an empty computer—all night if he has to—until Chelsea walks out of her office.

Someone needs to forgive him. *For what?* It's as if the whole world has conspired to condemn Jim without giving him a fair trial. Even Kat has become one of *them.* Hasn't anyone seen the news? Don't people know he's innocent? Although the FBI wanted to keep the story quiet during the investigation, bits have leaked out to the press. A few reporters tried interviewing Jim in Reno but he turned them down. Probably a mistake.

He sees a computer at a vacant desk next to Gerald's domain and heads in that direction. Gerald is on the phone but at least makes eye contact when Jim passes by. Easing into the empty chair, Jim tries to open his email. He can send Chelsea and Jerry a message explaining that he was indeed kidnapped, that the FBI and the Reno police can prove it.

Access denied. There is no user by that name.

Jim bangs his name and password into the keyboard again.

Access denied. There is no user by that name.

"Gerald!" Jim cries out. "What's wrong with the network? I can't get to my email!"

Gerald fidgets with the cord of his mouse, says he hasn't checked his messages in a while, doesn't know what the problem is.

Not you too! Apparently the whole staff at *Signal* became part of an alien squad overnight.

"Gerald," Jim says, keeping his voice low, "what's going on?"

Gerald takes off his black science-lab spectacles and polishes them with a corner of his shirt. "Didn't you read the column in Transmitter last weekend?"

Yeah. Like he'd had the luxury of Web cruising during his stay in Hell. "No, Gerald. It would have been kind of hard to get any reading done with a gun shoved into my head."

280

Gerald keeps buffing his well-shined glasses, staring at a trashcan underneath his desk. "Well, uh, it said you were fired," he mumbles. "You're too high a risk, too unstable. They're in the process right now of shuffling staff around to fill your position."

Nooo! Gerald has to be wrong. They wouldn't fire him without hearing him out. Gerald just wants to screw things up, steal his job. When last they talked Chelsea had said they'd discuss his future in a week—tomorrow. How could they have let him go after promising that they'd talk in seven days?

Before he can control himself he grabs a stapler, throws it at Gerald. "Fuck you!" he screams.

Gerald ducks and the heavy object hits another editor's computer, cracking his screen. That editor shouts at Jim, then runs off.

Jim needs to read the Transmitter article, rushes his mouse to a folder that opens the Web. He types the URL, clicks on "Transmitter Archives." The computer is too damn slow and he kicks a desk drawer in frustration, breaking its handle. Finally the page comes up, offering a link to archives.

Before Jim can click to back columns, a strong hand falls on his shoulder. Jim spins around, sees a stocky giant in a wrinkled security guard uniform frowning at him. The man has oily hair and the bushiest mustache Jim's ever seen in his life. Mandy is standing next to the guy.

Jim turns back to the computer monitor but loses control of the mouse, can't understand what's on the screen. He doesn't respond to his hostile visitors, hopes they'll go away.

Mandy moves to his side. "Get out now, or Bruce will throw you out."

"Who the fuck is Bruce?" Jim says.

"Security. We felt it was necessary to hire him until the El Tropical investigation is wrapped up."

El Tropical. So now they *do* know.

"I'm waiting to speak to Chelsea and Jerry," Jim says, keeping his gaze on the Transmitter site.

"It was in the paper, Jim. We know how much you gambled, putting all of our lives in danger by getting involved with the underworld. You're a threat to this company. No one has anything to say to you."

Jim finally looks up at Mandy and is sickened by her sadistic smile, an expression he'd seen many times before and had considered part of her professional charm. He turns his head, jerks his body away from the guard's grip. He jumps to his feet and pushes his chair into the giant. "Stay *away* from me!"

Jim runs to Chelsea's door, pounding his fists against it.

"Chelsea! Jerry! Let me in!"

Mandy and her mustachioed sidekick catch up to him. He's sure they're going to smother him, snuff the life out of him.

"You're fired, Jim!" says Mandy. "You should've thought about your future before you got involved with those drugger friends of yours. Now get out!"

The guard reaches for Jim but he dodges the large man, running to his old desk as if it were a sanctuary. He sees his clarinet case, starts waving it in the air.

"Somebody help me!" he screams, forgetting where he is.

Jim sees the guard approaching with a baton that's much longer than his clarinet case. He shoves a chair in his assailant's direction, leaps on top of a desk, screams at the top of his lungs. After the first scream comes another, another, he can't stop. It's like getting sick—once you purge, you've got to let it run its course. After the screams come the tears and the mucus and the saliva. He tries to wipe his face with his shirt but his arms are suddenly behind him, pulled into a tight bun.

Someone has turned off the stereo system, the room is dead silent.

Bruce nearly dislocates Jim's shoulders as he escorts him out of the building. Jim sees Rhiannon at the front door, wildly looking around to see what she missed. As Jim is bounced down the steps he wakes up from his delirium. The full impact of what he's just done hits him hard. Not only will he never work for *Signal* again, but he's just booted himself from all of South Park. Shit, from the entire world of multimedia. And Chelsea and Jerry didn't even have the courtesy to say goodbye.

52

"Hey Kat, what's going on with Starling?"

"Looks like we'll be bidding against Random House for his novel. His agent is supposed to call tomorrow," Kat says to Thomas Hagen as she checks to make sure her Air New Zealand tickets are in her briefcase.

Thomas hired Kat as his assistant over a year ago to work at CODE READ, *Signal*'s new book-publishing division. She'd still been interning at *Zenith,* frustrated that she had nothing to show for her time at the Berkeley mansion. The Empress, as bewitching and intelligent as she was, had a bad habit of scaring off advertisers. She'd bark orders at them, tell them their ads were too ugly for her magazine, and then refuse to return their calls. Sadly, *Zenith,* the grandmother of all cyber-rags, had shriveled into a catatonic relic, vanquished by the arrogant pubescent newcomers at *Signal*. Ironically, what it stood for— the melding of biology with technology, or "ribofunk," as some have called it—is now the latest paradigm of pop science. *Zenith* came and went before its time.

Signal, on the other hand, has mushroomed into a multi-million-dollar media empire, expanding into television, radio, and books and fostering other start-up magazines. With these

283

new divisions sprouting like a rampant virus, *Signal* has spread into several larger buildings on the other side of South Park.

A stack of unread manuscripts sits on Kat's desk, but they'll have to wait until next week. She looks at her watch. 10:08 AM. *Shit.*

"You'd better get a move on," Thomas says in his German accent, whisking past her with a phone plastered to his ear. He's angular and sexy in a '50s beatnik kind of way, but of course he's already spoken for.

"Yeah, I'm hurrying," Kat says to herself, popping a Rolaid and washing it down with the rest of her lukewarm coffee.

Kat sees an intern and draws a blank. She can't remember his name. "Excuse me," she hollers over the irritating safari music blaring over the loudspeakers. "Can you call me a cab please?"

The intern rushes to a phone. Kat would have called the cab herself, but she needs to make sure she has everything in order. She pulls her new rolling suitcase out from under her desk and sets it by her chair. Then she opens her briefcase, rechecks her tickets, makes sure she has the right contract and manuscript. Kat's finger taps a jackhammer's beat as she reads the manuscript's title page: *Signal to Noise,* by Jim Knight.

At first Jerry had told Kat to burn it. He'd been stunned at Jim's audacity to presume that CODE READ might publish the groveling account of his last week at *Signal.* Jim had masked the story as a fictional thriller, but anyone could see the close parallel between the world in *Signal to Noise* and the environment of South Park.

But Kat didn't burn it. Thomas intervened. He claimed that the book was an entertaining glimpse of digital culture and that CODE READ needed a book that poked a little fun at *Signal.* People were starting to frown on the magazine's serious know-it-all attitude. *Signal to Noise* might diminish the swelling backlash.

284

But it's not just the contract that Kat's bringing to the Cook Islands. Jerry is sending Kat to negotiate with Jim, see what it would take to rope him back in to *Signal.* It seems he's the best features editor *Signal* could ever hope to have. Jerry says he's one of the few who really "gets it."

Kat looks at her wrist. 10:11. She locks her briefcase, attaches it to her suitcase, and says goodbye to Thomas before running outside to wait for her cab.

Kat's nervous about going to the Islands. She hasn't spoken to Jim since the day he showed up at Kimmy's, and reading his novel opened up a floodgate of wet emotions. Is the horrific part about Goines and the bump truth or fiction? If it's true, why didn't he tell her right away? She maybe would've treated him differently in the end, had she known.

She closes her eyes and sees Jim on Kimmy's porch: wallowing on the floor . . . spittle strung across his face . . . puffy yellow eyes . . . cigarette smoke distorting his hysterical expression. . . . And then the wicked stories that raced through South Park about Jim's bizarre behavior his last day at work. Temporary insanity, he would have justifiably pleaded, had he accidentally killed someone during his delirium.

Kat's both curious and afraid to see him again. She'll have to make it clear from the start that their relationship is strictly business. The fact that he won't leave the Islands is too weird. She pictures him, his body pallid, holed up in a ramshackle beach hut, imagines him still obsessing over the day he took her to the movies, still pining for her. Thomas offered to make the trip himself, saying he could use a vacation, but Kat felt that she needed to end this chapter with Jim.

After 10 hours of flying and a night spent in a pleasant hotel on the main island of Rarotonga, Kat's charter plane finally touches ground on Aitutaki soil. With a population hovering around 6,000, Aitutaki is the second most populated of the Cook Islands, and it's where she'll be staying for the next four nights.

She looks out of the plane's tiny window but doesn't see Jim. She whips out her compact and powders her humid nose and cheeks. She applies a thin coat of icy lipgloss Clare gave her last Christmas.

Clare. Kat rarely talks to her old zine pals anymore. Chelsea and Jerry still haven't made up their minds about purchasing *Force,* actually have their eyes on a couple of new zines on the block. Once in a while Kat sees one of the Mikes sitting in South Park with people she doesn't recognize, but it's never a convenient time to stop and chat. Kat misses her friends—when she has time to think about them—but lately she barely has a moment to breathe. She hopes they understand.

The plane comes to a stop and six other passengers, all from New Zealand, elbow their way in front of her. Finally a jolly pilot helps Kat step off the plane. A tickling breeze sails around her.

Kat's eyes dart around the small crowd. Apparently he's late or she's early. Then she realizes that the grinning man standing near the white Jeep is him.

"Jim!" she shouts, running over.

"Hi Kat," he says with a relaxed smile.

"You look great!" she says.

She can't get over how different he looks. He's turned in his flaccid computer-geek body for a solid bronze model. His wavy hair dips below his shoulders and he's pulled the front of it back with a hairclip made from the same green fibers as his woven bracelet. He's even grown taller and Kat guesses his posture has improved.

"You look great too," he says.

Kat braces herself, wondering if this is an appropriate moment to remind him that she's here as a friend and business associate only. But he walks away from her, toward the plane, and picks up her suitcase, the only one left on the asphalt. He asks if she had anything else on the plane and she shakes her head, realizing how awkward it would be to talk about their relationship at this point.

286

"So how was your flight?" he asks, throwing her luggage into the back of the Jeep.

"Fine." She hops in the warm passenger seat and soaks in the salty air.

Jim talks about the island as they drive toward the town of Arutanga, which is part of Aitutaki but slightly separated by water from the mainland. She's happy to quietly listen as he points to various beaches, exotic fruit trees, nearby isles, and the little markets scattered along the road. They often pass clusters of men who apparently do nothing but sit and wave at the occasional passing car. Jim explains that half the locals on this island don't work, and the ones who do have jobs take many long breaks throughout the day. With an abundance of fish and wild fruit, and so little in terms of industry, "working" as Jim and Kat know it isn't a prerequisite for the good life on this island.

Jim stops talking and the humming of the Jeep pacifies Kat, reminding her of the high-school summer breaks she used to relish in Los Angeles. An infinite sky merges seamlessly into reef-lined water, which greets them on both sides of the road. As Kat loses herself in the turquoise that surrounds her the noise of San Francisco gets fainter and fainter. She asks Jim how it's possible that she can see the ocean on either side of the car and he explains that the island is an atoll: it's shaped like a bicycle tire whose center is filled with water, coral, and smaller islands. She can't believe a place this stunning hasn't been spoiled by commerce.

"Well enjoy it now," Jim says, frowning. "The Radisson has already cleared a chunk of the island for a resort. It won't be like this forever."

Again Jim and Kat fall into silence, but it's not uncomfortable.

Jim doesn't speak until they park the car and step onto a motorboat. He tells her it'll just be moments before they reach Arutanga, and he's right. By the time Kat finds a dry spot to sit on one of the plastic benches, the boat reaches the other side of the water.

Kat looks up and sees the Aitutaki Lagoon Resort Hotel,

their destination. She gasps. It's more beautiful than she'd expected, with draping feathery trees that fan the grounds, and charming wooden bungalows surrounded by long wild grass behind the hotel's reception lodge.

"Here we are," Jim says.

Kat's antennae perk up. *We?*

"Isn't this gorgeous?" Jim says. "I thought after we check in we could have some lunch here and catch up on things."

"Uh-huh."

They walk into a white, high-beamed lobby with panoramic windows and Polynesian prints on the walls. An old man with only a few strands of hair is playing the ukulele on a wooden platform but Kat pays no attention to him. She follows Jim to the front desk, where a bubbly broad-figured woman with wavy black hair smiles warmly at Jim.

"How are you doing today?" she asks him in a familiar tone.

"Just fine," he says. "This is my old friend Kat. She's got a room under Astura."

Kat relaxes. No *we* this time.

The woman wears a large sarong around her waist with a long-sleeved cotton shirt that seems too hot for 80-degree weather. She tells Kat that her bungalow won't be ready for another couple of hours but offers to store her baggage behind the desk. Kat hands the clerk her suitcase but hangs on to the briefcase. She can't lose the contract.

"Well, should we do lunch?" Jim asks.

Kat just ate a huge breakfast two and a half hours ago and tells Jim she'd rather walk around for a while.

"Well, here then," Jim says, taking Kat's briefcase away from her. He swings it over his shoulder and leads her outside.

The small islet of Arutanga is a paradise within a paradise and Kat can't believe it exists.

288

"Where'd you get the money to come here?" she asks.

"I had a little in the bank, and I sold my Rolex."

She rolls up her white cotton pants and follows Jim to the water, her body tingling at the sound of each gentle wave. But a small part of her eyes Jim suspiciously, wondering when he'll cave in and turn to mush.

Jim takes off his shoes and tells Kat to do the same. Her feet are pale and clammy-looking next to Jim's. They walk along the shoreline, each step orgasmic as the soft sand percolates in and out of her toes.

"Whatever happened to Gerald?" he asks.

"What?" Not a question Kat had expected. Then she sees the connection. "Oh, well, he's still at *Signal*. I don't really talk to him much."

Jim picks up a brown shell and tosses it into the water. "Is he still associate editor?"

So heavy so soon. But Kat can't lie. "No. When you left he became the features editor."

"Good for him," Jim says. "He was overripe for a position like that."

If Jim is harboring any ill will toward Gerald he sure covers it well.

They come upon a row of simple houses, each one sporting a large balcony that hangs over the sand. A family is playing cards on the first balcony and the father waves at them, asking Jim if Kat is the American friend he was talking about.

"Yeah," he says. "This is Kat."

The man smiles and asks if they'd like some iced tea.

"Not right now," Jim says, "but maybe we'll stop by later."

"Okay neighbor," the man says. "See you around."

Jim soon turns away from the water, cutting across the sand to the third house. The materials used to build it look cheap and the structure looks like something an army would slap together for the troops.

"Is this your place?" she foolishly asks.

Jim nods and opens the door for her. She enters and looks around an interior decorated like a suburban house from the '70s, with a warped Formica counter that divides the kitchen from the eating area, papered walls, a differently colored carpet in each room, and potted ferns that hang from the ceiling. The place is breezy and Kat feels at home.

Jim lays Kat's briefcase on the kitchen table and asks her if she'd like something to drink. She sits down, trying to ignore her escalating laziness, says she'd love whatever he has.

Jim sets two short juice glasses on the table and opens the refrigerator. Kat slowly unzips her briefcase, realizing she'd better deal with the contract before her business sense completely deserts her.

"The contract is twelve pages," Kat says, taking it out of its manila envelope, "but we can go over it pretty quickly."

Jim emerges from the fridge with a flask of red wine. He fills each glass and hands one to Kat.

"Cheers," he says, then turns his attention toward the briefcase and pulls out his manuscript as if he's never seen it before.

"Your book," Kat says.

"Yeah, I know," Jim says, grinning. "It's just that I've never seen it printed out before." Jim flips through his novel, admiring it like a proud parent. He stops at a paragraph, then laughs out loud. He doesn't seem to mind Thomas's red ink splashed across the pages.

"This contract is pretty standard," Kat says reluctantly, not wanting to spoil his enthusiasm, "but we should run over it anyway."

Jim sets his manuscript on the table and walks over to the sliding glass door that opens to the balcony.

"It's going to rain," he says.

Kat looks outside and is shocked to see a low-slung white ceiling over the ocean. How capricious the sky is here.

"Kat, let's just enjoy our wine first. We have four days to look at that contract."

Kat's a little embarrassed by her brusqueness. She tries to give in to her growing mellowness and tastes the wine. Not bad. Its rich silky texture evaporates in her throat. She notices Jim's clarinet balanced over a stack of books on the floor.

"Your clarinet! You're still playing?"

"Yeah," he says, still looking at the ocean. "I play a couple times a week on the main island at a tourist restaurant called

290

The Big Bamboo. The owner is a friend of my dad's. He's the one who talked me into coming here in the first place." Jim takes a sip of his wine.

"Unfortunately you're leaving the day before I play."

"Can you play something for me now?" Kat asks.

Jim doesn't seem to hear her. He slides open the door and steps outside. Kat follows him. He angles two lounge chairs so that they face the water and sits in one, patting the other as an invite for Kat.

The rubbery recliner props Kat's back up to a perfect ocean-viewing position. She watches a butterfly weave in and out of the plants that frame the rocky beach.

"Isn't this great?" Jim says.

"It's beautiful," Kat says, setting her half-empty wine glass beneath her chair. She sees other families puttering around on their balconies and some kids playing in the water.

She looks at Jim's even tan. If she were smart she'd ask him for sunscreen.

"Do you ever run into Mandy?" Jim says, turning on his side to face Kat.

Kat doesn't know why her heart jumps. She hadn't expected this question. Does he think about her? Is it *Mandy* that he's missed these last fifteen months? Thank God she didn't set down the "rules" of their relationship when she first saw Jim on the air strip.

"She left," Kat says. "Around six months ago, I guess. She went to New York to work at some huge ad agency."

"Wow! How did Chelsea and Jerry take it?" Jim asks.

"They were upset at first, but *Signal*'s doing fine without her."

Kat studies the stranger before her, tries to find pangs of remorse or sorrow at the mention of *Signal*, but she sees only curious eyes, clear and serene. Where's the old anal Jim? She decides to see how nonchalant about his prior life he really is.

"Jim, I've been meaning to talk to you about something," she says.

Jim silently waits for Kat to go on.

"Jerry and the rest of us feel that it's a waste for you to be hiding out here. You're too talented to lose and we'd love to have you come back to *Signal*. With so much expansion going on, a couple of cushy positions in editorial have just opened up."

Jim smiles. The cat is already out of the bag. Kat gets ready to talk numbers. He reaches for her hand and she's only a little guarded.

"Kat, I'm not hiding out here." He laughs as he says this, a laugh that throws her.

"I didn't mean it that way," she says defensively. "It's just that this place is so removed from the rest of the world. You're missing out on everything—new music, the business world, the news, technology. You're just not at the center of anything anymore."

Jim thrusts an upward palm in front of him. Seconds later Kat is covered with raindrops. Her blouse is getting wet and she sits up in her chair, ready to bolt into the house. Jim grabs her hand.

"Come on," he says, ushering her down some cracked wooden steps that lead to the sand.

Kat stiffly runs with Jim, fantasizing a warm dry beach towel wrapped around her. They reach the choppy sea, where two boys and three girls are jumping and splashing each other.

Letting go of her, Jim spreads his arms and throws his head back to catch the rain in his mouth. Kat smiles and watches him but doesn't participate. One of the kids recognizes Jim and splatters him with a mud-bomb. All of his friends point their fingers at Jim and roar with laughter. Jim mimics an angry adult and hurls a ball of wet sand back. A bucking wave sneaks up on him and knocks him into the shallow water. The kids scream with delight, tugging on his shirt to pull him in deeper, until a parent hollers for them to get into the house.

292

Bobbing in the water Jim motions for Kat to join him. She's tempted, but the thought of getting her clothes even soggier than they already are sounds miserable.

"Come on!" he insists, emerging from the ocean to capture her. He reminds Kat of the Creature from the Black Lagoon.

She shrieks and runs down the beach in a schoolgirl mock panic, but Jim catches up to her, traps her in his wet body. She makes an impotent attempt to struggle, teasing that if he doesn't let go she'll burn his contract.

"Then burn it!" he says, dragging her into the ocean. She screams and as they wrestle into the ocean with the rain pounding overhead the world momentarily seems upside down.

The sky crackles and booms as it spews even heavier sheets of rain. The emotional sky illuminates, darkens, illuminates, then darkens again, and Kat's breath catches her heart as her adrenaline rushes to the dangerous rhythm of the thunder.

Jim holds her from behind and for a few minutes they silently watch the electrical patterns rip apart the atmosphere above them. She's glad he can't see the tears spilling into the universe of salt water around her. They're not sad tears or even tears of joy, but rather a reaction to nature's savage celebration.

And then, as if someone suddenly pulled a plug, the rain stops. The clouds begin breaking up almost immediately, and denim patches of blue soon peek out at Kat and Jim. Birds twitter in the distance.

"Look," Jim says, pointing at the sky, his arms still wrapped around Kat.

A smear of pastels paints the drying sky.

"You see, Kat," Jim whispers, "I *can't* go back to San Francisco. *This* is my center. Look at what the rest of the world is missing."

Kat turns so her chest presses against Jim's. His hairclip is gone, perhaps drifting into a cove of coral, and she tucks the hanging strands of blond behind his ears. He watches her with a partial grin, and without thinking she grabs the back of his head and places her lips on his. His strong body pulls her into him, and Kat hopes this moment never ends.

293

Kat cinches the cotton robe around her waist and floats into the kitchen. She sees her damp clothes already hanging over the rail of the balcony. Jim is pouring hot water into a mug and says he hopes she doesn't mind Sanka. Of *course* she doesn't mind. She'd drink a cup of vinegar if he offered it to her.

The book contract is spread out on the table and Kat notices that Jim has already signed it. She sits on one of the yellow plastic chairs and asks if he read all twelve pages.

"Yeah, it looks fine," he says, placing a cup of Sanka, a box of sugar, and a carton of milk in front of her.

Infatuated with his tangible manuscript, Jim picks it up and plops into a chair next to Kat. He sets the novel between them and begins to read it to himself.

Although Kat's read it dozens of times already, or so it seems, she asks him to read it to her out loud.

"Really?" he asks, already angling the bound pages under the light. Without waiting for Kat to answer he begins to read it to her.

"*Signal to Noise*, by Jim Knight."

1

Jim Knight lights another cigarette and looks at his watch. Noon on the dot. If Rhiannon isn't here in five minutes he'll split. Jim skims the table of contents of *New York* magazine, oblivious to the tree-branch-filtered sun overhead. No article about him and his recent promotion at *Signal* magazine. Damn—they interviewed him over two months ago. Maybe next issue.

A weathered bicyclist wearing tight Lycra shorts and a yellow bandanna around his head rolls by with a shaggy sheepdog. He scowls at Jim's cigarette. Jim scowls back. The rider secures his bike and dog to a nearby bench and saunters into Caffe Centro. Jim reskims *New York*'s contents.

"Hey Jim," says a breathless voice.

"Hi Rhiannon." Jim sneaks another glimpse at his watch. 12:04.

Rhiannon places her cappuccino on the small green metal table before she takes a seat.

"I would've gotten here earlier, but I got stuck talking to Raymond. Guess who's going over to watch *Project Bluebook* at his house tonight?"

"Who?"

"Darren!" she says.

"Darren who?"